WIRE TO WIRE

WIRE TO WIRE

**A NOVEL
BY SCOTT SPARLING**

Tin House Books

Portland, Oregon & New York, New York

Published by Tin House Books, Portland, Oregon, and New York, New York
Distributed to the trade by Publishers Group West, 1700 Fourth St., Berkeley, CA 94710, www.pgw.com

Library of Congress Cataloging-in-Publication Data

Sparling, Scott.
  Wire to wire : a novel / by Scott Sparling. —1st U.S. ed.
      p. cm.
  ISBN 978-1-935639-05-3
  I. Title.
  PS3619.P372W55 2011
  813'.6--dc22

                                    2010045831

First U.S. edition 2011
Printed in Canada
Interior design by Diane Chonette
www.tinhouse.com

Lyrics from the following songs are used with permission from Gear Publishing Company (ASCAP). All Rights Reserved.

"2 + 2 = ?"
Written by Bob Seger
© 1967 Gear Publishing Company (ASCAP)

"Heavy Music"
Written by Bob Seger
© 1971 Gear Publishing Company (ASCAP)

"Lookin' Back"
Written by Bob Seger
© 1971 Gear Publishing Company (ASCAP)

MAY - 2011

To Harriet and Zane

If you seek a pleasant peninsula, look about you.

—MICHIGAN STATE MOTTO

In action, watch the timing.

—TAO TE CHING

The Tao that can be named is not the real Tao. The town of Wolverine, Michigan, described in this book is not the real Wolverine. Nor is it located near the real town.

— Prologue —

THE SCREENS IN Michael Slater's editing suite had immaculate reception. At night they showed him things no one had ever filmed. Sometimes, Slater could make the images go away, but he could not keep them away.

Screen three—a 1981 Sony Studio Master—showed a freight train rolling through a dark Detroit switchyard. Silver-edged clouds hid the moon. Up ahead, invisible in the dark, a power line hung low over the tracks, hustling a current of electrons endlessly onward.

Of the two fools standing on top of the train, one was Slater. A joint between his lips bobbed, unlit. Slater and Harp had their heads down, searching their pockets for matches.

The clouds were the River Above. Everything else was the River Below. At least that's what Slater had been told by a woman. It was all ninety-nine percent water, she said, and there was nothing you could do to change the way it flowed.

Standing on top of a moving freight was against the rules that Harp and Slater always followed. Still, there they were on screen three, perched high on a loaded woodchip car. Harp had his back to the power line, which was coming to slice off his head.

As the train began picking up speed, he found a pack of matches. I'll light it, you light it, let me light it, Harp said. The match flared in his hand. Slater bent down slightly to meet the flame.

At the last possible instant, the River Above shifted. Moonlight cut through a gap in the clouds and reflected off the wire. Slater saw it coming and pushed Harp into the woodchips. He tried to drop to his knees in the same motion, but he was not quite fast enough. The power line kissed his forehead. It lit him up like a torch and lit the joint with 33,000 volts, but Slater never had a chance to inhale.

— 1 —

NEAR THE SUBWAY entrance on Twenty-third, the charity-case street musician spun twice on his heel and flashed his electric guitar. No amp. Deeply gone, he chopped out "Purple Haze" wildly and soundlessly, complete with vibrato you could see but not hear, throwing his kisses skyward and singing to no one, while down the street three dark-suited businessmen and a black woman with fierce eyes watched for the bus. Quitting time. Heading home.

Slater dropped a bill into the open guitar case as he passed and the goateed musician gave a nod; his body bumped and jerked, riding the mad and silent jam.

Always the way it goes, Michael Slater said to himself. The best stuff, you never get to hear.

It was only six o'clock, but he'd already taken his second Smiling O, and the speed turned the city combustible. Ordinary wage-earners and six-figure swells jostled past him, squeaking. The lineup was frightening and all-inclusive. Corporate citizens with blank faces. Department store women. Workers in native garb, spear carriers from every walk of life. At the corner, a bum with no lower lip lay dozing, saliva leaking onto the walkway, adding to an already bright mosaic of gum, bird shit, and other unidentified substances. Except for the missing lip, the man bore an odd resemblance to Mr. Greenjeans. As far as Slater could remember old Greenjeans, that is. The amphetamines caused a certain amount of line interference where long-term memory was concerned.

Up ahead was the Flatiron District and the glass facade of the building that housed Spectrum Productions, where Slater edited video. He was roughly eight hours late for work. Not that anyone cared.

"Pollution all over the world," a man on the sidewalk said, "and we vetoed it." Without turning his head, Slater could see the flash of the man's gold fillings. The power line had altered his peripheral vision; on rare occasions, it proved useful. That very afternoon, an auburn-haired woman with a lopsided smile had sprayed mustard across his chest on Seventh Avenue. The condiment, well sealed, had misfired from its plastic pouch as she doctored her street-corner hot dog. Slater had seen it coming from the corner of his eye and stepped back, missing most of the blast.

"Don't worry, miss," he told her. "You only winged me." She turned away from him quickly—a speed freak wearing mustard. Now the yellow sash vibrated like bad fluorescent.

If this is reality, Slater thought, I'll take hallucinations any day.

Past Madison Square Park, in the shadow of the Flatiron Building, Slater veered off course, ducking into the shabby entrance of Paradise Squared, the old and usually empty strip club. At the table farthest from the stage, he ordered three Rolling Rocks as insurance against the speed. Beer, the anchor.

It was a plan, he told himself. Speed in the afternoon, a little more speed in the early evening, then tie down with a brew or two. Not a great plan, maybe, but a plan all the same.

The first dancer to come onstage was short and a little too plump for her G-string. She reminded Slater of someone he'd known in Michigan, a woman who went by the name Vulva Voom.

The other dancers at Paradise Squared were slouching around a door marked PRIVATE, chewing gum and adjusting their bikini tops. At first glance, one or two of them appeared Astoundingly Beautiful, but a closer look revealed ordinary women in extravagant underwear. It didn't matter to Slater. He wasn't there for the flesh. He was there for the dark.

After the second beer, the dark closed in around him. He drifted through it for what seemed like a long time, his mind blessedly blank. In the end though, Vulva Voom stepped out of a dim corner. She called for Slater to be shot, using the same flat tone businessmen use when they fire you. Come in. Close the door. Have a seat. Shoot him.

When Slater blinked, she disappeared. A freakishly skinny woman took her place. She was naked and seemed real, and she wanted money.

"This guy owes me for an Early Bird," she told the bouncer, who was standing over Slater. "He won't pay."

"I will pay," Michael Slater said. But it was too late. The bouncer hoisted him by the arms and a minute later he was backpedaling onto the sidewalk, sloshing beer on his jeans. He came to rest against a 1981 Pontiac Grand Am, so new he could smell the General Motors plant outside Detroit. Somehow, he still had a Rolling Rock in his hand.

Expelled, he thought. So much for the plan.

The Pontiac's window distorted his face. He brushed his hair back and squared his jaw under a slightly crooked nose. The night air was warm and smelled fermented. Someone had dimmed the lights while he was in Paradise Squared, but otherwise not much had changed.

The electricity in Detroit used Slater's body as a raceway, entering at his forehead and shooting out through his feet, rearranging molecules as it went. In the hours afterward, his brain began to swell. At Henry Ford Medical Center, a neurosurgeon opened Slater's skull to relieve the pressure. Only three surgeons in the country could perform the procedure, and the one who worked on Slater had taught the other two. His name was James Knoughlton III, but he made everyone call him Jimbo.

You lucked out, Jimbo said when Slater finally came to. Next week I'm going to Barbados. You mess up your head then, and you'd be dead by now.

Another interesting fact, Jimbo said, concerned cerebrospinal fluid—the soup between the brain and the skull. It was a much better conductor of electricity than blood. He gave Slater a wink: Your soup got supercharged.

There were burns, too, but they were limited, and there was morphine for that. When it was done and his skull was back together, Slater noticed a change in his vision; he could see almost the whole room without turning his head. This new ability startled him; he asked the doctor how it had happened but didn't get much of an answer. You're alive, Jimbo said. Beyond that, I wouldn't ask too many questions.

Ten days after being admitted, Slater was shipped out to rehab, to a program in Arizona that was supposed to be especially good. He left with a metal plate in his head and a small treasury of drugs. The pills were supposed to prevent seizures and hallucinations, but Slater didn't have seizures. Sometimes he saw people who weren't there, but who didn't?

Matthews was not at the guard desk when Slater finally entered the lobby of Spectrum Productions, and the new guard would not let him pass without his badge, which Slater had lost long ago.

"Hit the road, pal," the guard told him, eyeing the beer that Slater still carried. "You booze, you lose." Finally, Dimi Webster came down to vouch for him, and the guard let him by.

"That man is wasting his potential here," Slater said to Dimi as they stepped into the elevator. "He could have a job in a supermarket. He could be the guy who checks your check."

"Why do I bother with you?" Dimi asked. "Can you give me any kind of hint?" She touched a finger to the yellow crust across his blazer.

"Mustard," Slater said. "A woman did that to me."

"Left you scarred, did she? Where have I heard that one before?"

From a speaker in the ceiling of the elevator, Sinatra crooned his desire to wake up in a city that never sleeps. Slater had taken the idea to heart: he was living on uppers in New York City.

"Did you know that right outside our office Mr. Green-jeans is sleeping in the gutter? All those years of service to the Captain. And when he's old, cashiered."

"Amphetamines are not very good company," Dimi said. "I really wish you'd stop. If you won't do it for yourself, do it for the ones around you."

Slater took a moment to consider the idea. "Most of the people around me aren't all that real," he told her. "They're phantoms."

"I'm real," Dimi Webster said.

He looked at her and saw her realness. The curve of her smile, some kind of light in her eyes. He was afraid to go any further.

"Do you know what an Early Bird is?" he asked Dimi. "Because I'm clueless."

A tangle of wires led from Slater's edit suite. The biggest, blackest wire ran up to the ceiling and onward, to the River Above, where it was attached to the tail of an invisible cat. That was how Slater understood it, anyway, particularly when he was high. The Buddha-like cat knew everything and fed the screens their knowledge, from which the marvelous pictures of light were made—all the unfilmed and impossible images from his past that played out nightly.

The simple thing was just to accept it, so that's what he did. Everything had its own electricity, and that's all the images were. Photons and cathode rays. If you opened up the right frequencies in some deep part of your brain, you could tune into anything. And he did.

On screen six, a familiar line of boxcars turned from dusky red to crimson. The Northern Arrow. Train of no return. The silver tank car in the middle of the Northern

Arrow was leaking propane or PCBs or some such shit, though he hadn't known that at the time.

He hadn't known about the money hidden in the Ford, either, or about the girl in the freezer. But what he hadn't known then, he couldn't stop knowing now.

That was the thing about the past: it had such staying power, such a long shelf life. You could always count on the past to be there when you needed it, and even when you didn't. Especially then.

In the darkness of his edit suite, Slater tapped his keyboard, a three-stroke tattoo on EJECT, but the tape decks were already empty. To make the Northern Arrow go away, he did some real work, loading clips from various source tapes and arranging them for the night's edit—a horrid labor-relations piece called "Handling the Difficult Employee."

Thinking of Dimi, he resisted the urge to take another Smiling O. The little white pills were marked with a curved line inside the letter O—a smiley face with no eyes—and were rumored to contain equal parts of amphetamine and cornstarch. No matter; they kept him company when there was no one else around.

As usual, his coworkers were long gone for the night; nothing moved around him. The far end of the sixteenth floor was Spectrum's dumping ground for mismatched partitions, broken swivel chairs, and surplus office equipment, some of it left from a previous tenant. One corner had been converted into a cave for a video shoot years earlier; it was all torn papier-mâché and chicken wire now. Few employees could remember why the cave had been needed or what the shoot was about, though there were stories of trysts and conquests under the stalactites.

Cubicles occupied the central portion of the floor. Vinyl banners hung above them marking different departments: Plumbing, Garden, Electrical. The banners were apparently from a hardware store. How they related to the actual departments, Slater had no clue. Reality had only the smallest foothold on the sixteenth floor.

The edit suites were off by themselves, built against an outside wall. Stacks of tapes, empty bottles, and wrappers littered Slater's suite—the debris of midnight.

The late hours suited him. In daylight, the whole loop of time stretched out and became a straightway, and you got the crazy feeling that one day followed another, and there you were, stuck, pulling your sorry history behind you like a payload of rusted pipe.

But midnight was different. At midnight, the past, present, and future circled round like a train on a circular track and you could end up anywhere.

It was nearly morning by the time he put the labor-relations piece to bed. He played it one last time when he thought he was done, aware of the tricks he had used, of every corner cut. For his own satisfaction, he backed the audio off about a dB and a half, cleaning up the lower end, getting it just right. By then the Northern Arrow was back on his screens, bright as real video.

Sucking air through his teeth, he muted the console's sound. Dumbstruck boxcars rolled on all monitors. Soon, freight cars would be scattered all over the snowy hillside. Before that happy moment replayed, he wanted the whole mess off his screens. Gone. Kaput.

All right, Mike, he told himself. Relax. Take a breath. Find your hiss.

The hiss would be sharp. If he found it, he could drill little holes in the bottoms of his feet and let the bad memories drain. But before he could begin, screen two lit up with the Sonora desert. He had lived there once, on the edge of endless heat. Even on the monitor, the sky was so blue it hurt his eyes.

Under the early desert sun, Ed Dickinson propped his shovel in the dirt, removed his Stetson, and wiped the sweat from his forehead. Brittlebush and wildflowers bloomed along the ridge of the gulch. Beyond the arroyo, the cracked angles of the Santa Catalinas were blurred by heat.

Despite the heat, it felt good to move some dirt. It put him in the right frame of mind for what he needed to do.

Dickinson was a tall, barrel-chested man with the wide face of a butcher. The man beside him, Thomas Gorrel, was thin, nearly skeletal. A navy footlocker, battered and missing a handle, sat next to the trench they were digging.

"What about when it floods?" Dickinson asked.

Gorrel put his shovel down and pointed to a spot lower in the gulch. "Waterline's down there. It'll be dry up here."

It had been Gorrel's idea to bury the footlocker. It belonged to him and so did the money inside it. Dickinson's share was fifteen percent because he owned a couple of bars and he could make the money look like income. Plus his face scared people, and when they got scared they bled green. It was a useful skill.

Dickinson walked to his truck and got a paper bag with two bottles of beer. He handed one to Gorrel and stepped back, standing behind his partner and looking out at the desert. "I hope you're right. One flood would wash it all away."

"When the fuck have I ever been wrong?" Gorrel asked. "I know this desert."

"Butt or brain?" Dickinson asked.

"Say again?" Gorrel raised the bottle to his lips, tipping his head back.

"Brain," Dickinson said and shot him through the back of the head. The bullet shattered the skull and made the beer bottle explode. Gorrel dropped, landing half in the hole.

"Here's what happened," Dickinson said to the corpse. "You took the money and ran off. Guadalajara, Mexico City—who knows? Poor Cassie will be all alone in that sad house of yours. For a while." In fact, he had already slept with Gorrel's wife. Cassie was easily fooled, a convenient lay. She wasn't the point. The money was the point.

No need to cover the body, he thought—it was too hot for any more shoveling. The big cats and the vultures would take care of things, anyway. He finished his beer, adjusted his Stetson, and began dragging the footlocker back to his truck. He had a much better place to hide the money.

—2—

A LINE OF mesquite trees made a crooked windbreak for the small cinder-block house that was called the Addition. The trunks of the trees had been painted white against the sun and they shimmered in the heat of the Sonora. At night, the trees looked like ghosts; in the darkness, they danced slowly around the house.

As the sun went down, Slater went from room to room, closing the blinds. He turned on all the lights, then turned some of them back off. When he got it just right, he sat at the fake mother-of-pearl table in the kitchen and snapped his fingers softly by his ear. The rhythm calmed him, gave him something to hang on to.

The trees couldn't really move. He knew that.

Before Selda left, the trees hadn't bothered him. After rehab, he moved in with her. They'd sit on the steps together as the sun went down and watch the white trunks waver about. Nothing scared Selda. Ghosts, come get me, she said. I don't mind.

Sitting by her side, Slater didn't mind either.

Keeps the snakes away, she said.

What does? he asked.

The ghosts, she said. She ran snaky fingers up his back and kissed him.

That was before she decided he wasn't all there and left him in the Addition alone.

In the kitchen, he opened a beer. When it was gone, he parked himself on a chair and let the TV soothe him into sleep. A half dozen times he woke to the strangers on the box. After midnight he was greeted by a salesman and a preacher, followed by Elvis in black and white. At 3 a.m., he found himself confronted with the news in Spanish. He watched intently, not understanding a word.

When morning came, Slater stepped out on the porch and felt the heat change the map of his body: scalp, testicles, the bottoms of his feet. He thought that if he slashed his hand through the air, the hot land would ripple like water. That would be fine. Ripple all you want, he told the land. I'm leaving.

Across the scrubgrass, on the other side of the windbreak, was Cassie's place, a ranch house set back from the road. A pen next to it held two mangy horses.

Keeping an eye out for rattlesnakes, Slater crossed through the scrubgrass and mesquite trees. A 1968 Ford Ranchero—ten years old and badly rusted—sat in the shade near one of the trees. The Ranchero hadn't moved in months.

He rang Cassie's bell twice before she opened the door, dressed for work—tight jeans, red bandana, and a white blouse with the words *Ed's Steakhouse* on the pocket. Cassie was freckled and a year past forty. Her eyes were done up darkly, in a way that might work in the steak house.

Under the desert sun, she looked more ghoulish than sexy. She did not look happy to find Slater on her porch.

"Hey," he said, filling the silence. When she continued to stare, he told her he had come for his deposit.

"You can't just leave whenever you feel like it," Cassie said. "Notice has to be in writing. Says so in the lease."

"There is no lease," he said.

"Sure there is. Ed drew it up after Thomas disappeared."

"I gave notice verbally," he said. "When you came by."

The AC that blew out against his face was obscenely cool. "Is that what you call it," she said. "I know a different name for it."

A month earlier, Cassie had stopped by the Addition to collect the rent. Slater had just opened a bottle of tequila. It was late in the day; she looked good with the sunset behind her. The fact that she was fifteen years older than Slater and hard as nails made it more exotic. Not in a good way, it turned out.

Slater resisted the urge to snap his fingers. "That has nothing to do with it." But he knew it did. Once you mixed up sex and money, there was no unmixing them.

"Doesn't matter," Cassie said. "I don't have it."

"You don't have six hundred dollars?"

She jerked her head and led him to the kitchen, which was done entirely in yellow. A shoe box on the counter held a rat's nest of papers. Rooting through it, she produced the lease. "Says right here. One-year occupancy. Twelve months. No pets and all."

"I never signed that. You never even showed it to me."

"I didn't have to. Ed got it notarized. You can't break a notarized lease."

From the back of the house, a parrot squawked. Slater picked up a spoon from the table and weighed it in his hand. I made love to a woman who owns a parrot, he thought.

"Where'd you say you're going?" Cassie asked. "Minnesota?"

"Michigan." His T-shirt showed a railroad ferry sailing under a cherry sun. *Northern Michigan*, it said. *Enchanted Land of Cherries and Ferries.*

"Whatever. Just write down your address. I'll mail you the money when I get it."

"I don't have an address. All I want is the deposit."

Cassie stood eyeing him with a look that said she had slept with better men. "Tell you what," she said. "Take the Rolls Canardly."

She meant the Ranchero rusting under the mesquite trees. Slater had heard the joke before. Rolls down one hill. Can hardly make it up the next.

"I'm not taking a busted-up old car. I need the money."

"So do I. And when I have it, I'll sure let you know." She plucked an envelope from the shoe box and handed it to him. Inside was the title, registered to Thomas Gorrel. Her missing husband. "Things go wrong," she said, "men run off. Whereas if you're a woman, you have trouble alone."

Slater held the spoon between two fingers. It had an interesting heft. He could fling it and bounce the curved end off her nose. It was a talent he had.

"I'm not running off."

"Nice tits!" the parrot called. "I'm a shitbird." Cassie yelled for it to shut up.

"Listen," she said. "I'll throw in some speakers. High-end stuff. Go see Dr. Jack. Tell him Ed sent you."

"I'm not taking the Ford."

"Then you're not getting anything," she tried to say, but the parrot drowned her out with a chorus of "Nice tits!," followed by "Don't make me shoot you."

"Shut up, Sammy," Cassie yelled.

But the bird knew that one too and repeated it back.

On his way back to the Addition, Slater rocked the back of the Ford Ranchero and watched it bounce. The shocks were shot. No surprise.

The Ranchero was a sedan in front, a flatbed in back. Half car, half truck. The words FLASH ME had been written on the tailgate and then painted over, but the letters were still faintly visible. It was hard to believe anyone had ever been flashed in such a vehicle.

He circled the Ford, looking it over. Across a quarter mile of scrubgrass, a short line of cars undulated toward Tucson, sunlight glancing off their chrome. The road going north was empty. That was the road he wanted.

Sometimes in Northern Michigan, when the cherries were being harvested, a truck stacked high with crates would take a corner too fast and spill some of its load. He remembered dirt roads the color of coffee with a sprinkling of cherries at the corner. There'd be a summer shower, a slender girl, a flannel shirt open under the trees. The scent of sex and the smell of grass—not grass being cut, but living grass, down close to the ground where you could smell it next to the soil.

That was where he wanted to go. But that wasn't Northern Michigan. That was his youth. And there was no way you could get there in a broken-down Ford.

Dr. Jack ran a thieves' bazaar from a house outside Tucson. Slater parked the Ranchero in the drive and rang the bell.

Several minutes later, Dr. Jack appeared in a T-shirt and boxers. Kernels of popcorn were stuck to one side of his face; he seemed to be emerging from a deep nod, a sleep with luxurious, even tropical overtones. The air coming from the house had a rubbery smell; in the room behind Jack, Slater could see tires stacked to the ceiling. Before Slater could explain himself, Dr. Jack helpfully offered to rip him a new asshole.

At the mention of Ed Dickinson, though, Dr. Jack's face changed. An hour later, the Ford Ranchero was equipped with a refurbished tape deck and six mismatched coaxials. As Slater left, a Lincoln Town Car with tinted windows pulled up the drive. Dr. Jack also filled prescriptions.

At Safeway, Slater picked up a Styrofoam cooler, a six-pack, and several jugs of water. Afterward, he hit an auto-parts store on Ajo Way for hoses, belts, and a new set of plugs.

When he returned, he discovered a wheelchair preacher spraying drunken prophecy all over the sidewalk. By the tailgate of the Ranchero, the man scooped something from the sidewalk and held it up for all to see. A one-hundred-dollar bill. *Trees will tumble!* the man shouted. *Insolvable dichotomies will be transcended!* A bottle of Mogen David poked out from his grimy blanket.

Slater gave the man a wide berth and drove off. It takes more than a hundred dollars, he thought, before the insolvable dichotomies get small.

That afternoon, he moved the Ranchero into the shade of the Addition and replaced the fan belt and the hoses. By dinner time, he was done. He opened a beer and drank it quickly. Inside, in the tiny bathroom, he turned on the shower and lay down in the tub, letting the spray strike his chest. To his shame, he found himself growing hard thinking about Cassie.

It had been the bottom of the barrel, sleeping with Cassie. Getting there was not half the fun.

It was possible, he knew, to be aroused and disgusted at the same time. Once, after Selda left, he had made love to a woman simply because he liked her boots. They were delicately tooled, with a leather strap around the heel as if to hold a spur. Her feet, though, were stubby and square and made him want to stop, but he didn't. As with Cassie, the experience just made him feel more alone.

The worst part was in the middle of their humping, when Cassie told him to move his thumb, which, apparently, was pressing on her shoulder. Her voice was at the ragged edge of something, and it took him a moment to understand what she was saying. But he obediently moved his thumb. Then, to prove he was no fool, he moved it right back.

In the tub, Slater raised his hands beside his ears and snapped his fingers. It was a habit he'd started after the power line. He tried not to do it in front of others.

When he got out, he decided it was too late to leave. He passed the cool hours of the evening in front of the television, sleeping off and on, and staying away from the windows so the ghosts wouldn't see him.

In the morning, he gathered his backpack and two sturdy boxes containing his clothes and a few other possessions. The furniture would stay behind. Some of it had been abandoned by Selda; the rest was Cassie's or possibly no one's. When your belongings don't really belong to you, he thought, it's time to go. But when he opened the blinds, he saw Ed Dickinson outside, Stetson on his head, his hand on the back of the Ford.

Slater let the screen door close behind him. He stood on the porch in bare feet.

"Are you the dead man who moved my car?" Dickinson said. "Don't ever do that again."

"Cassie sold it to me," Slater said.

"Like hell she did. It ain't hers to sell. That heap of stink is mine." Dickinson's red face sat atop a pale yellow shirt and a bolo tie. The right side of his skull sloped up at an odd angle, a look suggesting violence. Mayhem given and received. "How much she con you for it?"

"Six hundred."

"Six hundred? Don't you know better than to trust a dumb bitch?"

"She owed me the money," Slater said. "I'm leaving town."

"I'll bet you are." Dickinson moved closer to the porch. "So I guess you looked this bucket of bolts over pretty good. Crawled underneath and all? Checked her out from tits to toes?"

"Not really. No."

"Huh."

Dickinson took off his Stetson and looked past Slater. "I don't suppose you've seen Manny's brown ass around here this morning. What do you bet he's shacked up with some two-dollar Mexican whore? No offense to your girlfriend."

"She moved out a couple months ago. And she was half-Mexican."

"Half-Mexican. Which half, I wonder." He put a hand on the Ford. "Tell you what. You keep the car. I'll square up with Cassie. You just help me load her goddamn horses in the trailer. They're stubborn as hell."

"I don't know anything about horses."

"All the better."

Slater tried to read Dickinson's face, but it was big and blank. To get him to go away, he agreed to help.

"That'd be a blessing." The big man winked. "Come up to the house when you're ready."

The word *blessing* nearly queered the deal. Whatever Dickinson was up to, Slater thought, there would be nothing blessed about it.

In the Addition, he washed up, pulled a clean shirt from his bag, and laced his boots. He put his backpack and two boxes in the Ford and took a last look inside the Addition. As an afterthought, he strapped the Blue Dart onto his belt. The knife was a Tru-Balance, made for throwing, with a handle that someone had hollowed out. Slater called it the Blue Dart because Ernesto had called it that.

Ernesto was Selda's uncle. He had come out to the Addition on Easter morning, pedaling a rusted green bike twenty miles. When he got there, Selda wouldn't let him in, so Slater made coffee and took it outside with some folding chairs. They sat in the shade, drinking. Eventually, Ernesto stood up and threw the Blue Dart into one of the mesquites.

Selda blamed him for her father's death, he said, because he was the one who heard that Phelps Dodge was hiring. He and Miguel had gone to Bisbee together, but Miguel was given the wrong job. He was a born mechanic, Miguel was, but Mexicans were supposed to work in the tunnels, not take machine jobs from white men. The first Friday evening, the other workers went looking for Miguel.

"Selda forgets that Miguel was my brother," Ernesto said. "She wasn't there. So she imagines how it might have been, and she decides not to know anything else." He looked at Slater. "She doesn't forgive."

The old man threw the knife and hit the same spot on the mesquite three more times. "This was Miguel's knife. He should have kept it on his belt. He shouldn't have thrown it." He waved his hand at the mountains. "That was ten years ago."

"Long time," Slater said.

"Long time for you. Not for a skinny girl like her. She doesn't eat because she has the grudge inside. It fills her up." His eyes turned to crinkly slits. "So I serve my purpose. I help her keep her figure, yes?"

Ernesto retrieved the knife and showed Slater the secret compartment in the handle. It was full of sand.

"I used to keep it filled with salt. You need salt in the desert. Without the weight, the knife doesn't throw." The old man opened his palms, accepting all the unfairness of the world. "That was what killed Miguel. He ran out of salt."

A clank of dishes came from inside the Addition. Ernesto threw the Blue Dart again. "Grip and stance," the old man said. "And fifty years of practice. You try it."

When Slater threw, the knife landed in the dirt. After ten more tries, he was able to bounce it off the tree. Because there was nothing else to do, Ernesto began to teach him. The next weekend he came by again, and the Sunday after that. Slater guessed the old man was hoping to see Selda, but she never came out. In the process, Slater learned the pinch grip, the finger grip, the hammer grip.

"You get your throw, then we work on distance. Most of all, you have to be fast. Fast enough to kill a snake, yes? One motion." His hand moved in a blur. "They never know it's coming till it's in them." He winked. "Like with a girl, huh?"

"That's not my style," Slater said.

The lessons were better therapy than anything he had done in rehab. Ernesto made him throw hard to get a good snap at the end. After one of their sessions, the old man ran his fingers along the handle where Miguel Sanchero's initials were engraved.

"That's you now. M.S.—Michael Slater." He held the knife out to him. "This is yours. Take it. Or it will end up in a box like me."

The gift made Slater work harder. He learned the half turn, the easiest throw. He could hit a tree reliably, but he had trouble sticking the blade.

"Your back foot moves," Ernesto said one afternoon. "Watch how I stand."

"I am watching."

"You're watching the tree. Watch my feet."

"I can see both."

Ernesto held three fingers in front of Slater and moved them toward his ear until he found the limits of Slater's peripheral vision.

"That's a new one," Ernesto said. "I haven't seen that before."

"I'm full of surprises," Slater told him.

"Just keep throwing. Don't get old like me."

— 3 —

A RAILROAD BRIDGE rose over the Mississippi near Winona—
an elaborate structure with steel trestles and wrought-iron
truss work, spanning a full mile across the river, tying
Minnesota to Wisconsin. The bridge had been built in four
sections, each forming its own arch. The second span, over
the deepest part of the river, could swing open to let ships
pass. Near the top of the span was a wooden bridgetender's
shack—a cabin up in the trusses where, in the old days, an
operator would sit with nothing but a radio and a flask of
whiskey, watching miles of open river. The shack was abandoned now, the bridge automated.

On the Minnesota side of the river, Harp Maitland
stood watching an eastbound freight approach in the night.
The train was a ways off and going too fast to hop, but it
would slow as it rolled onto the bridge. He would jump
it and ride across the river. Two days later, if things went
right, he'd be back in Michigan.

Getting ready, he moved back from the rails into the
higher weeds. His right arm swung wide as he moved—a

gunslinger walk formed from days of wearing a tool belt, a hammer at his hip.

Harp wore an army coat stained with creosote. His hair was held back by a rubber band. He had spent the previous night in the bridgetender's shack with a slender young woman named Melinda. If he had met her in a dream, she would have been some kind of winged creature carrying him off to the forest. Instead he met her in a bar. She was small and dark and not much over twenty-one, and she was getting revenge on someone who needed to be taught a lesson—boyfriend, fiancé, asshole. She found Harp in the Crosscut Bar, looking at maps and drinking Molson. What kind of maps are those, she asked.

"Railroad lines," Harp said. He pointed out the different cross-hatching. "These are the ones I've ridden. And these I still need to ride."

He moved his backpack and she sat down. Don't use your luck and it goes away. That was one of his freight rules. It applied to women as well.

They had three more beers while she told him about the jerk who had left her. She had long dark hair and a trilobite fossil on a necklace that she didn't take off when they made love.

It was tragic, Harp thought. The fossil against her flesh. The smallness of her hand. The way the night disappeared and was gone forever. You needed a really long freight ride to get a tragedy like that off your mind.

The train that was coming at him—the one that would carry him across the river—was a Green Bay & Western. The Snake, it was called. It curved across Wisconsin to the town of Kewaunee on the edge of Lake Michigan. From there, the cars would be loaded onto a ferry, the *Chief Tecumseh*—a mammoth ship that carried whole freight trains in its belly.

He'd had to help Melinda climb the ironwork to get to the bridgetender's shack. Cold rungs led up the trusses to a narrow catwalk along the front. The cabin had been closed for years but the door was unlocked, just as Harp had guessed. "You first," he said to Melinda. Her eyes were alive with the danger of it all.

She had wanted her clothes off right away and after she undressed they stood and looked out at the darkening world. The farms and roads looked like something from a model railroad. They could see a bottling plant on the Wisconsin side of the river, a miniature factory. The tiny lights of Winona. Even without a naked woman, the view would have stunned him.

As the oncoming freight grew closer, Harp pushed the image of Melinda away. On freights, stray thoughts and distraction could kill. What mattered was each new breath. It was why he loved riding trains.

When the headlight hit him, he spread his arms, not hiding. The engineer raised a gloved hand and so did Harp. Here I am, he said.

Very quickly, he spotted a Milwaukee Road boxcar, open on both sides. He jogged even with the train, putting a gloved hand on its side to feel its speed. He let the freight cars slip past until the open boxcar caught up to him. As it drew alongside, he threw his backpack into the car, grabbed the door frame with his right hand, and leaped. His eyes saw nothing—it was all by feel, legs swinging up as far as he could hoist them. He rolled in easily and got to his feet.

My Crosscut Hop, he thought. Something to make you feel alive.

As the freight crossed the Mississippi, the ironwork of the spans flashed past, cutting the river into frames. Out one side, the moonlit water rippled up, reflecting broken planes of light. The other way, south, the river was smooth black, a sheet of mica.

The idea was to ride the Snake all the way across Wisconsin. In Kewaunee, he'd hide in a freight car and let the *Chief Tecumseh* carry him across Lake Michigan. To Wolverine, and Lane, the woman he lived with.

He supposed he should feel guilty about Melinda, but he didn't. Sometimes you had to betray others to be true to yourself. That was just the way it was. If you didn't know that, or if you were afraid to face it, you didn't get much of a life. Sometimes you paid the price. Shit in all its forms would rain down, but shit would rain no matter what. You couldn't stop it by trying to please others.

On the Wisconsin side of the river, the train surprised him by taking a switch. Instead of rolling east, it swung onto the southbound tracks of the Burlington Northern, carrying him away from Michigan and into Iowa.

Clear of the bridge, the freight was already picking up speed. There was little time to sort things out. Harp grabbed his pack and crouched by the door, searching for a spot to jump, looking for switches that might snap an ankle or bust his head. But the darkness hid everything in shadow.

Even as he tensed to jump, part of him thought how he had never ridden the southbound rails. Iowa was full of railroad towns he hadn't seen. He hesitated a second or two longer before stepping back from the door. Letting the moment pass, letting the train decide where he would go. It was the right thing to do, he was certain. In another minute, the southbound was rolling fast, heading into the night and the dark mystery of Iowa.

Melinda had REPENT AND BELIEVE in ballpoint on the pale side of her forearm. She went to the Methodist college and she had written it there in class when she was bored. On the floor of the bridgetender's shack, with her arms up over her head, the church words made her seem even more naked.

The freight swayed through gullies, cutting through trees and overgrown brush. Pockets of cold blew over Harp when the track dipped close to the river. He got out a joint and lit it, remembering nights when he woke beside Lane and found himself wishing for the boxcar floor. He worried sometimes that the memory of her body, which he carried with him when he traveled, pleased him more than the real thing. It would be better, he knew, if he stayed in Michigan more. But there was no stopping the going.

The track seemed to get louder as he got high and soon he forgot about Lane. The night was empty—there was just the breeze and the glowing joint and the fleeting glimpses of the Mississippi. All the good people had gone to sleep. Except for me, he thought. Except for the Methodist-humping, to-thyself-be-true freight riders. We never sleep. The night is just too rare.

—4—

NO ONE ANSWERED the door when Slater walked up to Cassie's house, so he let himself in, calling for Dickinson. No reply. He wandered to the kitchen and filled a glass with water. He watched it sweat onto the yellow counter as he waited. From the back of the house, Sammy was squawking. "Shut up. Show me your tits! Shut up."

There's a new kind of hell, Slater thought. Your husband disappears, and a bird keeps repeating his insults.

After a few minutes, he decided to take a look. The squawks led him down the hall to a partially closed door. Cassie's bedroom, he thought. He pushed it open and went in.

Inside was a freak show. The ceiling was painted black with gold trim. A naked, muscular cyclops took up an entire wall. The cyclops wore a Budweiser cap; a smiling pixie hovered over his huge phallus, sprinkling fairy dust. Volcanic mountains erupted behind him.

On the opposite wall, the same artist had painted a unicorn, hog-tied and suspended above a fire. Pygmies in

Speedos were roasting the beast. The baseboards were covered in fake furry leopard skin.

Sammy—a blue and gold macaw—was in a wrought-iron cage covered with fine mesh. The cage sat opposite the bed and was nearly as tall as Slater. The base, lined with the *Tucson Citizen*, was at least a yard square and dotted with colorful poop.

"Don't make me shoot you," Sammy said.

On the wall near the cage was a cheap wooden plaque showing a romantic couple, arm in arm on a sunset beach. *I Love You More Today Than Yesterday*, the caption read, *But Not As Much As Tomorrow*. Someone had drawn a thick black line through the last part, so it read *But Not As Much As Tom*.

Thomas Gorrel, Slater thought. He was still looking at the plaque when Ed Dickinson appeared in the doorway. Slater saw him in his peripheral vision, but jumped anyway when Dickinson spoke.

"What the hell are you doing in here?" Dickinson asked.

"I heard the bird talking. I thought maybe you were back here."

"You thought I was a bird?" Dickinson tipped his head back, as if judging a midget act. "You seem to know your way around this house pretty well."

"I just wandered back. I never knew Cassie could paint."

"She can't. Her husband did all this. He was a kick-ass artist when he wasn't all fucked up."

"Good for him," Slater said. "I guess."

"You don't like me, do you?"

"I don't know you."

"You can pound sand up your ass. I know when someone doesn't like me.'

Sammy squawked.

"Make him say 'Show me your tits,'" Ed Dickinson said.

"He did that one."

"Make him do it again. Say, 'Show me your tits,' Sammy."

Before Slater could speak, Sammy repeated the line. The bird wasn't doing Cassie's husband, he realized. It was Ed all along.

A dented, mud-splattered trailer was hitched to a red-and-white Chevy pickup by the horse pen. The trailer was several shades of white, like someone had used house paint and a roller on it. Rust edged the flat surfaces where water collected. Next to it, the red-and-white truck seemed even brighter.

"1978 Silverado," Dickinson said. "454 engine, 4-barrel carb. Had it a month."

Cassie's two horses were already in the trailer, their heads visible above the rear doors. "I loaded them while you were screwing around in the house." Dickinson thumped the side of the trailer. "You just have to help me unload them."

"I need to get going. I was on my way out of town."

"Bullshit. This won't take long. Just a short ways into the scrub, toward the old Willow Place. Back roads. I never go alone. One little thing goes wrong, and you're at the mercy."

Slater looked across the scrubgrass to the highway. "Which direction?"

"North. You lead the way. Watch my signals."

North was the way he was going. He agreed to go along.

At the end of the dirt driveway, they turned onto Highway 77. Slater, in the Ford, kept his eye on Dickinson in the rearview. When they'd gone a few miles, Dickinson put his blinker on. Up ahead was a dirt road that led into the Sonora.

For a few seconds, Slater thought about accelerating, following the highway north. Let Dickinson chase him. But he turned onto the dirt road instead. He'd given his word, and even with a bully like Dickinson, keeping it might mean something. They drove into the Sonora and the highway receded in his mirrors, becoming just a heat blur. Soon even that was gone.

Dexter Photo Lab was a steel-framed building in the woods outside Traverse City, far enough from Lake Michigan to lose the cooling breeze. Near the employee entrance, Stuffer Jude stood smoking a joint. She wore a suede vest, short skirt, and black fishnet stockings. When Lane walked by, Jude offered a toke. "It'll make the day go faster."

"The day goes fast enough as it is." But Lane took a hit anyway.

"Everything fine in Black and White?" Jude asked.

Everything was not fine in Black and White. Lane's machine had shut down twice that morning—once when the paper broke and once when the Dektol got too warm, blackening the photos. Shutting the machine down was an offense against management; Stottle had come by personally to supervise the blaming. Her boss had a tongue from a low-budget porno flick, a little pink eel that wouldn't stay in his mouth.

"Some first-class people used to work here when I started," Jude said. "Now there's some first-class jerks."

"Stottle's okay," Lane said, "if you keep him where you can see him."

"He's a water boy with a tiny pecker. I should have cut it off when I had the chance."

Lane didn't want to think about that.

From the loading dock came the whine of an electric drill. "Seen your brother lately?" Jude asked.

"I don't see Charlie. And I don't run his drugs."

The stuffers spent eight hours a day at the conveyer belt, putting snapshots into paper wallets. It was minimum-wage work, and they all got high. Jude was more or less their leader.

"I'd go see him myself," Jude said, "but I'm *persona non grata*. Last time I went there, Charlie threw a pool float at me."

"Charlie doesn't have a pool."

"Well, he has pool floats. He throws hard, too. Maybe you could mention my name. I'd ask him myself, but you know what he'd say." She lowered her voice, doing Charlie. "*That's your problem, babe.*"

Lane took a last toke and handed the joint back.

When the break ended, she found ten rolls waiting to be run. The machine she operated was a black-and-white photo processor called a Silva—twenty feet of tanks and drums and torque. It was built through the wall, with one end in darkness and the other end in light. Her job was to splice large rolls of light-sensitive photo paper onto the dark end—while the machine ran continuously—and collect rolls of school photos off the daylight end. Dexter had the school-photo business from Michigan to Florida.

Timing was everything. As with life, there were lots of ways to fuck up. If the tension on the rollers was too strong, the paper tore. Too loose and the paper wrinkled. The chemicals had to be fresh, the temperature regulated. The speed of the paper as it moved through the tanks had to be just so.

She'd been hoping for an easy afternoon. Running ten rolls was a hassle even when she was straight. Stoned, it would be a royal bitch. The standard drill was to run them through the machine one at a time—racing to and from the darkroom, making ten splices with perfect timing. It occurred to her that she could combine them all into one monster roll, instead. Then she could kick back and let the Silva run for an hour while her head cleared. It seemed like a good idea.

But making the monster roll in the cramped darkroom took forever. The first nine rolls had to be unwound and by the time she was halfway done, coils of photo paper covered the floor. She was afraid to move her feet, for fear of tearing the paper. After a half hour the door from the light trap opened and Stottle thrust his head inside—a squinting apparition. He'd come in from the light and couldn't see her.

"Hey," he said. "What's going on?" His wet tongue came darting out. "You need any help, honey? Is anyone in here?"

Lane considered the possible answers to that. She was about to tell him to go to hell, but by the time she found the words, the squinting head was gone.

As they drove across the dry land, Dickinson pulled ahead, leading Slater deeper into the desert. Soon they were following a dry streambed, an arroyo. The two horses were shifting shadows above the gate of the dingy trailer. Until now, Slater had never paid any attention to them.

He'd had the blowjob dream the night before. Again. The first time he had it, he was on morphine, a 20-mg drip in Henry Ford Medical Center, and it was more like a vision than a dream. One minute the hospital room was there; then it shimmied and vanished, replaced by a sidewalk. A billboard showed a candidate for city council, a woman kneeling at his feet. HE'S GETTING A BLOWJOB, the billboard said. VOTE FOR SCHMIDT. Across the street, waiting for the light, two men were being done by two women. The stick-figure man on the WALK sign was getting head from a stick-figure woman.

In the dream, Slater crossed the road and went into a coffee shop. Three customers at the counter were all getting hoovered. Booths were filled with raised rumps and bobbing heads. A pretty twenty-year-old, chipper and fresh-faced, stepped up to take Slater's order. "Hey stranger," she said. "What can I do you for?"

Embarrassed, Slater avoided her eyes. "Cup of coffee," he said. "And maybe a blowjob?"

Everyone stopped. Her smile drained and she slapped him hard.

"That's disgusting," she told him.

Someone else yelled for him to shove off. The kneeling women murmured agreement.

At that point, the hot shame usually woke him up.

When he told Selda about the dream, she traced her finger around his skull, following the route of the cranial saw. "I know what it means. It means you're incomplete."

By the time she left him, that was all she ever said. You're missing something. And it's not a blowjob.

Driving through the desert gulch, he wondered if she was right.

The sides of the gully were lined with yellow flowers and brittlebush and desert lavender. In a flash flood, the gulch would swallow them instantly, Slater knew. But it was too narrow to turn around. Finally, they came to a slightly wider spot and Dickinson stopped. There was no ranch and no willow tree. Slater cut the engine and walked to the truck.

"A hundred and ten in the shade," Dickinson said, getting out. "That's why I never come out here alone. You ever shoot a horse?"

"I thought you said you were selling them."

"I never said that. Maybe I should sell them to you."

"I didn't sign up for this."

Dickinson got a rifle from the cab of the Silverado. "Don't matter what you signed up for. I'll do the hard part. Then we'll turn around and you'll be on your way."

"Count me out," Slater said.

Dickinson laughed at that.

The first horse out of the trailer was Buster, a blood bay with a white stripe between his eyes. Dickinson led him fifty paces down the gully and wrapped the lead around a viney shrub that Selda used to call a Jacob's Staff. The bright red flowers matched the truck.

"Why not just let them go?" Slater said. "You don't need to shoot them."

"That's real ignorance. You have no idea how cruel that is."

The second horse had welts and sores around its halter. Dickinson led him to the first and tied their leads together. Overhead, a Phantom broke the sound barrier. The thunder spooked the horses, but Dickinson calmed them with some soft, reassuring guff.

The fighter jets were from Davis AFB. Selda delivered vegetables there; Slater had seen the place. The sign by the gate said *Excuse Our Noise. It's the Sound of Liberty.* That was Selda's motto too. She could fill up one end of a bar with laughter. The best part was how she pointed when she laughed. Her head went back and her arm extended and you knew you had made her happy. Then she started pointing at others and that was not so good.

Their last day together was the loudest. You have a small crooked penis, she yelled. Your Jesus has a small crooked penis. You scratch at night. He denied it, but some of what she said was true. You're not a whole person, she said. You've got a head full of nonreconcilable bullshit, which was smarter than he thought she knew.

She was beautiful on fire.

Dickinson fed a magazine into the rifle, engaged the bolt and locked it. "We all got wants and needs, kid," he said. "I got mine, you got yours. Sooner we finish, sooner we'll both be drinking a beer."

He cradled the rifle with one arm and put a set of orange earplugs in his ears. "You know what COB is?" he shouted. "Corn, oats, and barley. It's what I'm sick of buying."

Before Slater could answer, Dickinson raised the rifle and shot Buster between the ear and eye. For a split second, the horse looked like a puppet on a string, all four legs jerking up at once. His neck snapped with a crack as his full weight hit the ground. The other bay reared, bellowing. Dickinson waited a horrible half minute, then laid it down with one shot. He nodded at his work, then turned to Slater.

"Sorry," he said, taking the plugs from his ears. "Should have given you some of these."

The second horse gave out a wet, groaning wail. Slater snapped his fingers by his ears, trying to keep the sound out of his head. He half expected the big man to produce a shovel and order him to start digging, but it turned out not to be that kind of movie.

"Go ahead now and lead the way out," Dickinson said. "There's a turnaround up ahead."

Slater dropped his arms, brushing the Blue Dart on his belt. The dying horse made a guttural sound that stopped abruptly as Slater got to the Ford. From the corner of his eye, he saw Dickinson put the earplugs back in. In a single, panicked second, Slater found time to marvel how good his freakish vision would be on a basketball court. By the time that image left, Dickinson was raising the rifle, aimed at his back. Slater turned with the Blue Dart in his hand and yelled as he threw.

Dickinson made the mistake of whirling, not diving. The knife struck him between the shoulder blades and went in deep. As he fell, he fired into the grille of the Silverado. Green radiator fluid shot out, hitting him in the chest. Both men were yelling now.

Slater ran to him and pulled the rifle away. Dickinson, on his knees, clawed at his shirt. He tried to stand but jerked back down and Slater grabbed the handle of the knife. The blade twisted as it came out. It took Slater a second to hear the words inside Dickinson's howl. "Don't leave me."

Until then, it had never occurred to him. He took the bolt from the rifle and threw it into the desert. Under the hood of the Silverado, he cut the distributor wires and sliced through the fan belt.

Dickinson, still on his knees, had worked his shirt off. His skin was fiery red where the fluid had hit him; his back was covered with blood. As Slater ran to the Ford, Dickinson tried to lunge at him, but seized up and toppled forward.

"I've got a million dollars," he yelled. "A quarter million. I got any kind of drug you want." He crawled toward the Ranchero, his gut heaving as he shouted. "I'll pay you anything."

The steering wheel burned Slater's fingers. It took him nearly a minute to turn the Ranchero in the gully, lurching forward and back. Dickinson managed to get to his feet and stagger a few steps toward him, his face squeezed tight in pain. "You bastard," he said. "I'll find you. I'll kill you."

A desert bird chirped. Slater drove off.

When Dickinson was tiny in the rearview, he stopped, knowing he had to go back. At low idle, the Ranchero's engine shuddered, missing slightly.

To hell with that, Slater said. He put the Ranchero in drive and followed the dirt track to Highway 77. By the time he got there, the sweat was dry on his face.

The road was empty. Slater looked both ways. Tucson was south. He could tell someone there, send medical help. The Blue Dart, still bloody, was on the floor. It pointed like a compass. North.

— 5 —

CHARLIE STOOD ON the balcony of Hidden Mist in sunglasses and a Hawaiian shirt, an orange-juice-and-vodka in hand. Breakfast. The sun was up on the Lake and the Spreadables had an early-morning party going in the boat. Probably they'd been up all night. The boat was zigging recklessly, a game of Don't Drop Me in progress. Fun for the guys.

The sky over Lake Michigan was cloudless; every little wave was lit. A perfect day, unless you were being squeezed by beady-eyed suppliers on one side and the undersheriff on the other. Charlie hooked a chair with his foot and sat. It was hard to make an honest living in drugs anymore.

The boat was a fifteen-foot Apache. As it passed close to Hidden Mist, he heard the squeals of the girls out on the water. Don't Drop Me was a parasailing game. Girls went up for a bird's-eye view. Maybe they did one of the fun drugs first. The guys drove as erratically as possible. To avoid stomach-wrenching drops, you had to shed a piece of clothing. By the end you were up in the sky wearing only a life vest. If that.

Of course, being naked at the end of a rope was its own kind of charge.

Despite their bravado, the guys were always the ones who got hurt. They drank and jeered and peed over the side, and pretty soon they went over. Most of them couldn't swim, but they kept a death grip on their Bud Lites as they splashed and gulped for air. Except for the liability issue, it was kind of funny.

Charlie took a pack of matches from his bathrobe. The bong was on the glass table. He lit a match and fired it up. Some of us ain't so carefree, he thought. Some of us gotta get up in the morning and solve problems.

The problem was Lazenbeck. The undersheriff was up for election and wanted TV spots. But TV was expensive, so Lazenbeck had given Charlie an ultimatum: Either you become my catch of the week, so I can haul you off in cuffs in front of the cameras and bask in free publicity, or else we double my royalties, so I can buy some airtime.

Royalties. The undersheriff thought *bribe* was an ugly word, so he used the fancy term.

Neither of Lazenbeck's options worked for Charlie. There was no extra money to up the payments. Lately, as the days passed, Charlie had begun to imagine the undersheriff coming for him, TV crew in tow, in the early hours of the morning. In movies, the big battles were fought at night, but in the real world they always came for you at dawn. But not this dawn anyway. There was that, at least.

He took another hit. A bikini top fell to the water. Before he could get a good buzz going, Tracy came clomping down the spiral stairs, heading for the kitchen. Her hair was stiff, and she wore a green and white jersey signed by every member of the Spartans' kickoff-return team.

"Whoa," she said. "Bong's out early. Must be serious."

Tracy was the shortest stripper Charlie had ever known—short and somewhat squat. In her club days, when she was known as Vulva Voom, she'd had a tendency to overcompensate with lewd favors. Tongue in the ear, under-the-table stroking, occasional dry-humping on the couch. She was endlessly greedy, a virtue in the world of vice. She and Charlie ran Hidden Mist together.

"Go back to bed," Charlie told her.

Tracy grabbed a Diet Coke and came out on the balcony. "This a private party? Or are you sharing?"

Charlie put his hands out, palms up, as Tracy took a hit.

The bong was a thing of beauty. Six hundred dollars of hand-blown glass.

"What's got you up so early?" Tracy asked. "Let me guess. The Stink."

The Stink was their supplier. Charlie was behind on his last three payments. Threats had been made. "Let me worry about this stuff," he said.

"Okay. But I got the answer for you. It's all very simple." She leaned over the bong and took a hit.

"Do tell."

Tracy held the toke as long as she could, then let it out in a rush. "Lazenbeck needs to bust someone, right? The Stink and his tribe need to get paid. Two negatives. Put them together and make a positive. Lazenbeck busts The Stink. We use the money we owe The Stink to pay Lazenbeck and throw a party with what's left over. Two birds slaughtered with one stone."

Charlie put his feet up on the table. In the distance, a naked girl tacked across the sky.

"That's brilliant," he said. "Except The Stink's opera-
tion is two counties away. Lazenbeck has no authority there.
If he goes after The Stink, the voters will rip him limb from
limb for wasting their tax booty on someone else's mess."
Charlie grunted at the stupidity of voters. "After which, The
Stink's tribe, as you call them, will come and kill me. And
then who would light the bong in the morning?"

Tracy made a duck face, pressing her lips together. "Alright. How about Chance?"

Chance Ballinger sold drugs to the gentry in the town
of Charlevoix, to the north of Hidden Mist. He was immensely successful and smelled of salad oil. Charlie hated
his guts.

"Nice idea," Charlie said, "but that mouse don't
squeak. Lazenbeck's got a slice of that action too. I'll bet
he's pressuring Chance just like us. The little jerk's probably pissing his silk undies right now, trying to figure how
he can shift all the pain on to us."

The Apache buzzed by on Lake Michigan. *The Big
Lake*, as it was called, or usually just *the Lake*.

"You have a better plan?"

"I'm thinking about the Whispering Sands."

"Oh, please." Tracy let out a puff of air. "That money's history."

The Whispering Sands were condos, or supposed to
be. The developers had given Lazenbeck and other officials
a private investment deal. In return, the developers got a
variance to build on the edge of Lake Michigan. The undersheriff had convinced Charlie to put some money into
the condos, too. It was supposed to be a sure thing, a ten-
to-one payout down the road. But it turned out there were
wetlands involved, and the specter of progress had flushed

out naysayers of every stripe. Now the condos stood half-built, covered in plastic and mired in three levels of lawsuits. Construction had been shut down for months.

"You're years from seeing any of that money, Charles. If ever." Tracy finished her soda and put the can on the balcony rail. "Your ROI is DOA."

"I'm not thinking about the condos getting finished," he said. "I'm thinking about blowing them up. Not personally, of course."

"Jesus, Charlie. You're stoned."

"Thanks for noticing. But think about this. The Whispering Sands are insured. If and when they explode, the project's dead. Everyone gets their money back, or a reasonable facsimile thereof. The Stink gets paid. Lazenbeck gets his bribe. You and I stay alive. You got a better idea?"

"And who's going to make them explode?"

"I haven't figured that out."

"You're insane, Charlie. It's the 34B Club all over again."

"I was young and foolish then."

"What was your slogan? *The Righteous Rack*?"

Charlie had once managed a topless club in Saginaw. One day, he saw a bit in *Playboy* about America's favorite tit size. Someone had done a poll. The winner, hands down, was 34B. Struck by inspiration, Charlie renamed the place and fired all the non-34Bs. Tracy was tired of dancing and her tits were overqualified, so Charlie made her assistant manager. The 34B Club went under in less than three months.

"I see the problem now," Charlie said. "When everything's perfect, nothing's perfect. Next time I'll have a few 36 double Ds mixed in for variety."

"Oh, please." Tracy took another hit.

"You can't follow a banjo act with a banjo act. That's what I learned." He moved the bong to the floor, out of her reach. "I wouldn't expect you to understand. It's Zen."

"It's bull. Men like big tits. That's what you should have learned."

Down below, the Apache docked. The girls, whom Charlie called the Spreadables, came in the back door and passed through the living room on their way upstairs. Two were naked. The third, Shannon, wore long sleeves and jeans.

"Pardon me for asking," Tracy said when they were gone, "but why do we let her stay here? She doesn't strip. She doesn't entertain customers. She doesn't sleep with anyone. She's so un-perv, it's scary."

Charlie shrugged. "She's a project. Under your tutelage, I'm sure her hang-ups will disappear. Along with her clothes. And then we'll see her righteous rack."

Tracy yawned. "I wouldn't count on it."

Charlie leaned forward and lowered his voice. "Okay, but dig this: I know what the Whispering Sands are whispering."

"Really? Tell me. I promise I won't laugh."

He looked at her without smiling. "*Boom.*"

Tracy snorted. "I thought it was going to be *Money.*"

"That too."

She stood up and pulled the Spartan jersey to mid-thigh. "I'm going back to bed. It's too early for me to be thinking up evil deeds."

"I've already thought up the deed," Charlie said. "All I need is the doer."

When she was gone, Charlie took a last hit from the bong and watched the smoke travel through the glass passageways. The smoke was trapped and could only go where the bong let it. It spiraled and turned and doubled back in the elaborate glass, following the unseen hand of the bong creator. When it finally escaped, it wafted into the air and disappeared.

That's what we need, Charlie told himself. Someone who could be tricked into following a path and then be gone. He took one last hit and a name came to mind. Someone headstrong and a little too honest. It was almost obvious, he thought, when you got right down to it. It wasn't that hard. You just had to think like smoke.

— 6 —

THE RANCHERO HAD a shimmy at 65, so Slater kept the needle at 70. He drove with the windows down and checked the rearview constantly for police. When he had covered two hundred miles, he stopped and bought a six-pack. In the parking lot, he held a sweating bottle against his head and tried to forget what he'd seen in the desert. But his head played it on a loop. Dickinson crawling, dying. Adjusting his wants and needs.

Back on the highway, Slater felt better. In complicated times, he told himself, make a simple plan. His plan was to get as far away from the desert as he could.

In a mountain town, he parked in the shade of a desert willow and stretched out in the flatbed. The wind coming over the ridge was cool and he slept close to the surface, listening to the rustling noise of the trees. Soon, he wasn't sure whether the sound came from inside his head or out and he slept the full, thick sleep of exhaustion.

When he woke, a moon had risen in the twilight sky. He got back in the Ford and found the highway again. *The Thing,* a billboard proclaimed. *500 Miles Ahead. Scarifying.*

In the Henry Ford emergency room, Slater's brain had been the subject of debate. One option was to put Slater into a coma and hope the swelling would go down. The other choice was to operate. Either way was risky. Jimbo liked to operate. He made a preliminary incision five centimeters above Slater's eyebrows, drawing the scalpel to the right ear and then to the left, cutting through burned skin. He did the same on the back of Slater's head, through all five layers of scalp. When he was done, he retraced the cut with a gleaming miniature buzz saw with three diamond-faced cutting surfaces. Humming to himself, he applied the instrument to the edge of Slater's left temple and cut counter-clockwise, opening him up.

For the next seventy-two hours, Jimbo and his team waited to see whether the brain would continue to swell—in which case, Slater would die—or whether the damaged tissue would begin to shrink. During those hours, Slater slept in a clear plastic tent—twenty-five cubic feet of precisely monitored, highly filtered, temperature-controlled air.

On the third day, the swelling stopped. By late afternoon, Jimbo had moved on to bigger challenges, calculating payments on beachfront property in Virginia under three different amortization schemes while mentally undressing the new Asian nurse manager. A second team put Slater back together, closing his skull with a titanium plate.

His burns were mild, considering. The ICU staff kept him on morphine for fourteen days. *You'll look ten years younger when we're done*, a nurse said, unless he dreamed it.

No one really knew what kind of long-term damage the voltage might have done. *I opened up your skull*, Jimbo said. *That voids the warranty*. There was a doc who could help, a genius who needed brain patients for his research, but he'd just taken a position at the University of Arizona. They could arrange to have Slater transferred.

When they shipped him out, Jimbo gave him a small vial, about half the size of a roll of pennies. Bone dust from the cranial saw. Slater kept it as a souvenir. After he met Ernesto, he poured it into the handle of the Blue Dart.

The Northern Arrow was back on screen two. The speed wasn't to blame this time, because he hadn't taken any for hours.

It was not the real Northern Arrow, of course. The real one was a passenger train: coach cars of velvet and varnish and white-gloved conductors to sir or ma'am you. That Arrow had once run to the tip of Michigan's mitten, carrying bold adventurers from Ohio. It was a tourist train, long gone, so Harp had reinvented it.

Harp's Arrow was a freight train that started where the original had left off, rising through Canada on the Algoma Central to the Canadian National, winding north and west and north some more, a thousand kilometers to the town of Churchill. As far as you could go by freight.

To distract himself, Slater decided to try working. Productivity, the businessman's drug.

One by one he sorted through his clips. Eventually the Northern Arrow faded and a battle appeared on his screens. The center monitor showed mortar rounds—firefights and columns of smoke blowing through a documentary he'd lost the thread of.

Ah yes, he said. The soldiers. The brave ones.

What music? he wondered. Something martial, probably. Maybe an anthem from the sixties. Somewhere there was an edit sheet listing the effects to be added. The producers' music choices were uniformly dreadful—up-tempo, cornball dreck with names like "Rousing Themes of Industry," or "Dynamic Moods of America." Listening to them too long could cause permanent damage.

But mine is not to reason why, he reminded himself. Mine is to dick around with graphics and smooth out the final cuts. That's mine. And then there's the past. That's mine as well.

Hitting a key, Slater made the war rewind. Atrocities flashed by in reverse: wounds healed, dead men rose, black smoke vanished over unbroken land. It all looked very lifelike, but it was not very much like life.

On screen three, a bridge exploded. Slater stopped the action, went back, and watched the bridge blow up again. Nice color. Fire-engine red. Sweet lens flare too. A young soldier was crouched in the corner of the shot with a look on his face that suggested revelation—one of those moments when everything changed.

In freeze-frame, the soldier waited for a touch from Slater to lead him on or take him back. Hell, Slater thought. He got out his stash, broke a Smiling O in two, and swallowed half. Just enough to get him going as he rifled through the edit sheet.

Working the keyboard, he curled the corner of the image and flipped it over like a page. Underneath was another part of the war, another group of soldiers. He checked his list and applied his arsenal of gimcracks. He superimposed a map. He rotated a company of infantrymen, shrinking them as they spun. He took scenes of politicians, joined them into a strip, and made the strip turn in a circle at the center of the screen.

As if effects were needed.

Working quickly because of the amphetamine, he assembled the remaining graphics and still shots on the black and whites, and laid the soundtrack under the action. The finishing touches took several hours. When he was done, he walked through the final edit, studying every crossfade, every cut. Close enough, he decided. According to the meters, the highs could go a bit higher, but only just. He could sweeten the audio later if anyone complained.

It was after midnight when he pried the lid off his second Rolling Rock of the night. Down the hall, the elevator sounded with a soft electronic ping. The doors slid open and a bank of fluorescents went on. In his peripheral vision he saw Dimi Webster.

Officially, Dimi was art department, acting assistant something, a victim of sexual politics—first promoted, then blocked by front-office rivals. At least, that was what he'd heard. She had short blond hair and a diamond pin through her nose, and a way of tilting her head that Slater found appealing. She came into his edit suite and sat on his couch, a cup of coffee in her hand.

"Long time no see," Slater said.

"I came up last night," she told him, "but you were asleep."

"Are you sure it was me? I was probably just resting."

"It was you." Dimi sipped her coffee. "Dunlap got the axe today. Graphics is in shambles. Nobody knows who to toady up to." The tiny diamond in her nose sparkled.

"I heard. Matthews told me."

Matthews was chief of night security at Spectrum. Part tabloid, part sphinx. Two or three times a week he came by to pass a joint and share the glad tidings of the working world—who just got fired, or who was about to get fired and didn't know it yet. It was Matthews who had provided Slater's couch, salvaged from the streets. A place for the working people of the world to park their butts, he said, though in fact only Matthews and Dimi ever wandered into Slater's dim lantern light, Matthews early, Dimi late, and their butts were nothing alike—one Barbie-doll cute, the other massive and black.

"You hear about our screw-up?" Dimi asked. "Every planet in the 3M video is labeled wrong. We'll be here all night fixing it."

"The stars are out of order. No wonder I feel fucked up."

"When do you not?" She sought out his eyes—looking for signs of the drug, probably. "What are you working on?"

"Men with guns. A war of some type." He put his hand on the drawer where he kept his stash. One more Smiling O would be perfect.

"So you know," Dimi said. "I heard a rumor about you the other day. From Erickson. He said a bottle of Ritalin is missing from his office."

"Erickson thinks I'm stealing his Ritalin? Jesus."

"He didn't say that specifically."

Slater watched Dimi take another sip of coffee. She made it look like the most ordinary thing in the world. Raise cup. Drink. He wished he had it on film.

"I didn't know Erickson was on Ritalin," he said. "Or I might have been tempted."

"He's a dangerous guy, Mike. He's not to be messed with."

Screen three was flickering. In a minute, the Northern Arrow would be back. "Fucking Erickson," Slater said. "We should take him down. We should fog his film."

North through New Mexico, Slater followed the path of
the Rio Grande. Beyond the lights of Santa Fe, moonlit
mountains rose. One of them wasn't really a mountain, or
so Slater had heard, but a hollowed-out armory. "Warhead
Warehouse" it was called. Who knew if the story was true?
It was the sort of thing people liked to believe. Maybe it
reminded them of how false the surface is. How much lies
hidden. Or maybe it was the idea of containment, the vault
sealed tight and all that.

He kept the Ford Ranchero at 70.

But there is no such thing as containment, he thought.
If you have explosives, sooner or later they have to explode. It's how the world works.

Around midnight, he stopped for fuel. The station was
nearly deserted; a radio in the office threw heavy-metal
lyrics out to the pumps. The skinny kid who took Slater's
money made change with simian slowness.

"A blonde, a black, your head in a sack," the kid said,
singing along. He had Dickinson's hateful eyes. Over the
door was a sign that said *Don't forget to ask for your free
slap in the face.*

A hundred miles later, on a twisting mountain road-
way, Slater noticed something fluttering at the edge of his
vision. The image caught the reflected light of a road sign
then fell back into the slipstream. It was the Woman With
One Eye.

Vanish, he told her. But the specter did not leave.

The Woman With One Eye had been the defining person in his father's life. Through his father, she haunted the
whole family.

In real life, the Woman With One Eye was Slater's aunt, his father's sister. As a girl, she had endured the meager joys of farm life and a pesky brother. The family was poor, the crops marginal. One day near the chicken coop, the boy approached his sister with a stick. He was six, maybe seven years old, and eager to play. His sister was not. Angered by the boredom of the farm, and defiant, he thrust at her.

Before the accident, she had not been a child who smiled much. Afterward, wearing an eye patch, she denied herself all pleasure. Perhaps she thought she deserved disfigurement, had done something terrible to earn it. Whatever—it wasn't her story that affected Slater. It was his father's story—never spoken but ever present. His father's story was that some terrible part of him had gotten loose and maimed his sister. To protect other innocents, the beast must never be let loose again. His father became a quiet, tightly constrained man. Nevermore did he parry or thrust.

As a boy, Slater knew nothing of the accident. His ignorance made him all the more vulnerable to its aftereffects. Through the magic of daily life, his father's restraint was passed to Slater. He developed a natural timidity.

But the Woman With One Eye wasn't timid. Just the opposite. She was going for the gusto, making up for lost time. She was for letting it all hang out. She taunted Slater, daring him to do the same. That's what he'd been doing on the freight train with Harp, the night he got hit by the power line: he'd been going for it. It was why he'd slept with Cassie. So far, the gusto hadn't exactly worked out.

Driving, he did his best to ignore the specter. But the night was lonely. It was hard giving up old ghosts.

Around three in the morning, he pushed a tape into the deck and congas burst from behind him. After an adjustment, the sound equalized, front and rear, until the beat came from within, became more feeling than sound. It mixed with the texture of the road and took him away from himself. Soon, he wasn't driving, just unrolling into the beat. To Raton, to Trinidad, and, after that, Pueblo and north, where water replaced the desert, where the cerveza became beer. The road piled up behind him, his headlights fit the night like pegs.

Along the roadside, another billboard rose up for The Thing. *The Inevitable Is Coming,* this one said. *300 Miles.*

At night, the railroad revealed its secrets and there was something to see everywhere you looked—if you were tough enough to be there in the first place. A curving track, a river of boxcars: Soo, Great Northern, Milwaukee, Chessie, Canadian Pacific, Short Life & Misery 050616—boxcar with a wooden floor, the boxcar carrying Harp across the upper Midwest, through the top of the middle, and the song of the wheels is ride.

Ride: past scrap heaps and factories and beaten bums waving, past the ends of towns, through empty fields and junkyards, past everything man has made and the things man can never make, eventually past light. At night Harp stood in the boxcar and a halo rode the train, low above the engine, while landscapes turned amber, half-finished, pristine, and never glimpsed again. In Minnesota, moons veered from safe trajectories, and the brightest lights of cities blew past like sparks from a half-smoked joint—*I'll light it, you light it, let me light it*—the air warm like Lane's body. Ride: in a soft cloth sleeping bag if you can, if they don't detrain you or ditch you or spot you at sidings or kick you over the hump; ride, then wake in the darkness with the clattersong loud, a stream of words launched from a sling, all tearing past at once, and from the deep part of the night one word rings clear, one word, an inscription—ride.

The Iowa train had taken him to East Dubuque and from there to Green Island and then the dregs of Davenport. Finally he caught a freight to the switchyard in St. Paul.

Some people said it was called the Pig's Eye yard. Some people said it wasn't. With trains, there were always things you didn't know.

A switch engine in the center of the yard was pushing a string of cars up the hump. At the crest, a hump rat lifted the coupler pin, setting each car free, to be shunted onto one of a dozen outbound tracks, sorted by destination. Harp's car moved slowly to the top of the hump, where it was cut loose. It gathered speed and momentum on its downhill run until it was flying. Finally, it banged onto a string of outbound cars—coupling on with such force that both doors slammed shut, sealing it in darkness. But by then Harp was already out of the car and watching from the shadows, knowing when to ride and how to wait, and that his fate was with the train.

$$— 7 —$$

AROUND NOON, TURKEY vultures found the two dead horses. Dickinson lay with his mouth in the dirt, dried snot
decorating his cheek. He had expected to die, and when
he didn't, he forced himself to crawl into the hot shade
of the trailer. A barbed pain ran up his spine and into his
teeth and eyes. A pair of dragonflies darted by his head,
tormenting him. When he decided the pain could get no
worse, he crawled to the truck and discovered the asswipe
had locked the cab.

Friend, he thought, I was planning to kill you, anyway.
But now it'll be slower and with more screams. All because
you had to be a prick and lock the door.

Still on his knees, he worked off his right sock and began inching forward, collecting stones. His skin was on fire
where he had been scalded, and spasms of pain sent him
down to his elbows twice, forcing him to rest his forehead
on the ground. Eventually he managed to fill the toe of the
sock with small rocks. Clenching his jaw, he rose to his

knees and swung the bludgeon hard against the truck's window. It bounced back. The pain nearly killed him; the air in his throat felt like razors. It took three more swings to break the window. He leaned against the tire when it was done and pictured the Ranchero driving away, *Flash Me* on the tailgate and a quarter million hidden in the side panels.

That got him angry enough to stand. He worked the door open and managed to flop into the cab, bent like he was waiting to be spanked. When he found the Percocet, he held the bottle close to his face and counted. Five left. He ate two, closed his eyes, and passed out.

The difference between driving a car and riding the rails, Slater told Matthews, was that the highway made you crazy and the railroad made you sane. That was the peril of the rails. Sanity in a crazed world.

"Tell me about it," Matthews said. He brushed marijuana ash from his broad chest. "I listen to crazy white people every day."

"And night," Slater added.

On the screens, a teenage drink-and-drive piece played, in need of grisly stills and statistics. Slater shuffled through the betas.

It was early in the evening and Dimi hadn't stopped by yet. Slater was telling Matthews about the blowjob dream.

"What was her name?" Matthews asked. "Selma? Selda? She got it all wrong. A dream like that doesn't mean you're incomplete. It means you need a blowjob." Matthews passed the glowing joint. "What I really want to know is where you hide the girlie films."

"There are no girlie films."

"So you say."

On screen one a red Camaro ran into a wall. The edit sheet told Slater to freeze the crash and overlay a chart showing alcohol levels, but in talking to Matthews he kept missing the moment. He had to run the crash four times before catching it right. Then he began sorting through clips, looking for the chart.

"Speaking of girlies," Matthews said, "they left together, your girl and Erickson."

"Who? Dimi? She's not my girl. And I doubt she'd be with Erickson."

"Have I ever been wrong?" Matthews asked.

In addition to his job at Spectrum, Matthews was also an amateur detective, video surveillance expert, and electronics hot-wire man. It was Matthews who had saved Slater at the end of his Michigan summer and got him his job at Spectrum. The two of them had hired in with Erickson's group, a month before the big bloodletting. The new management saw nothing to gain in the success of old ideas, and everyone in the group had been left to drift, including Erickson, who had abandoned all pretense of productivity to get his next show-around piece cut. Postproduction was a tangent to everyone, a ledger line of hundred-dollar hours, hardly noticed. That was the curse and the saving grace of working for Spectrum. Nobody cared.

Once more the red Camaro broke itself against the wall.

Slater put on his headset and began transferring narration from the source tape. Matthews watched the silent screens with casual, Sunday-afternoon interest, the way a man might watch neighborhood kids tossing a ball.

So that's where our national attention span has gone, Slater thought. Matthews has it.

But when he looked again, his friend was dozing and Lane was on screen three. In her left eye was a crescent of blood. The mezzaluna. When she got high, the crescent glowed. The glue made her skin warm and burnt through inhibitions, but you could taste the destruction in her kiss.

On screen three, her Jeep was in the ditch. *Another Woman for Peace* it said on the bumper, but that was some other woman, not Lane. That was someone who had owned the Jeep before.

When the image went black, Slater saw his reflection on the screen. The uncombed hair. Three day's beard. And the expression on his face like—what? A look mixing concentration and emptiness. Athlete at the free-throw line? Maybe—yes, a little. An idler constructing beer-bottle pyramids in the sun? Okay. There was that.

His sister, who lived in Denver, had warned him not to go back to Michigan. He had stopped for a meal and a shower during his cross-country drive and got the speech for no extra charge: It's all a mind game up there, she told him, all lost souls and losers. "People smiling and hiding their teeth."

He pointed out that she'd lived there herself once. She was the Petoskey Stone Girl then, a hippie chick who sold Petoskey-stone jewelry to the tourists and slept with the good-looking guys from downstate. One of them married her and bought her a house outside Denver. Now she had a cockapoo and was on the tango committee. Her view of Northern Michigan had changed.

"The woods and the lakes are nice," she said. "It's the people you have to watch out for. They all have ulterior motives behind their ulterior motives. Everyone's working an angle, and it's never the angle you think." Slater thanked her for her advice and got back in the Ford.

Looking at his reflection in the monitors, he tried to see what kind of motive might be in his eyes. Instead he saw green lights—railroad signals. Some kind of railroad scene from his past. But it was only the lights from the control board below.

He took a breath, trying to find his hiss. Remember, he told himself. This is only a test. This is only a movie. This is only your life.

A line of ants crawled up Dickinson's leg as he came to. He shook them off, sending a stab of pain up his back, even through the Percocet. When his head cleared, he staggered into the horse trailer to escape the sun. It was an oven inside. He quickly passed out again.

When he woke a second time, the sun was lower and he was viciously thirsty. He kept a gallon jug in the trailer, but the effort of lifting it caused more spasms; the container fell from his hands. A third of it spilled before he could right it.

The first cool hours of twilight brought some relief. But he knew what the night would bring. Coyotes would come for Buster and Bo. They'd draw mountain lions. Dickinson had seen a jaguar in the desert once. They'd smell his blood.

Hobbling, he managed to pull up the trailer's ramp and shut the doors from the inside. There was nothing he could do about the open-air windows. As the last light faded, he climbed into the nose of the trailer and sat rigidly.

Early in the night, something started eating the horses. Later, he thought he heard animals fighting, growling, and snapping at each other. He held a rock in his hand. Every time he fell asleep, he jolted himself awake. He was sure the cats would come for him, but they didn't.

At dawn he took the last Percocet, certain he would not survive another day. Without waiting for the drug to kick in, he took a coil of rope from the trailer and put a knot near the end. Kneeling, he worked the rope into the gas tank of the Chevy, stopping when there was only a foot left.

For the next half hour, he searched the sky, shading his eyes with his Stetson. The jets on their way to Davis were useless: they flew too high. Finally, a small plane appeared on the horizon. Its wings reflected sun that hadn't yet reached the truck. Dickinson pulled the gas-soaked rope out of the tank until the knot emerged. He left the last few feet in the tank and crawled like a baby away from the pickup, stringing out the fuse. In a few minutes, his new Silverado would be gone. A $10,000 flare.

When the plane was nearly overhead, Dickinson took a pack of matches from his shirt pocket. The pack had been soaked with radiator fluid and the cover came off in his hands. Three matches in back seemed dry.

The first lit and flared out. The second and third matches crumbled. Dickinson swore with a ferocity that hurt, then started to laugh. "Son of a ten-cent carnival whore," he said.

In spite of the pain, he stood and ran to the cab. Letting out a growl that was half delight, he punched the lighter into the dash and waited for it to pop.

Heading into Iowa, the Ranchero vibrated, one tire out of round. Nothing to do but keep going. Old days, you'd stop and find a tireshaver, shave the hump till the rubber was round. Not anymore. Supposed to buy a new one now, throw the old one away. Bad luck for the tireshavers. Gone with the wind, they were. Probably turn up at craft fairs next to the blacksmith and the glassblowers. *Gitcher picture taken with Ye Olde Tireshaver*, five bucks.

Slater was driving on coffee and nerves. Near Omaha, he was surprised to see his elementary school teachers crouching at the edge of the two-lane. One by one they sprang in front of his headlights like jackrabbits.

Only Mrs. Keyes, the one who had yelled at him about his penmanship, didn't make it. His headlights pierced her eyes: she froze and faced him in full frontal horror. A second later the grill popped her into a foul supernova, a streak of red and black swirling in his taillights.

That's the way you do it, he told himself. You pop 'em.

But a hundred miles later, Mrs. Keyes was crouched by the roadside again.

It was the way of the world, or at least the way of the world at night, when everything telescoped down to the car and the empty road. The place where he had left Dickinson was an overexposed memory, some other planet—real enough but far away. Maybe Dickinson had found some strength, managed to walk out. It seemed unlikely. However it happened, it was over by now. And not my fault, Slater told himself. He tried to kill me.

Outside Davenport, the sign. *Girls Girls Girls*. Why always three? Sometimes it was just *Live Girls*, but still plural. Depressing if there's only one. *Live Girl on Stage*. Not much of a show there. Better than *Dead Girl on Stage*, of course. But no one was that kinky. At least no one that he knew.

Taking a break, Slater stopped at Chick's Café next door. One table over, two women were drinking coffee. Late thirties and disappointed in life.

"She took his dirt bike and flipped over the . . ." The first woman drew a circle in the air with her cigarette to finish the thought. "When she woke up she thought Sam beat her."

"She better quit that," the other one said.

It turned out that Chick's was connected to the topless place. His waitress, in Spandex, was cheerful and sneezing. She called him Mike and filled his emptiness with coffee and pie. Dancers from next door hung out at the counter, smoking, and waiting for their turn to undress.

After Selda left, Slater had spent a few nights at the topless bar on Ajo Way. Crummy stage and colored lights and lots of empty tables. The draw wasn't sex; it was fear. The naked dancers scared him. They were comfortable in their nakedness, they blended in with the rest of the flesh. In contrast, his loneliness was on stark display. It was scary to be so exposed.

One dancer in particular had his number. She made him look left, she made him look right. She had him on a little string. She was extremely good-looking and the fear she inspired scoured a month of crap off his soul. The only thing he didn't like was when the dancers chewed gum. As if bewitching him was a bore.

And most of them did. Chew gum. It was a failure of the American educational system. Mrs. Keyes specifically.

The girls at Chicks ignored him and he finished up quickly. Clean plate, empty cup, and then back on the road and the contentment as pure as it comes—Iowa at night, all the comforts of the moving world, one tire out of round.

At Burnt River, he saw a shooting star. The conga tape repeated forever. He drove on, passing through Slaterville with barely a smile.

What he wanted most, he realized, was not a topless woman, but the dressed, inhabited kind. A woman with a fearless heart, the kind you heard about in songs.

Bad karma, he thought, to dwell on the unattainable.

You Just Missed The Thing, a billboard said.

— 8 —

AT THE SIDE of Highway 22 in Northern Michigan, a stylized Uncle Sam looked down at drivers, bushy eyebrows raised in smarmy indignation. *Who's Living off Your Taxes?* a headline above him asked. The question was meant to conjure images of burr-headed blacks jigging around a bottle of spodie odie in darkest Detroit. In fact, half of white Northern Michigan was on relief.

Past the billboard was a dirt road leading into the forest. Lane drove the road in her Jeep, bouncing as it turned into a two-track, heavily rutted. It was barely a mile long, but it always seemed to take forever—the two-track elongated time, making everything outside the forest seem far away. As she got deeper into the woods, Lane struggled to keep an image of herself in mind. Her brother's house— Hidden Mist—always tried to turn her into someone else.

When the forest ended, the road broke into meadow, rich with fading sunlight. At its edge, the Big Lake beat against rock and beach grass.

The house was farther down the beach. Its slate-gray facade was as ugly as she remembered.

Hit and Miss, she called it. Architecture by Frank Lloyd Wrong.

The angles of the house suggested a victory of violence, an elbow in the face of the civilized world. A way of living for which the rewards were obscenely high. Lane promised herself she wouldn't stay past sundown.

As she pulled into the drive, an emerald-green Karmann Ghia nearly sideswiped her Jeep. The woman behind the wheel waved distractedly and kept going. Charlie's silver BMW sat shining in the drive. Lane parked behind it.

Lane found the front door of Hidden Mist standing open. Entering, she was greeted by a coppery, antiseptic smell. In the hexagonal living room, Charlie was slouched in a rocker. He was watching a soccer match, a steaming dinner plate balanced on his lap. Behind him, a sapling grew through a cut in the floor. Propped by the door was a deer rifle, a .30-06.

"Pretty lax, Charlie. Good thing I'm not the cops."

Her brother spoke without turning. "It's not the cops I worry about. I've got them on retainer. It's the crazy people that scare me."

"You mean your customers."

"I mean my suppliers. My customers are respectable people."

Charlie sold to a good class of buyers. Vacationers. Downstaters temporarily upstate. Folks who needed a little toot to enjoy the pleasant peninsula.

"Who's the girl in the Karmann Ghia? She nearly ran me over."

"Shannon," Charlie said. "Our problem child. She won't S her T's."

Lane thought a minute. Show her Tits. "Your customers must love that."

"We're working on her."

He turned off the soccer game, and they walked to the glass wall facing the beach. Rolls of netting and aluminum riprap were strung in front of the house. Flexible tubing was installed at water's edge, supported by pool floats. The beige tube looked like an enormous condom.

"See how high the water is, sis?" he said. "Howard put in ten thousand dollars of reinforcement. He's worried about losing the house."

Howard Green was an auto-parts millionaire and the owner of Hidden Mist. His life's work involved putting a chrome silhouette of a busty woman on a set of mudflaps. After selling a pair to every long-haul trucker in America, he retreated to Thailand and a life of endless sin. Charlie had been encamped at Hidden Mist ever since. Officially, his title was caretaker. He and Lane owned a house in Wolverine that had once belonged to their mother. Lane lived there now.

Charlie motioned at the giant condom. "If it goes, the deck goes. After that, the house. Insurance has been canceled."

Lane sniffed. "What are you eating?"

"Coquilles Saint Jacques. Try some."

Lane shook her head and Charlie got her a beer instead. "We haven't seen you in who knows how long," he said. "And now here you are. Life getting a bit too lifelike for you? You've come to the right place."

"I don't want your drugs," she said. "Though Jude does. She's asked about you every day this week."

"Jude? I wouldn't let Jude polish my dick. Why would I sell her drugs?"

"I don't care either way, Charlie. That isn't why I came."

"The fastest way to go to jail in this business is to deal with lowlifes like Jude. People who rat you out the minute they get hauled in for soliciting."

"That's not why I came."

Charlie went back to his chair and sat down. "Well then. Do tell."

"A man came by. You jerk."

Her brother put his hands up. "You're mad about the house, aren't you? Don't be. It's just a big screwup." He gave her his phony smile.

"He said he's buying the place. He talked about charging me rent."

"It's all just a funny misunderstanding. I haven't sold the house."

"Don't give me your dumb-guy act, Charlie. That house is half mine."

"I put out some feelers. Just to see what it's worth. I haven't signed any papers."

"You asshole."

Charlie walked to the window and put a brotherly arm around her shoulders. "As long as you're living there, the house is not for sale."

The light was dimming, the Lake was steel-gray. It had been a mistake to come, Lane thought.

"Listen, kid," he said, "since you're here, why don't you stick around? I'm expecting snow tonight. The kind that melts in your mouth, not in your hand."

Before she could tell him to go to hell, his beeper went off. While Charlie made a phone call, she wandered upstairs. Below, Charlie went into full dealer mode, his voice drifting up: *Hey mo' fo', man with a plan, got what you're looking for.*

Lane had stayed at Hidden Mist when she first came north. At the top of the spiral staircase was the bedroom that used to be hers.

The wall-sized mirror next to the bed was the same. In the large, walk-in closet, a full-size gong hung from an ornate stand, gathering dust. The shelves held a collection of bongs and stacks of magazines: *National Geographic*, *High Times*, and *Asian Amateurs*. In the back was a framed photo, a picture taken when she first arrived at Hidden Mist. Her face was dirty, her eyes wild. A towel was slung over her shoulders. The picture made her look confident, indestructible. It was the kind of photo she liked—a little bit of truth that didn't stay true very long.

She had messed up worse than usual at work, running eight rolls back to back, forgetting to turn on the drying drums. The photo paper came out of the wash tanks dripping wet. It was supposed to roll over two large shiny cylinders, big as bass drums in a marching band, heated from within by gas flame. When the temperature was set properly, the hot drums baked the paper dry. But Lane left the gas off by mistake; her rolls hit the take-up spool soggy and mashed together, becoming the world's largest spit wad. Stottle came by to shake his finger at her and stare at her chest. When he was done, he carried the papier-mâché mash to the vending room, where it was displayed beside the bowling trophy as a marvel of employee stupidity.

In the parlance of the stuffers, she had fucked up. She came from a long line of fuckups, in fact.

Her father, Charles Sr., served three years in Jacktown for writing bad checks, the only charge that stuck among many, including manslaughter. On the day he was to be released, they all went down to Jackson. Lane's mother smiled nervously and chainsmoked during the drive. She was dark-haired and had light freckles, like something fragile kept in a dark place. Lane was fourteen at the time.

Charles Sr. was waiting for them outside the rec room at Southern Michigan Prison. He'd already had his hand-shake from the warden and was free; now he wanted a beer. They bought a six-pack and drove to a weedy park with splintery picnic tables and unmowed grass. Some kids were playing ball near a lagoon. Charlie, sixteen, helped himself to a Stroh's.

"Tastes like bull crap," he said, wiping his mouth.

"You don't talk that way in front of your mother," his father said.

Lane saw a look pass from her brother to her mom.

"Sorry," Charlie said. "I meant bull*shit*, not bull crap."

It was an old fight, fought the old way: Charlie striking fast and often, their father doing a slow burn. "You got a lot to learn, son."

"So do you," Charlie said.

Lane tried to smile at her father but kept imagining the baby. A crying baby she'd left inside a shopping bag. She watched her father across the picnic table. Even in the open air of the park, she could smell him—a combination of sweat and floor wax from the prison.

The day was sticky warm. Complacent bees flew lazy circles in the thick air. Charles Sr. lit a cigarette. Her mother touched his arm and told him again, without enthusiasm, how glad she was to see him. She kept a sweater around her waist to hide her stomach.

No one saw the bee fly into the Stroh's can. But Lane could still see it flying out of her father's mouth, bumping his upper lip and buzzing into the air. His face went red; he grabbed his throat and made unspeakable noises. Charlie rose, spilling his beer. Nobody knew what to do. Charles Sr. fell to the grass, arms and legs twitching. When he lost consciousness, they tried pounding on his chest. Nothing helped. Five minutes later, he was dead, his windpipe swollen shut.

"You stupid fuck," Charlie yelled at him. "Now what?"

Lane's mother dropped to her knees and started screaming, but Charlie grabbed her and made her stop. He dragged the body to the car and wedged it in back. In the grip of a great stupidity, they drove to the prison for help. Lane had to sit in the backseat with her dead father. She curled her knees tight into her chest, shrinking as far from Charles Sr. as she could get.

It was punishment for the baby, she knew. In the Pricebenders' bag. For the terrible thing she had done, which was all for nothing now.

The guards at the prison gate laughed at them. *So Charlie the Roach kicked the bucket*, they said. *Couldn't happen to a nicer guy. We don't take free men here, kid. Hey missy—yeah, you, what are you hiding from? Give us a smile, little missy.*

Life was a joke and it was always on you. That's what she learned from that.

At Hidden Mist, she closed the door to her old room and went back downstairs. Her brother had assembled a little package. "For Jude. Tell her it's the last time ever." He opened his arms wide. "Now, what can I get for my dear sister?"

"I get what I want from the hardware store."

Charlie pretended to be hurt. "I don't see why you insist on buying from strangers, when I can get you anything you want."

"Your deals end up costing me plenty."

"Hey, who got you your job in the photographic arts? And the job before that?"

When Lane was living at Hidden Mist, Charlie had wrangled her a job at the Sunday Market. Lane's booth sold toe rings. Charlie would often stop by to supervise. There was nothing finer, he used to say, than sitting on a stool on a sunny afternoon, looking down the blouses of college girls as they tried on toe rings. And selling drugs to their boyfriends. When the toe-ring business proved to be ephemeral, Charlie came up with the photo-lab job.

"It pays to have connections," Charlie said.

"Stottle's a pervert."

Charlie led them out onto the balcony, still using his dealer voice. "That's what you get for being female. Everyone wants a piece of your pudendum. Speaking of which, how's your boyfriend doing these days?"

"He's gone. And when have you ever cared how other people are doing?"

"I'm turning over a new leaf."

"You wouldn't turn over a leaf unless there was money under it."

"He's coming back, right? Your friend Harp?"

"He always has so far."

Charlie got two more beers from the cooler. They drank them at the rail, looking out at the Lake. It would be a beautiful sunset. The sky had turned blue and pink.

"Howard ever show you his special rock?" Charlie asked. "The one he carries in a little pouch?"

Lane kept her eyes on the horizon.

"It's from Atlantis. If he takes it out, he can make you levitate."

She snorted. "Maybe he should levitate the house."

"Watch out. It might come to that." He raised his bottle in a toast. "To the man who has everything and wants more."

"Keeping up with the Joneses. That's your whole life, isn't it?"

"It's gone way beyond that. We're foreclosing on the Joneses and taking their land. Outlive and outlast, that's my motto: Charlie Vancouver—Stayed Alive till the Other Guy Died."

"That's your epitaph, not your motto."

"Whatever."

Lane could feel her anger going soft. "It's his birthday today," she said. "In case you forgot."

"Who? Howard?"

"Of course not Howard." *Your fucking son*, is what she wanted to say. She couldn't make herself say *baby*.

Charlie let his shoulders droop. "Jesus, Lane. Give yourself a break."

"Give *me* a break? You think I'm the one who needs a break?" Her right eye throbbed the way it did on glue.

The Pricebenders' bag had moved like there was a kitten inside. *Here*, Charlie had said, *take it*.

"You would have been a horrible father," Lane said. "That's the only saving grace."

"Maybe so," Charlie said. "I got over it a long time ago."

"You were over it the minute it happened."

He shrugged in a way that was both casual and cruel. "That's *your* problem, babe."

She had walked right into it. He had said the same thing then, twelve years ago. *That's your problem, babe.*

He finished his beer and moved closer. "Listen," he said. "The past is past. Why don't you stick around for a while? You can have the Jacuzzi to yourself."

"Screw you."

"That cold front should blow in any minute now. We'll do some together for old time's sake."

"I don't want your sympathy. Or your drugs."

"You'd be doing me a favor." He did a little drumbeat on the balcony rail. "You could do the old meet and greet."

"Are you inviting me to sleep with these guys?"

"Of course not."

Her eye throbbed. "Leave me alone, Charlie. Get your dirty, vicarious thrills from someone else."

"That's exactly what I *do* do. I get my vicarious thrills from someone else."

Hidden Mist was getting to her. She'd stayed too long. "Just tell me you haven't sold the house."

"I wouldn't sell the house out from under you, sis. I would never do that."

She had no idea whether to believe him. For a moment she stood at the rail looking out at the Lake. It was getting darker.

"Charlie," she said finally. "Do you ever wonder if hell is full of people like us?"

Her brother nodded. "Here's an even scarier idea. What if it's not?"

She finished her beer. When Charlie got a phone call, she left. A minute later she went back in, grabbed the .30-06, and threw it in the back of the Jeep. Just in case Charlie really was selling the house.

It was Undersheriff Lazenbeck on the phone.

"I'm at that motel next to Fudge Mountain," the undersheriff told Charlie. "Every room in Grand Rapids is booked. There's a convention in town. I had to stay at this goddamn tourist trap."

"How's the sheriff? Is he bad?"

"He's dying slowly and surely. Emphasis on *slowly*."

Lazenbeck's boss was being treated for a rare type of cancer in Grand Rapids. Lazenbeck planned to run against him in the fall election. He was visiting the hospital to guard against a miracle recovery, and because it was good PR.

"The sympathy vote is gonna kill me," the undersheriff said. "How do you beat a guy with cancer?"

"Put it out of your mind," Charlie said. "I've got you the perfect perp. Friend of my sister's. A total loser."

Worry crept into Lazenbeck's voice. "Are we talking about the condos?"

"Exactly. What else?"

"And this guy is dumb enough to do it?"

"He's in love with my sister," Charlie said. "Case closed."

"Alright," Lazenbeck said. "But the timing has to be perfect. I don't want to rush it."

Charlie let out a breath. He needed the Whispering Sands blown up soon; he owed too much money to wait. "I won't have access to this guy forever. We should do it now."

"Negative. It has to be closer to the election."

An electronic beep told Charlie a vehicle was entering the long two-track from the highway. "We'll have to discuss this later," he said.

"I still need your help on the missing persons case. Sara Whatshername." Lazenbeck's voice went ugly. "I'm getting full-time grief from her parents."

"I put the line out. Nothing came back."

"I thought you knew all the goddamn junkies."

"She's probably down in PV getting a tan and driving the campesinos crazy. Probably ran off with her boyfriend. Happens all the time."

"According to her boyfriend, she was at your place."

"They all say that," Charlie said. "Listen, I'd love to stay and chat, but my ride is here."

"Roger that," Undersheriff Lazenbeck said. "We'll talk."

Charlie hung up and went to find the deer rifle. It wasn't where he'd left it. He grabbed the Browning from a closet instead, just in case, and listened for the car outside to park.

The meeting went badly. The Stink brought out the skewer again. He carried it into Charlie's living room and waved it about, red-eyed, like a conductor on PCP. What would Charlie's tiny balls look like on the skewer? The Stink wondered. How long would they need to be roasted? He spoke very loudly. Charlie had heard the routine before, but the skewer still frightened him. Something meaty had left a brown stain on the shank. Charlie had been forced to laugh along as The Stink poked the sharp end in his crotch. Worse, he had to fork over five thousand cash. Even so, The Stink wasn't happy, but he took the money and left.

The new girl might have helped—The Stink loved new girls—but Shannon was unaccounted for. Her absence pissed Charlie off. What was the point of being a Spreadable if you were never there to spread?

To calm himself, Charlie poured a glass of wine and took it out onto the balcony. He was good at a lot of things, he thought, but he was lousy at being alone. Old feelings came back to life when he was alone, and all of his old feelings had teeth. The only feeling he really trusted anymore was greed.

To hell with it, he thought finally. The day was already fucked; he might as well go check on Sara, Lazenbeck's missing druggie.

The entrance to the basement was from the back of the house, down a ramp to a steel door. It took a while to find the keys. When he got inside, he spent another few minutes just staring at the freezer. It was plugged in and running, and that was all that mattered. But he opened it anyway.

"Alright then," he said, "let's have a look how you look."

He raised the lid slowly. Inside, Sara was dressed in party clothes, her bare midriff frosted over. In her current frozen form, Charlie felt a small touch of affection for her. If she'd been dying, he would have told her, *That's your problem, babe*. But being dead made her a loser, and at heart Charlie liked losers. That was partly why he hadn't undressed her, though he should have: a naked body is harder to ID. Now that she was frozen it would be a bitch to get her clothes off and he'd given up the idea. Plus, if somehow he got caught, he didn't want anyone thinking he was turned on by dead chicks.

In ballpoint pen, an inch below her navel, were the words *There are no problems, only solutions*. The letters were quite small. Whoever had written it had spent some time down there, pen in hand.

The girl's honest-to-God name was Sara Lee. She was not supposed to be dead. She was supposed to be borrowing money from everyone she knew and spending it on Charlie's toot. She was supposed to be a walking, talking profit center. Like every other chick with a broken heart and a hungry nose.

Tracy had met her at a party and brought her to Hidden Mist around 4 a.m. one morning. It was an old story. Troubled girl cashes tuition check, gives it all to Charlie. Inhales, spreads, inhales, spreads. Everyone wins, except the girl, who was troubled to begin with. The night she came over, Charlie could see she'd been crying, a promising sign. But he'd done too much speed that night. He could do a little and be fine; one pill too many and things always ended badly. Every time, he vowed never again.

That night, he was hepped up on the beachfront video scheme. He even took Sara Lee outside to show her where the camera would go. She followed him from the balcony to the roof of Hidden Mist as the sun was coming up.

"Ask yourself," he said, his heart pumping. "What's the main thing you want in a beach house?"

"I don't know," Sara Lee said. "A guy who doesn't treat you like crap?"

"No," Charlie said. "The beach! If you have a beach house, you want it to be right on the beach!" He looked at her, hoping that she might rise to his dream. It was a mistake he almost never made. "And why is that?"

Her mascara-streaked face was flickering through the channels: Anger. Confusion. Loneliness. "I don't give a rat's ass, actually."

"That's cute. Now try to think like a pasty-faced forty-five-year-old with a spare tire and a hangover. You don't want to waltz out the door and go frolicking. You want to sit on your butt and watch other people frolic. Comprende?"

Sara Lee looked out at Lake Michigan. "No."

"Morning coffee, afternoon cocktails, BJ from the wife—it all happens in front of the big picture window. The sand and the surf!"

Sara Lee nodded, either entranced or not listening.

"Unfortunately for you, the beachfront is already taken. Everybody wants it, but not everybody gets it. That's where we come in. We install a broadcast-quality camera right here. Get our own cable channel so you can watch it right in your living room. Some good speakers for the surf. In reality, your crapshack is three feet from the highway, but who cares? Turn on the screen and you're at the beach."

He spread his arms wide, trying to hold the beauty of the idea. "And let's say you get a network of these roof cameras, and enough customers to purchase massive cable access. Hey, you want an apartment in London? Rio? Central Park? Just change the channel. Suddenly you can live anywhere you want."

Sara looked at Charlie. At the Lake. At Charlie. At the Lake. She seemed to be having a moment.

"Bite me," she said finally.

"Okay," he said. "Sure. That might work."

She opened her purse to get a pack of cigarettes. When Charlie looked more closely, he saw the cigarettes were not really cigarettes. They were a pistol. The gun looked real, though he couldn't be sure.

"Hold on," Charlie said.

Sara got to her feet on the slanting roof. The pistol swung around to the sky, to Charlie, to the Lake.

"That's not necessary," Charlie said. He rose, took a step forward.

"Stay back, stumptail."

Charlie tried his most charming smile. "Is that real?"

"My boyfriend knows I'm here. So don't try to mess with me."

"I wouldn't."

"I'm not some stupid cunt," she told him.

"Of course not." He took another half step. You're a stupid cunt with a gun.

She aimed the pistol at herself, placing the small silver barrel against the underside of her chin.

"No," Charlie said. "Don't do that."

"Why not?"

He shrugged and took a shambling step forward. When a seagull squawked she glanced away for an instant; Charlie lunged and wrenched the pistol from her hand. In the scuffle, Sara Lee backed up. Her momentum took her three more steps, the last one over open air. As her foot found nothing, her mouth formed a perfect O. And then she was gone.

Charlie looked over the edge in time to see her body bounce off the riprap. She landed facedown in the waves.

He watched for a moment. She didn't move.

"Shit, Sara," he said quietly. "Please don't do what you just did." He had her pistol in his hand. It was real. He opened the cylinder and saw it wasn't loaded.

He stood at the edge of the roof for a minute, waiting to see if the world would change. Nothing. The world didn't care.

The first thing he did when he got inside was wake up Tracy.

"You're going back to wherever you got Sara," he told her. "Find her boyfriend. Get a hotel, get him so high that the last decade is a blank. I want him waking up tomorrow afternoon trying to figure out what his name is and how his dick got so happy."

Tracy knew not to ask questions.

As soon as she left, Charlie went down to the beach. He turned Sara Lee faceup. Everything would be immensely more difficult if she wasn't completely dead. Mercifully, she had no pulse. He dragged her into the basement. As the sun rose, he put her in the freezer.

Her parents, he found out later, were John Birchers. That was a problem for Lazenbeck. A hippie chick could be ignored, but Mr. and Mrs. Lee were prominent right-wingers and rich. They expected the undersheriff to find their daughter. Instead, the weeks went by with nothing.

Charlie took a last look and closed the freezer.

In a world that wasn't completely cruel, he might have dropped the body where it could be found. But that was a risk he didn't need to take. He had a business to run and more important problems to deal with. Like making the Whispering Sands disappear, whether Lazenbeck was ready or not. All he needed was the doer. No problem there. His sister attracted doers like flies.

— 9 —

THE KID AT the Crown Z dock in Superior, Wisconsin, had a mock-Indian name. You-Want-Fries-With-That. Heartless coworkers had given him the name as a taunt. It was part of his mojo now. Eighteen years old, he had hair down his neck, a ring on his finger, and carpet in his van. You-Want-Fries-With-That worked the graveyard shift and he was angry. A new sign had been posted on the loading dock. *If You've Got Time To Lean*, it said, *You've Got Time To Clean.*

"Who the huckleberry are you calling lazy?" he asked the sign.

He was repeating the question when he lost control of the forklift, damaging twelve cartons of toilet paper from the mill, and hitting a silver tank car full of propane.

The crash brought the night foreman. An expert at deception, the foreman concealed the damaged toilet paper, tagged the forklift, decided the tank car was fine, and told You-Want-Fries-With-That he was fired. "Get your mojo and go."

⇌

Screen four in Slater's edit suite was an RCA broadcast monitor, removed from its chassis, with bad bayonet inputs so the picture often went to snow. On it, sharp for now, the railroad ferry crossed Lake Michigan. The ship was enormous, nearly four hundred feet long, rising sixty feet above the water. Inside it was a freight train.

Even when the RCA got snowy, the twin black-and-white smokestacks stood out against the green-gray of the water. In postproduction, Slater watched the ship make its slow but relentless passage across the Big Lake. What would be handy, he thought, was a freeze-frame. Something to stop the action, bedevil the clock. But freeze-frames, like cops, were never around when you really needed them.

At the Kewaunee ferry dock, someone tried the handle of the men's room and Slater heard a man's voice say, "Wait, Stevie." Unhurried, Slater tipped his head back and pissed with the deep satisfaction of those not dead. The still-alive crowd. Kewaunee was in Wisconsin, the last stop before he crossed to Michigan.

Leaving the men's room, he passed the doorknob rattlers, their faces set in father-and-son versions of polite attention.

"Boysenberry wine," Slater said, and their expressions scampered in opposite directions—the boy's to amazement, the father's to disgust. Watch out world, he said to no one in particular. Michael Slater, live and in person.

The bottle of Mad Dog he was drinking was actually blueberry, but he thought boysenberry had a more exotic sound.

Two dozen automobiles, including the Ranchero, were parked in the dirt lot by the railroad ferry. They were all waiting for the *Chief Tecumseh* to load. Slater had ridden the ferry before, but not for years. In the twilight, the ship seemed even older and more massive than he remembered. The double smokestacks, painted with the logo of the *Chief Tecumseh*, looked like they could vent the fires of hell.

Earlier in the afternoon, Slater had surprised one of the deckhands rolling a doobie in the lee of a storage shack. The worker had wild gray muttonchops, a short white beard, and a deeply lined face. For a half second, Slater took him for a vision, but the man turned out to be real. He gave the paper a final lick and turned halfway toward Slater. "Helps with the arthritis," he said.

Slater felt compelled to offer him a shot of Mad Dog. The man declined. "Never touch it beforehand," he said. "After we tie up, maybe."

The man introduced himself as Jack Brady. Slater asked him why there was no schedule for the *Chief Tecumseh*.

"It's all BS," Jack said. He took a deep, leisurely hit from the joint, then snuffed it against the shack and put it in the front pocket of his work shirt. He pointed his chin at the ferry. "The old twin screw. They don't want you to ride it. It's all for show."

Slater looked at him blankly.

"Twin screw. Two propellers."

"Oh," Slater said.

Jack put out his hand for the bottle. "Just a nip. What do you know about tariffs?"

It went back to the forties, according to Jack. The Illinois Central, which ran through Chicago, had the highest tariffs in the country. "This line here was cheaper," Jack Brady said. "You got something going cross-country, route it up here, cross the Lake on the ferry, and skip Chicago completely. Saved you a ton of money. We had three of these mothers running twice a day back then. Hell of a time, it was. Good honest work. You know what I mean?"

Slater had never done anything that the deckhand would have considered good honest work, but he nodded anyway.

"You know what's funny?" Jack didn't wait for an answer. "Some people think I'm scary. 'Cause of the way I look. Wild man, all that stuff. But there's nothing scary about me compared to them guys in soft shoes and haircuts. You see them guys coming, you better run. Those guys will suck you dry, and not in a way you're gonna like. I'll tell you that for sure."

He put his hand out and the 20/20 went back again. The sky had darkened and a few lights had come on around the *Chief Tecumseh*.

"So what happened is the Chicago boys changed the rules. Made it just as costly to route your freight up here. And once they did that, all the long-haul traffic went back to Chi-town. Hell, most of it's on the GD interstate now." He gave each syllable of *interstate* its own space, drawing out the word to expose its dark innards.

For years, he told Slater, the company that owned the *Chief Tecumseh* had been trying to shut it down. But legally it was a railroad, interstate commerce, and subject to federal rules. It couldn't be abandoned unless they could prove it would never make money. "So they go out of their way to drive away business. No schedule. No maintenance."

He got the joint out of his pocket, looked at both ends, and put it back in his shirt. Behind them came the far-off sound of a freight. The yard lights around the *Tecumseh* gave the boat a movie aura, a relic from another time.

"They told you to pay onboard, I bet. But you see if you can find the purser tonight. If you see him, you better tackle his fat ass quick. And tell him Jack sent you, okay? Tell him Jack Brady says he can go get screwed."

Slater swallowed the last of the Mad Dog. "I'll tell him."

"Well, I shouldn't be squawking. You know what time I came on the clock? Twelve noon. Sure as shit. By the time we shove off I'll be making double time. That's their plan, see. It runs up the labor cost, which they like. Twenty-eight years I been doing this. They're gonna lay me off before I hit the thirty-year mark, just wait and see."

Leaving, they shook hands. "Safe crossing," Jack Brady said.

To kill time before the ferry boarded, Slater walked back to the Ford and sat on the tailgate. A dozen or so passengers milled around their cars; workers talked in small groups, smoking cigarettes and drinking from paper cups. They were all waiting for the Snake.

In the night breeze, Slater let his mind wander. Closing his eyes, he had a passing vision of Selda—a night when they'd been sitting on the floor, watching TV, and she touched her foot against his. For no reason. Just a touch and nothing more. It was strange—how such a simple moment could make him feel so blessed. And so empty, once it was gone.

A few minutes later, he heard the Snake. The sound was muffled, then loud, as the headlight curved into sight. The train smelled like grease, farm manure, and raw, wet air. The Snake had come through rain.

Immediately, a winch went to work on the rear end of the *Tecumseh*, raising an immense section of the hull called the seagate. When it was fully up, Slater could see four lines of boxcars inside the ship. Those were the westbounds, newly arrived from Michigan. Workers moved to the switches and waved lanterns, guiding a stubby, yellow yard engine as it pulled the westbound strings off the ferry, starting with the two outermost tracks.

Within fifteen minutes, the hull was empty. The yard engine then went to work on the Snake, cutting it into four sections and pushing them onboard, filling the *Tecumseh* with MoPac, Rock Route, Cotton Belt, Southern, Canadian National, and Detroit & Mackinac.

When the freight deck was full, the seagate came down and two workers began loading the automobiles. One of the car hostlers, a young buck with a ponytail, came for the Ford. Slater gave him the keys and stood off to the side as the hostler drove it up a wooden corkscrew ramp to the *Tecumseh's* top deck. He and the other worker repeated the process until all of the automobiles were loaded.

Passengers boarded last. Most of them went straight to the holding room with its vending machines and chairs. Slater stayed out on the deck, watching the switch engine sort the westbounds into a single string. Near the middle was a Soo Line boxcar. Slater had kissed a girl named Sue Kline in high school. In tenth grade behind the dugout. A brunette, short hair, very shy about using her tongue. Delicious little nips. Since then, he'd always liked Soo Line cars.

Only two other passengers stayed on the deck—a short, roundish woman who spoke loudly and a tall woman with dark hair. From the way they argued, Slater saw that they were lovers. They stood ten feet down the rail, but paid no attention to Slater.

"Don't worry about Charlie," the tall woman said. "I'm not one of his girls. I'm just crashing there."

The other woman cradled her left arm as if it were broken, though the rest of her movements were quick. "That's how it starts, baby," she said.

"I don't have any options. And it's right on the Lake."

"It's the mouth of hell," the short woman said. "And Charlie is the monkey who dances outside."

The yard engine geared up, drowning them out. Slater moved a step closer, pretending he wasn't listening. The tall woman folded her arms, hugging herself. "It's cold. I thought we were getting a room."

The other woman turned suddenly, catching Slater eavesdropping. "Having a good time?" she asked. "Since you're so interested, how about lending us a hand?"

Slater was forced into the embarrassed grin that he tried to keep off his face. As a rule, he liked lesbians. There was the imaginary girl-on-girl raunch, sure. More important was the fact that they rejected his entire gender. It removed the specific threat of rejection, which was far worse. With nothing at stake, there was no way to fail.

"How long are your fingers?" the woman asked him.

Slater held out his hands. His fingers passed inspection.

"Follow me," she said.

They led him down a passageway to the purser's office. The service window was dark; beneath it, a wooden box was fixed to the wall—a key drop. With her good arm, the short woman tried to reach into the narrow opening of the box, but her hand wouldn't fit. "There are keys in there,' she said. "But my fingers are too short."

Slater looked at the tall woman. She turned away from him. "No way. I'm not putting my hand in there."

At the end of the passageway, two crew members paused to light cigarettes, in defiance of the No Smoking signs. Slater waited until they moved on.

"The rooms are pretty dingy," he said. "At least they used to be." He worked his hand into the opening and came out with a key to stateroom 8. The short woman took it from him. The tall woman was already moving down the passageway.

"That's a good trick," Slater said. "I might remember that."

"What did you say your name was?" the short woman asked.

"Michael Slater."

"Nice to meet you," she said. "I'm Rose. So would you like to join us for a three-way? Just kidding, of course. Have a nice night."

The two women moved off toward the staterooms laughing, apparently at him. When they were gone, Slater put his hand back in the key box. Nothing. There were no more keys to be had.

Abandoned, he went back to the rail and waited for the *Tecumseh* to leave. Before long, he began to feel lonely. The constant fuckery of the world was oppressive, he thought, the way things never worked out.

As the breeze grew colder, the water of Kewaunee Bay rippled and curled. The arc lights from the ferry slip leapt and flared in the water's reflection. The more he tried to focus on them, the harder they were to see. For a moment, standing alone in Wisconsin, he thought the water might actually be on fire.

In a boxcar on the freight deck of the *Tecumseh*, Harp stripped off his wet clothes. Rain had caught him riding a ladder on a Detroit & Mackinac. He had grabbed on, expecting to move inside the boxcar at the next siding, but he had misjudged the distance. He ended up clinging to the side of the train for half an hour as the rain pelted him. By the time they reached the siding, he was soaked.

The sound of metal on metal echoed through the freight deck as Harp changed into dry clothes. He listened carefully for any noises that might mean workers were coming. Crewmen sometimes came down to grab a smoke or to avoid working.

When he was sure the coast was clear, he hopped out. Rain dripped off the cars. Most of them were shut—he'd been lucky to find an open boxcar. As he walked between the strings, checking out the cars, he began to feel like he was in charge of the freight deck. It was his world, he thought, and why not?

String three, he saw, was not properly blocked. The chocks that should have been wedged against the wheels sat carelessly by the bulkhead. In a storm, the cars might move. If a big wave hit, they could ram the seagate, maybe even bust it open. They'd roll off into the Lake, maybe the ship would go down too. Of course, something like that would happen only once every hundred years. But that wasn't the point.

He was tempted to wedge the wheels himself. But rounding a corner, he glimpsed something rare on string two. It was a crew car of the Ann Arbor Railroad, painted in the dried-blood red of the line and built of wood. Five glass windows lined the side. The car looked to be thirty or forty years old. It couldn't possibly be in service; he couldn't fathom why it was being shipped.

He was walking toward it, exposed between lines, when he heard voices. He looked quickly for a place to hide, but the cars closest to him were closed. The only escape was a rung ladder going up the side of the seagate. He climbed it quickly; the voices grew louder. If he didn't move, the workers wouldn't see him. No one ever looked up. It was a trick he had learned long ago.

At the top rung, about thirty feet above the deck, he looked over the edge of the seagate into the dark froth of the Lake. There was no barrier—from the top, a man could dive into Lake Michigan and never be seen again. Eternity was what it was. It scared and fascinated him. You don't get that in your living room, he thought.

Below him, two workers came into sight. They were dressed in denim overalls, and they were righteously pissed. The taller one had a blond ponytail and held a clipboard. He was checking numbers on the freight cars and walking straight toward Harp.

"So Petey sits me down," Ponytail says, "and he goes, 'I'd like it if you made an effort to be more respectful.' And basically do all that kiss-up stuff he knows I'm never gonna do."

"Fucking Pete," the other worker said.

"So I go, 'I like it when your wife gets all spasmy around my johnson and says how I can have anything I want. That's *my* Kodak moment, you know what I mean? 'Cause after that it gets all dark and freaky.'"

The shorter man snorted. "What'd he say to that?"

"He said I need to be more punctual." Ponytail tapped his clipboard on a boxcar. "This is it. Two eight four one."

The other man took out a knife and twisted the metal seal of the boxcar until it broke. They slid the door back and peered into the boxcar. For a moment, they stood motionless.

"You said Panasonic. These boxes say Fort Howard."

"I can read," Ponytail said.

"Fort Howard is goddamn toilet paper."

"I know that."

"I can't fence toilet paper. I got all the toilet paper I need, Dick."

The ponytailed man was turning to go when he looked up and saw Harp. He thumped his friend on the chest. "Look at that clown up there. Hey, you. You enjoyin' the show? Come on down here and get your ass kicked."

Harp heard violence in their voices. They'd been caught trying to steal. Worse, they'd been caught failing. They would not be forgiving. The men moved to the base of the ladder, waiting for him, but he was not going down. Instead, he raised himself up and went over the seagate. Into the roar and the dark.

Halfway through the crossing, Slater pulled a chair onto the deck and sat in an alcove out of the wind. Above him was a mural of the *Tecumseh* in rough weather. A stab of yellow light illuminated the artwork. For some reason—a faulty switch perhaps—the light flickered erratically. The mural showed the bulkhead broken open and boxcars rolling into Lake Michigan.

The scene cast a witchy, frightening spell, and Slater's thoughts turned again to what he had lost. Selda, most recently. Good friends from here and there. And maybe Harp.

There was also the larger question of what the hell he was doing. While he was driving, the question hadn't come up. He had simply been chalking up miles, making time. The road was its own answer. But the boat encouraged reflection and, worse than that, doubt. There was the possibility he simply had nowhere else to go.

But that wasn't true. It was a big world. He'd been lots of places; he could go anywhere. Minneapolis. A one-room efficiency on Hennepin Avenue. No one would find him there. Assuming anyone was looking.

The ship pitched gently, and eventually Slater let his eyes shut. On the edge of sleep, he realized he was going back to measure what was left of his friendship with Harp. The way you went back to a house after it had burned. No other reason.

He put his backpack on his lap for warmth and let himself sleep. Somewhere in the night, he woke to discover the Woman With One Eye flying overhead, as big as the ship. Too tired to care, he dozed off again. When he woke later, she was gone.

Not long after that, the huge diesels of the *Chief Tecumseh* reversed, waking him fully. At the rail, he could see the dim outline of Wolverine, Michigan. A town he had spent some time in, growing up.

As the land grew closer, pinpoints of light dotted the north arm of the bay. To the south were the faint outlines of Pregnant Point. At the far end of the bay were three giant stumps rising high as the hills—Sunoco Oil tanks, no longer in use. He remembered when they were new. The ship's horn sounded, thunderous in the night. A minute later they passed the lighthouse into the bay, and for a moment the land seemed to be opening her arms.

— 10 —

IT WAS THE night Wallenda fell, and the stars came up full and a thousand normal things happened and in the same space of time small shifts were made in the stream of freight flowing across the continent. Short Life & Misery boxcar 050616 left Rhinelander on a Milwaukee Road freight. Slater drove up River Road until he came to a two-story farmhouse. He parked the Ford Ranchero in the dirt drive and walked toward the front porch.

It was late, but the downstairs lights were bright. A cut from *Electric Ladyland* seeped out and played faintly among the maple and beech. Where the forest floor neared the living room windows, light was caught in trapezoid patches, as if the house could not quite contain what it held.

Slater stopped a few feet from the porch and snapped his fingers by his ear. The piney air carried a trace of skunk. The Hendrix cut was "Midnight Lamp."

Better to come back in the morning, Slater thought. He was lonely enough as it was. Knocking on a strange door in the middle of the night would only make it worse. But before he could leave, the front door opened and a woman's voice came from behind the screen. "Rose? Is that you?"

In the next instant, the porch light came on and Michael Slater was once again a figure in the world of light.

Harp stayed in his boxcar while the yard engine pulled the string from the ferry. When he reached the far end of the yard, he jumped out. The night was cool. The air smelled like rhubarb.

One rail over, junked boxcars sat in waist-high weeds. Dim light from the ferry dock washed their dented sides. At the other end of the yard, workers were stowing equipment and locking down switches. The sound of metal on metal reached him across the weeds. It was something he liked: the stillness of a yard where nothing was happening.

He had escaped the two workers by hanging on to the outside of the *Chief Tecumseh*. There was a rung ladder on both sides of the seagate. He knew the workers wouldn't follow him.

The first few seconds, clinging to the outside of the ship, had made his heart race and the pounding nearly made him dizzy. He gripped the rungs so hard his hands hurt, and he told himself it was no different than ladder-riding the Snake. Either way, if he fell, it was over.

Only when he decided to climb back inside did he get really scared. Not of falling. Of letting go. Those few seconds before hitting the water—what would they feel like? He was frightened of his own curiosity, and the panic froze him. He was forced to wait another long minute, getting his mind right, before climbing into the safety of the *Tecumseh*.

Now, lifting his pack, he took a last look at the yard, the bad-order cars. He tried to think of Lane and how it would be to see her again. She would be upstairs in bed or downstairs with a bag of glue, getting fucked up. He had asked her to stop, told her she had to, and she had pretended that she would. But he knew that she was doing it more and more.

In the shadows at the edge of the yard was an Ann Arbor caboose with twin cupolas—raised areas that extended above the roofline. In daylight, sitting up in the cups, a brakeman could've seen the whole length of a train. In its day, the cab had gone everywhere the Ann Arbor went. Thompsonville, Cadillac, Clare, Owosso. All good towns. Now it went nowhere. Teenagers used it at night as a place to drink and grope.

Harp was tempted to go in. But the cups looked out onto the half-built frame of the Whispering Sands. The work of downstate investors, men who didn't give a slippery shit about anything, as long as their return on investment was high.

It was pretty clear how things were going, he thought. What used to be the world was becoming the marketplace. Anyone could see it wasn't square.

He cinched up his pack and started walking. The road through town was empty. He passed the gun shop and the barbershop, and the Odd Fellows hall. Only the Sawhorse was open.

Across the street, someone had taped a sign in the window of the IGA. *Frozen Hamburger, Half Price. Why It Lasts.*

Sure, Harp thought. Let everyone know we're a bunch of idiots up here.

The music was loud inside the house and at first it seemed
to leave no space for Slater—even when Lane invited him
in and sat him at the kitchen table while she heated water
for instant coffee. He knew before she told him that Harp
wasn't home; if he'd been there, he would have cut a space
through the guitar. The music, with its wild fluorescent
colors and startling prisms of light, was there to fill the spac-
es left empty by Harp. He sensed that without her saying so.

"Here," she said, placing a cup and a bottle of whiskey
on the table, "put some Jack in that. That's how it works
when Harp's away." She leaned against the refrigerator,
curved at the top like an old-fashioned gas tank, the word
Refrigamatic in chrome script.

"Do you know when he'll be back?"

She turned to him, pushed her hair back. "Yesterday.
Last week. Who knows?"

After a few sips, they carried their cups and the bottle to the living room. A lamp with a water-stained shade
stood at one end of a green couch. Stuffing showed through
in two places.

"I heard you drive in," Lane said. "I thought you
might be someone else. My friend Rose."

Slater offered to come back later, but she brushed it
aside. "You're here. You might as well stay."

He sat on the green couch and she sat on the floor by
the coffee table. One leg of the table was broken; its stub
rested on a copy of *The Fountainhead*.

"You're the one who rides freights with him, aren't you?"

"I used to. Before I learned better."

"I've heard some stuff about you."

She was all raw material, Slater thought. As if she'd never learned the poses people struck, or had discarded them. Her hair fell across her face in strands and there was a crescent of blood in her left eye.

"Harp and I go way back," he said. "We were pretty close. We did some crazy things. One night we stole a dozen bowling balls and lined them up on the pier, just to see what the fisherman would do the next morning."

Behind her, on the other side of the room, a black-and-white TV played without sound. Two men were chasing each other through a warehouse. Slater recognized one of them as Mannix.

She refilled their cups and he told her about Tucson, leaving out everything important. A baggie of white pills sat on the coffee table.

"Quaaludes," she said. "Not for me. For someone at work." She talked about Charlie, the house called Hidden Mist, and the rock that made it levitate. "Today's the birthday of someone who would have been my brother. Harp goes off on his merry trips so he misses these anniversaries."

Her pupils were black and very large. Don't just look, they said. Swim right in. He dropped his eyes to the broken table leg. "Is that a library book?"

"I was going to read it, but I couldn't get into it. It's been there for months. I don't think the library wants it back. They've given up on *The Fountainhead.*"

"Right," Slater said. "A lot of people do."

The whiskey coffee burned. He hadn't slept a real sleep in days, and if he drank much more, he wouldn't be able to get up.

"Harp told me about the power line." Behind her, the TV detective took a round in the shoulder. Hendrix played "Little Miss Strange."

"Did he tell you I saved his life?"

There was a small paper bag under the coffee table. She reached for it and put it on her lap. "He told me how freaky you looked with your hair on fire."

Slater took another drink. "That would be true of anyone."

Lane's feet were bare and her big toenails were painted plum; she wore a silver ring on one toe. Her sweatshirt was printed with a large smiling pie and the words *Cherry Hut–World's Best Cherry Pie.*

"So what did the fishermen do?" she asked. "When they found the balls?"

"Nothing. They fished."

Lane smiled. She took a tube of epoxy from the paper bag. When she spoke, her voice was all lower register, no spark of nerves anywhere. "So, Michael Slater," she said. "Do you do glue?"

The Sawhorse Tavern was full of hammer guys. Wedgeheads, Harp called them. One or two of them nodded at Harp from under ball caps, and a few called him by name. They were all good guys. The kind of guys Harp didn't want to be.

Once, on a hammer job, one of them had explained how to build a salt trap. It was simple enough. You find a tree with the right kind of branch and nail some boards up in a V. The salt lick gets rigged up behind it, so the only way the buck can get to it is through the V. When the trap's done, you go back to the double-wide and watch the game. Eventually a deer comes along and works his antlers through the V to get the salt. After that, he's not going anywhere. By the time the Lions have stunk up the place, you grab what's left of the six-pack and hike out to your trap. You feel like crap, pulling the trigger, but at least you come home with some meat.

The ball-cap guys reminded him of that. Not the trap builders, but the bucks. Wedgeheads. They were stuck in their lives and they didn't even know it. He shot a game of pool with two of them—guys he'd built a deck with once. Later the bartender asked where he'd been. "Traveling," he said.

When he left, he walked around the back of the building to take a piss. The sound of it hitting the dirt was a wonderful thing.

In the old days, the land behind the Sawhorse ran to weeds and rusty rails all the way to Wolverine Bay. The emptiness was part of the town and seemed to be fine with everyone. But then money took over, and money didn't like emptiness. The land behind the Sawhorse wasn't earning any income, and that attracted bulldozers. The Whispering Sands.

Someday when it's too late, Harp thought, we'll all be sorry we didn't tell money to go to hell. He zipped up and started walking. The house was two miles out of town and the night was warm—a good night for putting one foot in front of the other.

The baby was a boy, Lane said. It was five days old and they had to get rid of it because their father was getting out of prison early. He had lied to the parole board and the dickheads believed him. He wouldn't be happy about the baby.

That's how Charlie put it. He gave her a pill that day and made her swallow it. *People do this all the time*, he said.

No they don't, Lane said. *People don't leave babies in bathrooms*. But Charlie said, *They take babies to adoption agencies all the time. That's all this is. This is just a different way of getting it there, so they don't come and hassle us*. He gave the baby half a pill so it wouldn't cry.

We don't have time for an adoption agency, Charlie said. *We have to do this now*.

Then you do it, Lane said.

But they couldn't leave the baby in the men's room. *Men are jerks*, Charlie said, and she knew it was true. *Who knows what men would do? They might leave it there crying all night long. We have to put the bag in the women's room. So you have to do it. It's all up to you.*

Slater was looking at her feet. The plum toenails, the silver ring. The TV was going soundlessly behind her. Hendrix played "Return of the Voodoo Child."

The worst part was when Charlie dumped out the scarves she had put in the bag. They didn't have any baby blankets, so she'd made a bed of scarves in the bottom of a Pricebenders' bag. *Not a good idea*, Charlie told her. *We might need these next winter*. Lane's face got hot because the baby needed padding and she wanted them in but Charlie said no.

The worst part was the French-fry smell and the antiseptic and the stall door creaking and the terrible bathroom floor. The worst part was coming back to the car empty-handed.

The Hendrix cut ended and she leaned forward, put her face over the bag. She inhaled deeply and held her breath.

When her head came up, her cheeks were flushed. The crescent of blood in her eye, the mezzaluna, was on fire.

"That'll kill you," Slater said.

She looked at him with a fractured smile. "What'd you do? Read a book?"

On the southern edge of Wolverine, Harp made his way past the abandoned A&W and a transmission shop, long out of business. From there, River Road began to rise. He hoped Lane would be asleep when he got home. Otherwise, she'd be stoned. Glued, actually.

A lot of guys would go for it. He knew how it was. Instead of strange pussy, they settled for a strange woman and called it good. A quick trip to the twilight zone, just to ride the weird energy. The problem was, that kind of thing never stayed fun very long—the crazy high went away, but the crazy woman hung around.

Lane wasn't like that, though, not really. She was okay when she wasn't on glue. More strong than crazy. Some days, when things were working, he could look in her eyes and see the connection between them as strong as anything. Other times it was just gone. Lately, it had mostly been gone.

He had been on the road for three weeks. The Northern Arrow would be even longer and Lane would have to find a way to deal with it. That he was strong enough to leave was the reason he deserved her.

He didn't understand people who turned their back on luck and then claimed they didn't have any.

In the bridgetender's shack, he had licked the word on Melinda's arm. REPENT. From the T to the R and up where nothing was written. He didn't have anything to repent.

At the last streetlight before the dark, a car pulled up beside him. The two workers from the *Tecumseh*. The tall one tripped getting out and hopped twice before getting his balance. The other man, coming around from the driver's side, looked on in surprise.

They left the car doors open, which Harp took as a bad sign. He put his thumbs under the straps of his pack, so his hands would be up and ready.

"You again," the ponytailed man said.

"Downstate," Lane said, "people are constantly finding new ways to fuck you over." She pulled the neck of her sweatshirt forward, ducked her head, and sniffed herself. "They tell you *yes*, but what they really mean is *uh-huh*. They have it down to a science."

She moved next to Slater on the couch. She was a train wreck, he thought—too dark and fucked up for Harp. I'm the one who likes things fucked up.

"They say, 'It's not the heat. It's the humidity,' but that's just bullshit." She let the glue bag fall off her lap. Across the room, the screen showed grainy footage of a man walking across the sky.

"So," she said to Slater. "Why'd you suddenly decide to come back?"

Slater didn't answer. He was looking at the screen. The walking man was in trouble. The wind whipped his shirt and he juggled his pole. Jimi's guitar rose, spraying jagged chords that burst and drifted down like fireworks. Wallenda took one more step along the wire, then stumbled and fell.

The camera zoomed in, trying to track him, but lost sense of up and down. Lane put her hand on Slater's arm, her fingers warm. Then, almost instantly, Wallenda was back on the wire in replay, taking his last wavering step and preparing to fall again. He dropped the pole in slow motion and the scene froze. A red circle showed his hand closing around the wire. For a moment, his grip held. Then the pole knocked his hand away, and Wallenda began falling and Lane made a sound in her throat.

After that they understood that Wallenda was dead and had in fact been dead for a while.

"Jesus Christ," Slater said.

Lane moved closer to him. Her face looked different. Where her cheeks were, Slater saw the meat on her bones. He could feel the place on his arm where her hand had been, and she moved her lips to his. Slow, so the part before touching was almost the best part.

He thought about yes or no, but by the time that thought came she was already in his arms, the couch taking their weight.

Her skin was clammy and very warm. She took off her sweatshirt and dropped it on the floor. She opened his shirt. The wayward light of the TV threw its changing shades on their flesh. Somewhere near the kitchen, Hendrix clutched his Stratocaster and sang about hit and run.

Walking up River Road, Harp shifted his pack, moving the straps away from the pain. He was tired now and angry at the road for being long and uphill. The beer didn't help, or maybe it was going home that made him tired.

They got him once in the face, but it was his shoulder that hurt. They were idiots, the deckhand guys. Glorified wedgeheads. Probably figured they'd cream him. Two against one. But it wasn't about numbers. You just had to decide how much pain you were willing to take.

Harp's father had died in a corn silo. Fell from a catwalk when Harp was in high school. The fall didn't kill him—the silo was nearly full and the drop was barely ten feet. Another worker, who came to help, told Harp that his dad seemed more embarrassed than anything. He stood up quickly, dusted himself off, and started to gasp. It had been a dry year: the corn was full of nitric oxide. Silo gas, heavier than air. Minutes later, he was dead. The farmer who owned the silo was a prominent man in the county. Road Commissioner, Farmer of the Year. He never did anything for Harp's mom. She moved to Florida, covered the ceilings with foil, and called the president every day to check on the weather. That was how much pain she was willing to take.

The deckhands were bullies; they weren't willing to get hit. They each landed a punch, and when Harp swung his flashlight like a club, they quit. It wasn't that bad. He'd been worried they'd take his pack, but in the end they settled for insults, shouted from the car as they roared off.

Left alone, he crunched along the gravel, one foot in front of the other. No other cars came down River Road. Even the raccoons were hiding.

A railroad map as large as a flag was taped to the wall of Harp's room. In the darkness, the map seemed to glow. Slater and Lane lay on the mattress beneath it. The hall light made a yellow stripe under the door. As they humped, Lane's ass rose and broke the line—once, twice, then many times. The yellow stripe became a far-off horizon, a wire. At the end, inside the textured weave of orgasm, was a scrabbled mess of dark and light.

For a few moments afterward, Slater felt guiltless. The map seemed to float over him. As the reverb of sex faded, the room turned back into the room.

"Hello, sunshine," she said.

They slept for a while. Soon enough, he saw the power line coming and woke. She was curled beside him with her head on his chest. Outside, branches creaked. "They had our number," he said. "The police in Canada."

Her head came up. She looked at him to see who she was with; it took a moment for recognition to show on her face. When it did, she seemed neither pleased nor unhappy.

In Canada, he told her, they got taken off trains constantly and every encounter included the words *you two*. As in, *You two, get on down from there. Where do you two think you're going? Do you two know how dangerous that is?* It was the You Two Tour. The phrase took on a secret meaning. If a waitress asked, *How are you two tonight?* they exchanged knowing looks.

In Manitoba a constable spied them in a boxcar and drove them to the nearest town, a dot on the map where they could get a bus. He told them to stay off the trains and wished them good luck.

"You too," Harp said.

When the constable drove off, they walked from the bus depot to the tracks. It took them two days to catch a freight. Slater could no longer remember the name of the place, though he could picture the bottle of whiskey they drank in the park and the two teenage girls who walked by twice, giving them a look. In his memory, the name of the town was Canadian Farm Girls.

There were no boxcars in the yard, so they slept on the ground. The next morning they walked along the track until they came to a trestle, where they sat and did nothing. After an hour or so, they heard the rumble of a westbound. At the same time, about fifty yards off, a line of cows moved toward the track, head to tail. They were moving slowly, on a collision course with the oncoming freight.

"Shit," Harp said.

The lead cow reached the track bed and hobbled over the rail. The second and third cow crossed. The fourth. The fifth. The freight seemed to be right on top of them.

The last cow stepped directly in front of the oncoming train—a sure collision. But it was a trick of perspective. The cow cleared the track with thirty seconds to spare.

"I was disappointed," Slater told Lane. "I wanted to see the cow explode. Things start to go wrong and I like to watch."

Lane propped herself up on an elbow. "And I'm the cow?"

"You're the train."

Outside, crickets chirped.

"Tell me what happened in Detroit." She put her head down. "I heard you screamed like Jesus."

Even in rehab, he hadn't really talked about it. No one had asked.

The electricity in Detroit wanted down, he told her. Down to the ground, and it didn't matter how it got there. To the electricity, he was just a bigger, softer kind of wire. But some of the million barbed electrons were still inside him, trying to get out. That was the thing. He was leaking electricity.

Some of the electrons were in the Hill Rom Century

bed. The Micro Infusion Pump. The Servo-Ventilation Unit. The Vacutron Suction Ensemble. And *The Dating Game*. A horrible, endless loop of *The Dating Game*, showering down on him from above. It turned out to be a TV mounted above his bed, though it had seemed like some kind of radiance at the time. Something flickering in the mist of a cosmic exhaust pipe. Dainty music set to a mincing beat. A woman in a paisley dress.

Slater couldn't change the channel, but with a 25-mg morphine drip, he didn't need to. Lights strobed, sound split into strange fragments. Harp never came by, but he was visited by many others. A man with a knife for a tongue. Someone who looked exactly like Slater climbing a rope ladder made of snakes. A red-haired woman who shot Ping-Pong balls from her vagina and stared at him with the face of Raymond Burr. The more morphine they gave him, the stranger it got. Ordinary lightbulbs turned on and off 120 times a second. He could see alternating current.

Harp reached the drive and stopped, the pain in his shoulder gone numb. A rusted Ford Ranchero sat parked in the gravel. It took him a minute to see the Arizona plates.

Jesus, Mike, he said. Welcome back to Bumfuck. Took you long enough.

He put a hand on the tailgate of the Ranchero, getting the feeling of it like he would a freight. There was something dark in the gravel beside the car—a shape that looked like money. When he picked it up, he saw it was not a one, or even a ten as he had hoped, but a hundred-dollar bill. One Ben.

Somehow, he knew it was a bad sign. But he put it in
his pocket just the same.

⇌

In Slater's dream, everyone wore stethoscopes and you
couldn't tell the wounded from the well. A nurse who looked
a lot like Lane took off her scrubs; she was about to speak
when he woke and saw Harp standing in front of the map.

"So you're back," Harp said. "Obviously I've missed
some shit."

Slater propped himself up on an elbow. Lane was gone.
"Christ," he said. "How long have you been standing there?"

"About a minute. How long have you been sleeping
there?"

"I don't know. About an hour."

When he'd pushed Harp down in the woodchips, he'd
seen a flash of surprise on his face, and something else—
something like the need for revenge. Harp couldn't see the
power line coming. It was an attack, unprovoked, as far as
Harp knew. They were close enough to the edge of the car
that he might have rolled off; Harp couldn't know for sure
as he fell if he was going to be killed. In that instant, there
was fear in Harp's eyes, but it was betrayal that Slater saw
most, a look of accusation as he saved Harp's life and risked
his own. It was the final scene before the electricity arched
from the wire to Slater's head, the last deep impression the
world made before he woke up three days later. He wondered if the electricity had fixed it there, hardened it in his
circuitry. And now that he had truly betrayed Harp, he saw
nothing but friendship on his face.

Harp stepped carefully across the darkened room, put

his backpack in the closet. "You meet Lane?"

The question required a lie, a perfect one. "She let me in. Jesus, it's late. Where have you been?"

Winona, Harp said. Iowa. He sat by the bottle of whiskey Lane had left and had a drink. There was a yard in Aberdeen, Harp said, where a brakeman yelled, *You're gonna die doing that* and then came back and shouted, *You wanna trade places?* You would have liked it, he said to Slater. There was a morning when he woke up with dew dripping from the boxcar roof, hitting him on the forehead. And Melinda, and the bridgetender's shack.

That was a different kind of betrayal, Slater thought. It made him wonder what the story was with Lane. It was the kind of question that couldn't be asked.

When Harp stood up, Slater offered to give him the mattress. Harp shook his head.

"I'll be next door." He paused in the hallway, looking into the room. "If you seek a pleasant peninsula," he said, "you're about a hundred years too late."

After that, Slater couldn't sleep. He spent a long hour on the mattress, eyes open, trying to extract meaning from the slender noises of the house. A door that opened and closed. A teasing laugh that held both meanness and seduction. Once, something heavy hit the floor. He imagined a stray foot upsetting a bottle. Muffled voices rose gently. To make himself stop listening, Slater brought his hands up by his ears and snapped until he had to stop.

Once, when he'd been snapping in a Tucson Tasty Freeze, he heard a woman with a small child say, "He oughta buy a clicker."

He considered it. A clicker would be nice. Easier on his hands.

Before the power line, it had been different. He needed no clicker then. In Winnipeg he had flown between boxcars. He had wings.

They were riding through a yard with a second freight moving on the track beside them. Both trains were rolling slow, the same direction, though the other freight was going slightly faster. Each time one of its boxcars passed by, the doors of the two cars lined up for an instant.

If he timed it just right, Slater thought, he could jump from one train to the other. Just to see how it might feel, he moved back a few strides. He measured the time two running steps might take.

"Don't," Harp said. "Don't mess around like that."

Without deciding to run, he ran. Midair, the two doorways lined up. Before he had time to get scared, he was landing in a crouch on the other train. An angel of the freight yard.

But then he had to jump back. No way was Harp gonna follow him.

By the time he got set, both trains were going faster. He backed up farther for extra speed and fear took hold in his body. Screw up in some small way, catch a toe, and the rest of his life would be a scream. He let a couple good chances go by, too tight to move. When it was almost too late, he bolted. His second jump was better than the first.

That night at a siding stop, Harp said, "That showoff stuff will be fun to look back on when you're hopping around on one leg."

A week later the power line kissed his head. Now he was wide awake on a mattress that wasn't his own. Now he was mortally screwed.

— 11 —

SLATER WOKE IN the morning with the sun in his face and a headache building behind his eyes. The house was quiet; the floating map was back on the wall.

Downstairs, the furniture had been moved. The couch, where he and Lane had wrestled out of their clothes, was by the window now. A phone book was under the coffee table's short leg.

There's a reason, Slater thought, that only broken people get in bed with you. There's a reason only broken people will take you.

When no one else came down, he made some instant coffee and carried it to the porch. The morning light was mildly reassuring. The question of what he should do next would get worse as the day went on.

Leaving his cup on the porch, he walked into the yard. A breeze brought the scent of pine, reminding him of the forest where he and his high school girlfriend first made love. It was not very far away. Things had been simpler then. Pine needles made a brown bed; Boones Farm seemed like an exotic wine. They drank a half bottle, then turned to more potent stuff, making age-old discoveries with first-time tenderness. She whispered something and used her teeth, but gently. It was a moment time left propped up on blocks.

A shame I didn't realize how fleeting it all was, he told himself. You thought life was going to be an unending series of such pleasures. But of course it wasn't. You couldn't discover a girl a second time. You couldn't open her shirt with the same desire. Once you knew about opening shirts, it was grasping, not discovering. Awareness would have ruined it. Lack of awareness was what the forest floor was all about.

As the sun got higher, Slater got the Blue Dart from the Ford and found a maple to throw at. The knife rotated once and stuck.

He retrieved the knife and threw it again, stepping back farther each time until he started to feel better. The doomed, he decided, have no need for guilt.

Harp woke and started to speak, but Lane drew a finger over his lips, stopping him. She slid off her bracelets as they kissed. Soon he was floating, in between worlds. Lane and boxcars, and other memories of the road. A milkweed seed that floated in the still air of a boxcar, while the land blasted past outside. The agent at Portage la Prairie who showed him where to wait so he wouldn't get caught. The bridgetender's shack.

Lane got on top as the land rolled by in his head. Trees and crops in corrugated rows. Rain-splattered loading docks, one faded number painted on the roll-down door and a different, fresher number in new paint up above. And RE-PENT AND BELIEVE. And the muscles in Lane's arms and how he missed her when he was gone, and how he wanted to go out there again. And the name Melinda, which worked its way to his lips and out of his mouth at the end.

They were in the kitchen when Slater came inside. Lane, at the sink, had her back to the room.

"It's not supposed to feel safe," Harp said. "But that's not the point. I don't do it for the danger."

Lane put a plate on the plastic rack. "So it's the thrill of meeting hobos. And hobo women."

Harp let out a ragged breath. "Explain it to her, Mike."

Slater leaned against the doorway, watching Lane from behind. He knew the attractions of the rails very well, and he had succeeded in not thinking about them for almost a year. It wasn't the danger, he told her. If you did it right, the danger was small, but you had to do it right every second, and that was part of how it made you feel alive. The things you had to do were always simple—don't get set out, hide from the tower, find water—but also hard. To get information you had to talk to workers, but talking to workers was how you got caught. You had to solve a lot of problems, but there was no bullshit. That was the best part.

Lane put the last dish on the rack. "Whose idea was it to stand on top of a boxcar underneath a power line?"

Harp took a drink of coffee. "We're going to the Saw-horse," he said. "Mike and I." He stood up to go.

"Actually," Slater said, "the best part is what the train shows you. In a car or a truck you face forward and see what's coming, but a boxcar makes you look out the side. It's all now, now, and now."

"Like sex," Lane said.

Long after Matthews left, Slater sat in front of the console. He put his finger on the power switch, but he couldn't make himself turn it off. The power switch was connected to a wire that ran to the outlet, the copper nipple on the wall, through which it sucked dry rivers and coal plants and even the energy of atoms. The outlet was connected to feeder wires, which were connected to transmission lines, interties, trunk routes, other feeders, other outlets, other consoles. That's how it works, he told himself. We're all connected by copper wire.

12

THE DOOR TO the Sawhorse Tavern had an ax embedded in it, the blade stuck in the wood as if someone had hurled it from afar. Slater grabbed the handle and stepped inside. Instantly, he caught a whiff of the past.

Up front, the bar was lined with a dozen stools. A painted nude reclined above the hard liquor. The Sawhorse had been built to store cabbage—thousands and thousands of cabbages, which were shipped everywhere by rail in the '30s and '40s. Now it was full of denim—locals out of work or working-class guys up for the summer.

Harp led the way to a booth in the back. Razkowski, the bartender, came over to take their order.

"Gentlemen," he said.

"Give us a minute, Razz," Harp said. Toward the front of the Sawhorse, a short man in a red and white Hawaiian shirt sent Harp a little nod of recognition. Harp returned it and looked away.

"You did glue with Lane last night," he said.

"She did glue. I watched."

"That stuff is deadly. I like to get high like anybody else, but glue will kill you. You should try to make her stop."

"Me?" Slater said. "What about you? I just got here."

The waitress floated up to the table. She was firm-jawed with blond hair to her waist and an expression of imperturbability.

"Mike Slater," Harp said, "Linda LaGood."

She gave Slater a blissed-out nod and Harp ordered a pitcher of Labatts. They both turned to watch her blond hair sway as she floated away.

"Remember Katie?" Harp asked.

"No," Slater said. "I don't remember Katie."

He did, of course. Katie was a rich girl, of high Ford or GM lineage, and wild. She was from the music camp down the road; they met her in the Sawhorse on the night Neil Armstrong walked on the moon, but she went home with Harp. Slater ended up on the beach alone, watching Neil Armstrong without the aid of a TV. Later, they heard she'd been expelled.

"Those were the days, huh?" Harp said. He pulled out a hundred-dollar bill and put it on the table. "I found this by your car last night. You lose it?"

Slater took it and looked at both sides. "It's not mine," he said. "Maybe it's Lane's."

"She doesn't have this kind of money."

Slater watched Harp's face for clues. He decided to take a chance. "How long have you been together?" he asked.

"A while."

He waited for more, but that was all there was.

"I've got a job lined up tomorrow," Harp said. "I'm building a pole barn for Howdy Broodson."

Broodson had been their high school guidance counselor. "You're kidding me," Slater said. "Broodson's still alive?"

"Apparently."

Linda LaGood brought the beer. Harp used the hundred to pay for it. "He told me I was bound for woe," Harp said. "Those words exactly. What kind of guidance is that?"

"Maybe he said it to everyone. He'd have been right half the time."

They drank to that. There was woe spread all over Northern Michigan. They'd seen plenty on the road into town. Abandoned farmhouses in fields of purple wildflowers. Rusting double-wides with big cars in front. A long stretch of fence posts where no fence remained. And the signs. *Stump blasting. Worms for sale. I do drywall.* People piecing their lives together.

The summer tourists brought money, but it was unreliable and never enough, and besides the tourists clogged everything up, rubbernecking at the scenery, buying postcards and taffy. On the drive in, Slater and Harp had gotten stuck behind some of them—a slow-moving Cadillac full of senior citizens. We're here to serve tourists, Slater had said. I like mine medium rare. Finally, the Caddy came to a complete stop in the middle of the road. A granny in tourist stripes and bluish-white hair got out and stood blocking the way while she took a picture of a one-room schoolhouse that had been converted into a junk shop. *10,000 Hubcaps Inside* the sign out front read. Harp reached over and hit the horn. "Jesus Christ," he said. "Now they want our hubcaps too?"

Slater emptied his glass and poured himself another beer. The afternoon sun slanted through a dirty window overhead.

"So," Harp said. "How was the desert? They get you fixed?"

"You mean, do I drool or anything like that?"

"Lane said you seemed solid enough."

"Really? What else did she say about me?"

"She said she looked deep down in your soul. And she saw a yellow-bellied woodpecker inside."

He couldn't tell if Harp was joking. And maybe it was true. Maybe he was a yellow-bellied woodpecker.

The power line could have killed him, he thought. People died all the time from less deadly stuff. A slip in the shower, a piece of meat in the windpipe, a bad choice of words. He'd survived 33,000 volts, but only by chance. If the line had been just a little lower, it would have sliced through his neck and sent his head bouncing along the track, an electrified grin on his face. The fact was, he'd been given a second chance by the grace of God or whatever random bingo caller happened to be running the show that day. All he had to do now was not fuck it up. So of course fucking it up was all he ever did. With Selda for sure. The horror with Dickinson. And now this. He had reached a point, it seemed, where the faintest whiff of his own life set him to convulsively snapping his fingers. He should just tell Harp what he'd done— say it and take responsibility. I did something bad with Lane. I slept with your girlfriend.

"I went to a topless bar in Tucson once where the women did backflips," he said instead. He threw his hands up slightly, as if to flip.

"That doesn't sound sexy," Harp said. "Got a quarter?"

"You just found a hundred-dollar bill."

"I need fifty cents for the pool table."

Slater dug in his pockets and came up with two quarters. Harp picked up the coins and left, taking his beer. "Private meeting," he said. "Wait here."

"So you got my message," Charlie said. He took two cues from the rack and handed one to Harp. "I take it that means you're interested."

Harp examined the cue Charlie handed him and took a different one from the wall. "I didn't say that."

"You might get interested when you see what I brought you." Then he turned to the booth where Slater sat alone. "Who's the doofus?"

"A friend of mine," Harp said.

"You brought a friend to our meeting? That concerns me."

Charlie racked the balls and bent over the table to break. His stroke was wild and barely nicked the cue ball. "Do over?"

Harp shook his head.

"Good," Charlie said. "I don't like do-overs. Get it right the first time or die trying, that's what I say. The thing is, champ, I worry more about friends than enemies. I mean, he doesn't look too hazardous to me. But who knows? He could be a talker. And then we'd be in trouble."

Harp sent the three-ball into the side pocket. "He's not a talker. And I trust him."

"Even worse. Trust will kill you every time."

Harp's combination off the rail didn't fall. He walked to his standing spot at one end of the table. Charlie came and stood beside him.

"Here's the deal, champ," he told Harp. "I need something unbuilt. Blown to bits, you might say, if you get my drift. I thought you might be my man." He motioned to a paper bag sitting next to his Budweiser. "I brought that for you. Don't look inside just yet, but I'll give you a hint. It's a bag full of boom."

Harp snorted. "I don't know who you think I am. But I don't do that kind of shit."

Linda LaGood passed by collecting bottles. Charlie put a hand on her shoulder.

"Hey, sweet thing. You ever see the sand dunes down by Wakashi Lake? Beautiful dunes. Miles of pure, fine sand. Almost as beautiful as you are."

Linda LaGood looked at Charlie's hand. He removed it from her shoulder.

"There are no sand dunes at Wakashi Lake," Harp said.

"Not anymore," Charlie said. "Somebody moved them."

Linda LaGood floated away, untroubled.

Charlie stepped up to shoot and overpowered a finesse shot. He leaned against the table, facing Harp.

"Let me ask you this, champ. What would you do with the most beautiful sand dunes in America? Lay out there and smoke dope? Build sand castles? Maybe take my sister out in a dune buggy and try not to get sand in the wrong places? Something like that? Am I right?"

"That's none of your fucking business."

"My point is, you'd go out and enjoy yourself. Dig the natural beauty. But not your average businessman. He looks at these dunes and you know what he sees?" Charlie moved closer to Harp. "Concrete. A million tons of high-grade concrete. He creams his pants thinking of what he could build with all that."

Harp lined up a shot and missed. "You're a weird fucker, Charlie," he said.

"That I don't deny. But do you know what they did, these businessmen? They hauled away every last grain of sand from

Wakashi Lake. And the sad part is that people like you and Miss Honey Britches over there have no idea the dunes were ever there. It's like they never existed. All because some jerk-offs in fancy suits figured out how to turn sand into money."

Harp returned to his standing spot. "It's your shot, Charlie. Take your turn."

"Ever been to Chicago?" Charlie asked. "'Cause if you have, you've seen the sand dunes of Wakashi. In a slightly more solid form. A more money-friendly form. The concrete that built Chicago is made from that sand. Some say it's a very exciting city, Chicago. Now go look inside the bag I brought you."

Harp picked up the bag. Inside was a metal lunchbox with scenes from *The Parent Trap* on the sides. Hayley Mills in pigtails.

"Nice, huh?" Charlie said. "I got it from Shannon. One of the new girls. Latest addition to the Spreadables." He lowered his voice to a whisper. "There's five hundred dollars inside and one stick of dynamite. That's just for yuks. The rest is in a storage locker across from Molly Hogan's bar. When I give the word, someone's going to haul it all over to that piece of crap known as the Whispering Sands and wire it up and solve a whole mess of problems for everyone. The five hundred dollars is just a down payment. Basically, it's a delivery job and the person who does the delivery gets a whole lot of money. That person might as well be you."

Charlie shot and scratched. Harp shot a tough combination and almost sank it.

"Why are you talking to me about this?"

"You're friends with sis. Keeps it in the family. I need that lunchbox back when you're done, by the way."

"You can keep it, Charlie. I'm not interested."

"We haven't talked real money yet." He pulled a tattered paperback from the back pocket of his shorts and wrote a figure on the inside front cover. The book was called *The Price of Beaver*. "Here," he said, "read this. You might find it illuminating."

Harp tossed the book down on the table. "You're wasting your time. You don't know me. And you have no sense of right or wrong."

Delighted, Charlie stamped his foot. "Right or wrong! Right or wrong! That's so fucking quaint!"

A couple heads swiveled in nearby booths. Charlie gave them the finger. He watched Harp shoot, then draped an arm around his shoulder.

"Think of it this way, champ. Imagine Wolverine ten years from now if you do this thing we're talking about. If we stop these bastards in their tracks. It'll be a town full of places like this place, full of people like you and me. Now erase that and picture Wolverine full of condos." He gave Harp a moment to picture the tourist town Wolverine would become. "Two futures. Is one right and one wrong? Who can really say? See, it's not about right or wrong. It's about power versus power. Yours and theirs. These money guys from Chicago, do they have the right to flush away our future? Hell, no. But they have the power, see, and that's all that matters."

Charlie took a drink and wiped his mouth. "And you have the power to stop them. Their power is green and yours is more like red, if you know what I mean. But get this: their power destroys what's here, and your power preserves it. Okay? And make no mistake, champ, they're gonna use their power. No fucking doubt. The only question is, are you gonna use yours? That's the only thing that cuts a good goddamn, you know what I mean? You see a girl at a party, right? I mean, is she gonna take off her panties or not? That's all that matters. It's all about what happens next—that's the only thing that counts. So tell me to blow it out my ass if you want, but don't say you don't have the right. 'Cause nobody has the fucking right."

Harp stood for a while and looked at the table. He'd forgotten whose shot it was. "Maybe I'll think about it."

"On a thing like this, champ, there isn't any thinking," Charlie said. "You're either in or you're out. I need to know which."

Harp went back to his standing spot. Charlie followed him with the lunchbox.

"When?" Harp asked.

"Soon." Charlie turned the lunchbox in his hands. "Great movie, by the way. You ever see it? Same kid played both parts."

The door to the Sawhorse opened and a new group of wedgeheads blew in. A batch just like them were at the other pool tables. Oblivious to everything. They'd end up in mobile homes with pregnant girls from Durand and Onondaga. In a year or two they'd be slugging quarters into Maytags while their girlfriends changed diapers on orange tables by the dryers. They were durable guys, made for hard wear, and they would get it. Meanwhile they shot pool and swung hammers and their share of things got smaller and smaller and they didn't even seem to notice. Their minds had been vinylized, Harp thought.

"Tell me something," he said. "If this is such an easy job, why don't you get one of your druggies to do it? Or maybe one of your whores?"

Charlie called a tough combination and shot it perfectly.

"The Spreadables aren't whores. They're nice girls who sleep with my vendors. No one's forcing them to do anything." He made another shot and waved his stick in the direction of Linda LaGood. "It's the American way, pal. Who do you think Goody Two-Shoes over there is banging to keep her job?"

"No one."

"Except maybe the bartender and the beer man. And half the liquor board, I bet." He took a bead on the twelve.

"Just because you're that way, doesn't mean everyone is."

Charlie straightened up and sucked in his cheeks. "If you're thinking about Lane, champ, don't worry. She was different. She didn't bang the vendors. They all wanted her, of course. But she was too temperamental."

"Just shoot, Charlie."

"Only a stud like you could tame that girl."

"Just finish your turn."

Charlie called a ridiculously hard shot—cue ball off two rails, kissing the eight. He shot it effortlessly and won the game. Turning, he put a hand on Harp's shoulder and sought out his eyes.

"You're my man unless I hear different. Wait till I say go," he pointed at Slater. "And not a word to Mr. Lonely over there."

Harp held his gaze, then casually picked up the bag. He was halfway across the bar when Charlie called out to him. "Hey champ—you know how they got all that sand to Chicago? By train. Lots and lots of trains."

On a high pole above the Sawhorse Tavern, a cast-iron weathercock with burnt-ocher eyes gazed over the yellow wedge of land along the bay. Near the tavern, at the thick end of the wedge, railroad tracks spread like the tines of a pitchfork. The tracks there were lost in weeds—a grave-yard for dead freight. The rusty rails held a dozen junked boxcars and a caboose the color of dried blood.

Officially, the cars were *awaiting disposition*—the rail-road euphemism for being left to rust and ruin. Had the cars ended their usefulness elsewhere, they might have been melted for debts. Stranded in Wolverine, they simply sat. By day they were junk; by night, they became secret shelter, places of alcohol and sex.

Beyond the cars, but still within the weathercock's purview, sat the construction equipment and the half-built skeleton of the Whispering Sands. Farther on, three decrepit docks protruded through marshland into the bay. Past an abandoned drive-in from the '50s, the view gave way to for-est—mottled evergreen spreading and rising in both direc-tions, ending in the bald patch known as Pregnant Point—*where biology and geology meet*. Just beyond the point, out of sight from the weathercock, was Lake Michigan.

The normal wind, a sou'wester, spun the weathercock's tail as Harp and Slater left the Sawhorse. Harp led the way through knee-high weeds, passing dead freight and scaring up quail.

Of the twelve junked cars, five bore the emblem of the Great Lake Central, the bankrupt line that had left them for dead. *Safety Pays* was stenciled on the side of one of the cars. Daylight stabbed through gaps where the metal was torn. Weeds grew through the floorboards. The cars had been stilled by the departure of the dollar sign—the force that runs all trains and which vanishes at the end of a railroad's life as surely as the soul departs the body, striking rolling stock immobile.

Harp walked to the edge of the dead storage yard, where the skeleton of the Whispering Sands rose, covered in huge sheets of plastic. His right arm swung wide as he walked.

"Welcome to the Whispering Sands," he said. "Watch for snakes."

Slater stepped gingerly through horsetail and meadow grass.

"Where we're standing will be covered parking," Harp said. He pointed at a Chicago & Northwestern boxcar with the words *Do Not Hump* on the door. "Over there, they'll have the croquet court."

"What about the snakes?"

"This will all be paved. But they'll hire some wedge-heads to kill snakes, just to be sure."

"You're joking, right?"

A line of seagulls came from the ferry dock and crossed over the condos. "It's just about making the numbers add up. A rat in the house may eat the ice cream. That's all it is."

"Ice cream?" Slater said. "What the hell?"

"*Arithmetic.* Money plus money. That's all they care about."

Wind snapped the plastic over unfinished construction. The Visqueen logo repeated endlessly along the seams.

"View of the bay," Harp said. "Worth half your pay. Unless it all comes down and hits the grit. Then watch out."

"What are you talking about?"

"'Get you a foxhole, a place to hide.'"

It was Northern Michigan shorthand. Seger, trains. "I give up," Slater said.

Harp shrugged and headed back to the road. "This whole town is bound for woe."

13

IN POSTPRODUCTION, THE dark seeped through walls and covered cubicles. When the console was silent, Slater could hear the place creak. A haunted house in the middle of Manhattan, a hall of mirrors just for him.

When Dimi or Matthews came up, it was better. Alone, he was a genius of regret. It was an inherited trait, he thought, a gift from his dad—wielder of the sharp stick, the farm kid who poked out an eye—but Slater had perfected it in the disloyalties of that summer. He owed Harp nothing but friendship; after sleeping with Lane, he at least owed her honesty. He could have been loyal to one of them and walked away from the other. Instead he tried to split the difference; the result was pretense folding in on itself. Surely none but a maestro could pull that off, Slater told himself, and that was me: I did it my way.

On screen four, the past continued to play. Selda. Rehab. The biofeedback lab.

In rehab, Slater always chose the blue helmet with the decal of Underdog on the side. He wore it when they played

Tilted, a biofeedback game for patients with brain trauma—
the Rewires, they were called.

The rules were simple. Two players sat on opposite
sides of a table with a rubber ball in the middle. The hel-
mets measured brain activity. Low-frequency alpha waves
meant you were relaxed. Faster beta waves showed stress.
The idea was to keep your waves low and tilt the table the
other way, rolling the ball into the loser's lap. A neurolo-
gist, Dr. Gert, had wired the table herself and adopted ten-
nis rules for scoring, which no one ever followed. Tilted
was competitive relaxation; the trick was not to care. Slater
didn't. His alphas were the lowest—he could drop the ball
into the lap of any mental defect on the ward. Selda was
the only one who ever beat him, and she wasn't a patient—
she was the housekeeper's cousin.

Every Sunday night, against ward rules, Rita and Selda
played Hearts and Screw Your Neighbor in the occupational therapy room. Their laughter and horseplay was a
highlight in the dull life of the ward. Selda usually won;
she was lucky at cards and loose with the rules. "This girl
will cheat you," Rita said to Slater at the table one Sunday.
"Watch your back, Rewire. She don't play fair."

Most of the patients on Two East were stroke victims
or diabetes amputees. The Rewires like Slater were the
stars. They all liked Selda. She was confident. Loud. Her
parents had been migrants; when she was a child, her family lived in a car. She worked for the food co-op now, driving a van and making deliveries.

"You're never gonna beat me," she said to Slater one night
at the card table. "If I win again, you have to lick my toes."

Slater took the bet. "But not at cards," he said. "Tilted."

Rita let out a whistle, getting a rise from the onlookers.

"Brain waves don't lie," Slater said. "You can't cheat at Tilted."

"Selda can," Rita said.

The biofeedback lab was in the basement. Rita took them downstairs and opened the lab with her housekeeping key.

A mobile of the solar system hung over the table. The walls were dark blue. It was supposed to be calming, but it didn't help Rita. Her nervous laughter was the product of very fast betas. Slater put on the Underdog helmet and beat her five times in five minutes. He called the game Slacker Take All.

Selda went next. Rita adjusted her helmet and showed her how to fasten the electrodes. Her face was all curves and laughter; it never settled.

They hit the switch and Selda started to hum. The ball hovered in the center of the table, held by their dead-even alphas. Then it rolled a half turn toward Slater. "You're in trouble now, Rewire," Rita said.

In postproduction, the game played across screen four. The ball rolled one way, then the other. Slater let out a deep breath and the table seemed to tip toward Selda. Then she did her smile.

On the monitors, Slater saw people's tics. The hand to the forehead. The mouth wipe. The nose rub. The screen caught any habitual move and accentuated it. Except with Lane. With Lane, the screen accentuated her stillness. Her only tic was when she ducked her head, pulled out her shirt collar, and sniffed herself. The glue made her sweat. Her nonchalance stunned Slater. I have a body, here it is, I can smell it. Eventually he figured out that she wasn't checking to see if she smelled. She was checking to see if the glue was working.

Selda, on screen six, did almost the same head duck. It began pixel for pixel the same, but it ended differently. She didn't pull her blouse out and sniff. Instead, she raised her eyes and smiled at Slater.

It had been a while since anyone had looked at him that way. When his doctor showed a smile, he heard the ominous hum of assessment. But Selda's smile was real. It lit up every shriveled nerve in Slater's recovering brain. She could have raised her shirt and it wouldn't have wrecked his game the way the smile did. The ball reversed direction, rolled his way, and fell into his lap.

A half-hour later, in the food co-op van, Slater was down among the vegetables, tongue working. A lick for each toe.

When he got out of rehab, they moved into the Addition. Six months later, Selda threw an orange at him and hit him in the stomach. He threw it back and broke her figurines of Mary, Joseph, and Scooby Doo. After that, he lived in the desert alone.

On screen one, Harp. On screen two, Lane. It was that kind of night—images floating in from all over. Slater wondered if the brain doctors in Detroit had cobbled things up. Red wire to blue wire by mistake. It would explain a lot.

On screen one, Harp swung onto a brown hopper, a grain car with a platform at the end. He put his pack by his feet and stuck his head out, looking up and down the train.

He had rules when he rode. Never hop a train running full out. Go for the forward ladder, not the rear, so if you slip, you fall against the side of the car and not between them. Take your gloves off when you're talking to brakemen; let 'em see your hands. Fill your water bottle every chance you get. Stay awake. Check the air hoses. Never stand on top of a moving train. It was Harp's rule and he was the only one who could decide when to break it.

On screen two Lane sat in the kitchen, a red scarf around her neck, a pile of white sugar on the table. She jerked her head, looking quickly over her shoulder, and began to squeeze epoxy into the sugar bowl. Start with yes, she'd said. Everything else is pain, so start with yes.

For Harp, there was always a new train on the way. New tracks rising like an underground stream breaking into daylight—darkness and then suddenly steel, twin rails cutting through thistle and alder shoots, running fast and clear across the land. Harp's rails ran through valleys and lumber towns, over mountains, and along rivers through the middle western flatlands and prairies. Montana, stars. North Dakota, snow. Minnesota, green and sometimes rolling. In Wisconsin, the tracks led to the hull of the *Chief Tecumseh*. Harp showed Slater all the secrets of the rails—which trains to ride, which cars to jump, and how a fast freight could blow the lines right off the calendar and change your sense of time. But it was Lane who told Michael Slater to start with yes.

— 14 —

"YOU SLEEP WITH him," Dickinson said, "and then you give him the car." He backed Cassie up against the horse pen. In his hands he held the blue and gold macaw. "Like I'm an idiot," he said.

It wasn't like that, Cassie said. She begged him not to hurt Sammy.

Dickinson tightened his hands around the bird. "Tell me where he is."

But Cassie claimed not to know. Snot ran from her nose. She wiped it on her hands and then on her jeans. Minnesota, she thought. No—Michigan. Fairies. Something about fairies and cherries.

The crying and the gibberish made Dickinson madder. He threatened to snap Sammy's neck unless he got an address and then he did it without thinking. His hands twisted the bird's head, and he wished they hadn't.

When he dropped the bird, Cassie fell to her knees, wailing. She picked Sammy from the dirt like he was a baby. Dickinson walked away. He felt worse about killing the bird than he did about shooting her husband.

The undersheriff was on the phone again. He told Charlie to wait on the Whispering Sands. Time it closer to the election.

"Not an option," Charlie said. "We're already in motion. The fuse is lit."

"Then unlight it."

Charlie held the phone away from his ear. At heart, public employees disgusted him. They were always so inept.

Across the living room, Tracy and one of the Spreadables were watching Bonanza and playing Nerfball. Shirts and skins.

"The thing is," Charlie told Lazenbeck, "our guy is itching to go. I don't know if I can stop him."

"So get a different guy."

Apparently, it was Amateur Hour. "Listen, I hate to get all technical on you," Charlie said, "but you can't change guys. It isn't done."

"Why not?" the undersheriff asked.

"The goal is to have no leftover pieces at the end. This guy is our doer. If he doesn't do anything, we're left with an unused doer dicking around. It's bad for security. Don't they teach this stuff in crime school?"

Tracy banked a shot off the screen. The ball hit Hoss Cartwright and fell through the hoop. She did her old Vulva Voom dance for Charlie's benefit. She was playing shirts, the other girl, skins.

"Trust me," Lazenbeck said. "This whole deal will be worth a lot more if it happens later. For you and me both. Just keep our doer occupied till I give the word."

Christ, Charlie thought, if I wanted to kowtow to cops, I'd get a real job.

As he hung up, Tracy shot the Nerfball again. Ben Cartwright glared down at Tracy and the topless Spreadable. "Not on my land," he said.

— 15 —

AT FIRST LIGHT Harp sat on the bed, watching Lane sleep. Her face was pale and he didn't want to leave. But Trick Bradley was picking him up in five minutes so he could go swing a hammer.

He brushed Lane's hair back from her ear. Jesus, he said quietly—the things money makes us do.

They hadn't said anything more about Melinda. She wouldn't bring it up and neither would he, but it was in the air. That was the problem when you went about things by feel. There was something weird about Mike, too. But that was always true.

He got his tool belt from the closet. Downstairs, he sat on the porch and waited for Trick. Two days ago he'd been riding freight. Now this.

He'd agreed to the job on another early morning, before leaving on his freight trip. He'd been sitting outside, watching the dew burn off, thinking about the road and where he might go. For no real reason, he started picturing the freight yard in town. A crew would be standing about, a yard engine snorting behind them. From the porch, he had imagined the marina and the pickups parked in front of Dewey's. People were going to work and he started to wonder why he wasn't.

Work, as he conceived of it, left a stinky puddle at your feet, and in return you got a paycheck. But the people he imagined that morning didn't seem crushed. In the blessed early light, they seemed industrious. Why not me, he thought. Why not get up with the sun, grab a rope, and do some pulling with the others?

After a few brilliant moments of that, he had gone inside and made a phone call. He told Trick he'd do the pole barn, Howdy Fucking Broodson and all.

Almost immediately, he regretted it. Slanting light, instant coffee, and suddenly he was full of the ripest possible bullshit. Most people searched their souls at night. Thanks to that morning, he wouldn't be allowed to enjoy this one. That was piece of crap number one.

Trick Bradley was piece of crap number two. Tricked Badly, Harp called him. A glorified handyman. Half-assed in everything except salesmanship. Trick couldn't nail his dick to the wall, but he had a contractor's license and the gift of gab. Even in bad times, he could get jobs. He just couldn't do them without someone to tell him which end of the hammer to hold. So he relied on Harp and others who knew what they were doing.

But Broodson wouldn't see it that way. Harp knew exactly what he'd look like to his old guidance counselor: Trick's sidekick. A Class B wedgehead.

At six fifty—twenty minutes late—Trick's green van pulled up in front of the house. A ladder was roped sloppily to the top.

"Your chariot awaits," Trick said. His collie, Lass, rocketed around the back.

Of course, bring a dog along. Standard wedgehead procedure.

When Harp got in, the collie pushed its wet snout against his ear. He shoved it away. The van smelled of oil and gas from the chain saw.

"How much do we get up front?" Harp asked.

"We're making twelve hundred total," Trick said.

"How much up front?"

Trick rubbed his nose. "There's a little issue with that."

"It better be a very little issue. It better be at least as little as your dick. If that's possible."

They passed the schoolhouse-turned-junk store with its 10,000 hubcaps for sale. "He was gonna hire Peters," Trick said.

"So?"

"It's a three-day job. He'll pay us as soon as we're done."

"Of course he will. Jesus, Trick."

The dog farted. They followed Highway 626 halfway to Traverse City, passing Murdock's Biblical Garden. The garden was built on an old miniature-golf layout. Each small fairway had been remodeled and peopled with religious figurines. Noah's Ark was threatened by a windmill, its arms laden with storm clouds. The sign out front said *Admission One Dollar, U.S. Currency ONLY*. Most days, Bernie Murdock sat toadlike in front of the garden, scaring off visitors.

At Bass Lake, steam ghosts rose into mist. Trick sang as he drove. *Mrs. Brown, you've got a dog-faced daughter. Her eyes are blue and she's the wettest thing since water.*

Five minutes later they turned into a drive by a well-groomed lawn. Broodson was there waiting, gesturing them forward like he was guiding in a plane. By a pile of lumber, he gave the stop sign.

"Jesus," Harp said. "We'd never have made it without the hand signals."

Trick went up to the house to talk with Howdy while Harp sorted through a stack of lumber, pulling out warped pieces. A pole barn was simple work. They would square the corners, set the poles. After that, it practically built itself. He pictured studs, beams. Once you got past the bullshit, the raw work appealed.

After about fifteen minutes, Trick sauntered back with powdered sugar on his chin. He opened the back of the van and Lass shot across the lawn.

"Let's get something straight," Harp said. "If you want to front-end Broodson, fine, but not me."

Trick stood looking at him for a moment. Then he fished a five-dollar bill out of his shirt pocket. "This is all I've got. Here you be."

Harp took the bill from the idiot. At least he wasn't working for free. He started driving stakes, placing the corners. He had just snapped a chalk line when the first raindrop fell.

When Slater came downstairs the smell of glue hit him. Corrosive, like gasoline, but with the tiniest vein of seduction ribboned through it.

Lane was at the kitchen table. Her skin was flushed; in front of her was a model railroad car, still in the box.

"I buy the cheapest one I can get," she said, holding up a Soo Line boxcar. "You can't just go in and buy glue all the time, or they get suspicious. You gotta buy a model once in a while, too."

The crescent of blood in her eye, the mezzaluna, was bright.

"I thought you worked," Slater said.

She hooked a finger in her shirt top and sniffed herself. "It's Monday. I'll go in late."

There was water on the stove, still hot. Slater poured some in a cup and found the jar of instant coffee. When he sat across from her, he could feel the pull of her eyes.

"Besides," she said, "I don't like to drive when I'm like this."

"You mean when you're wrecked on airplane glue?"

The paper bag from the hobby shop was on the chair beside her. Instead of answering, she put her head over the bag and took a shallow breath.

Slater drank his coffee. Behind her, past the kitchen, was a screened-in porch. In the small backyard, an ax leaned against a chopping block. Near it was a bit of fencing around a tall water pipe. An outdoor shower.

"I wanted to get an airplane or a rocket," Lane said, "but they cost more. And I never put them together anyway."

A few months before the power-line accident, Slater had walked right in front of an agent's truck in the Winnipeg yard. Not paying attention. The agent was parked, reading the newspaper and was as surprised as hell to see Slater. He and Harp got thrown out of the yard as a result. They were driven to the edge of town, betrayal and stupidity oozing from Slater's pores. Watching Lane get high, he felt the same way.

"You moved the furniture," he said.

She wadded up the bag and put it in the trash. "So?"

"Where's Harp?"

"Working. He does that from time to time." She went to the sink and rinsed her face. Still dripping, she announced she was going to work.

"I'll drive you."

She made him some eggs first. Slater was used to making his own food, but he let her do it. Not since Selda had someone cooked for him. She put the plate in front of him, then went outside carrying a towel. A minute later, the shower came on. Slater sat with his back to the porch, listening to the water and picking shells out of his scrambled eggs.

County Road 629 cut S-curves up the bay. Lane let her head fall back against the seat. Her hair was still wet. Slater asked what kind of job she had.

"A job I don't like."

Out over the Lake, storm clouds were stacking up. Thick droplets plunked on the windshield, outmatching the Ranchero's wipers. Rounding a corner, they passed a rusted VW camper. Two yellow shapes passed a lit cigarette behind rain-smeared glass.

"Those guys were there when I left," Slater said. "They've been passing that joint since 1969."

When she laughed, it reminded him of Selda. "Screw going to work," Lane said. "I have a better idea. Let's watch the storm come in."

What the hell, he thought. Michael Slater at your service.

They took the road up to Cat Head Point, gaining ground as they drove north until they were a hundred feet above the Lake. At Peterson Park, Slater pulled into an empty picnic area. They had run ahead of the rain, but not by much.

"I'm getting out," Lane said.

"The storm's coming. You'll get soaked."

"Good." She headed to the railing at the edge of the park. Beyond it there was a patch of grass and a slick, rocky drop-off, pretty much straight down. She crawled under the rail and stood close to the edge. Slater hesitated, then ducked under the fence and followed her.

"Look," she said. "You can barely see the islands."

The sky was dark over the Lake. In the distance, the Manitou Islands were bleary smudges in the storm. The wind was picking up and the rain had started again.

Lane took Slater's hand and pulled him closer to the edge. "You know the story? That Sleeping Bear shit?"

"Everyone does. It's on all the postcards."

"You buy it?"

Slater couldn't remember if he bought it or not. He certainly had as a child.

Sleeping Bear was a Chippewa legend but it wasn't told by Chippewa anymore. It was mainly printed on place mats and anything tourists might buy. A Great Darkness came from the West, according to the story, destroying everything. To escape the darkness, a mother bear and her two cubs were forced into the water. They swam for days, crossing the Lake. When they were finally in sight of the shore, the young bears gave up and drowned. The mother reached land, looked back, and died of sorrow. To honor her, the Great Spirit Manitou transformed the cubs into islands. The mother became Sleeping Bear Dune. The postcard industry had named this story *The Legend of Sleeping Bear*. As tourist legends went, it was kind of a bummer.

The rain came harder. It made glittery streaks in the corners of Slater's vision. He wanted to go back to the Ford.

"The other night," he said. "When Harp came home."

"I heard the front door open and went across the hall." She gave a small laugh. "Thirty seconds to spare."

Lightning flashed over the Lake. The wind had grown fierce.

"You think he heard you?"

"I'm not as worried about Harp as you are." She started to turn to him, but as she did, her feet slipped out from under her. Slater caught her arm and she flipped over, grabbing at wet grass as her lower body slid over the edge. Slater dropped to the ground and got her other hand. He pulled up, but she slipped back a little. For a moment he couldn't tell which way they were going. During that instant, her eyes went through three layers of panic. He tightened his grip and pulled her to him, rising up on his knees. Finally they fell back onto flat ground.

She was missing a shoe and crying out in pain or shock. The next instant she was holding her middle and laughing, the toes of her right foot wiggling against the sky. Her shirt was streaked with blood. "Jesus, Mike. I scraped the fuck out of my stomach." She put her face in his, and her eyes were as open and raw as any he'd ever seen. He thought he'd seen naked things before, but never anything like that.

As lightning flashed, they crawled back to the railing.

"That glue is going to kill you," he told her. "It's going to turn you into a vegetable."

"Don't be an old lady," she said. "I slipped."

She wouldn't get up. He tried to pull her to her feet, but stopped when he saw a flickering image in the corner of his eye. A man stepping out from a tree. When Slater turned his head, the vision disappeared.

A minute later, as Slater was starting to shiver, she stood up and they went back to the Ford, out of the rain.

People who don't do glue don't understand, she told him. Outside your body, glue makes things stick together. But inside, it makes everything dissolve.

"And that's what you want?"

"Everything dissolves anyway," she said. "Sleeping Bear Dune isn't even there anymore. The wind's blown half of it away. It doesn't look anything like a bear. It looks more like a giant turd. But Sleeping Turd doesn't sound as good on the postcards."

The windshield fogged up, making the Ford smaller. "You sound like Harp," he said.

She told him about the River Above and the River Below then. How it all just flowed and you couldn't fight it. If she had gone over the cliff, it would just be because things happened and that was that.

That sounded like Harp, too, he thought.

The man behind the tree, the one who wasn't there, had been Dickinson. The Stetson gave it away.

In Iowa, someone had left a Praise Jesus brochure under the Ford's wipers. It had been on the floor ever since. Slater picked it up and used it to wipe the windshield. *Will You Be Ready?* it asked.

"Take me home," Lane said.

He put the Ford in gear and they headed back to Wolverine. Between wiper strokes, Michigan looked soft.

Hixton Party Store sold beer, packaged liquor, and chips. It had the wet air of a school gym. Slater bought a six-pack and drank one as they sat in the parking lot watching the rain. He offered Lane a beer, but she took the paper bag and emptied a tube of glue into it.

He didn't try to stop her. She put the bag between her knees and bent forward without speaking. When she came up, she held the bag out to him. The bottom held a gluey shine. Are you in or are you out? it asked him. It was a question he had heard before.

Selda had left him for a man they both called Thomas Promise. A Marxist from the food co-op. He talked about the dictatorship of the proletariat and felt her up. She encouraged it. She told Slater she was tired of living with someone who was always watching and holding back.

The glue smelled like the entrance to evil. Maybe it would be like the cliff, he thought. Maybe I could go in, put my arms around her, and pull her out.

The windows were fogged, the parking lot empty. Slater put his head down and inhaled. The burn surprised him. The second time down, the harshness was gone, and he was somewhere else. Like being inside a cavern, but with everything glowing and warm. How beautiful flesh would be, he thought, backlit by light like this.

After three hits, she took the bag from him.

A couple miles away, he discovered he was driving. Either he had kissed her recently or imagined kissing her. Either way, he could taste it. Cars honked and made sandpapery sounds. The road was a playful thing; the rain seemed to be a friend. In the side of his vision, Lane sniffed herself. Whatever she was smelling fired in his brain too. He told himself to remember to sniff her as soon as he had the chance.

She reached over and steadied the wheel as they skittered around the road. The crumpled bag on the floor was their first joint possession. Its jagged geometry next to her naked foot was the most beautiful thing he'd ever seen.

Everyone seemed to honk at him, and their horns were all different. Somehow, they made it back to the house. He left the Ford across the center of the drive and they tumbled out, teetering through the rain at an odd angle to the world. Lane had only one shoe; her shirt was streaked with blood from where she had scraped herself. She hopped along the drive, holding on to him. Halfway to the porch, they started laughing and she fell into him.

They had almost gotten things sorted out when Harp came around the side of the house, shirtless, wet, and holding the ax. He looked at their foolishness for a moment, then turned and walked back the way he'd come.

Slater put that in the category of not so good.

Holding each other, they made it up the steps. Slater discovered a chair that apparently had been there all along. He sat and pressed his thumbs into his eyes and everything disappeared. When he looked up, Lane was wiping rain from her face with her T-shirt, exposing her breasts. She looked completely asexual, like a person wiping rain off her face. He had never seen a body look so much like a body, so uncolored by desire.

"Epoxy Lady," he said.

He spent the afternoon on the porch. The lazy play-by-play of a Tigers game drifted over him, then Hendrix blasted out. Just as abruptly, the music went off. Staccato shouting followed. The word *fuckwads* went back and forth, but Slater was only partly listening. He was waiting for the glue to wear off, trying to let Time happen, but Time had taken the day off and stolen a car. Time had his arm draped around The Woman With One Eye; he was wearing her eye patch and laughing. The gleaming, potholed highway was actually a Möbius strip.

Eventually he noticed that the argument had stopped. He drank two more beers. For the hell of it, he raised his hands and snapped his fingers, trying to remember what was so good about that. Then he slept.

When he came to, Lane was in the chair beside him opening a carton of ice cream. She still wore her bloody shirt. "Hey, Harp," she yelled, though Harp was not there. "A rat in the house may eat the ice cream."

But the ice cream was too hard; the spoon bent. She threw it from the porch. It sparkled like a crazy metal butterfly before disappearing into the grass.

Inspired, Slater got the Blue Dart. He stood in the yard, twenty feet from the maple and threw. His head was polluted with glue and beer, but the knife hit the tree and stuck.

After his third throw, he caught sight of someone in the driveway: a roundish woman with dark hair. For an instant, he expected her to disappear, but she turned out to be real. He recognized her as Rose, the woman from the ferry.

"I see the circus has come to town," Rose said. She pulled the knife from the maple and gave it the evil eye. She looked at the initials on the handle and then up at Slater before handing it back. "Put this away," she said.

As she climbed the porch steps, she pointed at Lane's shirt. "You're bleeding," she said, "Let me see."

Lane tipped back in her chair and folded her arms. "It's nothing."

"Did Harp do that?"

"Of course not. I slipped."

Rose knelt down and delicately lifted Lane's shirt, keeping her back to Slater. "That hurt, I bet."

"I told you I'm okay."

Rose pulled the shirt down and turned to Slater as if he were an annoying bird who had just landed there. "Is Lane teaching you to be a gluehead? Or were you one already?"

"No," Slater said. "I'm just a guy who likes to help people."

Rose turned back to Lane. "It's Monday, babe. In case you forgot."

There was a moment of silence before Lane stood up. "Monday's Family Chicken Night at the 7 Spot," she said to Slater. "We go every week, Rose and me."

That made as much sense as anything else. Slater walked to the porch and sat while Lane went inside to change. When she came back she was wearing a light blue top with thin burgundy trim. She had washed her face; her eyes seemed clear. She glanced at Rose before turning to Slater. "Come with us if you want."

Slater shrugged. It had been a day for bad ideas—one more wouldn't hurt. But three steps from the porch, he felt his stomach rise. He knelt in the grass and vomited.

"This'll be fun," Rose said. "How about the drifter who calls himself your boyfriend? Is he coming too?"

"Harp's upstairs," Lane said. "Incommunicado."

Rose looked up at the window. "Good. Maybe he'll stay that way."

Their table at the 7 Spot was in the back by the juke-box. The smell of fried chicken hung in the air, bringing the edge of Slater's nausea back.

"Okay," Lane said to Rose. "So what's the story?"

Rose was a dispatcher in the sheriff's office. She knew the news of Wolverine. Often, she reported on the sexual and moral misdeeds of certain cops. And she kept a running list of wife beaters.

"Slow week," she said. "House fire out on Dupertail Road. You probably saw it on your way home."

The waitress, an older woman with deeply set wrinkles, greeted Rose and Lane by name and took their drink orders.

"I didn't go in today," Lane said. "We went up to Cat Head instead."

Rose sat with her hands clasped, the right holding the left. "Well, that's sweet." Her voice managed to be both kind and judgmental. "Skip work, do some huffing with the new guy, and head out on the road."

"It wasn't like that," Lane said. "We had fun."

"Come what may."

Lane played with her fork. "Rose knows how to live, and I don't."

"Not true. You know exactly how to live."

The waitress's name was Elsie. She brought white wine for Rose and bottles of Rolling Rock for Slater and Lane.

"To each his own," Slater said. He raised his beer.

"God," Rose said. "He sounds just like Frank."

Slater waited for her to explain, and then gave in. "Who's Frank?"

Rose moved her chair, inching closer to Lane. "Frank was the last guy I ever pretended to like. An impossible jerk. There was no limit to his needs, and they all ended the same. He'd do the dance of a thousand fuckups, and when I called him on it, he'd go, 'To each his own.'"

The Rolling Rock did not mix well with glue. "Excuse me," Slater said.

The floor of the 7 Spot men's room was hideous. The fact that he didn't care was even more fascinating. He spread his hands on the tiles, smelling the black grime that would never come clean. His second heave missed the bowl completely.

When he was done, he stood and looked in the mirror. He looked like hell. Where he had hoped to see confidence or strength, he saw a Rewire sprung to bits; disconnection everywhere. It was Rose showing up out of nowhere, he thought—undoing everything with Lane. The world letting him feel like he had something and then snatching it away. But he couldn't blame that on Rose. It was just the way of the world, the very fucked-up way.

He took another breath and tried to pull himself together. The night wasn't over yet. The most terrible sort of shit happened and you adjusted. What else could you do? He put his hands to his ears and snapped his fingers. He had to do it a while before it helped.

When he got back to the table. Lane and Rose were eating. Rose gave him the kind of look you'd save for a mangy dog.

"Frank had a line for everything," Rose told him. "First time he asks me out, he says, 'Let's go for a little stroll.' Like this is 1930 and we're in River City. So we *stroll* out to the lighthouse, and of course he kisses me, except he's not the least bit interested in the kiss. It isn't a kiss, it's an opening gambit. The next minute, he's got his hand under my blouse. And you know what he says?"

Slater looked from Rose to Lane and back. "Ooh la la?"

Rose leaned in to him. "'I'll just unhitch the team.' That's how this Romeo conceives of my breasts. As *horses*. He's got his strolls, he's got the phony kiss, he's got his little line of patter, and everything is take take take. And I'm supposed to be too dumb too notice."

The jukebox played Johnny Cash. "The Junkie and the Juicehead." Rose drank her wine. "And that's why men are scum."

Lane drank from Slater's Rolling Rock. "Did you let him unhitch you?"

"Neigh. I said, 'Neigh, Frankie.'"

The beer passed from Lane to Slater.

"Every man on the planet has the same script in his head." Rose turned to Lane, squeezing her hand. "Don't you get bored to tears? How do you stand it?"

The waitress came by and Rose ordered another Chardonnay.

"It's getting late," Lane said.

"Harp will still be there when you get back, sweetie. Who else is gonna buy his groceries?"

Slater straightened up, starting to feel angry. "If you hated this Frankie guy so much," he said, "why did you see him?"

She showed him her eyes until Johnny Cash ended and Alice Cooper began. Then she pursed her lips, making a decision. "I have to tell you this in all honesty and humility. I liked the fact that my mother liked him." She smiled very faintly. "I was a different person then. My name was Cheryl."

"Oh," Slater said.

Lane played with an empty beer bottle. "Go ahead. Tell him what happened."

"Really?" Her eyes sought Lane's. "Really, babe?"

"Sure. Long as we're not going home."

Elsie brought the wine and two more beers. Slater didn't remember ordering more, but he drank it anyway.

Rose raised her glass to Lane. "Here's the only thing you need to know about men, babe. If you don't sleep with them, they'll eventually slither away."

"But not Frank," Lane said.

"Not Frank. He didn't slither off. He shot me in the head."

Slater put his beer down.

With her right hand, Rose put her left hand on the table. She couldn't move it on its own. "Your eyes are like a rat's," she told him. "Did you know that?"

"Now we're going," Lane said.

But Rose made no move to leave. "I got sick of his bullshit, so I told Frank to stop calling me. Of course, then he has to call to ask me *why* he should stop calling. It's pathetic, when you think about it. I mean, here's a guy who has never learned to moderate his need. The need is all he knows. So one night he calls and he's been drinking. He's sorry about calling me, sorry about pressuring me for sex. He doesn't even want sex anymore, he just wants me to touch him. Touch him where, I ask." She ducked her head, smiling at Lane. "I know, babe—I shouldn't have done it."

"Duh."

"Anyway, he tells me where he needs to be touched. He doesn't really say it, you know, because honesty would be too much to ask, but he hints about his precious prong. I let that sit for a minute, and then I tell him I'd rather stick my hand in a meat grinder."

She laughed loud enough for a couple at the front to turn and look.

"Suddenly a hand job's not good enough for Frankie," Rose said. "No, sir. Now he wants to turn me around and give it to me where it hurts. I don't need that kind of filth, so I hang up on him."

"Don't mess with Rose," Lane said. "Wait—were you Rose or Cheryl then?"

Rose reached out, touching her shoulder. "Don't worry about it, sweetie."

The way she said it made Slater realize they were lovers. Past or current, he couldn't tell.

"To be honest," Rose said, "I felt kind of bad about the whole thing. Not about Frank's feelings. He only had one feeling, which was basically 'Gimme.' How can you hurt a feeling like that?" She took another sip of wine. The 7 Spot was nearly empty. "I felt bad because I once knew a girl who lost her hand in a meat grinder. Working in East Lansing. She reached in a little too far. There's no hand to put back after something like that. That's what bothered me—taking the worst day of her life and turning it into an insult. Especially for Frank. He didn't deserve special insults. A third-grade insult would have hurt him just as much."

"Really," Lane said. "Let's go home."

Rose ignored her. "The next day, I get to thinking about all the vile stuff he said. And it hits me—that was the only true passion I ever got from the guy. Everything else was straight out of *How To Pick Up Chicks*. But that night, when he went ballistic, we were actually communicating. Admittedly, at an exceedingly crude level. I mean, the violence didn't appeal to me because I'm not a masochist. Which is why I don't sleep with men. But getting real passion from a guy, even at that level—I felt it was an accomplishment."

Slater pushed his chair back and eyed the door.

"And the next day he shot me."

It should have killed her, she explained. A low-caliber shot, point-blank. By chance, it found a route that left her only mildly disabled.

Rose held her glass over the table and smiled at Lane. "So who wants to kiss the luckiest girl in the state?"

"I have to pee," Lane said, standing.

She left them to silence. Chairs were going up on tables. The sound of a night train came from outside. Slater closed his eyes and listened, the way he hadn't since before Detroit. There was a time when he had loved the sound of a train.

"Maybe you think you're some kind of hotshot with that knife of yours," Rose said. "But take my advice. The world doesn't need hotshots. And whatever else you do, don't mistake glue for love. Because real love has nothing to do with screwing while your head is filled with fumes." She held his gaze in a way that made it hard to look away.

"I wouldn't think a thing like that," he told her.

"You're a man. And men have scripts."

Lane came back to the table and stood, waiting for them to rise.

"And then there's Lane," Rose said. "She's a sexual dyslexic. First the fucking, then the flirting. But that's why we love her, right? She drinks straight from the blender."

"Is that good or bad?" Slater asked.

"Rose is always slamming me for doing glue," Lane said. "Which she's never tried."

"Believe me, babe, I don't need to." She put a twenty-dollar bill on the table. "That's what no one gets. I had the brainfuck and it was a rousing success. Shooting Cheryl was the best thing Frankie ever did. You think I'd go back? Not for anything."

"Where is he now?" Slater asked.

"In prison."

Lane led them to the door. "He's probably the one giving the hand jobs now."

"Damn straight," Rose said. "Pardon the language."

Slater looked at her. "Damn?"

"*Straight.*"

Outside, the night was clear and windless. Lane scanned down the tracks.

"You missed it, babe. It came while you were in the john." Rose put a hand on Slater's arm. "Lane wasn't home when the train went by. Harp will be pissed. Do we care? Not very much."

Lane got in the car without answering. Slater opened the door for Rose.

"Just remember," she told him. "If you can't hear the angels sing when you make love, you're not doing it right."

Screen five lagged behind the others. It showed Harp at a pool table. Chalking his cue, the slow sizing up, his encouragement when Slater missed. *Nice touch. Close. In the neighborhood.* Then calling his own shots: *Seven, here. Off the rail. Combination. Back here, Slate.* Harp would move his eyes away from the ball in motion even before it fell, the rumble of one ball under the table while another rolled on the felt. When he missed, he'd walk to the wall, one arm swinging wide, and stand in the same spot every time.

In postproduction, Slater watched Harp rack up a new game, in command of his world. That was the Harp he had fallen in love with. At certain points deep in the night, he didn't mind putting it that way. It was true.

In Slater's drawer, along with the Blue Dart and his stash of Smiling Os, was the book Charlie had given Harp. *The Price of Beaver.*

Despite the title, the book had nothing to do with pussy. Just the opposite—the short volume was a moralistic history. It traced every bit of Michigan perfidy, every miscarriage of justice to fluctuations in the price of beaver pelts. The betrayal of the Potawatomi and the Council of Three Fires. The destruction of pine forest. The extinction of the passenger pigeon. The Detroit Lions. It all went back to beavers and the greed that their pelts inspired.

Set against this treachery was the warrior Tecumseh, heroic but doomed. *The Price of Beaver* presented Tecumseh as a lost hope. His name meant Panther Streaking across the Sky. He spoke four Indian languages and English. His favorite book was *Hamlet*. He was educated in astronomy and predicted an eclipse—a day when night would fall at noon. When the eclipse occurred, Tecumseh's power grew.

Of course, in the real world, there was a fine line between noble warrior and crazed loner.

On screen five, Harp cut the three-ball to the end pocket and lined up his next shot. The monitor to the right showed him in a freight yard, standing by a Great Northern boxcar. Army jacket and pack. In quick, short strokes, he scratched his name on the boxcar with a stub of white chalk.

In pool and on the road, Harp said, the trick was to leave yourself in position for the next shot, or the next train. That meant paying attention, thinking ahead. Noticing whether the hoses were hooked, or if the road engines had moved, or how many pickups were parked by the crewhouse. Collecting clues like rust on the wheels or on the tracks, or a brakeman's mark—*L* for Lincoln, or Laramie. Sometimes the cars were stenciled to tell where they'd been or where they were headed—*When Empty Return to Ann Arbor R.R., Saline, Mich.* Most of the marks came from other riders: *Nomad, Spider Rider, Iron Legs Burk*, usually with a word or two like *Cold*, or *Going home*. Harp took it all in, tried to make it mean something. The only thing he didn't care about was the number on the side of the car. Those numbers were for people keeping track of money.

On screen six, Harp slipped the chalk into his army coat and moved on.

Harp hated Family Chicken Night. He lay on his mattress alone, waiting for Lane to come home. When the room grew dark, he turned his police flashlight on and off, making a circle of light on the ceiling. The circle pleased him. Its sharp edges suggested clarity. Clarity wasn't that hard once you got your mind right.

After watching the circle of light come and go a hundred times, he decided that Slater doing glue with Lane was not such a big problem after all. Slater could get tangled up in a T-shirt; it was just like him to step in whatever there was to step in. It didn't change anything. Mike wasn't strong, but he was stubborn, and that was almost as good. At least stubborn you could count on.

Unlike Trick. They'd just gotten started when the rain came. Harp wanted to keep setting the corners, but of course the sissy Trick said no. He called it off for the day. Instead of going home, Harp got a ride to Molly Hogan's, a bar outside Traverse. It was a wedgehead place, but Harp didn't go in. He waited until Trick drove off, then hunched his shoulders and walked through the rain to the chain-link gate of the Cherry City U-Store.

A bone-thin dude with a scraggly goatee stopped him at the entrance. Harp showed his driver's license, signed in, and wandered through the lot until he found the unit marked 26B. He'd been given the combination only once, but it was easy to remember. 13-7-13. A lucky number with an unlucky number on either side. He rolled the door open and stepped in out of the rain.

The shed was stacked with Stroh's cases. Harp opened the ones on top. Each held ten sticks of dynamite in wood shavings.

"Fucking Charlie," Harp said.

He'd need a truck, that was clear. If he was really going

to do it, he'd need Slater's help.

Sitting on one of the cases, he listened to the rain strike the tin roof. Blowing up the Whispering Sands was Charlie's craziness. He had no reason to involve himself. Charlie was counting on him, but the guy was a weasel and there was no crime in lying to weasels. Still, with the cases all around him, he could see how it might feel.

Everybody talked about the California gold rush. But the rush to cut down Michigan's pine trees had been just as fierce. An entire state, clear-cut. It was all laid out in *The Price of Beaver*.

The storm drummed down. Harp left the shed. No one but the goateed dude paid him any attention. Cars hissed by on the road to Wolverine.

Back at Molly Hogan's, he had a beer, then hitched a ride home with another rained-out crew. When he got back, the house was empty and his nerves were too hot to sit still. He paced in the backyard and smoked a joint, and when he could feel it in his chest, he picked up the ax and stood by the chopping block.

The rain had stopped. He took the tarp from the woodpile and got to work.

He liked to get stoned and chop wood. It was a comforting thing. True, there were moments of horrifying fright, particularly mid-stroke, when he forgot where he was and what he was doing, and then the blade came flying down in front of him, busting the log and scaring the cold-water shit out of him. But it was cleansing, a good, natural fear.

Mostly, it was escape. He'd spent hundreds of hours swinging the ax. It was all muscle memory, and it actually worked better when the mind went away. Like making love, when everything tunneled down, first to pussy, and then to something unnamable. Chopping, everything became grip. Set, swing, chop. If no one stopped him, there'd be half a cord of split beech on the ground before he looked up.

Eventually, his arms began to ache, and he followed the ache into his hands. From there, he worked until he was sweating and dizzy.

They didn't even have a woodstove. It was all for Rose. Every year, he cut and stacked enough to get her through the winter. It didn't matter that he didn't like her, or that she didn't like him. He did it because she couldn't, and she was Lane's friend.

When he was done, he took a long breath, smelling the wet soil, the forest. He stripped and stood under the outdoor shower.

The shower was a strange piece of work. A single pipe rising from a slab next to the back porch. It was enclosed on three sides by rotting, waist-high fencing.

The cold tap ran nearly to ice. An hour of splitting wood got him out of his body; the first shot of cold blasted him back. The secret to it was simple: Don't fight the cold, because fighting makes it sting. Welcome it. Make your appetite for cold bigger than the cold itself.

This time it didn't work. He stood under the rusted showerhead, shivering. The day had some strange hex on him. Maybe it was Trick and the smell of his damn dog.

He pulled his jeans on and was putting the ax away when he heard Lane and Slater in the front yard. Their laughter should have tipped him that something was off. Instead he'd wandered into the front yard unaware, still holding the stupid ax. If he hadn't been stoned and embarrassed, he would have asked them what the fuck they thought they were doing. But he kept it in, for a while at least.

All afternoon, he'd been wanting to talk to Slater about the dynamite. He ended up shouting at Lane instead, fighting about glue and pissing her off. Then they left without him. It was one more way the day had done him wrong.

In his bedroom, he turned the flashlight on and off. After what seemed like a long time, he heard the freight. A southbound, heading to Owosso and Durand and Ann Arbor.

It would be louder in Lane's room, so he went there and opened the window, hoping she'd come home while the train was still passing.

Sometimes he was scared when he was riding. Certain rare nights. When that happened, he did what he always did. He followed the rules. He counted the yard engines, stayed close to his ride, and said *yes sir* to the agents, especially the ones who let him stay, which was almost all of them. The train demanded strength, so that was what he gave it. A bulkhead flat gave no protection from things that could kill you, but there was no Howdy Broodson to make you feel small.

The southbound passed and Lane did not come home.

It's how it was in the world outside of freights, he told himself. You want a little comfort and there ain't shit to be had.

— 16 —

OUTSIDE THE SIXTEENTH floor at Spectrum was a small open-air landing where employees were allowed to smoke. A half wall, waist-high and two cinder blocks thick, lined the edge. Slater sat on the wall, dangling his legs out over the city. He often went there to relax.

Below him, cars and buses traveled through the night in streaks of red and white, lighting up the marvelous grid. Other men had lived there once, he told himself, when the night was darker. Now people were going all places at once, living in loops of happiness and pain, making wondrous connections and foul. Their individual designs were plain or fantastical or beautiful or crude, but from where he sat they all looked beautiful. The marvelous grid looked soft.

After a while, he decided to stand on the ledge, to remind himself how it felt.

His feet were bare. He liked to take his shoes off when he edited. His console had uncanny sucking power. It sucked up hours of his life in single gulps; it would consume him entirely if he let it. Whenever his body started to disappear, he'd curl his toes against the carpet's industrial weave and find himself again.

The ledge was cool under his feet. A light breeze pressed against him. Slater raised his hands to his ears and snapped.

It wasn't a daredevil thing. If he wanted a rush, he'd go back and watch the monitors. The screens were full of adrenaline. Lane undressing, the Northern Arrow exploding. Compared to that, the ledge was calming. Even when the night rippled and curled, he enjoyed it. Sometimes the Woman With One Eye floated over the city, trying to cast her impulsive spells. But she rarely bothered Slater anymore. It was hard to imagine her frightening anyone these days. There were so many more powerful spooks around.

For five minutes or more, he watched the lights below—the city as neon Etch-a-Sketch, himself as the eye in the sky. For some reason beyond his ken, he found himself listening to the voice of his driver's ed teacher—a bully of a man who was also the high school wrestling coach. *Life is what you make it*, the voice said. Slater burst into laughter at the folly of such a man.

It was true in a way, of course. But not in any way the high school wrestling coach could have meant. That was what made it so funny. It was gumball-machine wisdom, fortune-cookie stuff. A clear case of those who say don't know.

After a moment, a fresh wind blew up, carrying Slater's laughter away. He was about to get down from the ledge when the door opened behind him.

"Oh, no," Dimi Webster said. "Not again."

"Just charging my chakra."

"Would you please get down from there?"

"Why?" Slater kept his eyes on the lights. "You can see everything from here. You can see the accidents before they happen."

When she didn't answer, he turned and stepped down beside her.

Below, a car stopped in the middle of the intersection, backed up, and then turned left.

Some nights, when he had the headphones just right, he could hear Harp on one side, Lane on the other. The rumble of freights, the whisper of glue. Isacoustic. Two sounds of equal intensity. The fact that he had ended up in one world and not the other was pure luck. The careen of chance off sharp edges.

"Life is what you make it," he said. "My driver's ed teacher said that."

He looked to see if the idea amused her. For a moment, she looked like someone he was going to kiss. Instead, he looked at her until the moment passed.

"Let's go." She put a hand on his elbow, guiding him. Leading the barefoot man inside, like he was back on the ward.

She stopped in the break room for coffee and drank it in his edit suite. The tape on Slater's screens was titled "Your Vasectomy and You: What Every Man Should Know." He had spent the previous two hours timing the audio. The narrative stank of lawyers. Screens four and five showed a graphic labeled "The Male Reproductive Organ."

"Christ," Dimi said. "It's everywhere."

"Well, you've got your frenulum there. Then there's the coronal ridge. And of course the shaft."

"Stop. I've dealt with enough pricks tonight."

"Erickson?" Slater touched a key and made the penises disappear.

"He asks for your buttons," Dimi said. "That's how he starts."

Erickson had a reputation for sexual harassment. It had never been proven.

"You know that silver cup on his desk?" Dimi asked. "He tells you to put your buttons in it."

Before going out on the ledge, Slater had swallowed a Smiling O, and now an odd light was screaming across his screens. Harp in the freight yard on two. Lane on screen one, up to her knees in Lake Michigan.

"Why does he want buttons?"

"He doesn't. He wants control. How many times have you seen a naked woman, Mike? Counting pictures and fantasies?"

On screen one, Lane knelt, dipping her hair in the water. They went naked for days on the island. "Counting fantasies? A million."

"How many times have you seen a woman take a pair of scissors and cut the buttons off her clothes? On demand."

"Never." Sharp, skittery bugs were crawling up his legs. He reached down to brush them away, in case it wasn't the drug.

"That's the point," she said. "And he has to hear them ping into the cup. That's the big turn-on. Hearing the ping."

"Right." Slater ran his tongue around his mouth, feeling how his gums gripped his teeth. It was a good, tight, amphetamine feeling.

The pill turned everything herky-jerky, but Slater could suss out how it was. There was defenselessness everywhere. Everyone seemed to have some. It could feel good, defenselessness—it's why he stood on the ledge. And then people like Erickson came along and ruined it. Made you cut off your buttons.

Dimi put her coffee cup on the floor and pulled her legs up under her. She looked almost perfect there, like she belonged nowhere else. And yet every night she came and left, and he never found a way to sit beside her. Never even tried.

Rose was right, he thought. Men are scum.

AFTER FIVE DAYS in Michigan, Dickinson could feel things growing on his skin. The humidity was a nightmare.

The bars were even worse. Dickinson had never seen so many homos. Men were stronger in the desert, back in God's country. "Tell me, friend," he said to the clerk at the Holiday Inn Express. "Is there something about the humidity that makes everyone in this town queer?" He didn't wait around for an answer.

Cassie had said Michigan. *Where the fairies go*. Dickinson had decided to check it out. It wasn't much of a plan, but neither was waiting in the desert for Slater to return.

He started with the university towns. It was easy enough to pick up the rags that catered to perverts. In his hotel room, he made a list of gay bars and dug out a photo Slater had left behind. The punk and his spic girlfriend. Slater's face had the shit-eating grin of someone who got too lucky and knew it wouldn't last.

Dickinson hit Diablito first, then the Side Track. As a bar owner himself, he felt he was due a measure of respect.

It wasn't forthcoming; the bartenders he talked to were dismissive. 'You sure he's gay?' they asked. Dickinson hated the word *gay*. It was a homo word.

The 57 Club and the Equator were filth traps. The queers on barstools repulsed him. They laughed at his Stetson. But Dickinson's disgust for them was no match for his greed, and even that paled next to revenge. He'd scour a thousand scummy ratholes if that's what it took.

By the fifth night Dickinson had worked his way to Detroit. The bartender at the Admiral greeted him with a too-familiar smile. "Hello, Cowboy."

"You don't have a clue in the world what that word means."

He had figured out that queers did everything backward. If they thought you were a steaming pile of crap, they were extra friendly, and somehow everyone in the place was in on the joke.

Dickinson pulled out Slater's photo. "I'm looking for a guy."

"Aren't we all, Cowboy?"

"A hundred dollars if you help me find him."

The bartender inspected the snapshot and passed it down the bar. The customers made a show of holding the picture to the light.

"There's a happy haircut."

"In real life, does he have eyes, or just two black holes in his skull?"

The bartender gave the picture back. "I don't mean to be presumptuous. But why are you looking here?"

The knife wound in Dickinson's back itched, but he was not limber enough to reach it. "It's a free country," he said. "Thanks to people like me who fought to keep it that way. You know a better place to look?"

The bartender walked away, and one of the loud-mouths took over. "That depends. What's he into?"

Dickinson turned to the man, squared up his shoulders. "He's driving a Ford Ranchero."

The man shook his head like he was talking to a kid. "We need specifics. Is he a spanker or a spankee? Cut or uncut? Is he into twinks? Latex? We're not all carbon copies, you know."

"Have your fun," Dickinson said. "You walk into my place in Tucson and I guarantee you won't walk out."

"Stink or sniff? Cuddle or drool?"

The bartender came back and set a beer in front of Dickinson. "On the house."

"He said something about cherries," Dickinson said.

"That could be anyone."

Dickinson didn't touch the beer. He looked toward the door, then back at his tormentors. "Just tell me this. Where do fairies go in Michigan?"

The bartender blinked once. Twice. "To hell, I guess."

The next morning, Slater woke to the sound of running water and knew it would be her. He rose from Harp's mattress and stood by the window in his boxer shorts, watching Lane in the outdoor shower. From his high vantage point, the rotting fence hid nothing.

The angle foreshortened her. Slater could see the vertebrae of her spine and the curve of her ass in the sunlight. Desire grew and he did nothing to resist it.

She finished examining her foot and began washing herself—her legs, armpits, her neck, her small breasts, her flat stomach, her crotch, all without a hint of self-consciousness.

Her movements were so routine that Slater barely felt he was spying, though he was ready to jump back instantly.

When she was done, she crossed the yard to a ragged lawn chair and took a towel from its back. Leaves blocked his view; she moved and her nakedness was revealed in patches. She dried herself, put on a robe, and walked through sunlight to the house. Below, he heard the back door slam.

Slater leaned against the giant map and forced himself to breathe slowly, not wanting to make a sound. He stood that way for a while, waiting for his erection to be gone.

Afterward, he sat across from her at the kitchen table and pretended nothing had happened. He drank coffee and read the *Town Trumpet*. The police blotter reported the brief history of losers. Fuckups who fucked up. Car theft. Custodial kidnapping. Uttering and publishing. The perps were all males and all from small towns. Men who gave the whole world a royal fucking didn't get their names in the weekly paper; the *Trumpet* didn't play that song.

"Your problem," she told him, "is you've forgotten how to want things. That's what happens when you do what you're told. You lose your instincts. It fucks up your brain." She emptied a tube of epoxy into a bright yellow gift bag.

"And glue doesn't?"

She leaned over and inhaled. When she came up her skin was flushed and she kept her eyes on Slater. *This is my need*, they said, *I don't care if you see it.*

"I'm late for work," she told him.

She handed him the bag. Without really making a decision, he inhaled.

It turned out to be a mistake. Once she left, he was high and alone. He tried to take a shower, but the water was too cold. After a while he found himself upstairs, standing in her doorway. Staring at her bed, unwilling to cross the threshold. The world was full of places where he didn't belong.

Late in the afternoon, Trick and Harp pulled up as Slater was tossing the knife at the maple. They needed to make a supply run into Traverse. Harp convinced Slater to come along.

After the lumberyard, Trick dropped them off at Molly Hogan's. A beer and a burger. When it was dark, Harp took Slater across the street to the Cherry City U-Store. The gate was locked, so they went around back. Away from the streetlights, they hoisted themselves over the chain-link fence.

"Fort Knox," Slater said. He felt like they were back in a freight yard.

Harp opened up a unit and pulled the door down behind them. It was dark for an instant; then his flashlight went on. Slater looked over the stacked cases.

"It's not Stroh's," Harp said. "It's dynamite. Have a look."

Slater opened one case and then another. "Fuck," he said. "Let me out of here."

"It's not gonna blow. The fuses aren't wired." Harp took a joint from his pocket. As he lit up, he explained Charlie's plan.

"That's insane," Slater said. "You can't be serious."

"It's going to happen whether we get involved or not." He passed the joint.

"Are you out of your mind? We could go to jail just for standing here."

"No one's going to jail. The fix is in. It's all lined up and approved."

"Or else they're setting you up."

"Maybe I'm setting them up. Maybe that's a possibility too." He pointed at the joint. "Take a hit or pass it back."

The marijuana was very strong and Slater ended up coughing it out. "Jesus, Harp."

"I can't move this by myself," Harp said. "I'd need something like Trick's van. Or that thing you're driving."

Slater rolled up the door. "Let's get out of here."

"There's enough money for both of us."

"I don't even want to know."

The joint came back, glowing in the dark. This time Slater held it in deep.

They left the shed, scaled the fence once more, and started walking. For a while Slater wasn't sure where he was. The night air smelled damp. It went a million years back and was full of dead things and live things.

"You did glue with Lane," Harp said.

Christ, Slater thought.

"I know what she likes to do when she gets high."

The Woman With One Eye was floating in the darkness ahead of him. She was naked in bright, cartoon flesh tones, as if she were painted on the fuselage of a bomber, full of promiscuous desire. Slater tried to blink her away, but it didn't work. "Nothing's going on with Lane," he said. "We did some glue, is all."

"That's not nothing."

The ghost winked with her good eye. A pair of red panties hung from her left ankle.

"Look," Slater said. "You can't imagine what it's like for me. I see sparks every time I blink, okay? But I'm not sleeping with Lane, if that's what you think."

"I didn't say that," Harp said. "I just said you did glue with her."

To keep himself from snapping, Slater put his hand on the Blue Dart. His denial didn't seem completely like a lie.

Surely there was a difference between what had happened on impulse and what he would do in the future. The past was cluttered with all sorts of circumstance. Random crap and do-it-yourself lighting. All sorts of fuck-ups happened that way. It wasn't a true test.

"Where are we going?" Slater asked. "How are we getting home?"

Harp pointed into the darkness. "Freight yard. This way."

An hour after sunset, Rose arrived on the porch with a bottle of wine and let herself in. Lane was in the living room; a paper bag was on the coffee table. The TV was playing silently in the corner.

"So where are the two penises tonight?" Rose said.

"I wish you wouldn't call them that."

"I'm a real person, so I use the real words. I don't buy into the whole *cock* bulldoody. It's a penis. It's a little piece of the small intestine. It should be washed."

Lane took the bottle from her and went into the kitchen. "There are other things you can do with it."

"You. Not me." She sat on the couch, cradling her left arm. "You aren't doing epoxy tonight, babe. Or ever. Bring some glasses."

While Lane opened the wine, Rose turned the TV set off. "I'll bet they didn't even tell you where they were going, did they?"

"They went out."

Rose looked in the paper bag and took out the tube of glue. "This is one of the few things worse for you than Harp. I've told you what it does. People our age with liver damage.

People who shit and piss themselves because they're vegetables. Heart failure. Instant death."

"I'm giving it up," Lane said. She came and sat across from Rose, bare feet on the coffee table.

"Yes, you are." She took Lane's foot in her good hand and removed the silver toe ring, dropping it on the coffee table. "This is meant to attract men. I like you unaccessorized."

"There's nothing wrong with toe rings."

"Let's go upstairs," Rose said.

Lane looked toward the wall as if she could see through it. "The two penises could show up anytime."

Rose rose. "I hope they do come home. They'll see how obsolete they are. Come on."

Lane followed Rose up the stairs. She left her clothes on the floor of her room and lay on top of the sheet as if she were a subject, a specimen. A blue ceramic bowl was on the bedstand. Rose dumped Harp's keys out of it and filled the bowl with wine. She dipped the fingers of her right hand in it and traced from Lane's forehead to her lips, between her breasts and across her belly. Soon there was no boundary; it was all one thing—the sex, the kisses, the drinking of each other. Rose, with her one good arm, led them to a place they'd been before, and Lane did not retreat.

Afterward, when the night air began to feel cool, Rose put on a shirt and rested her head on Lane's hip.

"You should go," Lane told her.

"I should stay." She ran a finger down Lane's thigh. "Did you ever hear of Koro, babe? It's a mind disease. Men with Koro think their penis is disappearing. They think when it disappears completely, they'll die. Some of them do."

Lane held a pillow against her for warmth. "You're making that up."

"You've never heard of dying for what you believe in? Men do it all the time." She brushed her lips against Lane's skin. "I just wish I'd known about this when I was with Frank. I would have enjoyed torturing him. *It looks smaller today, honey. I'm getting worried.*"

She dipped her fingers in the wine, held them over Lane's mouth, and let a drop fall to her lips. Just as Lane closed her eyes, the phone began to ring.

"Don't answer," she said, but the receiver was already in Rose's hand.

The joint produced an overpowering, confused thirst in Slater. "I'm not riding a freight back," he said. "I don't do that anymore."

"It's the local," Harp said. "This isn't Detroit. It's safe as shit."

They were walking along the road in what Slater assumed was the direction of the freight yard. A sign in the distance advertised DANCERS.

"I don't care," he said. "I'm done with all that."

"If you don't want to ride freights," Harp said, "why'd you come back?"

The pot made it hard to explain. He couldn't ride freights anymore. It had to do with the stuff still trapped inside his head. Hopping a train would complete the circuit, fry every atom in his skull.

As they got close to the sign, he saw that it read "DANVERS." The sign marked a Chevrolet dealership, closed. There would be no water there, probably, and certainly no dancing girls.

"Did we lock the shed?" Harp asked.

"I don't know. I think you did."

They walked. Nothing mattered except his thirst. His throat was a dry riverbed, his brain a dying crop.

"So," Harp asked, "what's the deal with the dirk?"

"The what?"

"The knife. Where'd you learn to throw it like that?"

"Therapy," Slater said.

Past the dealership was a Pancake Shanty, still open. A large plastic boy with a spatula rotated by the door. "Wait," he said. "I'm going to get some water."

"Jesus, don't go in *there*."

An American flag waved outside. Land of the Brave. Home of the Sticky.

"I'll be right back," Slater said. "Wait for me."

The interior of the Pancake Shanty on grass was a nasty trip. Teen girls in brown uniforms buzzed around like bees. The clatter of plates, painfully loud, seemed to have no physical source, as if it were piped in off a soundtrack.

The girl behind the counter didn't do water. "May I tell you about our specials?" she asked. She had more teeth than seemed normal for one mouth. The marijuana was bending one world around the next.

Slater stood listening to the soundtrack before noticing that he had slipped into some kind of freeze-frame. Finally a boy with a red clip-on tie floated up. "What's the problem?" the boy asked. His teeth were not nearly as plentiful.

After further dickering, Slater paid for a soda and went outside. Harp was gone.

Abandoned, Slater thought. Alone in a plastic world. He checked the shrubs that lined the lot, just in case Harp was in their shadows. The shadows had never been so empty.

What's the deal with the dirk indeed, he said to himself. He had no idea where the freight yard was. He decided to call Lane for a ride.

Inside, he found the pay phone and dialed the house, knowing Harp would see it as another betrayal. The line rang four times and Rose answered.

"Who is this?" she asked.

"Good question," Slater said. "Let me talk to Lane."

"She's resting now. You can call her in the morning."

Slater was about to hang up when Lane came on.

"It's Mike," he told her. "We're at the Pancake Shanty and they put something in our syrup. We thought you could come and pick us up."

The *us* part was a lie. But the night was full of them.

It turned out there were three Pancake Shantys in Traverse City. Slater let the phone dangle and went to the counter to find out which one he was at. When he returned, one of the brown-uniformed waitresses was holding the phone. The back of her tan legs shone.

"Try washing him," the girl said into the mouthpiece. He decided she was not talking to Lane.

Outside under the neon, Slater threw a small salute to the rotating statue. "You are a child of the universe," he told it. "You have a right to flap jacks."

He waited a few minutes for Harp to step out of the darkness. When it didn't happen he started walking.

The road to Wolverine ran uphill and then down. At the top of the first hill was a large, old-fashioned farmhouse, the downstairs windows dimly lit from within. The sight made him feel more alone. A single light pole lit a tractor, a pickup, and a universe of bugs. The sheer bulk of the place suggested to Slater a life he would never know. Family dinners and a dog.

A couple miles farther on, he heard cherry cannons boom. He'd forgotten about the cannons. They were set up in the orchards during growing season. The noise was supposed to sound like rifle shot to scare deer, keep them from eating the cherries. It reminded Slater of Dickinson. He didn't like to think about that.

A few minutes later, the edge of the sky began to shimmer. A yellow-green light with the briefest flashes of pink. The aurora borealis. He hadn't seen it in years, and had never seen it so bright. He stopped, watching the sky. Soon a single car came over the rise. It slowed, made a U-turn, and pulled up beside him. Lane leaned over and opened the passenger door.

"Where's Harp?" she asked.

"I don't know. He got pissed and left."

"Why?"

Slater climbed in. "Because the world won't stop being the world."

The engine idled. She looked at him in the strange light and he kissed her. It surprised him to realize that he had decided to kiss her way back in the dynamite shed and he was just now catching up to himself. When the first kiss was over, he took a breath and reached for her again. He remembered how it felt, the first night he was back, on the couch and then upstairs, when there was no way to stop. Holding her in the Jeep, he closed his eyes and opened them, looking into hers. He saw no guilt or fear.

Driving home, they looked for Harp but the road was empty. Just before Wolverine, Lane slowed for a turn and one of the roadside shadows became a deer. For a strange moment, the deer looked at Slater full on, with a look that said we're broken and we go running through the night. Just as quickly, the angle shifted and the shadow changed and Slater wasn't sure he had seen a deer at all.

On screen six, the Northern Lights flickered green and yellow. Harp lay on top of a flatcar stacked with lumber, the two-by-sixes lashed together and marked *Northern Michigan Lumber*. Above, the sky opened and closed, a magic show.

The track he rode was strong, aged, worn, broken, sturdy, hard, and cold—one part of a larger track, a mainline that crossed the state like stitchery, cutting a scar across the land. On it, train cars mixed and turned, a shuffle of freight that was never at rest. And there was always a train on the way.

Slater didn't need the monitors to remember Lane. All he had to do was close his eyes and he was back inside the Jeep, holding her while the night sky flashed yellow, green, and pink.

You're looking for a safe place, she told him between kisses. But there isn't any. It's all a tightwire and you never get to come down. You just get used to it, she said. You just move from wire to wire to wire.

— 18 —

THE ONLY WAY to pay Lazenbeck and take care of The Stink, Charlie said, was to sell the house in Wolverine. Which meant Lane had to move back to Hidden Mist. And she'd have to *want* to move back, he told Tracy, or it would never work. We have to invent a problem and make Hidden Mist the answer.

"Or have her killed," Tracy said. She had the bong out again.

Charlie ignored her. He watched the smoke pass through the intestinal loops of the pipe, considering the angles. What sort of emptiness could he conjure that could only be filled by Hidden Mist?

The solution, when it came to him, was both pleasing and obvious. Money was his problem, so he'd make a solution out of the same material. He'd make Lane's job disappear. Stottle could be convinced to fire her. Charlie already had a plan to make her boyfriend vanish. With no money and no hard-on hanging around, Lane would be forced to come asking for shelter.

"One problem," Tracy said. "Stottle will want something in return."

"That's where you come in."

"Oh no," she said. "Not with that weasel."

"It's *quid pro quo*," Charlie said. "You're the *quo*."

Tracy stood up. "Fuck that, Charlie. What about Shannon? Isn't she living here for the express purpose of *quo*? Make her put out for a change."

"You know she won't," Charlie said. "Listen, I'll make it right for you. You'll get tons of free snort out of this deal."

"I already get free snort," Tracy said. "Just thinking about his tongue makes me sick."

That's your problem, babe, Charlie thought. He picked up the phone and dialed. "I'm sure you'll figure something out."

She glared at him while they waited to see if Stottle would answer. When he did, Charlie put on his dealer's voice. "Stottle, my man—got a question for you. You like what the astronauts drink? 'Cause I got some 'tang here you wouldn't believe." He winked at Tracy and mouthed the words *free snort* to her.

When he hung up, Tracy lit a Marlboro and took a deep drag. "Are you sure your guy is in? Your mad bomber guy? What if he gets cold feet and the condos don't go boom?"

"He'll do it. I fed him a sad story about sand dunes and cement. An epic battle between good and evil. Guys can't resist that."

She blew smoke toward the ceiling. "I want ten percent of whatever you get for the house."

"Five," Charlie said. "Believe me, this could work out beautifully."

"I'll tie him up." She gave a long, disgusted sigh. "At least that way I'll be in control."

"That's the spirit. Eat the rich."

Tracy raised her middle finger. "I've eaten the rich. They're too gamey."

The hayseeds in the Hell Café were arguing about show cows. Straight backs and perfect tails. Well-formed udders. Dickinson sat at the other end of the counter, making extra work for the waitress, who was bored, young, and pretty.

"You probably don't serve barbecue here," he told her. "Am I right?"

"If it's not on the menu," she said, "we don't serve it."

Her green eyes showed no expression and she spoke from far away. Body present, mind gone. The way he liked 'em. She reminded him of Cassie that way. Younger and prettier, but just as dumb. He ordered soup and watched her backside as she got it.

The gabby queer at the gay bar had said Michigan fairies go to hell. Probably, he meant the real place. But the road took Dickinson through the town of Hell, Michigan, so he had stopped to check it out.

The minute he parked the rental, he knew he was wasting his time. Hell was a one-stoplight town. Bar, gas pump, boarded-up hardware store, and the single, sorry café. The bar wasn't worth checking. No one under sixty would be inside. Except for the young thing serving coffee, the café was pointless too.

At the other end of the counter, the farmers continued their griping.

"You see that big ole ugly vein down her teat? No way was she a first place."

"They go by the face. And she walked good."

"The hell she did. She won 'cause she's Farley's. You or I show that cow and we'd get laughed at."

"Farley's Farley," the second man said. "Always has been."

The two old fools were about his age. Dickinson was afraid he and the men would seem like three of a kind to the waitress. That was why he had asked about barbecue. To show he was a different breed, despite how things might look. He reminded himself that he had killed a man and slept with his wife. Not many men could say that.

After a while, the girl came back and refilled his coffee. Most of it sloshed in the saucer. Service was not her passion. Dickinson drank it quickly and stood up to pay.

At the register was a rack of postcards reading "Greetings From Hell. Wish You Were Here."

Cutie-pie was not quick enough to avoid his fingers when she made change. He decided to ask her the question, just to have something to say.

"I don't suppose a sweet young thing like you would know anything about fairies and cherries?" he said.

Her green eyes didn't light. "You mean the car ferry? That's in Wolverine. I guess they have cherries up there too."

"Say again?"

"Wolverine," she said. "Where the car ferry docks."

Dickinson had been about to put his wallet away, but now he took out a twenty and put it on the counter. "That's for you, honey. For all your good service."

She picked it up quickly.

"You stuck with these bulldogs here?" he said. "'Cause you and I could go get frisky somewheres if you've got the time."

"No, thank you," she said. "And barf."

Dickinson leaned over the counter. "Next time you see me, you might be begging me to repeat that offer."

She turned to the two men at the back. "Dad," she said. "Little problem."

The hayseeds looked up. Dickinson gave her a wink and was out the door.

Slater reedited the vasectomy tape every night for a week. Higher-ups couldn't decide how much of the procedure to show. A note from the producer read, "We want to prep patients, not scare them to death."

He ended up trimming the cauterizing scene. When he was done, he added screams to the soundtrack just for kicks, but set the volume at zero. Silent screams. Always the best. He finally put it to bed and moved on to something even more horrifying—a sales piece glorifying the income-producing talents of two master salesmen from Korea, proponents of an eight-point plan.

Despite the topic, he liked the work. Most productions had to be a certain length. Exactly this or exactly that. He was constantly nibbling at the beginnings and ends of scenes. Shaving five frames here, seven there. With his nervous, rodentlike eyes. It was like whittling in a way.

The most amazing thing was to edit laughter. Ten frames of a laugh were the same as the gasp a man makes when a knife hits his chest.

After an hour of solid work, he stopped and checked the transitions. For a hack job, they were fine, better than the piece deserved. Reviewing the tape, it seemed to Slater that neither of the Korean salesmen had ever known hard work. As they described the rich rewards of their eight-point plan, he imagined their children as ne'er-do-wells, driving red cars into walls and requiring vasectomies.

When he was done, he took a Smiling O and washed it down with a Rolling Rock. The idea was for the beer to funnel through the amphetamine like a spout, and then to put his attention in the center of that spout. It was a one-point plan.

The Bowl of Hiss, he called it.

While he was waiting for the spout to form, the transient nature of his position hit him. He was sitting in front of a console. Someone had sat there before him, someone would after. Once, the room itself had been a place where birds flew and rain fell. Someday, certainly, it would be again. The vision was as quick as it was terrifying. That was the problem with emptying your mind.

Touching the keyboard, Slater tuned each screen to a precise shade of gray. He cupped his hands and closed his eyes. Put silence where silence should be.

At his pelvis he envisioned a ceramic bowl. He felt the beer and the buzz and let it funnel into the Bowl of Hiss.

When he opened his eyes, the screens were flickering. World War II. A milkman. A gray-haired woman bringing a pipe down on the head of an intruder.

Hey, Slater said. This is not my past. Whose freaking past is this?

Closing his eyes, he tried again. Just the wind blowing in some strange signals, he assured himself. No surprise if it includes some lives other than your own. Merely a reminder that we sit at the communal table. But if it's not too much trouble, he told the hiss, I'd prefer to relive my own past.

For the time being, it seemed to work. Screens flickered. Boxcars slammed. Purple haze.

—19—

THE MORNING BREAK was in progress when Lane arrived at work. Some Simple Simon had put up a sign in the vending area: *You never fail until you stop trying.* Simplistic, she thought, and untrue. It ought to say, *You never stop falling until you hit.* And you hit with the slopping pop of a bursting pumpkin, only louder.

At one of the tables, Stuffer Jude was holding forth on the origins of Stottle.

"He comes from a donut factory in Ohio," she told two other workers, hippie girls in braids and fringe. "He was raised by donut people. He was one of those pimply-faced kids who work in the windows mixing batter. That's what makes him so mean."

Lane made past it them without speaking to Jude. She had just done a bag and wanted to get to the darkroom before anyone could talk to her. The glue was messing her up more each time and it wasn't wearing off the way it used to.

Past the double-door light trap, the Silva hummed. In the darkness, the sound guided her. If a roller was set too

high, or if the fixer tank got low, the pitch changed. Different grades of paper—eight-inch, four-inch, twelve-inch—
vibrated differently. Once she tuned into the hum, she
could locate everything around her—the clock, the sink,
the splicing knife.

Without waiting for her eyes to adjust, Lane loaded the
first roll onto the feed spool and threaded it into the machine. When she went outside to check the drying drums,
the film ladies erupted into a flurry of clucks. She was on
the shit list more or less permanently now. Stottle licked his
lips more vigorously every time he saw her.

Feeling a trace of dizziness, she touched the drying drum
quickly to make sure it was hot. The scorching metal stung.

When she went back into the darkroom, she heard a
rasp and knew that the roll of photo paper had twisted;
there would be a kink down by the developing tank. Unless
she straightened it quickly, the paper would tear when it
hit the rollers. The machine would shut down and the film
ladies would have to reshoot the roll. The flapping of their
wings would draw Stottle for sure.

Working by feel, she ran her hands along the paper until she found where it was twisted. She attempted to flip it
straight, but the paper resisted. The only option was to cut
the twist out and splice the two ends back together while
the paper was still moving through the machine. A rolling
splice, it was called. It took perfect timing and dexterity.
Lane had done it many times and never missed

She took the splicing knife in her right hand, but as she
reached for the twist, the darkness shifted under her feet.
It pressed against her and became liquid. A wave, a lake
of darkness. Was she inside water or was the water inside
her? Still fouled with glue, she held the paper and applied

the knife, but the blade went too far and sliced into her palm. The pain surprised her and she fell against the wall. A shock rang through the water; red seeped into the black, a school of strange fish turned as one.

Bleeding, she found herself in daylight still holding the knife. Curiously, Stottle was there waiting for her. He held an envelope in his hand. Behind her, both doors of the light trap were standing open. "Goodness," one of the film ladies said.

Stottle's questions came on the upbeat and her answers on the downbeat. *What are you doing out here?* Can't bleed in there. *Why not?* It's full of sharks.

His white shirt had a glow to it, like an immense field of snow. She extended her hands. The splicing knife fell to the floor. She touched the cool white snow and felt a gentle thump. When she took her hand away, one side of his shirt was monogrammed in blood.

Stottle's heart, she thought. I've discovered Stottle's heart.

"You're fired," he said, licking his lips. "Leave before I call the police."

Harp balanced on the roof joists and cast his eyes on the work they had just finished. The angles weren't right. "We're out of square," he said. "I know we are."

Trick slid a two-by-six up to him. "If Howdy says we're square, we're square."

"If Howdy said a beehive was pussy, would you put your dick in it?"

Trick retracted his head, turtlelike. "That kind of talk is why you have trouble getting jobs."

From the half-finished roof, Harp could see the mess they had made of Broodson's pole barn. Miscut boards piled in a heap. An overturned can of nails, a hammer left in the dirt. Trick worked sloppy. His craftsmanship sucked, so he fell in love with the mess he made. Worse, he let Broodson make every decision. The old fart had actually picked up a hammer and moved one of Harp's markers when they were setting the corners. Now they were out of square.

"It's gonna leak," Harp said. "And I don't want to hear about it when it does."

The day was only half gone when Trick let a two-by-six slide off the roof onto the power line. It pulled away from the main house with a shower of sparks. Instantly, the compressor on Broodson's AC shut down. A minute later he was out on the porch, moaning, *Oh my lord,* and *What are you sons of bitches doing?* Trick stood and stared for a moment, a creature caught in his own chaos. Finally, he climbed down the ladder and said, "Don't worry, Howdy. We'll pay for the damage."

The billboard on the road to Hidden Mist said *In the Welfare State, Equal Rights Means the Right to Your Wallet.* Lane, in the passenger seat of the Ford, touched Slater's knee with the fingertips of her bandaged hand. "Turn here," she said.

Slater steered the Ford onto the two-track, bouncing in his seat. "Where are we going?"

"My brother's whorehouse."

In the forest, the air grew humid. The canopy threw constantly changing shadows over Lane's face. Eventually they came into a clearing and he could see the house.

"The hand of man," Lane said as they parked. "If you're a big enough asshole, you get a really big house. You won't take what Charlie offers you," she added. "Girls or drugs."

"Of course not."

She entered without knocking and led the way to the living room. Charlie was standing by the large stone fireplace, eating noodles from a carton and talking to the Spreadables. The three women, in shorts and bikini tops, sat as straight as soldiers on the couch. A pale, skinny man with the angular features of a falcon slouched beside them.

"I was all set," Charlie was telling them, "to put an ad on every stripper's butt in America. Red Man. Chewing tobacco. You've heard of it, right? Tattooed right there on the booty, so when the panties come off, there's your message. And you sell the stuff right in the clubs. Point-of-purchase dream. You know what stopped me?" He gestured with his chopsticks. "The surgeon general's warning. Where do you put it? The human butt wasn't made for fine print. Not the butts you get in strip clubs, anyway." He got a laugh from the Spreadables, and turned to face Lane. "What can I tell ya, sis," he said. "The cancer crowd stole my dream."

"Don't talk about your dreams, Charlie," Lane said. "Nobody wants to hear them."

Charlie turned back to his audience. "My sister, the girl with kaleidoscope thighs." He jerked a thumb toward Slater. "And you, you're Ed McMahon."

The falcon-faced man laughed.

"This is Michael," Lane said. She put a hand on his forearm. "He's Harp's friend. And mine."

"Like I said, he's Ed McMahon." Charlie walked toward Lane, but when he spoke it was to the helper on the couch.

"Hey, Leonard," he said. "Take the girls outside, will you?"

"They want to go in the boat."

"So take the boat. But make them wear life jackets."

One of the girls groaned. "They're so ugly."

"Uh-huh. So are insurance attorneys, and that's all I'll see when they drag you from the Lake. Put the jackets on."

The women followed Leonard out, complaining.

"Six tits, three pussies, one brain," Charlie said when they were gone.

"That's good for you, isn't it?" Lane said. "That's the way you like them."

Charlie bounced up and down on his toes. "You think *I'm* cynical? They'd rather risk their lives than screw up their tan lines."

"Whereas you don't mind if they drown, so long as you don't get sued."

"Touché." Charlie motioned them to the couch with his chopsticks, but Lane didn't move. "It's about your job, am I right? I don't think I can help. I heard you attacked Stottle with a knife."

Through the floor-to-ceiling window, Slater watched Leonard load the girls into the boat. None of them wore life jackets.

"I know it was you, Charlie," Lane said. "Stop jerking me around."

Before he could answer, a short blond woman came padding down the white spiral stairs. She wore a shirt that said *Slippery When Drunk*; her hair was matted on one side. She walked to the counter and turned the coffeemaker on.

"I'm not jerking anyone anywhere," Charlie said. "If you want answers, talk to Stottle."

"If you can stand the smell of him," the short woman said.

"Shut up, Tracy," Lane said. "No one asked you." She turned to her brother. "Why is she involved in this? What does she know about Stottle?"

Charlie stepped between them. "Nothing. Go back upstairs, Trace." To Lane, he said, "It's a small world. Stottle's a customer. Why do you think you got hired in the first place?"

"I suppose that's why he was always drooling on me."

"Hey, I'm not responsible for the man's lust. You know the old saying: 'A man, a plan, a vagina.' Isn't that right, pal?" He put a hand on Slater's shoulder. "What'd you say your name was again?"

"Michael Slater."

"Michael Slater, the Action Man. Welcome to our little club." He turned back to his sister. "Listen, I'll call the guy if you want. But I don't think you'll get your job back."

"I don't want the fucking job back. I want money."

"Oh, is that all? No problem. Just take mine. I'm joking, of course."

But Lane was already going up the spiral stairs.

"Hey," Tracy said. "Stop her."

"Let her go. I'll fix it later."

Tracy gave Charlie the finger. She held the pose until the coffee was ready, then went out on the balcony. Slater found himself stuck in the living room with Charlie.

"So what's your story, pal?" Charlie asked. "How do you figure in all this?"

"Just a friend."

"That so? A friend of Lane's is a friend of mine. Let me know if you need the slightest little thing." He winked. "The lady on the balcony there is the famous Vulva Voom. Ever hit the clubs downstate? Maybe you've seen her dance. And those chicks you saw earlier—very primo."

Slater shook his head. "If they're that primo, you should keep them for yourself."

Charlie raised his hands as if he were the victim of a holdup. "Not me, pal. I'm on the stimulation side. All itch and no scratch. All that BS about satisfied customers? Forget it. Once they're satisfied, they're not customers. Gratification is for losers."

He walked over to Slater as if to shake hands, but at the last instant put something into his shirt pocket. It was a joint. "Compliments of the house."

Lane came down the stairs in time to see the exchange. Charlie asked her how much she'd taken and she told him.

"It ain't right, sis. But I'm always glad to help."

"You're so full of crap."

"I make no bones about who I am."

"You make no bones, period," she said.

"Telling secrets, huh? And I thought you valued discretion." Charlie turned to Slater. "You met Lane's so-called friend, the famous Rose, yet? The Cunnilingus Queen of Wolverine? She's a lesbian *and* a cop."

"She's a dispatcher."

"For the cops."

"She's got her own life. She doesn't live the way you live, and you can't stand that."

Charlie's face lit with a deep viciousness. "I knew someone once who didn't live the way other people lived. She had a great voice, but you hardly ever heard it unless she was drunk."

Lane took Slater's elbow, pulling him away. "Shut up, Charlie."

"She had great spirit, this woman. But she made mistakes. And some glue-sniffing do-right never forgave her for it. That's what killed her."

"Fuck you," Lane said. "We're leaving."

Charlie faked a loud, dramatic sigh. "How come no one has spirit anymore?"

Slater took the winding two-track too fast, hitting bottom a half dozen times before coming to the main road. Lane's eyes were fixed straight ahead.

"Did you see his whores? Sitting there so straight?" Her face was scrunched up.

"I didn't notice."

"All his little hookers have to have great posture. He can't get it up, so he has to have girls who sit around like little erect cocks. And that greedy witch he works with."

"Vulva Voom," Slater said.

"She's worse than Charlie," she said.

When she turned to him, the red crescent moon in her eye was glowing and her cheeks were wet. "Just once I'd like to make him admit what's he done. I'd like to hear him say it."

"He's a jerk," Slater said. "Forget about him."

The geometry of Lane's hell was five-sided. Charlie, her mother, her father, herself. And the baby.

When they got back to Wolverine, Lane took Slater upstairs, pointed to the bed, and told him to sit. Before the baby was born, she said, her mother used to get drunk and sing. Three rum and cokes and the songs came out. Once the manic energy was spent, the days ended badly.

"When I was little, she used to put me to bed by singing," she said. "Later the shouting would wake me up."

When her dad went to prison, things changed. Something happened between Charlie and her mom. She pictured it starting in anger. "I can see her slapping him for about a hundred different reasons. Or Charlie slapping her. Because she was drunk or because she brought men home. Or just because he's Charlie."

She looked at her hand where she had cut it with the splicing knife. The crusted streak was long but not deep.

"At first, it's just fighting. You might not even notice it change. You might feel a hand pulling you down, and not be sure—is it still fighting or is it something else? And you might not know until after it swallowed you up. I can see it moving kind of slow and kind of fast. She was drunk and he was a reckless little shit. Maybe it was nobody's fault, the first time."

"How old was he?" Slater asked.

"Sixteen."

She got a tube of glue from the bedside table. "You're always watching me. I want to watch you this time. I want to see you get high before I decide anything."

She closed the bedroom door. A shirt, one of Harp's, hung on the back.

"But the second time had to be on purpose," she said. "She unzipped him, or he unzipped her, and they both knew what they were doing. That's the part that makes me scream."

She handed Slater a white paper bag and squeezed the glue into it. "Charlie would never talk about it. Every time I tried to ask, he'd put his hand up." She held up her wounded palm, as if halting traffic. "It took me years to realize he wasn't saying stop. He was saying five times. They only did it five times. As if that makes a shit's worth of difference."

She pushed Slater's head over the bag and waited for him to inhale. Then she made him undress. Pants first, shirt last. "I want to see this baby-making equipment. I want to see what's so special about it."

While Slater took off his jeans, Lane did the glue bag.

The baby was born five days before her father's parole, she said. Sometimes she could hear Charlie's words coming out of her mother's mouth. *Wouldn't she like to have a house they could stay in, a nicer house? Where she could make some friends? Wouldn't she like to see her dad and stop moving all the time? But they couldn't do that with this baby. This baby deserved to have a better life too.* She saw her mom's mouth move while Charlie opened the Pricebenders' bag. The words smelled like glue.

She put on Harp's shirt and got on top of him. When she bent over, bringing her breasts to his mouth, the unbuttoned shirt made a curtain around his head.

"Charlie's right," she told Slater. "I never forgave her."

Slater was listening for Trick's van. He asked if they were safe.

She found the scar at his hairline and touched it. "We're never safe." Her voice came from her belly, reaching him through some slow narcotic wave. He had no choice but to believe her.

It was more than skin on skin. The sex was like a promise, in the time before promises became lies. The first time they did it, she'd been glued and he'd been straight. Now they were inside the glue together. Inside a red-soaked room. She tapped a finger at the center of his forehead. The mezzaluna glowed.

When he closed his eyes, her Lane-ness vanished. Other women—Selda, Cassie, women he hadn't met yet—skipped in and out of her shape like flickering video. The radiologist in Detroit, an angel of a radiologist who had turned his head, adjusting the angle. Her hands were wonderfully warm.

He put his hands on Lane's hips as she came. When he opened his eyes, he was surprised to see he was still in her room. A bottle leaned against his armpit and beer had sloshed onto his chest.

Lane was crying and trying to talk between sobs. Her mother got drunk and hit a tree, she told him. That's how she died.

He held her while her breath went from ragged to soft. She finished crying and told him that she loved him. He felt sure it was true.

She told him she was dying, that she wanted to die.

No, he answered. Don't say that.

Bury me here, she said.

"Why the hell," Tracy asked, "did I sleep with some middle-aged moron just so your sister can waltz in here and take all the money she wants?"

Charlie rested his chin in his hand. She was sounding less like Tracy lately and more like Vulva Voom. "Because she's my sister."

"And I'm your partner."

God help me, Charlie thought.

"I don't know if you've forgotten," she said, "but we need cash or we'll be out of business, or dead. Or both."

"Look," Charlie said. "The money sis took won't last. I'll put the house up for sale. The jerk she lives with will try to save the day by doing a little job for me. Bang—he's dead, we're rich."

"I know the plan. I'm asking why we aren't sticking to it."

Charlie hunched up his shoulders. "If it was up to me, we'd blow up the Whispering Sands yesterday. Lazenbeck wants to wait. I don't make the rules here."

"And you don't do the heavy lifting, either."

"What? Stottle?"

"Who else? The fucker hurt me."

"Stottle likes the rough stuff? Little dickweed Stottle?"

Tracy lit a Marlboro. "Stottle wouldn't know rough stuff if it bit him on the ass. He thinks the missionary position is wild and crazy."

"Then how'd he hurt you?"

She took a slow drag. "He called me a name. He used a word I don't like."

"Well, that bastard." Charlie stuck out his jaw, surprised by her tenderness. *That's your problem, babe*, he thought.

That night, Harp paced the living room as cherry cannons boomed. Lane had moved the furniture again.

"Trick knocks out the power," he said. "Then offers to work the rest of the day for free. I don't know why I didn't kill him."

"If he's such an idiot," Lane said, "don't work with him." She held a glass of cherry wine, which Harp refused to drink. Slater sat on the couch, pretending to read the *Town Trumpet*.

"Next we're gonna hear that it leaks," Harp said. "First time it rains."

A muffled boom came from over the hills. Each time a cherry cannon fired, the insects went silent. It was like someone kept switching the night on and off.

"I can't take this much longer," Harp said.

"Maybe you should go find a boxcar to live in. Maybe then you wouldn't have to deal with the rest of us."

"Maybe I should quit my job and get high every day."

"I didn't quit. I got fired. Ask Mike."

Slater kept his eyes on the newspaper. He was remembering Kaytee, an amputee from the rehab ward in Tucson. Her right leg had been crushed by a soda machine that frat boys tipped over, trying to get a free drink; she happened to walk up at the wrong time. Despite her troubles, she was never bitter, and she did more good than the rehab staff. Everyone loved Kaytee. She lifted the spirits of Korean War cripples and shiny-chinned stroke victims. She made you feel special just by looking at you.

One day Kaytee was helping a navy vet with his catheter bag. The bag was full to goddamn hell, he shouted. Code fucking Blue. The vet's name was Durwood. Code Blue meant absolutely nothing. The orderly was nowhere around, so Kaytee pitched in. She had just gotten the bag off when Durwood jolted forward, knocking it from her hand. Urine washed the waxy floor and soaked Kaytee's only leg. She didn't recoil. She was bending forward, struggling to pick up the bag when Slater arrived. Her blouse was bunched up in front. Stopping to help, Slater leaned slightly to his left to get the best viewing angle down her shirt. Kaytee turned her special eyes on him as he did.

Shame wasn't the word for it. She was an angel. She had practically no tits. He could never forget the look she gave him, or how it made him feel. He had done other dishonorable things in his life, but for raw self-disgust, that was the bottom. Until today.

"You got fired because you show up wasted every day," Harp said.

The cherry cannon went off. Robert Mitchum was on the TV.

Of course, in rehab all kinds of crap was excused. You could take a man's interest in mammaries and translate it into recovery. Showing an interest in life again. Real progress. But this wasn't rehab anymore. The treachery of sleeping with Lane, and now his brutal, casual silence, denying to himself that it meant anything—it was beyond shameful. It was the worst thing his soul had coughed up yet.

"I had a boss who could barely keep his tongue off me," Lane said. "But I went there every day so we could pay the bills. While you were off riding freight."

"So it's my fault," Harp said.

Lane picked up the bottle of cherry wine. "Maybe it's Mike's fault."

On the black-and-white, a blonde in pearls slapped Robert Mitchum. Mitchum slapped her back. But there was something in his drink. Soon he was very sleepy.

"Say something, Mike," she said. "We're all waiting."

Slater folded the *Town Trumpet*. "I'm not the one who got fired. I didn't work on the pole barn. What do you want to me to say?"

Lane handed him the bottle. "How long since you had a really good roll in the hay?"

At the bottom of the *Town Trumpet* was a one-sentence filler under the headline "Touches Five Continents." "About five minutes ago," he said.

"Mikey has a rich fantasy life," Lane said.

"I hope they've got money in that fantasy world," Harp said.

The vast Atlantic Ocean touches the shores of five continents, the filler read. *Africa, Europe, South America, North America and Antarctica.*

"I got five hundred from Charlie."

"What did you have to do to get it?"

"Nothing."

The cherry cannon fired. Harp walked to the window. "God forbid anyone should want to sleep when the cherries are growing."

Lane looked at Slater and he held her gaze. *Who are you?* it asked.

Harp's face nearly touched the glass of the window. "There's too much rain. There's not enough rain. It's too cold; it's too hot. The wind split the cherries. You know what they moaned about last year? The weather was too good. The poor farmers had more cherries than they could sell. So they all lost money again."

The distant gun fired three times.

"The poor retired businessmen. They come up here to get back to the earth, and every way they turn, they lose. 'Course, that's how it's all set up. They have to lose money or they don't get the write-offs. That's what they're really growing. Not cherries." He turned to Lane. "That's write-off wine you're drinking."

"We know that," Lane said. "I know that."

"You should hear these guys wail, Mike. *Woe is me, woe is me*—and every year they plant more ground."

Lane moved next to Slater on the couch. She put her arm around his shoulders. "It's a sad, sad story that makes my baby want to cry," she said.

"So," Harp said. He turned from the window and faced them. "You've got five hundred dollars and I've got nothing plus half of whatever Broodson pays Trick and Mike's got a bottle of wine. Is that about the size of it?"

Lane met Harp's eyes. "That's exactly what the size of it is."

"Good," Harp said. "I'm taking my room back."

The black-and-white switched to Mitchum's point of view. Everything was spinning out of focus.

When Harp went upstairs, Slater went outside. He sat on the tailgate of the Ranchero and lit the joint Charlie had given him.

It would be so much easier, he thought, if Lane were someone like Selda. Someone who made a small place for him, and you could see the end in the beginning, so when the last day came, at least you had always known it was coming. But Lane had no small places—for him or anything. Her world had no rules, no walls you couldn't go past—they had burned down a long time ago, thanks to Charlie. Now she went where she wanted. If he wanted to go there with her, he couldn't be who he used to be.

He was holding the Blue Dart when she came out on the porch. He saw her in his side vision. She wore a lavender nightgown.

"It's all cardboard, you know," she said.

He threw the knife at the big maple. The blade stuck.

"Whatever story you're telling yourself in your head. It's just cardboard scenery. I've seen it from both sides. It isn't real." She leaned against the tailgate, her thin gown ghostly in the dim light.

"It felt real to me," Slater said.

"Is that why you're pretending it never happened?"

She took the joint and had a hit. Upstairs, the light went on in Harp's room. "I told you not to take anything from Charlie."

"I should leave," Slater said.

"Really? Where you gonna go? Someplace pretty?"

He threw the knife again. The blade hit very close to where it had hit before.

"Teach me how to do that."

"I wouldn't know how," Slater said. "It's just something that I do."

She raised the joint to her lips. "That's the part of you I like," she said. "The part that just does shit."

"Does he know you're out here?"

"Probably. Since I told him I was coming out."

"Did you tell him about us?"

"What should I tell him? That you're both sleeping with me? If you guys can't figure that out without my help, it's not my problem."

He threw the knife again, harder. Full turn with a good snap. As he retrieved it, he heard a distant rumble. In a minute it drowned out the cherry cannons.

He hadn't expected the train. He hadn't expected Lane to take off her nightgown.

"C'mon," Mike, she said. "Come over here. *Doncha ever feel like going insane?*"

She leaned back on the tailgate and he knelt in the gravel, burying his head in her as the train passed, every loud and soft car, train sounds muffled by her thighs, the clatter of the cars and the maple creaking and afterward he slumped on the ground by the Ranchero. *There*, he said. *There. There.* He thought about snapping his fingers, but he was too far gone.

Even after he turned out the light, Harp could see the railroad map. Spidery veins climbing north. The longest line extended all the way to Hudson Bay. The Northern Arrow. At sixty below, the rail shattered like glass. Bears stalked the line. An impossible train. And so the train he had to ride.

Most people were happy to point their lives down safer paths, he thought. They lined the path with condos and coffee shops and all the distracting crap they could buy. They paved the damn thing. But it was still a cow path, and leaving it was the last thing they had in mind.

Through the open window, he could hear the passing freight, every part of the sound. The rail near the house had a pattern: a piece of track that gave a little under the weight of the train, followed by a rail that didn't. The rough joint was a drumbeat played by each set of wheels. Other rails, farther off, played other beats, which Harp could hear under the first. And on top of it all, softer than everything but just as urgent, was Lane.

He had known they were headed for this moment from the day Slater arrived. He realized that now. The surprise was how far away he felt from the pain. That was a good thing. They were on the path that they were on, the three of them. Things happened the way they did, and that was all there was to it. No one could change it.

— 20 —

DIMI LAY ON the couch, eyes closed, as Slater worked the screens. She was wearing a Mets shirt with the number 14 on the sleeve and very small hoop earrings. The small diamond in her nose caught a faint ray and glowed like a pilot light. Like something with a current running.

Slater was shaving frames off a training film about workplace disruptions and had the sound off. The monitors had been jumpy all night. Screen three showed the flaking cabins of the Wolverine Tourist Court. The window of the main cabin was broken and the setting sun was fractured in its spires.

"There aren't any wolverines left in Michigan," Slater said. "They call it the Wolverine State, but the actual wolverines are gone."

"What about the cherry guns?" Dimi asked.

"Cherry cannons," Slater said. "What about them? They were loud. They kept us from sleeping."

Dimi laced her fingers over the stripe of flesh between her shirt and her khakis. "They sound fairylike. I see them spraying ripe red cherries through the night. Buckets of cherries."

"They aren't really cannons," Slater said. "Just some PVC pipe connected to a propane tank and a timer. But the deer get used to the noise. They eat the cherries anyway."

This, Slater thought, looking at screen three, is where the color goes bad. The effects get weird. The picture was etched full of angles, and the shadows were too dark.

"No cherries in the cherry capital?"

Screen three showed the peeling red door of the tourist cabin. A barrel-chested man in a bolo tie and a Stetson stood beside it. Slater tapped the keyboard.

"A lot of years the cherries come from out of state," he said. "Oregon and Washington. They ship 'em in for the Cherry Festival. The tourists never know the difference."

Always an angle, Slater thought. And never the angle you think.

"I like that," Dimi said. "Boxcars full of cherries. So Mike can have his pie."

The phone rang early the next morning. It was Trick Bradley, with news that the barn leaked. Broodson had declared that no money would be paid until it was fixed. Harp swore and put on his tool belt.

Trick pulled up twenty minutes later. They drove in silence to Howdy's, then wasted an hour rigging hoses. The plan was to wet down the roof in sections and watch where the water came in. But Broodson's two hoses fell short. Howdy borrowed one from a neighbor; when that wasn't enough, he pointed to a hose that lay coiled in weeds at the edge of his property. Harp recognized the plants as poison ivy.

"That hose leaks," Broodson said, "but I suppose you could tape it."

There's a lot of things we could do, Harp thought. With that hose and an old fart like you. Before Harp could stop him, Trick bent down and picked up the hose. "Okeydokey."

Broodson joined Trick in the poison ivy. Harp backed away. "I'll get the tape," he said.

He went to the van, but instead of getting tape he sat in the driver's seat and watched the two fools. Broodson got some tape of his own and the two of them wrapped the fouled hose.

The world had a hundred ways to mess you up, he thought. The poison ivy was just a sign.

It's not the train that kills you, he had told Melinda. It's the space between cars. The slack. The engineer could pull the slack out fast, like a whip going through the train, and if you weren't braced for it, the jolt could throw you right out of the car. That's the shit that kills you, he told her. His fingernails traced circles on her back. She made a sound in her throat to show she was listening.

After fifteen minutes, Trick raised a beckoning arm and Harp returned.

"What were you doing in there?" Trick asked. "Taking a nap?"

"Jacking off."

He picked up one of the clean hoses and dragged it toward the barn, letting Trick handle the taped hose. When Harp got up on the roof, Broodson fastened the whole arrangement to the spigot.

I should stay up here and never come down, Harp told himself. It was almost interesting, looking down on the two morons. Like owning an ant farm.

There was a holdup getting the water on. Finally, Broodson opened the line.

Harp felt the water shushing along, sending a stiffening twitch through the hose. He divided each slope into thirds and doused them methodically. Despite his mood, he liked being the roof man. It gave him control. It required discipline.

He soaked the roof for ten minutes with no word from below. Finally Trick came out and gave a thumbs-up.

"Found it," he said.

Harp climbed down and went into the barn. A portion of the gravel floor was wet. Drips ran from three different beams. "Where's it coming in?" Harp asked.

Trick looked up, swaying like he was trying to catch a bug in his mouth. "I had it a minute ago."

Harp wiped his forehead. Above Broodson's workbench was a shooting target—a paper bull's-eye with the profile of a black man. Thick lips and a bushy Afro. The target was labeled *Michigan Jigaboo*.

"That's the end," Harp said. "We're done here."

"That's just a joke, Harp," Trick said. "Don't let it get to you."

Harp looked up at the beams and the joists he had crafted. He was finished with it now.

"Don't tell me it's a joke," he told Trick. "I have X-ray vision. I can see through lies."

Early's Bakery and Bait Shop sat on the rough edge of Wolverine, across from an abandoned drive-in and the five rundown cabins of the Wolverine Tourist Court. Six or seven fisherman were at the counter when Slater walked in. He had spent the night in the flatbed of the Ford, curled in his sleeping bag. He woke when Harp come out, but didn't stir until Trick's van pulled away.

Not wanting to go in the house, he drove to Early's. The place sold donuts, coffee, and worms. Past the booths, behind a little barrier, was a rack of adult magazines. Early's was a crew-cut place. In the old days, Slater would have been suspected of being a hippie. But tough times had taken the fight out of Wolverine's fisherman. Slater bought an apple fritter without even a dirty look from behind the counter. He took it outside to eat with his coffee.

The morning held no more answers than the night. It still came down to go or stay. The question called for some kind of plan, of which he had none.

Next door, at Red's Auto Repair, a mechanic with waist-length hair was cursing a bone-white Mustang on the lift. "You scroungy dog," the man said. "I know what you're up to."

When Slater was done eating, he wandered over to the repair shop. The mechanic was wearing bib overalls and no shirt. Under the Mustang, he was going at one of the U-joints with a wrench.

"You Red?" Slater asked.

The mechanic answered without looking at him. "Red left. About eight years ago."

"Oh," Slater said. "Okay."

"If you find him, ask him if my ex-wife still snores. Bitch used to snore like a wounded rhino. Ask him how he stands it."

The man chose a new tool from the sea of mallets and screwdrivers spilling off his bench and pointed at the Mustang. "This one here don't snore at all, but she's just as bitchy."

"Anyway," Slater said, "I got that Ford over here. It's got a shimmy."

The mechanic walked from the bay and circled the Ford as if it might be a snake. After a moment, he said, "You want me to flash you?"

"Not really."

"Could be the universal." The mechanic crossed his arms. "Alignment. Toe-in. Could be a lot of things."

"I thought it might be the tires," Slater said.

"This here's your all-time drug car." He gave Slater the same suspicious gaze he'd given the Ford. "What are you gonna pay me with?"

"Cash."

That seemed to be the right answer. "Come back at noon. I'm gonna get this little momma purring. Then we'll put your rig on the rack and take a look at her unders. See what we see."

Slater sniffed to show that his interest was casual and told the man he'd be back.

"Name's Ron," the mechanic said, sticking out his hand. "Red's my brother. Was, anyway."

As Slater drove from the lot, his way was blocked by a delivery truck. He waited as the driver loaded supplies, then cut through the Tourist Court. Highway 22 led him to a forest of birch and a dirt road with no name. At the end of it was Good Harbor Beach. Unknown to the tourists.

A century earlier, Good Harbor had been a logging town. Nothing remained now except a line of wooden pilings going out into Lake Michigan. The parking area at the end of the dirt road held only four cars.

What he should do, Slater thought, was turn the Ranchero around and drive. Get to a truck stop three hundred miles away and then take a long look in the mirror.

Instead, he parked the Ranchero and got out.

Walking along the beach, he was forced to admit that his shame was a false front. A cover. The real feeling was fear. Not the cleansing kind, but the cancerous stuff. He was afraid of what would happen if he tried to be with Lane. And afraid of the emptiness if he didn't.

Past the spit of land called Good Harbor Point, the beachfront rolled into smaller dunes, making pockets for sunbathers. In one, a lone woman was watching the shoreline. Slater avoided eye contact but switched to his Man-With-Many-Friends walk. When he was past her, he settled back into Man-Alone.

That was the problem. There were all sorts of Slaters, none of them real.

Farther down still, the beach narrowed and the dunes rose into a single, formidable bluff. He decided to climb it.

It took fifteen minutes of sweating to get a third of the way up, but the wind coming off the water was intoxicating. He dug and clawed for another half hour, moving more slowly as he got closer to the top. At one point he came within three feet of a thick and very menacing-looking snake. He backed up and made a wide detour in the sand.

What had happened with Lane was more than sex, he was certain of that. The world spun chaos, but she inhabited warmth. She held a tarp in the shitstorm and made her own space. And he couldn't be with her, and he couldn't turn away. There was a term for that. It was called being royally fucked. Where every move you make is wrong.

At last, he made it to the top. Standing there, he stripped off his clothes and stood facing the Lake, letting the breeze dry his sweat, honestly naked.

Totally Nude. Live Boy on Dune.

He raised his hands and snapped his fingers by his ear. It was impossible not to think of her.

It was the first day of July. He'd stay until the Fourth. It was a plan, he thought.

When he returned to the parking area, the familiar wind was back, a nor'wester to raise the waves. It blew something green across the sand and gravel—a bill, Slater thought. He started to chase it, but a gust took it over a patch of poison ivy and into the woods. Gone.

The shimmy was as bad as ever on the drive back to town. A new crop of signs had sprung up beside the road. *Elect Lazenbeck*, said one. *Retain Hultch*, the others answered.

At Red's, the hoist was empty, but the mechanic was gone. Slater parked out front and looked around. Maybe, he thought, he could run the Ranchero up on the lift himself. It ought to be simple enough. He could at least take a look.

He was poking around in the bay when the mechanic came charging out of Early's.

"You son of a monkey," the mechanic screamed. "Get the hell away from my tools."

Slater raised his hands and backed out.

"If there's a single screwdriver missing," the man yelled, "I'll run an air hose up your butt."

Slater got in the Ford and started the engine. The world had gone crazy, he thought. He had only himself to blame.

The green indoor/outdoor carpet in Cabin 5 had a deep, ferocious stain covering half the floor. Like maybe a calf had been born in the place, Dickinson thought. He was carrying his shaving kit into the cramped, underlit bathroom when he heard a commotion outside. Pushing the brown curtains aside, he saw a hippie in bib overalls running toward the Ford Ranchero. In the next instant, he spotted Slater.

It took ten seconds to grab his bag. Inside was the Beretta. He ran shirtless to his rental car, a Chevy Nova, but when he pulled out, a white Cadillac Seville blocked his way. Four gray-haired tourists inside the Caddy were passing a map back and forth. Dickinson tried to get around on the right, but a group of fishermen was standing on the shoulder. The Ranchero went around a curve and was hidden by pine trees. Finally, Dickinson was able to pass, sending up a spray of gravel. But by the time he reached the stop sign at River Road, the Ford Ranchero was gone.

THE CONSOLE SHOWED fireworks, but the explosions wouldn't stay on the screens. The flares made Slater flinch. He worked the keyboard, but got no relief.

Late in the night, Matthews came up. He sank into the couch and pulled a pack of rolling papers from his pocket.

"You know, Mike," he said. "I think you got bigger problems than you admit."

Slater kept his eyes on the screens. "I don't see them as problems. I think of them as pharmaceutical challenges."

"Dimi been by tonight?"

"She was here. Then she left."

"So every night this sweet young thing comes up here to take your temperature," he said, "and you spend all your time staring at stuff that's not really there."

"That's what I get paid to do."

A minute passed. Matthews rolled his cigarette and put it back in his pocket. "You know, you were a clueless little pup when I first saw you on the highway. You with your little white thumb sticking out. I almost kept on driving, but something made me stop."

"Random chance," Slater said. "A fluke."

"Maybe. But at least you had some spirit then."

"I was running," Slater said. "That's all."

He had been leaving Michigan when Matthews picked him up. They ended up driving to New York together. Slater's only goal was to get away, but that wouldn't cut it in the Big Apple, Matthews said—the city required some kind of paycheck. During the twelve-hour drive, he talked Slater into applying at Spectrum, a dork-work job in the security office. But the company had just landed a cost-plus contract from the Department of Tourism, and the head of production scratched out *Office Assistant* and wrote *Video Editor* on his application for the sole purpose of inflating the budget. Slater caught on quick. He made some serviceable and completely obvious edits involving Lady Liberty and the Staten Island Ferry. Some groovy jump cuts. He'd seen lots of movies; it was hardly rocket science, at least not the way Spectrum did it. Standards were low. Some people found editing swill to be tedious and an outright mindfuck, but Slater turned out to be a natural. He excelled, in fact, when he was straight enough to work.

"You had some adventure left in you," Matthews said. "Unlike now."

Slater checked the screens. "I've lost all my mirth," he said.

"I know bullshit when I hear it," Matthews said. "You haven't lost anything. You've given it away, so you can sit here feeling sorry for yourself."

Screen one glittered with a bottle of cherry wine. The bottle was a vicious dud of a firecracker, waiting to take a finger from the first hand that touched it. Lane had bought it for the Fourth.

"I can change," Slater said. "Maybe I will."

Matthews gave him a look; he could make breathing seem like judgment. After another moment, he got up from the couch. His two big legs made Slater think of earth-moving equipment. Massive hydraulics and power. "Alright, friend. Don't say I didn't make the effort."

"Tomorrow," Slater said. "I'll get it together."

Matthews walked down the hall. When the elevator pinged, Slater turned back to the screen and watched himself reach for the wine.

Harp commandeered the couch, his feet on one armrest, his head on the other. He showed no sign of getting up.

"Today is not the Fourth of July," he said. "I checked. Today is Sunday, the third. Tomorrow is the fourth."

Lane stood by the door, a Mexican blanket draped over her arms.

The blanket thrilled and scared Slater. He imagined himself on it with Lane.

"Well, we could go to the beach tomorrow night," Lane said. "But the fireworks will be over and the beach will be empty."

"Fine with me. I don't like crowds."

The Fourth was being celebrated on the third. It was all money, Harp said. By Monday night, the actual fourth, the tourists would be gone. They'd be downstate unloading their cars, vacation over. Getting ready for their jobs on Tuesday morning.

"You can't just change the holiday," he said. "I suppose the Revolutionary War was fought on weekends so the soldiers wouldn't have to miss work. This is not about freedom. It's about selling hot dogs." He looked at Slater. "Don't go with her, Mike."

"I already said I would. I thought we were all going."

Harp was holding a baseball. Lying on his back, he tossed it straight up so it almost touched the ceiling. He did it twice more while they all waited. "The entire town should stay home. Show 'em they can't fuck with our holidays."

"As far as most people are concerned, they can fuck with our holidays all they want," Lane said.

Harp tossed the ball. Straight up, straight down. Outside, a woodpecker drilled for an evening meal in the fading light.

"I'm going to the beach," Lane said to Slater. "Are you coming?"

Slater picked up the bottle. "We'll let you know how it comes out."

"I've seen fireworks before, Mike. I know how it comes out."

Ed Dickinson pulled his Chevy to the side of the road and fished a heart-shaped pill from his shirt. Dextroamphetamine, five milligrams. Pinks, he called them. He split it in two and put half back in his pocket.

Chewing it got the drug into his blood too fast, made his hands jump. But he couldn't help chewing. The Beretta was in his coat pocket, but he didn't want to touch it yet.

He was parked in front of the barbershop on the only road to the beach. Anyone going to the fireworks would drive right past him.

The smart thing, he knew, would be to grab the Ford and forget about the kid. Then, when he was a few miles out of town, he could take the money and ditch the car. It would look like a joyride. What kind of cop would give a tapered turd about a thing like that? None.

The truth was, he respected most cops. The ones he'd met were good people. He was sorry, sometimes, to be on the other side of things. The hippie-shit and sleazeball side. The guys he had killed all fell into that category. The way he figured it, he had never killed a guy that a good cop wouldn't want dead.

After another ten minutes of waiting, he got out his handkerchief and dabbed the corner with water from the jug he carried. There was a thick black streak on the front of the glove box. Shoe polish from a passenger sitting cross-legged. The rental company hadn't bothered to clean it off. Dickinson reached over with his handkerchief and rubbed it carefully until it was gone.

Better, he said.

The problem was, he couldn't just take the money. The kid had to pay. The punk had to end up with one eye, three teeth, half a dick, and two broken legs, watching while Dickinson porked his spic girlfriend. She had to say, *Thank you, can I have some more?* And that was just Day One.

He waited a little longer, then took the rest of the dexy. It wasn't smart, but it was the only way he knew.

By 9 p.m., Charlie's silver BMW was parked at Pregnant Point, overlooking Wolverine, along with another dozen cars.

Charlie had the best spot. He'd paid one of his dopers half a gram to stand in it all afternoon. He wanted a good view of the action.

To pass the time, he leafed through a copy of the *Town Trumpet*. The police blotter was always good for a smile: the naïve hopes of amateur lawbreakers on display. They stole a car and drove to the mall. If something worked once, they did it again! It was kind of charming. And there was always a woman. If the paper were honest, every blurb would have been headlined, "Man Destroys Life for Pussy."

Twice, Charlie had fallen in the province of poontang. Once with his mother, of course. And then with Krystal.

They'd met in bankruptcy court, in his downstate days. She had four brothers, which meant she learned the predator/prey stuff early in life. The double-cross. The illusion of safety followed by the trapdoor. False mercy. It must have been like playing the piano, Charlie figured—start when you're young and it becomes second nature. As an adult, Krystal began to turn the tables, and she laced the games with sex. Suddenly, *she* was in charge of the trap, the exquisitely timed betrayal. A succession of jerk-offs thought they were sticking it to her big time. She rang them like bells. Like surrogate brothers.

But she and Charlie got on perfectly. They were equally dishonest, so it worked. Except, regrettably, in bed. She liked the rough stuff, ropes and such, and she was always dinging Charlie for not getting her there. Like he was supposed to know where *there* was.

In the other cars at Pregnant Point, young couples pursued their urgent business. Charlie got an envelope from the glove box and considered a little snort, but thought better of it.

He had gotten away from Krystal just in time, he

thought now. Your standard doof would have kept going till he ended up dead or in jail.

It was the same story everywhere you looked. First, the world-on-fire perfection of poking some dangerous chick. Then, the glorious fuckup of your choice, followed by orange overalls on a county work farm. Spending your day with a #2 Idiot Spoon suitable for ditch-digging and dreaming about the possibility of parole.

Not for me, Charlie thought. Not anymore. The only thing he did anymore was money. As a driving force in life, money beat sex hands down.

At ten minutes after nine, the passenger door of the BMW opened and Undersheriff Lazenbeck slipped inside.

"Damn it," Lazenbeck said. "You couldn't drive something a little less flashy?"

"You don't drive a beater and expect a girl to take her pants off," Charlie said. "I'm just trying to fit in."

"I didn't come here to talk sex."

"Imagine my relief." Charlie wiggled the envelope. "Mind if I do a little snort before we start?"

"Out of the question. I'm here on business."

"You don't get their pants off that way, either, boss. Besides, drugs *are* my business."

Lazenbeck open the passenger door and started to get out. Charlie put a hand on his arm.

"Okay. Don't get all twisty on me. Everything's set up. I've got witnesses lined up who will finger our guy."

"I can't use druggies. I need respectable people."

"In this town?"

"Don't start, Charlie."

"Okay," Charlie said. "I got this guy Stottle. He's a big shot out at Dexter."

"What'll he say?"

"Hard day at work. He stops at the Sawhorse to lift a few. Comes out, sees our boy Harp dragging a crate into the condo site."

"No," Lazenbeck said. "He sees the perp, *then* he goes to the Sawhorse. Otherwise, I've got a witness who's been drinking."

"He'll say whatever we tell him to say. He'll pick our boy Harp out of a lineup if you want."

"You said you've got witness*es*. Plural."

"I'm working on it," Charlie said.

Lazenbeck looked at Charlie as if he were an interesting bug. "Listen to me. Every day that goes by, I take more heat over that Sara Lee girl. I ask for your help and instead I get your silly smirk, which doesn't fool me one bit. Meanwhile her parents are all over my case. You want me to drop my drawers and show you the grill marks? I need a win here, understand? Whatever we do with the condos, it has to go off without a hitch. I need a perp and I need it ironclad. This guy of yours must have made a few enemies. Find someone who hates him."

Charlie took a straw from his coat pocket. He opened up the envelope and had himself a snort. He was done taking orders from cops.

"Well," he said, "there is someone who hates his guts. But it's a little bit sensitive. You might have to get personally involved."

"Not possible. The less I know, the better."

"Actually," Charlie said, "she works for you."

"Christ. You mean the lesbian? Rose? She hates everyone."

"Trust me. She hates Harp even more."

The undersheriff shook his head. "Rose is a goody-goody. She won't lie for us."

Charlie finished his snort and tucked the envelope away. "People do crazy things for love."

Lazenbeck closed his eyes and massaged his right temple. "Find someone else. Are we finished here?"

"The money," Charlie said. "I need to wave some more cash in front of our guy."

"Take it out of my monthly."

"No can do. I need the cash."

"So do I. Take it out of my monthly."

Over the Lake, the first of the fireworks went up. Charlie put his hands on the wheel. He flicked the wiper lever on and off.

"We should light the fuse on the condos," he said. "Soon. Now. It's dangerous to wait."

"We've already talked about this. You're wasting my time." Lazenbeck made a little show of checking his watch. "You aren't the only person on my list tonight. I have a rendezvous with your competitor Chance Ballinger tonight."

"Fuck Chance," Charlie said. "He's a schmoozer, not a dealer. He's not tough enough to last in this business."

"He's lasted long as you have. For booze and broads, he throws the best Fourth of July party in the county. And he's never late on his payments."

Charlie turned to Lazenbeck. The undersheriff wouldn't meet his eyes. "Payments won't be an issue after the condos. That's why we should do it now."

"The timing hasn't changed. We go when I say go."

A car rolled up to Pregnant Point and idled. Charlie watched it in the rearview. "The thing is, this isn't like a water faucet. I can't turn it on and off. Our guy's ready to go."

"We'll talk in a week," Lazenbeck said. "We'll make the final decision then."

"*Decision?* We made the decision! This thing's happening. You can't unring the bell. Not with something like this."

Before Lazenbeck could answer, the dash of the BMW lit up blue and red, and Charlie saw the patrol car in the rearview. At first he thought it was a bust. Some sort of vicious double-cross. But the cops were just hassling the make-out artists. They had a handheld spot and they were moving it from car to car.

"Jesus Christ," Charlie said. "Don't your guys have anything better to do?"

An amplified voice urged everyone to move along. The spotlight was coming their way.

"Put your arm on my shoulder!" Lazenbeck said. He leaned in toward Charlie. In the next instant, the undersheriff's face was nuzzled against Charlie's chest. There was a hideous smell of cologne.

"Christ," Charlie said. "Take it easy." Lazenbeck's bulk, so close, was repugnant.

"Break it up," the amplified voice said. "Zip-up time."

The instant the light went out, Lazenbeck straightened up. "Get away from me," he said. "And don't you ever laugh at me again."

"If you think I was laughing, boss, you really do need help."

The patrol car rolled away and Lazenbeck got out. "They'll be back. You better move along. Don't let anything happen till I say go."

Charlie started the engine, but left the car in park. He waited until the undersheriff was gone, killed the engine, and sat back to watch the show.

Slater drove River Road into town, headed for the beach. Lane, beside him, had the Mexican blanket on her lap. The cherry wine was on the seat between them.

"He's pissed," Slater said.

The night air carried the tang of skunk, somewhere not close by. To Slater, the smell seemed dark and full of life, though it was really a death smell.

Lane scooted closer, put a hand on his leg. "Harp sees shit in a lot of places where ordinary people are just trying to live their lives. But that's what we love about him."

"I know." It was something they had in common. The difficulty of Harp.

In town, traffic slowed to a crawl. Police and volunteers were waving people through the intersections, getting the line of cars down to the beach. Slater and Lane passed the barbershop, then veered off toward the abandoned Coast Guard station. That section of beach was farther away and more private. It was where the lovers would be. Teenagers, mostly. Watching the fireworks with their eyes closed, turning passion into time, unaware where that alchemy led. And not caring. Just living with their hands. The idea very much appealed to Slater.

The old CG station was a white, two-story building, now boarded up. A half dozen cars were parked there, and a group of teens milled by the steps, smoking cigarettes and passing bottles. Slater parked and led Lane away from the building, over a five-foot dune toward the Lake.

Lane took Slater's arm as they climbed the loose sand. "Save some of that for me," one of the kids yelled.

"Fun group," Slater said.

"That's what the British said about us."

On the downhill side of the dune, the street lamp lost its battle with the night. They crossed two more small mounds and found a gully where, half hidden, they could lean back and watch the sky. "Here?" Slater asked.

"Here is fine."

As Lane spread the blanket, Slater uncorked the wine. He walked toward the waves as he drank. A half moon, a mezzaluna, lit the skin of the Lake. The Lake at night always got to him. After dark it was a totally different creature. Reptilian. Of course, it didn't really change—the whole effect was done with light. That was what really stunned him.

Far out in the darkness were the minuscule lights of a freighter. The idea of men laboring on the ship—inhabiting the same night he inhabited, but in another, unreachable place—opened up a tunnel through which the future momentarily appeared to him. He saw where things led with Lane, and in the vision he saw loneliness. Maybe, he thought, loneliness was at the core of everything anyway.

It was nothing more than a flickering thought. A wave crashed and the future left.

Turning around, he saw the dark square of the Mexican blanket in the sand. A shadow in a shadow. He could see Lane's shirt, which was white, and the faint outline of her jeans. He wondered if she was truly waiting for *him*. Or just waiting for whatever happened next.

If loneliness *was* the core, he thought, there was no point in playing it safe. There was just time and opportunity. And a woman who, for whatever reason, had come with him to the beach.

As his eyes adjusted, he saw another lone figure like himself at the Lake's edge, about twenty yards off. The sight made Slater nervous. He crossed the beach and rejoined Lane as the first rocket burst, forming a red and silver star. She was on her back, looking up. If there was a path, he thought, a way to go, he had no idea where it was.

"How's the wine?" she asked.

"Brutal."

"Give me some."

He drank from the bottle, then bent, giving her the wine in a kiss. A flare lit her face. Behind him, he thought he heard a voice. *Get her ready.* The kids, he thought.

Her eyes, when they kissed, were more frightened than he expected; the crescent of blood jumped. She pulled him on top and wrapped a leg around him and it was crazy, but he didn't stop. If you want action, he found time in the havoc to think, this is how it goes.

Reaching for the wine as he pushed back against her, he saw the shadow, silhouetted, but closer now. The man was watching them.

"Christ," Slater said, "is that Harp?"

Lane sat up. "Hey," she called.

"Hey your fucking self."

Slater heard something he knew in the voice. He stood up and the man stepped forward and for an instant everything froze. Lake, silhouette, desire, guilt—all caught in a freeze-frame. And then the night exploded and the sky was filled with flames and the red-hot rebar of the Whispering Sands.

Everyone ran. A last volley of fireworks exploded as burning Visqueen fluttered to the beach. The young hoodlums from the Coast Guard station came tearing down the beach waving flashlights and beer bottles, shouting,

"Incoming!" and "The end is near!" Beach grass was ablaze on one of the smaller dunes.

Slater started toward the water, thinking Lane was beside him, but when he turned he saw the man had her by the wrist. She broke free just as of the one of the kids collided with Slater, knocking him to the sand.

When he got up, Lane was there and the man from the shadows was gone. A bullhorn was telling everyone to clear the beach. A second wave of people had already arrived; one of them grabbed the Mexican blanket and began using it on the grass fire.

"What happened?" Slater asked. "Who was that guy?"

"Some asshole. Let's get out of here."

They ran along the waterline, staying out with the crowd until they got to the Coast Guard station. The lot was deserted.

At the main road, they could see the Whispering Sands. Most of it had been blasted away. The rest was on fire. Seagulls, disturbed by the explosion, circled in the sky above it. Slater sat in the Ranchero, staring, until a horn sounded behind him.

"Christ," he said. "He did it."

Dickinson shouldered his way through the do-gooders who were slapping at the beach fire. He had dropped the gun during the blast. By the time he found it, Slater and the girl were gone. She wasn't the spic from the Addition. That had surprised him. But it didn't change his plan one bit.

The roads leaving town were clogged. To escape the traffic, Dickinson cut through a gas station and waited. Ten minutes later the Ranchero crawled by. He bullied his way in behind it, cutting off a young couple in a Dodge. When they honked at him, Dickinson put his arm out the window and raised a finger.

This is for you, Farmer Brown.

Traffic crept slowly. Tourists and kids on foot cut through the line of cars, stalling things further. But a few blocks ahead was the darkness of River Road. When they got there, he would force them off the road and bring out his Beretta.

Tapping his fingers on the wheel, he realized the little jerk hadn't found the money. If he had, he wouldn't still be driving the Ranchero. You poor ignorant sucker, he thought. You're gonna die for nothing. But you're still gonna die.

In front of him, men in overalls were running about, trying to turn a fire engine around. To clear a lane, a cop stepped suddenly in front of Dickinson and held up his hand. Dickinson hit the brakes at the last instant. The cop gave a shout and glared at him while the Ranchero went on. The fire truck reversed. Went forward. Reversed. The cop kept his hand up. The Ranchero disappeared.

— 22 —

CARL RUSSELL SLAMMED his gear bag into the locker at the Owosso station house. A thirty-year railroader, he knew the regs forwards and back, and he was royally pissed. Working the Fourth of July would have meant double-time. Working the day before got you diddley-squat, even though everyone was celebrating on the third.

Russell, an engineer, was called for the northbound. So he'd miss taking his grandkids to the Lansing Fairgrounds and for that sacrifice he would get nothing beyond his regular pay. His buddy Duhl would be at the fair, pounding down beers in the grandstand. Duhl would show up hungover on Monday, deadhead the slugtrain, and stuff his pockets with holiday pay. Good old Duhl.

"Something stinks here," Russell said, loud enough for the stationmaster to hear. But the stationmaster couldn't do anything. The regs were the regs.

On the call-board, Russell saw he'd been given a rookie brakeman, a kid by the name of Leo. He found him outside and they walked together to the engine.

"Hope you got your dancing shoes, Leo," Carl Russell said. "We'll be Ringing the Bell tonight."

Ringing the Bell was working twelve hours, which meant the railroad paid you double-time. Twenty-four hours pay for twelve hours work. Bring the train in at eleven hours and change, and you only had yourself to blame. Normally, the two-hundred-mile run to Wolverine would take eight hours.

"This is your lucky day," he told Leo. "If you want to make a living at this, you might as well learn young. It ain't about working the trains. It's all about working the regs."

They got in the engine, got the papers in order, and rolled out of Owosso under the green light. Ten miles north of town, Russell took the northbound onto a siding. "Blew an air hose," he told the young brakeman.

Leo, who wore a goatee and a Raiders jersey, cocked his head. "I didn't hear it." The brake hoses carried pressurized air the length of the train. When they blew, they burst like a rifle shot.

"You're about to." Russell winked at the kid. He backed the train up thirty feet, with a touch so gentle it felt like standing still. The slack between the cars compressed.

"Ready?" he asked. "Hang on." He slammed the throttle full forward and the train seemed to jump out of it skin. Leo was tossed backward. His head knocked against a metal divider; it shook the word *motherfucker!* from his mouth. The jolt kept going, passing from car to car down the length of train like a giant game of crack the whip. At the end, they heard a distant blast.

"Got one now," Russell said. He slouched back in his seat and put his feet up on the mudhop's chair while young Leo jumped out, new air hose in hand.

"Check 'em all," Russell called. When one broke, you were supposed to inspect the rest. Section 43, Rule 5.

The regs were the regs, and you could use them to run slow. There was a name for that too. It was called Fucking the Dog.

When they got back to the house, the Jeep was gone. Slater stood in the drive and looked at the spot where it was usually parked.

"Now it's gonna rain down shit," he said. "The police will be coming for him. Your brother set him up."

"Charlie? Why would he care about condos?"

"You should ask him that the next time you see him."

He put an arm around her, but she pulled away. "I need something first."

"Sure. Get trashed. That'll solve everything."

"You liked it before. Come upstairs with me."

"You're killing yourself, you know. You're gonna end up a pretty-looking cabbage."

"You coming or not?"

"In a minute," he said, not sure if he meant it. As she climbed the steps of the porch, he saw patches of sand on the seat of her jeans. It was a sight he thought he would remember.

Five minutes passed and he didn't go in. If I go upstairs now, he thought, there's no way back.

Upstairs, the lights went out. The porch light beside him drew moths by the dozens. The boldest of them flew directly into the bulb and died. Their burnt wings made a random arc on the porch floor.

It took him a while to figure out how he felt, and when it came to him, he was surprised. He felt left out. Harp had screwed up mammothly. Without him.

The realization called for a beer. He got one from the fridge, returned to the porch, and drank it slowly. He was ready for a second when headlights came down River Road. Harp turned into the drive, parked the Jeep, and got out. He was holding a bottle of Vernor's by the neck.

"Where's Lane?" he asked Slater.

"Upstairs."

"Why aren't you with her?"

"I don't know."

"You see the blast?"

"We saw it. We're scared shitless now."

"No reason to be."

Harp took an empty Stroh's case from the Jeep and carried it around back to the burn barrel. He lit it and they watched the flames crack.

"Charlie will turn on you," Slater said. "You know that, don't you?"

"I've got nothing to do with Charlie," he said. "Anyway, I'm leaving in the morning." He poked a stick in the fire. "You should come with me."

The flames lit up little pieces of the Stroh's case and turned them to ash, yet the light promised a kind of hopefulness. He had no reason to say yes or no to Harp. Offers came and went; usually he did what was easiest, or whatever scared him least. He could let Harp go and stay with Lane. But without Harp, it wouldn't work. They needed him as an obstacle. In the heat of the burn barrel, he was certain of that.

"Sure," he said. "I'll go."

In town, a volunteer fireman dragged a hose toward the condos. His muddy boot stepped on the iron weathercock, blown to the ground by the blast. Elsewhere, trains started and stopped. Purple-eyed moths burnt themselves and fell to the porch floor. Undersheriff Lazenbeck, satisfied and spent, slept beside a young prostitute at Chance Ballinger's Fourth of July bash, his beeper flashing in a pile of clothes. In Cabin 5 of the Wolverine Tourist Court, Ed Dickinson knelt on his bed and masturbated. The big maple creaked. The cherry cannon fired. Harp and Slater packed. And Howdy Broodson's pole barn blew to fucking smithereens.

$-$ 23 $-$

AT 6 A.M., Ed Dickinson took half a dexy and drove down River Road, pausing to check out every garage and every carport, looking for the Ford. This would be the last day, he thought—the last day he'd have to spend in Michigan and the punk's last day anywhere. He pictured loverboy in the woods, buried up to his shoulders. A talking pumpkin. Drop a couple dexies in the piehole, get him amped up, then duct-tape the mouth. Watch the eyes go wild. The punk's girlfriend could be involved; she could put on a show. With Dickinson's help, Miss Skinny would make noises no man has ever heard. After that, nightfall. Leave him to the bugs and beasts. Coyotes. You shake 'em off, they come back harder. Claws going for the soft parts. Pretty soon, your face ain't a face. It's food.

Surprised by his anger, Dickinson leaned forward and checked his eyes in the rearview. The pupils were small and mean. Screw it, he thought. The fucker left me for dead. He gets what he deserves.

Lane spent the night in her clothes. In the morning, she took off her jeans and sat cross-legged on her bed in panties and a sweatshirt. Her head ached from the night's dreams, which had been poisonous. When the phone rang, she was not surprised. It was Rose.

"You have to get out of there, sweetie," Rose said. "They're coming. You have to come over to my place right now."

"Who?" Lane asked. "Who's coming?"

"Lazenbeck and some others. They're on their way. If you're with Harp, you'll be an accessory. You'll go to jail."

Lane looked out the window. The road in front of the house was empty. "I didn't do anything."

"They don't care. Don't even get dressed. Just go out the back door and walk over to my house. Go through the woods."

Lane picked up her jeans but didn't put them on. She heard voices in Harp's room and went in. Harp was closing up his backpack. Slater had the knife strapped on his belt. Both of them stopped what they were doing and looked at her legs.

"If they ask," Harp said, "say we left yesterday."

Her troubled sleep seemed to have left some spell on her, and for once she could see them for what they were. They were boys. She tried to remember which one she loved, but nothing came.

"Rose said the police are coming," she said. "What the fuck?"

"Put your pants on," Harp said. "We need you to drive us."

Lane pulled on her jeans but couldn't find her shoes. She went out the front door barefoot, walking gingerly on the gravel, grabbing onto Slater's arm to keep from falling. They loaded into the Ranchero, Slater in the middle, and she drove them down River Road, toward the rail crossing. Harp had taken a cantaloupe from the kitchen and rolled it in his hands.

"Maybe we should go back," Slater said.

Lane kept driving. None of it made sense, but she wasn't sure it mattered. Rose had told her to run. She was doing the opposite. Sometimes that worked.

Harp pointed to a turnout by a historical marker; she jerked the wheel and pulled in, nearly hitting it. The tracks were nearby.

"Okay," he said.

"Okay what?" Lane asked. "What am I supposed to do?"

"Go home." Harp said. He took his pack from the flatbed and disappeared into the bushes.

Slater sat there, like he was waiting for something else to happen. He reached for her hand, but she took it away.

"I'll take care of your car," she said. "Don't worry about that."

North of Cadillac, Carl Russell got lucky. A journal box on a Rock Island flatcar started to smoke. The box was supposed to lubricate the axle; smoke meant it was out of oil. The kid Leo was sent out into the predawn light with an oilcan. By the time he got back, Russell was asleep. He sat up when the door clanged shut and pointed to the clipboard on its hook. "Log it down. Number, milepost, and time."

The kid filled out the form and Russell checked it over. "The number one thing to know about fucking the dog," he said, "is there ain't no shame in it. It's like jacking off. Everybody does it. But you sure as shit don't want to get caught."

Leo shook his head. "My jack-off days are over."

"That so? My condolences."

"Oh yeah? For what?"

He gave the kid a slow once-over. "For being dumber than I thought."

Thompsonville was the last stop before Wolverine. The plywood mill there normally had a cut of three cars to pick up. This time, the siding was empty.

"Damn it to hell." Russell got on the radio, hoping they might have to wait for the cars. But the mill had cut back to a single shift. There was nothing to pick up.

"That's it then," the kid said. "We're screwed."

Russell displayed a mouth of fine, yellow teeth. "Never doubt me, kid."

Harp led the way through milkweed and brush as a light drizzle fell. He stopped at the tracks. The rails were scabbed with rust; weathered ties lay at off angles. One-a-day rails.

"We can grab the westbound here," Harp said. "They'll load us straight onto the ferry."

"*Here?* There's nothing here."

Harp shifted the cantaloupe from hand to hand. The signal tower was dark. But he had the feeling he thought of as Go Dive Four.

In high school, he had played defensive end on the football team. One season only. He hated the position and spent most of the time on the bench. At a meaningless point in a meaningless game, the coach put him in. He crouched at the line of scrimmage, ready, and saw the play unfold before anyone touched the ball. Halfback through the number four hole. Go Dive Four. When the play came, it came in slow motion. Harp was in the backfield before the halfback could blink. Somehow, Harp had slipped ahead in time, just enough to feel things before they happened. It never happened again on the football field, but sometimes he felt it on the tracks. It was a current he locked onto. Train coming. No sound, no light, no plume of smoke, but he could feel it. Go Dive Four.

The crazy thing was, the guy had scored. The halfback was an Ojibwa named Jay Jay on the Traverse City team. He gave Harp the badfoot, slipped the tackle, and ran twenty yards for a TD. The coach sat Harp back down. But he never forgot the look in Jay Jay's eyes when Harp surprised him in the backfield. An animal look. Desperation and cunning.

"This used to run three times a day," Harp said. "In a year or two it won't be here at all. And for what? Some trucker's exhaust. It's always, rip 'em up. You never hear anyone say, fix 'em up."

"Maybe I shouldn't have come," Slater said. "I didn't think about riding freights."

"We'll be fine," Harp said. "As long as we stay on the tracks, we're invisible. No one will see us."

"That's not what I'm saying," Slater said.

"If you're worried about the condos, forget it. I didn't blow up the Whispering Sands."

"Well, somebody did. We saw it. Did you take Charlie's money?"

"Some of it. A little."

"Christ, Harp."

"I have an alibi. I was blowing up a pole barn at the time."

"Don't tell me," Slater said. "Don't say another word."

"Screw it. I don't care what anyone thinks. I'm right where I'm supposed to be."

The silver tank car, leaking propane, was waiting to explode on Slater's screens. A diamond-shaped sign warned of danger: *Easily ignited. Do not breathe vapors. Keep upwind of fumes or flames. If exposed to fire, tank car may rupture and rocket.*

Slater hit EJECT, but nothing happened. "There used to be a disease called Railway Brain," he told Dimi. "It was an occupational hazard for conductors. Back in the 1800s. The tracks bounced your brain around in your skull and messed you up."

Dimi stood behind him and massaged his shoulders. "There's a million ways to feel bad," she said. "Especially if you spend your time looking for them."

"It was in all the medical books. Frightening dreams. Loss of appetite. Hallucinations. Melancholia. And heaviness of loin and limb."

She gave his shoulders a squeeze. "Loin and limb," she said. "I'll keep an eye out for that."

Slater was about to suggest leaving when the signal light turned green. The westbound, like Harp had said. As the train approached, they hid under a small trestle that crossed the Betsy River. The ties were close enough that Slater could reach up and touch them. Fat drops of creosote-stained water fell down on them.

The train was louder than anything Slater had ever heard. With a scream, the engine exploded overhead, sucking up the air and blocking the sky. Slater yelled but his voice was swept away. He looked up at the underside of boxcars as Harp put a hand on his shoulder and mouthed something.

After the engine passed, they scrambled up the bank. Harp pointed at a St. Louis & Missouri boxcar with open doors. He gave the cantaloupe to Slater and ran beside the car. He swung his pack in and made the jump. Once he was in, he crouched in the doorway with his hands out, motioning for the melon.

Slater shook his head. He jogged beside the train, letting it pick up speed until it was past the point where Harp could have made the jump. At the last instant, he broke into a run.

With his right hand, he touched the side of the car. In his left he held the cantaloupe. He grabbed the door frame and slowed his pace for an instant, letting the train jerk his arm forward. Then he pulled back hard, slingshotting his legs up and ahead of his body. His right foot got in the box, and he hung there for an instant, feet in, butt and torso hanging out. Twisting, he rolled into the car. A top-speed jump with backpack and melon.

Harp shouted something. It sounded like "freak."

Slater set his pack next to Harp's. Hemlock and white pine ran by the door. I don't belong here, he thought. I'm a goddamn fool.

Almost immediately, the train clanked hard. The jolt jerked Slater forward, nearly off his feet. The train was slowing, getting ready to stop.

"What the hell?" Harp moved to the front of the car and pounded on the wall. "Roll!" he said. "Goddamnit."

The police, Slater thought. They've found us. He felt the rush of fear that had been waiting to catch him all morning.

Harp kept pounding the wall, trying to push the train forward. "They can't be stopping because of us," he said. "They couldn't be."

They *could*, Slater thought. He'd had almost no sleep and though it wasn't cold, his teeth were starting to chatter. As they crawled past River Road, he found himself caught in the doorway. Harp yelled at him to get back.

"No one saw me," he said. "The road's empty."

The train pulled past the crossing and came to a stop a half mile farther on, near a stand of young birch. The trees bordered a trailer park where tourists and sportsmen camped in Winnebagos.

"Let's get out of here," Slater said. "We can walk to the ferry terminal."

"They'll see us for sure if we do that."

"Maybe they've already seen us. Lane might have said something to Rose."

"No," Harp said. "I don't believe that."

They stood like deer for a moment, breathing quietly, waiting. No footsteps came. No sirens.

"We're alright," Harp whispered.

Slater let his breath out, not sure. Rain fell lightly outside their car.

On one wall, a boxcar artist had drawn some pussy. There were three pubic triangles, labeled *Good*, *Better*, and *Remember the Alamo!* The drawings were identical except for the amount of bush. The illustrator had signed his work *The Toledo Snatchman.*

"I'm staying with the train," Harp said. He held up the cantaloupe. "Let me see that knife of yours."

Slater passed him the Blue Dart and Harp opened up the melon like it was the most natural thing to do, as if they were waiting out a normal siding stop. He drank some water and sliced up a hunk of cheese, eating it off the side of the blade. Since there was nothing else to do, Slater got out some tuna. Outside were patches of blue sky where the day might clear up.

When the melon was gone, Harp pointed out the door with the knife. Two plastic lawn chairs sat near the tracks. The remains of a twelve-pack were scattered around them.

"Look," he said. "Who do you suppose did that? A couple of so-called *sportsmen*, I bet. They come up here to shoot their guns, and when they're done they sit in their plastic chairs and throw their empties by the tracks. We're a garbage dump to them."

He knelt down, drove the blade of the Blue Dart into the wood floor, and jumped out of the car. The knife stood there erect, a stake in the ground.

The chairs were on the other side of a shallow ditch. Harp jumped it, grabbed both chairs, and held them up like they were trophy fish.

"We don't need chairs," Slater yelled.

"Yes we do." He jumped the ditch again and jogged back to the train.

"C'mon. Help me up."

Harp set the chairs up near the rear of the boxcar and gave them a looking over. They were identical. After a long pause, he said, "Dibs on the good one."

The yokels had a radio station that played polkas at six in the morning. The hectic, noisy music banged against the dexy in his blood until he could barely stand it. "The Yellow Rose of Texas," done up like a whore.

He drove River Road for half an hour and discovered nothing. In the small rental, his legs started to numb up. He stomped against the floorboard, trying to get the feeling back. Men his age should be doing 'ludes, he thought. Not Johnny Go Fast. The go-pills were for young guys with soft veins.

As he reached down to switch off the radio, the Ranchero came over a hill. A woman was behind the wheel, alone in the car. Dickinson did a U-turn and followed her.

A half mile down the road, she turned right into a gravel driveway. He slowed, giving her time to get out of the car, then pulled in behind her. She was already on the porch. When she heard him, she turned around, looking harmless enough. She'd look quite different in a matter of minutes.

"Stop right there," Dickinson said. He walked toward her, pausing at the Ford to look under the fenders.

"Hey," the girl said. "Who are you?"

"Come over here," he said. "I got something to show you."

He was about to take out the gun when a patrol car pulled in beside him. A plainclothes cop got out of the passenger side. Another officer stood by the car.

"Undersheriff Cliff Lazenbeck," the plainclothes man said. "Who the hell are you?"

Dickinson raised his hands to show they were empty. "Just a tourist. Saw the young lady and stopped to ask directions."

The dumbass didn't bother confirming his story; the girl had gone inside.

"You a friend of Harp Maitland's?"

"Never heard of him."

The cop gave Dickinson's rental the once-over. "This is police business. You don't want to be here."

"Not a problem." He got back in the Nova and drove slowly onto River Road. The cops turned to watch him leave and he gave them a wave. The assholes. He had killed better men than them.

Not far up the road, he stopped by a historical marker. He got out, paced around, and took a piss on the spot where Marquette had lied to some Indians, or some such shit.

He'd give the cops ten minutes. Now that he knew where the car was, he wasn't going to lose it.

He couldn't make himself stand still. Up ahead, tracks crossed the road. As he waited, a freight came into view and crept slowly through the crossing. Dickinson was about to turn away when he saw the punk who had left him to die in the desert standing in one of the boxcars.

No, he told himself. Go for the Ford. Get the money. Don't be a fool. But the dexy made him walk toward the train.

THE AIR HOSES hissed, but the train didn't move. Slater sat in one of the chairs near the back of the car, eyes closed. He could still taste the cheap wine from the beach. And behind it, Lane's kiss.

Waiting stirred up his doubt. He had given no thought to his decision to leave—he was just following Harp's momentum, like always. Only in the Ford had the choice seemed to hang in front of him—go or stay. He reached for her hand and she took it away. If she had held on, he thought, he might not have gotten out.

Harp warned him not to go to sleep.

"We could just go get the Ford," Slater said. "It's better than waiting here to get caught."

Harp started to speak but stopped before the words came out. Footsteps were coming down the track. "Brakeman," he mouthed.

He stepped lightly and noiselessly to the corner. Slater tried to stand but the chair scraped on the floor and Harp signaled him to freeze.

Seconds later, a stocky man in a cowboy hat appeared outside the door. The man saw them and ducked instantly out of sight. When he reappeared, he was holding a gun. It was Ed Dickinson.

Slater got to his feet.

"Sit down, asshole," Dickinson said.

"Wait," Slater said. "Wait a minute."

"Tell me to wait one more time and I'll shoot your dick off." He stood in the light drizzle, holding the gun in a two-handed grip with his arms inside the car.

"We don't want any trouble," Harp said.

"Good. Then you'll do exactly what I say."

He made them stand and face the wall. "I'm coming in now," he said. "I'll be putting the gun down for a few seconds. Go ahead and rush me if you think you can make it."

Slater turned his head slightly, enough to see Dickinson hoist himself into the car. Harp turned and took a step toward Dickinson, but froze as the gun came up.

"You're an unlucky guy," Dickinson said. "You know that?"

"No," Harp said. "I don't."

Dickinson crossed the car and backed them against the wall. He made Harp sit in the chair and left Slater standing, the gun aimed at his chest. Slater's brain was a hive with one terrified bee.

"You're a living dead man," Dickinson said. "I'm with the living dead here."

In his mind's eye, Slater saw the hole the bullet would leave in the wall, a small nipple on the outside of the car, barely noticeable. Inside the car, a scum of bone, flesh, and brain stuck to the metal.

"Your friend stole my car," Dickinson said to Harp.

"He fucked me up and left me in the desert to die."

"You can have the car right now," Slater said. "I'll take you to it."

"I know where it is. I just saw it at your girlfriend's house. That little whore you were humping on the beach last night. After I shoot you, I'm going to go back there and finish the job. How about that? You like that idea?"

He took a step forward so they were less than a foot apart, the gun between them.

"Take the car," Slater said. "Take anything you want."

"I will. But you won't be around to see it. I spent two days on my knees because of you. Crawling around like an animal." He jabbed the gun at Slater's chest. "I had to blow up my fucking truck."

Far off, there was a low roar—the sound of the train engine straining and then slamming forward. At the front end of the freight, cars clanked rapid-fire as the slack whipped through the train. Harp turned and met Slater's eyes for an instant.

When the whiplash hit them, their car exploded forward. It blew Slater off his feet; his forehead smashed Dickinson's face. They tumbled down together, a knee in Slater's gut, blood in his mouth. There was the sound of a shot that was either an air hose or the gun. He slid to the center of the car, holding on to Dickinson. When they stopped, Dickinson tried to sit but Slater fell onto his chest. Amazed that he wasn't already dead, he looked for the gun and saw it in Dickinson's hand. At the same moment he heard Harp's voice.

"Knife," Harp said.

The Blue Dart was stuck in the floor where Harp had left it. A shred of cheese still on the blade. Slater grabbed the handle, lifted the knife high, and drove it as hard as he could through Dickinson's chest.

When the blade went in, Dickinson's eyes came open wide; he looked like he'd heard a joke he didn't understand. The gun dropped; blood sprayed from the wound. Even then, the man tried to sit.

"Stop it," Slater said. "Stop."

Harp was still in his chair. He had slid almost the length of the car. "Get the gun," he said.

There was no need. Arcs of red spurted from Dickinson—a fountain synced to the pulse in Slater's ears. The Blue Dart was still in his chest. Dickinson tried to lift his head and Slater put his hand on the man's forehead, feeling the last bit of life leave. Even then the spurts came, but weakly.

Finally, they stopped and Dickinson was no more. He was gone, not to return. He was with the dead dead now.

First you kill him, then you hide the body. That was how it worked. There were other ways to do it, but they all ended in disaster. It wasn't a question of right or wrong, Slater thought. They had to get rid of him.

They dragged the body from the car and carried him down the track, Slater on the front end, Harp holding Dickinson's feet. The gravel was loose, and twice they nearly dropped him.

One car down was a refrigerated fruit car. Harp broke the seal. Pulling together, they managed to open the door. Inside, Harp restacked a group of cartons, making space for the corpse. Slater shoved Dickinson's head and shoulders into the car and Harp dragged him the rest of the way by the belt. Their work left a trail of blood on the gravel, but the rain was coming harder, washing it away.

When they got back to the Short Life & Misery boxcar, Harp fashioned a handle out of yellow strapping material that had been left stapled to the wall. He looped it around the outside latch and used it to pull the door shut. The car went black.

"That's the first dead guy I've ever touched," Harp said.

In less than a minute, the train began to move. It crept slowly at first, then started to roll. Crossing bells greeted them as they came into Wolverine. At what must have been the ferry yard, the *Tecumseh's* air horn blew.

"So," Slater said. "We're good, right? We'll be okay?"

Harp's footsteps tracked back and forth across the dark car.

"Oh, we're good," he said. "Screwing Lane. Bringing assholes into my life. Murdering guys. We're really good. You got any other secrets you want to tell me about?"

On the ferry, they left their boxcar and went back to the body. The door of the refrigerated fruit car opened with a slow screech that seemed to fill the entire freight deck. Slanting light cast a dim tombstone on a crate of Michigan cherries inside. The words *Broods Orchard—Perishable Goods* were printed in block letters. Beside the crate was Dickinson's corpse. They climbed in quickly and looked down at the body.

"Forget it," Slater said. "Let's just leave him."

"We can't."

A loose chain clanked against a wall on the far side of the deck. They were twenty minutes out from Wolverine and the *Tecumseh* had started to pitch. The motion made Slater slightly sick.

"Three days from now this car's going to be out West somewhere," Harp said. "California. Texas. They'll open it up and find this guy. For all you know, he's got your name tattooed on his dick."

Slater nudged the body with his boot. A dusting of frost whitened Dickinson's eyebrows and slack cheeks, like he was made up for a play. Brown sludge covered most of his chest.

"We have to dump him in the Lake," Harp said. "Burial at sea."

The body seemed heavier than before. At the base of the seagate, they realized he was too big to carry up the rung ladder. They quickly returned him to the car.

"Take his stuff then," Harp said. "Anything that could identify him. Wallet, watch, ring. They can't trace him to us if they don't know who he is."

Slater stood over the body while Harp sat on the crates.

"You're not going to help?"

"You killed him, Mike."

The car's refrigeration unit cycled on. Slater knelt and put his hand in the dead man's slacks. He pulled out his keys, a pack of gum, a container of pills. As he got a grip on the wallet, Dickinson let loose a blast of gas. They put everything in a plastic bag Harp had brought.

"The string tie, too," Harp said. "And take his boots. It'll look like hobos killed him."

When they had everything, they went back to the seagate. The rungs were cold and held the thrum of the ship. At the top, the pitch and swell of the Lake made Slater's stomach worse.

Over the seagate, he saw a view of the Lake he had never imagined. Like a planet of churning green water. Wet air mixed with the smell of diesel. Slater clenched his jaw, trying not to be sick.

On the rungs below him, Harp passed up the bag. Then the boots and the Stetson. As Slater sailed the hat over, he twisted his head to look up at the car deck. Anyone standing there might have seen a cowboy hat in the middle of the Lake. Sucked into the churn, then surfacing in calm water, then disappearing forever. It would be a puzzling sight, Slater thought. But there was no one on the car deck to see.

He started to climb down, but Harp stopped him. "Wait there. I'll be right back."

Slater gripped the rungs and kept his eyes in the middle distance, nothing in his view but water. It was a place completely absent of all the things that could fuck you up.

When Harp returned, he had the chairs. "You were right," he said. "We don't need these."

Slater said nothing. One at a time, he slid them into the Lake.

The flashlight cast a circle of light on the ceiling of their boxcar. "Six hundred dollars," Harp said. "God works in mysterious ways." He was counting the bills from Dickinson's wallet.

Slater wrapped his arms around his chest, trying to get warm. "I'd leave God out of it if I were you."

"It's right here. *In God We Trust.* He gave the money to Slater. "You killed him. You take it."

"I didn't kill him to get his money. I shouldn't even be here. I should be anywhere but on this train."

Harped flicked the flashlight off. The boxcar went black.

"It's true. Whether you want to know it or not."

"I'm just saving the batteries."

"For what? For getting arrested?"

"For the Northern Arrow. Where the hell else do you think we're going."

"Jesus, Harp. I just killed a guy."

The whiskey had made him thirsty, but he didn't have the energy to move. He leaned against the wall and tried to remember the image of the Lake from the seagate. The endlessness. As the ship settled into a regular pitch, he felt himself drifting off.

"Sometimes I think it would have been better if that power line had killed you," Harp said. "None of this would have happened."

"Really? Sorry to inconvenience you by being alive."

"By being with Lane, you mean? On the beach."

"It's not like that. Anyway, it wasn't about the sex."

"Of course not," Harp said. "I love this act of yours. *I'm hurt. I have a plate in my head. Sleep with me and make me feel better.*"

"I don't do that."

"You should thank me for that plate. That crap is a free pass, so you never have to ask for it. Which is good, because you don't know how to ask for it."

"That's not true," Slater said. "None of that is true."

Their boxcar creaked on its frame.

"It doesn't matter to me, Mike. Let's ride the Northern Arrow and see how things go."

Slater didn't answer. He considered apologizing about Lane. But that would require words. They'd float out in the dark boxcar and get trapped.

After that, the darkness took over. It grew deeper and Harp disappeared. At times, Slater could hear him breathing. At times not. The vibration of the ship was all there was. Hours stretched out, wider than the Lake.

At one point, suddenly, Slater sensed they were not alone. A chemical breeze made him open his eyes. He was not surprised to see Dickinson standing above him. Cherry glaze covered his torso, spurting from a hole in his chest. A jack-o'-lantern grimace distorted his face. He looked angry. Someone had stolen his boots.

After that it was clear that the car, which had been hard metal, was actually a block of ice, wet and shiny, and it turned out then that it had always been ice, not cold necessarily, but hard and ready to shatter, with an ice pick poised above it at angle to strike, patient, indifferent to time, waiting only for a moment or for as long as a tree might grow until the mallet would fall, shattering the car and his life into dozens and hundreds of soft-sharp shards.

In the blackest darkness, time could mesmerize, stutter-step, turn the shiv, and fly.

— 25 —

THE ABANDONED KEWAUNEE Engine House was cavernous and haunted with light. Seagulls flew through sections of open roof; the afternoon sun sent spikes of dust through knotholes. Along one wall, a row of ancient, dented lockers remained. Slater spread his belongings in front of them, emptying his pack. The Blue Dart was missing.

"We left it in the fruit car," Slater said. "We're dead meat."

"Don't give me that," Harp told him. "Whatever else you do, keep that precious shit to yourself."

They had moved to the engine house soon after the *Tecumseh* docked. Through a crack in a boarded-up window, Harp kept an eye on the yard, waiting for the Snake to come. They planned to ride it to Green Bay.

Frantic, Slater emptied Harp's bag next to his own. A pair of boxer shorts topped a pile of jeans, gloves, T-shirts, crayons, tuna, trail mix, maps, a melon, and whiskey. A bag of food. Extra clothes. No knife.

"Maybe you threw it in the Lake," Harp said.

"It has my fingerprints on it. And my initials."

"Lots of people have those initials. Anyway, we're not getting back in the fruit car. Take a look."

Slater found a knothole that faced the yard and peered through it. A worker with a blond ponytail was standing by the refrigerated fruit car. He looked nervously over his shoulder to be sure he was alone.

"What the hell?" Slater said. "Why is he checking cars?"

The ponytailed worker gave the door a tug. It opened half a foot.

"I know that guy," Harp said. "He's not checking cars. He's a thief. He's trying to steal some cherries."

Charlie was on the phone when Lane let herself in. He rolled his eyes and motioned for her to sit on the couch, so she stood in the corner instead. It was a glue place.

The world was pretty simple when you thought about it: just don't be in the places people expect you to be. You could solve all kinds of shit with that one trick.

Charlie made a jabbering motion with his hand, mocking the caller, while he held the phone to his ear. The Spreadables were on the balcony with a couple of men. Two of the girls had their tops off. The third girl was fully dressed.

"Relax, boss," Charlie said into the phone. "You're running against a guy who's on a ventilator, for Christ's sakes."

The other trick was not to follow the normal order of things. First the fucking, then the flirting, as Rose would say.

"My part was to get the guy," Charlie said. "It's not my fault if he shot his wad prematurely." He winked at Lane. "I warned you he wouldn't wait."

The caller spoke and Charlie made the jabbering motion again. From the balcony, Tracy said, "I bet you have a very strong heart."

The man she spoke to was wearing a black shirt with silver piping, as if he were a country-western singer. He put his hand on her back. "It could always be a little stronger." Everyone laughed except the tall girl.

"As luck would have it," Charlie said, "a confidential source just walked in the door. A very confidential source." He looked at Lane again.

The other man touched the tall girl's butt. She quickly pushed his hand off.

"Negatory on Sara Lee," Charlie said. "That trail is cold. But the minute I get a lead on your guy, you'll hear about it." He rolled his eyes and held the phone away from his ear for a moment. "Sure, boss. The instant I know."

When he was done, he turned to Lane.

"Your boyfriend has disappeared," he said. "On the very day Lazenbeck is desperate to find him. I don't suppose you came here to turn him in."

"Lazenbeck already talked to me. I told him Harp didn't do anything."

"Really? I heard he was a disgruntled hothead who blew up the Whispering Sands. Lazenbeck wants to arrest him *tout de suite*. He claims time is of the essence."

"I think it was you, Charlie. It's always you."

"Can you believe that shit? Who does he think he's talking to? Let me tell you something, sis. Time is not of the essence. I've been to the essence and there ain't no Father Time there."

"You did it and made it look like Harp."

Before Charlie could answer, Tracy and the other topless girl led a little parade through the living room, taking the men up the spiral staircase. The tall girl, still dressed, went downstairs toward the sundeck.

"Take this one example from your own little life," Charlie said. "You're in bed with some guy. Doesn't matter who it is. You've got it going, and you've forgotten who you are. It's not about him, it's not about you, it's not that place between your legs. It's the moment before the moment when you know you're going nova. Womblike pleasure everywhere. No unmet need, no plan, no purpose, nothing at all in your mind. That's the essence. Time is not of that. In fact, time destroys that."

"I'm taking that as a yes," Lane said.

"Hey, your boyfriend was up to something. Because I counted one less crate of dynamite in the shed. And one less barn out on Coon Hill Road."

Charlie poured himself a glass of wine. Together they watched the tall girl settle on a chaise lounge.

"Shannon never gets naked," Charlie said. "It's a bit of a problem. Tracy thinks she's embarrassed about her tits. Everyone else here has fake ones."

Lane looked at Charlie. Charlie looked back.

"If you haven't seen them, how do you know?"

He shrugged. "It's not my theory. Ask Tracy."

Lane met the suggestion with a tiny scoff. Tracy was totally fake. She was a walnut painted like a woman.

"I need a ride home," Lane said.

Charlie peered into his cabernet. "Think of it this way, sis. You are home. Why don't you stay?"

"I don't live here," Lane said.

"Don't worry about Harp," he said. "What's done is done. And it really doesn't matter who did it. Except to Lazenbeck. He thinks he has to arrest somebody. I'd rather he didn't. Let him stay clueless, at least until the election's over. I like him better as undersheriff anyway. He'd be a total pain in the ass as sheriff."

Tracy appeared on the stairway, drinking a beer. She wore a T-shirt that read *Kohoutek: Comet of the Century!* "I'd like him better pinned to a piece of Styrofoam," she said.

"I thought you were entertaining our friends."

"I was. We're done."

"That was fast."

"The performance wasn't exactly stellar. I took off my panties and he popped his cork."

Charlie turned back to Lane. "The postgame show. Another reason I abstain. I never liked the cuddling and I don't need the criticism."

Tracy wiggled her beer in the air. "Are you sure, Charlie-boy? How long has it been, anyway? I'm sure the girls could help you Summon the Badger."

"The Badger's retired," Charlie said.

"It lowers the risk of heart attack, you know."

"Uh-huh. Here's a hint. Guys will say anything to get you in bed."

"It *does*. Orgasm does something for your heart muscle."

"Yeah, well," Charlie said, "I'll take my heart attack early. It's all supply and demand. You got old guys who need new hearts. You got young guys crashing cars and snapping their necks. Instant organ donors. Now look ahead a few years. Think there's gonna be enough careless young bucks around to supply hearts for everyone? No way—it'll be first come, first served. Eat right and exercise and by the time you need a transplant, the cupboard is bare. Meanwhile, I'll be on my second ticker eating like a pig."

Lane folded her arms. "Jesus, Charlie. Only you could figure out how to screw thy neighbor by having a heart attack."

"It's all in the timing."

"How about a ride home? Do you have time for that?"

Charlie walked onto the balcony and called to Shannon below. "Excuse me, miss," he said. "I have a very small errand I'd like you to do. It doesn't involve being friendly, so you might enjoy it."

Tracy jerked her head toward Lane. "Why doesn't she drive herself home?"

"I've been wondering that myself," Charlie said. "But I'm afraid to ask."

"I'm leaving Mike's car here," Lane said.

Charlie walked to the front door and looked out. "That ugly bucket of bolts that's leaking oil on my drive? That car?"

"Every time Lazenbeck sees it by the house, he stops and asks questions."

Charlie squinted at the Ford. "Why not drive it into the Lake instead? Why sully my world with that piece of junk?

"Because Lazenbeck won't come out here. As you well know."

Charlie shut the door and waved his hand at her. "Fine. Park it in the shed. If I decide to go out in the world posing as a drug dealer I might need a rig like that. Or we could give it to Vulva Voom. How 'bout it, Trace? Need a new old car?"

Tracy gave him the finger. Shannon entered just in time to see.

"What did I miss?" she asked. "What did he do now?"

Tracy retreated up the stairs without answering. Shannon went off to find her shoes.

"They don't seem to appreciate your leadership," Lane said.

Charlie refilled his wineglass. "C'est la vie," he said. "It takes a while to get to know me. Five or ten years. A lot of people can't be bothered to make the effort."

As the afternoon grew hot, a smell of grease and wet metal settled over the Kewaunee Engine House. Except for a crumbling concrete apron where the tracks used to be, the floor was dirt. Wildflowers grew under the broken roof and a bush with tiny red berries hugged the wall. Slater stood at the front of the engine house, watching the freight yard through the good knothole. When his neck grew stiff, he looked down at the berries and wondered if they were poisonous.

The corpse had been discovered in the refrigerated fruit car. The ponytailed thief who opened the door called to his buddies and showed them the body. Pretty soon the yard boss bellied up. Within fifteen minutes, three squad cars arrived.

As Slater and Harp watched, the body was removed on a stretcher. If the knife was there, no one seemed to find it. Photos were taken, the fruit car was strung with yellow tape. After an hour, two police cars left; the third remained parked in front of the ship.

"This changes the plan," Harp said. "We can't risk riding freight now. They'll be watching all the trains."

"Maybe we wait until dark," Slater said. "Walk into town and get a bus."

Harp took a string of licorice from his pack. "This is a small town. There's a limit on strange behavior. Only one strange thing per month. First, they find a dead guy. If they see two freaks with packs at the bus station, they're over the limit. They'll take our names and figure it out. Then we're finished."

At the far end of the yard, a switch engine sorted cars. Short Life & Misery, the car where he had stabbed Dickinson, was shuffled into the mix. The bloodstains on its floor would be a puzzle for a policeman in some other town.

"You have to go back and get the Ford," Harp said.

"How the hell am I going to do that?"

"The police aren't looking for you. They're looking for me. Take the ferry over and back. Get the car and pick me up in the morning. We can drive into Canada until it's safe to ride freight."

"I don't know." He pictured the knife, the blade still red, the initials M.S. on the handle. He started to pace.

"Don't do that," Harp said.

"Don't what?"

"Don't pace. It sets up ripples."

He took two more steps and stopped, afraid to move. Dust motes filled a shaft of sunlight that angled through the broken roof.

"I've ridden all these lines," Harp said. "I've ridden Green Bay, Kewaunee, Rhinelander. I've ridden Manitowoc to Kenosha, down and back, a couple of times. When the crew sees me, they wave. It's like they're proud when someone comes along who loves trains." He leaned against a wooden support column. "That's over for now. The only way we get out of here is with the car."

Slater couldn't think. He concentrated on not making ripples.

When Harp decided it was dinnertime, they moved deeper into the engine house. There was a second room with a concrete floor and a grooved concrete berm that had once held heavy equipment. Above it, half the roof was gone. They leaned their packs against the berm and ate. Two cans of tuna, beef jerky, and a carrot. Some whiskey.

As they ate, a robin perched along the far wall, then flew off under sunset clouds, lit from beneath. The image was perfect in its simplicity, as if the engine house and the sky had been conjured for just that purpose.

"Okay, I'll go back," Slater said. "We'll drive out of here tomorrow. If you think it will work."

Harp nodded. "I'm sorry about what I said on the ferry," he said. "About the power line."

Slater looked at the whiskey bottle sitting on the concrete. "I'm the one who should be apologizing."

A horn came from the lot, and distant, cheerful voices. More people were arriving.

"The truth is," Harp said, "I would have done everything you did. Only better." He pulled a baseball cap from his pack. It was purple and faded from the sun. "You want the whiskey hat?"

"Will it help?"

"Sure."

The front of the cap said *Party Animal*. Slater put it on.

"One thing," Harp said. "If you're not coming back, tell me now. Don't leave me waiting if it's not gonna happen."

"I'm coming back, Harp."

"You might change your mind."

"I won't even go in the house."

They shook on it. As the sun got low, the switch engine started up. They moved back to the front of the engine house.

Passengers were already waiting to board. The parking lot held a dozen automobiles. From one, a radio played. The Ronettes. Halfway through "Be My Baby," a crow began cawing. The squad car was still parked by the ship. Slater would have to walk past it to get to the ramp.

"You might as well get moving." Harp stood half in shadow. He opened his arms to the gloom all around him. "Kick out the jams, motherfucker."

"Always."

The daylight was nearly gone as Slater approached the *Tecumseh*. At the ramp, he fell in with a group of college kids. One member of the group—a boy with wolflike eyes—was having fun hiding a bottle under his coat. When he thought no one was looking, he would pass it to the others. Ten minutes later, a worker opened the ramp and they boarded the ship.

The crowd headed down to the purser's office. To Slater's surprise, it was open. He got in line with the others and paid with Dickinson's money. Returning to the deck, he passed the staterooms where Rose and her friend had spent the night.

By the rail, he allowed himself a glance at the engine house. It was nothing but a shadow at the edge of the dingy yard. A place for rats and bats. He nodded once, in case Harp was watching.

Inside, the college kids had taken over the passenger lounge. Their bright laughter clashed with the shabby interior. Slater found a chair at the periphery of their group, hiding in plain sight. For the next hour or so, the kids played what seemed to be strip poker where the players only pretended to undress. Hoots and hollers followed every hand.

Later, as Slater walked back from the vending machines, the wolf-eyed boy called him over to the table and pointed at his head.

"How much for the hat?" he asked.

Before he could answer, one of the girls folded her hand. She had short red hair, and she moved in a way that was angular and quick. She stood, mimed removing her top, and twirled the imaginary shirt above her head. She dropped it on an imaginary pile of clothes to catcalls and woofs. She was as far from his type of woman as you could possibly get, he thought.

Wandering about, he thought he saw Jack, the bearded crewman he had shared a doobie with at the beginning of the summer. He tried to follow him, but the man disappeared down a passageway.

Finally, toward the end of the crossing, Slater encountered the redhead from the card game in the men's bathroom. She was standing between the sinks and urinals, looking about as if contemplating a purchase.

"I'm a decorator," she said. "Those fixtures there— you just don't see stuff like that anymore." She turned in a little circle, absorbing the charm of the ancient men's room.

Slater offered to come back later. She blew a little puff of air and pointed at the urinals. "Don't let me stop you. After all, you were looking at me naked."

He stepped past her and unzipped, not sure if she was still naked or not.

As she left, she called him a freak with such conviction that he looked down to see if he had turned into a lizard.

In postproduction, a blur of red. A pulsing light on an otherwise black screen. On, off. On, off.

When Slater boosted the volume, the edit suite filled with crickets and the sound of a turn signal. The screen showed Lane's Jeep, angled into a ditch. The driver's door had sprung open and her foot was sticking out. The red turn signal lit the faded sticker on the bumper in slow, relentless rhythm, washing the message in weak crimson light: *Another Woman for Peace.*

In postproduction, Slater could almost smell the glue.

The *Tecumseh* reached Wolverine after midnight and had trouble docking. The foul-up cut into Slater's time; he was forced to walk double-time to the house. When he saw the Jeep, he called Lane's name and broke into a run.

She was sprawled sideways across the seats and there was a bag of glue on the floor. The Jeep smelled strongly of vomit. He touched her face and she opened her eyes.

"Bury me here," she said.

Her skin was clammy, but there was no blood that he could see. Slater worked his arm around her back and tugged. He managed to pull her from the Jeep and they tumbled into the ditch together.

"Get up, Lane," he told her. "It's Mike." Finally she woke up enough to stand. She looped both arms around his neck and he walked her crablike to the porch. He sat her there, propping her on the steps, and ran to get the Ford, but the Ford was gone.

The Jeep was the last car on the ferry. It had taken an hour to free it from the ditch, and precious more minutes to get Lane strapped in. She fell asleep immediately without asking where they were going.

As they boarded the *Tecumseh*, he pulled the brim of the Party Animal hat low on her brow. She rested her head on his shoulder and kept an arm around his neck. It was 6 a.m. and she might have passed for sleepy.

At the key drop, he stuck his hand in and tried Rose's trick. Maybe it was everyone's trick. The key he plucked out opened stateroom 6.

The small rectangular room held a card table, a sink, and a metal-framed bed. He put Lane on the hard mattress and sat at the table. Everything was going to be okay, he thought. It was under control.

A fog had blown in with the morning. As the *Tecumseh* left Wolverine, the dingy porthole was filled with wisps of white. Well before they hit open water, Lane was soundly asleep. Her breathing was deep and regular.

He was filled, quite suddenly, with confidence. The ship would dock and the three of them would work it out. He'd stop sleeping with Lane, be an honest friend. Everything that had happened—it would all be forgiven. They'd ride with the windows down and a fifth of Jim Beam on the seat, and it would be sunny. It would be sunny even when it was foggy.

His optimism was so strong that he couldn't sit still. He stood by the bed for a moment and touched Lane's hair. After a while he walked out to the deck.

The morning fog had not burned away. The ship, which he had expected to find bright, seemed empty and pointless.

The coffee vending machine was the saddest thing he'd ever seen. Black electrical tape covered most of the buttons and an angry sign said *Use At Your Own Risk*. Slater put two quarters in. As his cup filled, he saw his face in the dull shine of the machine. He looked like a convict. Unsteady. Untrustable.

Back in the stateroom, his confidence fled as quickly as it had come. He took one sip of coffee and poured it out. The knife was out there to be found, the initials in the handle.

There was nothing he could do about it except get into bed with Lane. For warmth, he thought. But once they started, there was no holding back. Buttons fell open, fingers grasped. Every touch led to another; behind every kiss was a deeper kiss. Somewhere in the middle of things, Lane moved down in the narrow bed and went at him with her mouth and tongue, and then accidentally with her teeth. He came quickly, certain it was the right thing to do.

Before worry or fear could catch him, he slept. Later— it seemed like quite a while later—he was hard and inside her without being fully inside himself. Waking more completely, he discovered her body as he reinhabited his. Her head was turned; he trailed his fingers from her jaw. Her mouth was open, the mezzaluna on fire. Thrusting, he said to himself *this, this, this.*

When she started to come he looked out at the water, trying to keep himself, but at the end of her orgasm, his began. He rocked into her softly, the knife still sharp in his mind. Then he slept.

SEAGULLS WOKE HARP at five, raising confident squawks and dropping their birdshit by the rear wall of the engine house. Roused, Harp moved to a patch of cold sunshine and pulled his army jacket on. He could not help but wonder what bed Slater might be rising from.

The yard was empty, so he left the engine house and climbed a hill that overlooked the ferry slip. From the top, he could feel the wind and stand lookout. He was hungry and wanted coffee, but he resisted the temptation to walk into town.

There'll be bacon and eggs tomorrow, he told himself. And the highway. After a couple of weeks, they'd ditch Slater's car and get back on the rails. He plucked a stem of grass and ran it between his fingers. The Northern Arrow, and who knows where else. He could think of a thousand places he'd like to go.

Around six, a pickup truck entered the ferry lot, and Harp retreated to the engine house. Hiding made him feel guilty. He resented it. All he'd done was take apart a barn that Howdy Broodson hadn't paid for. It was a fair enough deal. If Broodson had wanted the barn, he should have cracked his checkbook and squared up, like an honest man.

What would hit the spot, he thought, were some pull-ups. About five would do. But there was nothing to grab on to.

The ferry came into the harbor on time. Harp watched through the knothole as it docked. He found a clean t-shirt to put on, placed the packs by the door, and waited. It took another half hour for the boat to begin unloading.

The happy tourists came first. Their shorts and striped shirts angered Harp. They would not ride out on the line for what they believed in. You could count on not being able to count on them. Of course, if jokers like that rode out on the line, the line would be too damn crowded.

After the tourists came the stragglers. A woman got off the ship with a golden retriever, a plum-colored pack, and a bandana. A man with a cane worked his way painfully down the ramp. A family with toddlers. No Mike.

Before long the crew began bringing cars down the corkscrew ramp. A Dodge came down and the ponytailed worker got out, his day of glory over. He left the engine of the van running. As a family of five claimed the Dodge, he walked to a rope elevator at the side of the ship and rose forty feet up in the air.

To Harp, the contraption looked like a death trap. A set of parallel ropes ran on pulleys, rising straight in the air, all the way to the car deck. A small piece of wood, not much bigger than a doormat, was strung between the two ropes, which never stopped moving. A platform, three steps off the ground, led to the edge of the rope elevator. The trick was to stand on the platform and step onto the wooden doormat at the precise moment it came around, and ride it to the top. A daredevil trip for sure. The pony-tailed car hostler made it look easy.

After the Dodge, a Taurus came down the ramp with Ponytail behind the wheel. Without waiting for its owner to reclaim it, he left it in the dirt lot, engine running, and went back up the rope for another car. Working alone, he brought down a Chevy van. A New Yorker. A Pontiac Tempest.

No Ford. No Slater. The last of the passengers were off the ship.

So, Harp said. Mike had stayed with Lane after all. Maybe she'd lured him into bed. Maybe Mike's paranoid instincts had been right and the police had him. Either way, Harp thought, I'm a sitting duck here.

The woman with the golden retriever looked like she might share a ride, a lift out of town. He had known women with dogs before. He knew how she would smell. The dog was a negative. He decided to give Mike two more minutes. After the first minute, he gave up.

That was that, he thought. Over and out.

The ponytailed hostler brought down a green Comet. The woman with the dog got in and left. Another future gone. The crowd was getting thin. If he was going to make a move, it had to be now.

A Pinto came down and no one stepped forward to claim it. Without stopping to think, Harp swung his pack onto his shoulders, stepped into the sunshine, and headed toward the driver's seat. Car theft would be an interesting new experience. All he needed was thirty miles; he could ditch it in Green Bay and go from there.

He was four steps from the driver's door when a man in a Levi's jacket appeared, keys in hand, looking concerned.

Harp gave him a friendly nod and kept going toward the ship, as if he'd been heading there all along. The rope elevator was dead ahead, humming like a hornet's nest.

Jesus H. Christ, Harp muttered. A little mercy here.

It was hell on a stick, but there wasn't any choice. He climbed the stairs and waited on the platform until the doormat-sized step came around. When he got on, the upward jolt drove his knees toward his stomach, but he gripped the rope tight, knowing not to look down. Finally, the car deck appeared. Stunned, he stepped off a second late and ended up on his hands and knees. He hadn't thought to put on his gloves and his hands scraped on the rough deck, bringing some blood.

When he looked up, he saw a green Buick, an Olds 88, and Lane's Jeep. Parked in a line, bumper to bumper. The Jeep was blocked by the other two. It made no sense, but there was no time to sort it out. He couldn't get caught on the car deck.

He moved the Buick first, backing it out of the way and leaving the engine stalled. He was running to move the Olds when the ponytailed hostler stepped off the rope elevator.

"Hey," the guy said, "what the hell are you doing?"

Harp pushed him down, jumped into the Oldsmobile, and gunned it for the ramp.

Slater woke to cracked plaster. An unknown ceiling in an unknown room. For a long, unhappy moment, he had no idea where he was. Then he saw Lane standing at the sink. She was naked, washing her face. The ferry was docked.

"I thought I'd let you sleep," she said.

Slater struggled to his feet and found his watch. Eight o'clock. "Shit," he said. "Get dressed. Now."

Their clothes were spread across the floor. She picked up her shirt and sniffed it. "How did we get here?"

Slater grabbed her shirt and tried to force it on her—right arm, left arm. She waved and swatted at him. "Okay," she said. "Stop."

They burst out of stateroom 6 fastening buttons, laces wild. The ship was empty and the long passageway smelled of bathroom sanitizer. When they made it onto the deck, the sunlight hit them like a fist. Below, the parking lot was nearly empty. He gripped Lane's hand, pulling her to the rail. "Where's the goddamn Jeep?" Slater asked. "It's got to be down there."

They ran down the gangway to the dirt parking lot. The engine house was lit with morning sun. Slater took two steps toward it, but Lane jerked him back. Behind him, a blue Olds 88 was screaming down the ramp. It scraped the side rail, bottoming out as it hit dirt. "That's my car," a man yelled.

As the Olds raced passed, it slowed just enough for Slater to see Harp behind the wheel. The brake lights flashed, as if Harp was thinking about stopping; then a horn sounded and a second vehicle came roaring down in pursuit. Harp hit the gas, racing the Olds out of the lot.

Slater turned just in time to see the Jeep coming off the ramp. He stepped in front of it, hands up, forcing it to stop. The ponytailed hostler jumped out, demanding to know what kind of ignorant fuck Slater might be. When he got no answer, he asked again, louder.

Slater took Lane's hand in his own. "This is our Jeep," he said.

Lane's shirt was misbuttoned, and she looked at him exactly as she had the night they met—eyes that took in the pointless world and asked for nothing by way of mercy.

Stepping around the car hostler, he got her in the Jeep. "We fucked up," Slater said. "He's gone."

— 27 —

FLOWERS IN FLAG colors wreathed the big hotel. Manicured beds, larger than Slater had ever seen, extended like fingers down the sloping lawn, ringing the pool, the gazebo, and the walkways of the Grand Hotel. At night, the blossoms looked like foam. Their first evening there, Lane led him out a side door and into the beds of fire pinks and bluehearts. Near a hedge of huckleberry, they made love in the shadows. The happiness he felt was huge and unconscionable.

Kewaunee had turned into a black hole, an expanding depression with its center in Slater's chest. After Harp disappeared in the Olds, they drove to town. It was pointless, of course. They went to Dick's Bucket, where the beer tasted like hoof-and-mouth disease. In the flicker of TV and broken pinball machines, Slater saw the shambles he had made.

"We could try to find him," Lane said.

"Good idea. You check North America. I'll check South."

He couldn't finish his beer. Eventually they got back in the Jeep. Lane drove. Slater slept. After an hour, he woke up and asked where they were going.

"We're going home the long way. We're driving around the Lake."

"Why?"

"It's what people do. Everyone should do it once and I've never done it."

They spent the first night on a deserted beach north of Menominee. The air was cold by the water. Grabbing a tarp from the back of the Jeep, he discovered a .30-06.

"What the hell is this?" he asked.

"Charlie's rifle. I stole it from him."

"Why?"

"Who knows?" She took the sleeping bags and laid them side by side next to a knobby, bleached log. They were out of the wind at least. Lane rested her head on his shoulder as she slept, but he felt separate and lost, as adrift as he had felt in the dark boxcar with Harp. Invisible waves hit the shore. Instead of offering comfort, they deepened his sense of isolation. If they would stop, he thought, he could get some sleep.

Finally, he went to the Jeep and got the rifle. By the water's edge, he flipped the safety off.

He fired the first shot over the Lake for Harp. The second was for Lane. The third, just for the hell of it, was for Selda. The fourth and the fifth were nothing. Empty clicks. Holding the stock with two hands, he swung the rifle hard and launched it out over the Lake. It disappeared into blackness, hanging for a satisfying interval before making a distant splash.

When he got back to the log, Lane was sitting up in her sleeping bag. He lay down without speaking and she curled close against him.

The next day was warmer. They made it all the way to the straits and took the tourist boat to Mackinac Island.

The ship, barely a quarter the size of the *Tecumseh*, was thick with tourists and a few hippies mixed in like raisins in white bread. One of them, a Jesus figure still holding some toke from the sixties, approached Slater as if recognizing lost kin. "You have the seeds," he intoned. Slater wasn't sure if it was a statement or a question.

When they docked, Slater hired a carriage to take them to the big hotel. Purple-draped horses clopped absurdly around a grand promenade; even the horses radiated arrogance. It was the last place on earth Harp might be.

The hotel required coat and tie after six, confining them to their room. Lewis, their bellhop, carted in dinner and a local wine. He treated them as old friends. He was forty, had bellhopped fifteen years; his father had known Ellsworth Taylor.

"Are you here for the wedding?" Lewis asked them.

"We were," Slater said. "But I forgot the ring."

Mankato was a tub of heat. Harp camped at the west end of the yard, betting that the local would stop to throw a switch. But the engine blew off at the east end, so Harp picked up his pack and walked the length of the yard. By the time he got there, he was choked with sweat. He found a boxcar and climbed in. Then the whole train pulled forward and stopped right where he'd been waiting all along. It didn't bother him in the least. It was just what trains did.

After three days on the road he was floating. Not angry, not worried. Riding the locals filled him with simple tasks: watching the engine, staying with the train, finding food, waiting. Sometimes he thought about Slater, but inside he knew that he was better off riding alone. As for the police, if they were looking, they weren't looking where he was.

Leaving Mankato, he passed a switchman combing his mustache. The train took him past loading docks, trailers, ditches, and finally into a lightly forested meadow. On one side, field grass waved in afternoon sun. Out the other door was a darker, denser forest.

They stopped three times: once to pick up a boxcar, and twice for no reason he could see. It was the heart of railroading. Stopping, waiting, moving. All the pride and glory stuff, all that Ride with a capital *R*—that was mostly talk to impress women. The real thing was slower, harder, and simpler.

Halfway to New Ulm, he saw a kid with a hose wetting down the bluff that dropped to the tracks. The kid saw Harp and raised the hose in a friendly salute, letting the water arc high. A rainbow shimmered behind it. Harp waved back.

Connection enough, he thought.

The porch of the Grand Hotel was seventeen hundred feet of white pine. A plaque said it was the world's largest wooden porch. Their table overlooked the staging area for the carriage line. Farther off was a gazebo where a wedding was in progress.

"I don't suppose," Lane said, "you've thought about what happens next."

The waiter placed two flutes of champagne on the table. His jacket was red, but when he walked to the other end of the porch, it turned blue. Some trick of light.

"Rose is moving to Boston," Lane said. "She wants me to go with her."

Slater put his elbow on the table. "Don't do that. It's a terrible place."

He could see her life in Boston—the bedrooms, the alliances, the betrayals. The late nights and the later mornings. He thought about telling her, laying it all out, but he didn't have the energy.

"Have you ever been there?" she asked.

"No."

In the staging area, a horse pissed. A song wafted up from the wedding party.

"I wonder if there's anywhere around here that sells glue," Lane said.

For dinner that evening, they ordered lobster Newburg from room service, spending Dickinson's money. When Lewis came in with the cart, Slater was cross-legged on the bed, his face bent over a paper bag. His shirt was off and he was sweating. The bellhop's dignified friendship didn't slip. "Is he all right?" he asked.

"He will be," Lane said. When Lewis left, she took the bag and inhaled.

Later they lay on the bed and let the lobster get cold. The ceiling went out of focus. Nowheresville, Lane said. That's where we're going.

The best thing about Nowheresville was that there was practically nothing there. No bricks, no Boston, no Grand Hotel. Nothing was allowed past the borders of Nowheresville, though somehow the clop of horses made it in. Lane took off her clothes and tied a white scarf to her ankle, a blue scarf to each wrist. I am where the scarves are not, she said. The colors flowed, silk tangled. Slater rounded his back to the ceiling, on top of her; tuxedoed horses clip-clopped up his spine. Don't leave, he said. He kept seeing Lewis or Harp or the lobster in his peripheral vision, and it screwed up his mojo. Finally she bit him on the ear. Go into the guilt and out the other side, she told him. They humped a long, soaring melody while someone knocked on the door, requesting quiet and making threats. They wrapped themselves in ignorance, in fine oblivion. The scarves tangled, the bed shook. They made love in five forward speeds and reverse.

Harp left Cedar Rapids at noon, riding a flatcar. When the rain came, he covered his bag with a sheet of plastic, but the wind ripped it to tatters. It snapped and shivered behind him, a transparent hippie flag.

His train started and stopped, but Harp didn't rise and the crew didn't care. He woke at odd times and heard men walking past. A thin line of saliva ran down his cheek as he lifted his head from the flatcar floor. Each time he woke, his strange position surprised him. After each stop, his memory was washed by the wind.

Riding the locals made him insignificant. Trainmen answered his questions with straight-faced nods and grunts. His questions were simple. When does it leave? Where is it going? He was living in freight time. He took advantage of what came. A boxcar, a local going south, a piece of cardboard. The dynamite had come his way and he had blown up Broodson's barn. He didn't expect others to understand, not even Slater.

That evening, standing on a flatcar at a siding, he felt a humble righteousness. If you were strong enough to walk the solitary path, you could hear the world turn. Once you did that, it was easy to see the future.

He knew the world would not forgive him and he didn't care. He wasn't like Slater. He was hungry and his shoulders ached from nights on the ground. All stuff he could deal with.

Late in the afternoon, he found an open box and rode it to Sleepy Eye. The sun came in from the side so that the forest was projected in moving shadows along the inner wall of the car. Five miles from town, the engine pushed all the cars onto a lumber-mill siding. Harp could see he was going to be stranded. He considered grabbing on to the engine and riding it to the next yard. The crew probably wouldn't mind. But he had a rule against riding engines. He waited until it left, put on his pack, and started walking.

The track was moderate gauge and rusted, shiny here and there where it curved. Without regret, without the slightest edge of pity, Harp stepped up on the rail and walked heel to toe through the quilted light, never stepping off, never looking up.

They left the Grand Hotel the next morning, checking out early before Lewis could tell them they had to leave. After the ferry docked, they drove south along the Lake, passing through Cross Village and Good Hart. Near Little Traverse Bay, a cowboy on a billboard advertised cigarettes. *Come to Where the Flavor Is*. It seemed to Slater he had spent a long time where the flavor wasn't.

A couple hours from Wolverine, he stopped the Jeep at a marina where a daily boat went to Manitou Island.

"It's a nature preserve," Lane said. "There's nothing out there but nature."

"Nothing suits me."

A small boat took them across. Three other campers rode with them, all with full gear. Slater and Lane had a sheet of plastic, a rope, and a bag of sweet corn. The other campers headed west; Slater and Lane hiked east. They camped at the edge of the island in sand and marram grass, draping the plastic over the rope for a tent, anchoring the corners with rocks. Lane boiled the corn in a dented pot they borrowed from a ranger. A makeshift store by the small dock, open at odd times, sold them coffee and apples.

They stayed for three days and saw no one on their end of the island. Every day was sand and skin, and sunlight reflected off water. At night Lane held him and accused him of leaving. "You and your going-away eyes."

"You're the one going to Boston," he said. "Not me."

Days were glueless. It was a new and unspoiled life. Harp and the Blue Dart weren't part of it.

On the second day, Slater discovered a beach they called Nameless Beach. They swam naked, then lay drying in the sun. He told her about Ed Dickinson. About putting the knife in his chest.

She brushed a fly off her hip bone. "How did it feel? Killing him."

His answer surprised him. "Wonderful. It felt wonderful that it was him dying, and not me."

Lane made a noise like a hum. Slater put his hand between her breasts and felt her heart beat. It seemed like a requirement, to be aware of each beat.

They lay there all afternoon, listening to the Lake and the sound of their breathing. The island was bliss, she said.

Actual bliss. She had been there, and not on glue either. It was a real place. Sometimes, if you were lucky, you could slide yourself in.

Slater asked her what it was like. "It's not anywhere you've ever been," she told him. "It's like falling. It's like being halfway down and knowing there's still a long way to go."

When the deputies went home at six, Rose locked the doors of dispatch. Barely ten minutes later, two high school kids, a guy and a girl, came up the steps and hovered around the entrance. The glass was made so they could not see in, though Rose could see them.

Freaks, she thought at first. Looking past the crop-top and platform shoes, she decided the girl was a wide-eyed innocent, dressed according to guys' taste, but otherwise sensible. The dude looked more like the real deal: a mohawk in Northern Michigan. Must be a lonely life, Rose thought. She almost identified with him. At the same time, she wanted to tell the girl to run.

There was a button and speaker box beside the door where drunks and concerned citizens could make after-hours inquiries and demand relief from whatever perplexed them. Rose pressed the corresponding button on the dispatch unit to eavesdrop on the Youth of Today.

"No, baby," the guy said. "I told you before. We don't go running to the Man with this. We keep the bitchin' thing ourselves."

Happily, the girl was secretly in charge. She agreed with her boyfriend every chance she could while she played him like a matador with a little red cape. Her skill both encouraged and depressed Rose. Why can't we ever just confront them? Why does it always have to be eyelashes and smiles?

The girl's going to make a wonderful wife someday, she thought. Goddamn it.

When they finally pressed the button, Rose buzzed them in. The guy began talking first. They'd been out on the tracks, he said, just hanging.

"Taking a shortcut home," the girl corrected.

"Right. And we found something interesting. We decided to give it to the Man."

"I'm the Man," Rose said.

He paused and then said, "Cool."

The bitchin' thing was cool, too. It was Michael Slater's knife, she was sure. Rose recognized it from the initials. The blade was crusted with dried blood.

"Is there a reward or something?" the guy asked.

"There is," Rose said. "You have the satisfaction of knowing you did the right thing. I'll make sure this gets logged in."

The girl bought it. Mohawk looked disappointed, but he was forced to play along.

Run, Rose thought.

— 28 —

"WRONGFUL DEATH," MATTHEWS said.

Slater tapped the tines of a plastic fork against the console. Matthews had a hundred wrongful-death stories.

"Two guys," he said. "Joe and his pal. Let's call him Devilish Don. Names changed to protect the innocent. These two guys do everything together."

It was someone's birthday; a few craggy pieces of sheet cake had been left in the break room. The piece Slater was eating had the letters C-A-R on it. He didn't know any Carol or Carl or Carter. But there were plenty of people he didn't know. Matthews, on the couch, had his own piece of cake.

"These two guys go to the same school," he said. "They think the same thoughts, dream the same dreams, date the same girls. Especially a little whirligig named Sandy. Sweet little Sandy. One day Joe whips out a diamond and marries the girl. So his pal Devilish Don has to make do with her sister."

"Wife Swappin' Guys Meet the Blister Sisters," Slater said. "What'd they hire you for? Surveillance? Skip trace?"

Matthews put his plate on the cushion. A former PI, he still worked the occasional case. "I told you before. I don't do skip trace."

Slater checked the monitors. On screen five, Rose was doing a bit called Men Are Scum, Part Two. On the other screens, a researcher dressed in white used a low voltage wire to make a monkey ejaculate. The piece was interesting visually, but the voice-over killed it. Highest standards of humane treatment, et cetera, et cetera, in big-ass vowels and crisp consonants.

"By the way," Matthews said. "I saw your girlfriend downstairs. She's working late, all by herself."

"She's not my girlfriend," Slater said.

"Well, she should be. If you had any sense."

Slater was thinking of taking the monkey-spunk clip and sticking it in the puff piece he had just finished for the Dairy Council—*Wholesome Goodness from America's Dairy Farmers*. With yet another voice-over he didn't want inside his head.

"Well, boss," Matthews said, "these two guys, Joe and Don, are driving a one-lane logging road. Going hunting. No one around but God, maybe not even him. Got the ice chest open and they're working on a few Heinekens. Pretty soon, they start to feel the call. So Joe stops the truck, steps to side of the road, and unzips. Don takes the other side. No one around for miles."

Slater stole a glance at the monitors. Screen three sparkled with sunlit water. Manitou.

"The woods are quiet. Big trees, clear skies. Maybe a distant chain saw and two men peeing in the dirt." He pointed his fork at Slater. "And that's a beautiful sound."

They had no need for clothes on Manitou. The island was Lane on top of him in a clear plastic tent while ten thousand stars tried to get in. She said she felt lonely. That it was all about sex. That it was all about Harp. That the path led nowhere. He said he felt lucky and doomed and guilty and scared, but never lonely. Not when he was with her.

On the other side of the island, coyotes howled. They were spirit coyotes, or how else could they have gotten to Manitou?

One morning he woke and she was eating the last of the Granny Smiths. You'll always love him more than you love me, she said.

"Get to the death part," he said to Matthews.

"You know," his friend said, "everybody else up here has three screens. You've got six. Why the hell do you need so many?"

"I'm a scavenger," he said. "What happened to Devilish Don?"

"Nothing. He takes a piss. Then he hears a crack, looks over, and sees a tree come down on Joe. Dead. Right in the middle of doing his business."

Slater pressed the fork gently into his lower lip. If we had stayed on the island, he thought, I would have figured out how to make her happy. There would have been sweet corn every night of our lives. I would have stolen the names from the stars and invented jazz. We didn't need glue. We didn't need Harp.

"A tree falls in the forest," he said. "So where's the wrongful?"

"That's what Joe's family asks. They start in speculating. Maybe Joe didn't meet his rightful end. Maybe his fate was misdelivered. I mean, the only person who saw it is Joe's good pal. The one we call Devilish Don. Maybe this devil had something to do with it. All we know for sure is that he's a long way from help. Fifteen miles before he can get to a phone. The sheriff and deputy meet up with him and they all drive back to Joe. And guess what?"

Slater moved the shuttle control. The color bloomed on screen three. "Joe's gone. A talking fish wins the lottery."

"Yeah, right. You sit here all day watching this stuff, and pretty soon nothing's real anymore. You ever think about that?"

Slater looked at his screens. "It's real to me."

Matthews shifted in his seat. They listened to the hum of speakers. "Listen, Mike. Memories are wonderful things. But you've got too many of 'em."

Matthews dug into his coat pocket and came out with a videotape. "I brought you something real. From Erickson's office. The guy's crooked in about twelve different ways. I set up a camera, but there's no signal on the tape. Thought maybe you could work some magic."

Slater put the tape in the drawer next to his canister of amphetamines. "So where's Joe?"

Matthews smiled. "Joe's still there. His soul's gone, but his body's right there under the tree. Naturally, the hunting trip is off. Our man Don drives back and breaks the news to Joe's wife, the lovely little Sandy. Extends his sympathy. Gives her his warmest regards. A touch of human kindness. Gets her pregnant."

"I knew it." He wanted a Smiling O. But not with Matthews there.

"Fast as you want, they're married. And now Devilish Don's got all the nice things Joe used to have. Decent truck, wildcat wife, nest egg from the insurance company. Can't drink Heineken anymore, but hell, there's lots of beers to choose from." Matthews picked up Slater's plate and finished the cake. "This is America. You don't like one beer, drink another."

"And then along comes Matthews," Slater said. "I suppose you proved it was all a setup. It was Sweet Little Sandy out there with a chain saw, putting that tree down so she could run off with Devilish Don. They planned it together."

Matthews shook his head. "Don was innocent. Sandy, too. Maybe they didn't wait long enough after Joe's death. But the man knew what he wanted and he went for it. Got a nice set-up now."

"That was your big discovery? That's what you told Joe's family?"

"I wasn't working for Joe's family. I was working for Devilish Don."

"But you said –"

"Huh-uh. You assumed. Now think about it. A man stops to answer nature's call, and he ends up answering Nature's Call. What's that suggest to you?"

Slater hit rewind on the monkey piece. "Bad luck. A guy stops for a piss and a tree blows down on him."

"I never said the wind was blowing."

"Falls."

"I never said falls."

"You said it wasn't cut."

"I said Sandy wasn't the cutter."

Rose was on screen one. Slater would not see her again. Not in this lifetime. He swiveled his chair until he was facing Matthews. "You called him Devilish Don to make me think he was guilty. To mess with me."

"Devilish Don is what everyone called him. Besides, isn't that *your* job? To confuse and mislead?"

"*Every Day We Bend the Truth*. It's chiseled in stone over the door."

"Damn right." Matthews sat back, arms out wide like a man who caught a big fish. "Okay. Turns out there's some shaggy-ass logging crew running loose. That far-off chain saw? These jokers don't even know what part of the woods they're in. They're bringing down trees that don't belong to them and that's big, freakin' shit—that's major dollars if you get caught. When they hear the truck, they wake up and hightail it. But one of these maples is hung up in the canopy. Then Joe comes along with his bladder full of Heineken." Matthews gave a low-octave grunt. "They were wrongful from start to finish, the shaggy-ass bastards."

"Did they pay?"

"They paid until it hurt, thanks to Matthews here."

"But the money went to Sandy, right. And Don. Not Joe's family."

"Money's easy. Satisfaction's the hard thing. His family found out the real story. What more do you want? Wasn't nothing gonna bring Joe back."

Matthews got up to go. "By the way, someone you know is getting fired next week. Advance tip. The body bags are piling up."

— 29 —

AFTER MANITOU, THERE was nothing but rain. They got soaked on the ferry; the Jeep smelled like wet wool. The plastic tent was wadded up in back.

When they got back to Wolverine, they found the door to the house standing open. A notice said the electric would be shut off in five days. It was early afternoon and they went to Lane's room and slept without touching. An hour later the phone woke them. It rang for what seemed like forever before Lane reached for it. Slater saw that her shoulders were sunburned; the skin beneath her arms was pale. Gathering her clothes, she carried the phone from the room. When she returned, she leaned against the wall, her head tipped back. Her hair fell across her face, her shirt hung open. She seemed skinny, and tired to the point of exhaustion.

"It was Rose," she told him. "Some kids found your knife."

Slater sat up, the sheet bunched around his waist. "Kids? What kids?"

"Rose will take care of it," Lane said. "She'll make a deal. But you have to leave town."

There was sand between his toes. "I can't leave," he said. "I don't know where to go."

She gave him her deerlike, empty-eyed look. "Don't worry. I thought of that too."

That evening, Slater gathered his belongings. Rose came over to watch him go.

"Men have a plan for you," she said to Lane. "It's their plan, and it's not even a plan they like."

Slater put a box of his belongings in the Jeep. Rose stood in the drive, the sky purple-orange behind her.

"Be nice," Lane said.

"You leave for ten days without a word to anyone. Running around with Thing 1 and Thing 2. And you want *me* to be nice?"

"Michael's leaving," Lane said. "Isn't that what you want?"

"The thing is," she said, "they don't even know it's a plan, because they're too horny to see beyond their own erections. They walk around in these six-inch force fields, too dazed to realize what's really going on."

"Why don't you let us say goodbye," Slater said. "You can come back and gloat later."

"Basically, they just want to be fed. You start out holding hands and end up shoveling shit, while Mr. Right sits on his mile-wide butt watching golf on television. Men don't want love. Men are scared shitless of love. The best that can happen is they drink at home and jack off in the shower." She moved closer to Lane. "I don't know why you put up with them."

Slater put the last of his stuff in the Jeep. "Maybe it's my six-inch force field."

"Maybe it's your imagination."

"I want my knife back."

"Technically, it belongs to the county. *If* I log it in, that is. Whether that happens is completely up to you."

Slater looked at Lane, but she didn't meet his eyes.

"Just be prepared," Rose said. "Because we don't have to follow the plan. We can burn down the old and make a plan of our own."

"Now you sound like Harp."

"I sincerely hope not. Harp was one of the biggest male chauvinists I've ever had the misfortune of knowing." In the trees, a woodpecker worked. "He treated you like a hood ornament, babe."

Lane blinked. "He treated me okay."

"Was that before or after the felonies?"

Slater turned to her. "Harp didn't blow up the Whispering Sands. Charlie set him up. You might want to tell your boss that."

Rose was delighted. "Jesus, Lane, you're right. He really doesn't know shit from Shinola."

Lane didn't answer. She had her eyes closed.

"Listen," Rose said. "Telling Lazenbeck about Charlie is like telling the sun about the sky. Why not tell fish about water? Guess what? They've already met." She looked at Slater triumphantly. "Charlie and Lazenbeck are two halves of a whole. The only question is who's doing who. When I figure that out, some people are going to be very surprised."

The sun was nearly down; moths were beginning to circle the porch light.

"Harp was my friend," Slater said. "Is my friend."

Rose raised a palm in the dimming light. "I understand completely. You have very poor taste in men. You're a lot like a woman that way."

Lane opened her eyes, but she was far away. She was looking where the sunset had been or at the things inside her eyes. Contained. She was contained, Slater thought, and he would never get back in. Even if he stayed. There'd be sex and glue, and there'd be nights chasing things, and maybe once in a while he would get up close enough to sniff the person inside that skull, but he was never getting in. Not really. And neither was Rose. And neither was Harp. Harp would have known that from the beginning.

"Because I'm a nice person, I'm going to give you two hours to leave," Rose said. "If I ever see you near this house again, your ass will be incarcerated."

Harp rode into Granite Falls crouched in a coal car, a gritty bin funneling down to two huge chutes. The slanting sides made it impossible to sit, so he squatted and tried not to think about what would happen if the chutes came open. The grit came at him in the wind, sharp as the stars overhead.

When the train stopped, he left the yard for a nearby gas station. Inside, there was crap for sale. Every place had crap for sale. There was a huge crap factory somewhere, churning it out. Harp, a black beast from the yards, strode past the shelves of crap and picked up the dowel with the key.

In the men's room, he stripped to his underwear. With a bunched-up T-shirt, he sponged the soot from his chest, arms, legs, and feet. Water flooded the floor; his pack hung on the doorknob. At the last minute, he decided to leave his face sooty. It seemed natural and right.

When he stepped outside, he was amazed at how bright the night was.

Fuckin' A, he said. Granite Falls.

Here I am.

The restroom door said *Men*.

After Rose left, they made the porch their bed. Cedar beneath, stars above, Lane in between. He rested his hand on her back, on the spot he loved, the low valley just before the rise. She didn't move; her breathing was slow. Slater's left hand held a Stroh's. Off and on, above them, he saw the old coot from the Hixton Party Store, the wooden fortune-teller with the concessionaire's stare. He had to keep blinking him away.

Still on top of him, Lane reached for the bottle. The beer on her breath mixed with the smell of her flesh. In the big empty hangar of his mind, he imagined his erection, illuminated by Lane's strange light. He tensed, she answered. Under the comfort of her weight, her sharp and cutting hip bones, he drifted into a coral-colored world. When he came to, he saw the knife, his initials on the handle dulled by rain and etched with brown blood.

To make the world go away, he took her head in both hands, aware of the full length of her. He kissed her in the coded language of the rails. Two long kisses—releasing brakes. One long kiss and two short—second train following. One long—approaching station.

At the end of the last kiss, he poured the rest of the beer on her back and she came down hard, her teeth hit his, her skeleton knocked at his pelvis. He spread the cold beer over his favorite spot on her back, felt the cold on his balls, warm mixing cold until it burst. That's all being alive ever was, he thought, just one long thrusting kiss. All the parts in between were dreams.

His time was nearly up. The party store coot floated above them. "It's quiet in here now," he said, his wooden face come suddenly to life. "But wait till the bars close. Be a regular pig pile here then."

Finishing, he wrapped his hands around her back and pushed into her. But the release that promised contentment brought paranoia instead.

ALONE IN THE guest room at Hidden Mist, Slater stared at the curtained wall. At the other end of the room, a glass wall provided a private view of Lake Michigan. A money view. No one but the gulls and gods could see in. Slater felt out of place with such privilege, though he'd been given the room by Charlie. Welcomed, practically. The room had been Lane's room in the days when Lane stayed at Hidden Mist.

On the curtain beside the bed, six or seven couples were outlined in various stages of sexual union, all of them unlikely. *Gymnasts at Play*, it might have been called. A Beardsley rip, or maybe it really was Beardsley. The men were certainly huge enough. When he pressed a button on a remote, a motor hummed and the rippled lovers disappeared into folds of gray silk. Behind the curtain was a mirrored wall. In it, Slater saw himself, remote in hand, a scared look on his face. Awaiting disposition.

To pass the time, he read Harp's book, *The Price of Beaver*. He was halfway through already. The hero was an explorer named Etienne Brulé. An advance man for

Champlain, Brulé lived in the wild, scouting for the French. One day, he said fuck a duck and walked away to live with the Algonquin. He was tired of trading for beaver pelts. He had enough pelts to fill a lifetime. He wanted to wake up in the high country of Lake Superior and live by his wits and prayers. Brulé had no attachments. He was also a double agent. He liked to screw around. Naturally, he came to a very bad end.

Slater had just started to read when Charlie appeared in the doorway. He was wearing a red and yellow Hawaiian shirt.

"Pretty fabulous, huh, champ? Did you take a gander at the curtain?" Charlie unfurled the silhouette of a woman giving head to a half beast with antlers. "Mirrored wall, free liquor." He let the curtain go and stepped back. "You can test out this little setup later. We're going out tonight. You, me, and the Spreadables. Dinner."

Slater put the book down. "I know why you're letting me stay here. You think Harp will get in touch. I'm bait. That's the truth."

Charlie walked to the balcony. He opened a slider that immediately came off its track. "The truth isn't all that serviceable in my particular line of work. Maybe you've noticed. And you're wrong about Harp. Lazenbeck would like to flog his naked ass in the town square, true. But that's his psychosis. I'm more about sticking it to the undersheriff."

"I heard you were in cahoots."

Charlie's eyes got wide and merry. "Cahoots! I love it! What decade did you say you were from, pal? No, I like the undersheriff just where he is. People get too much power, it's a dangerous thing. You got anything a tad more cheerful you can wear tonight?"

"I think I'll pass."

"This is life, champ. You can't pass." He gave up on the slider, leaving it open. "Good food, good drink, pretty girls. Yours is named Shannon. She doesn't put out, but she's allegedly quite nimble. She can put her foot behind her ear. Or so I'm told."

Slater couldn't help picturing it. "Told?"

"By her husband. Her ex, actually. To whom I owe ten large. Which is why we put up with Shannon." Charlie waggled his eyebrows. "That and the hope that she'll put her foot behind her ear."

"Not in the mood," Slater said.

"I can fix that." He took some capsules from a pill bottle and put them into Slater's shirt pocket. "Take one of these, champ. No charge, I got plenty."

"Maybe some other night."

"Another interesting fact about Shannon," Charlie said. "She has friends in queer places. I think you've met Rose? The town thespian?"

"I don't care about Rose anymore."

"Me neither," Charlie said. "I'm not interested in Rose the human being, with all her nasty little juices. But Rose the office eavesdropper interests me a great deal. She seems to know exactly where Lazenbeck gets his hush money. Plus I hear she has something sharp and shiny. Something you might want." Charlie walked to the doorway. "We have reservations at seven. I'll find a shirt for you."

Slater waited until Charlie left, then measured himself again in the mirror, looking at his eyes for signs of anger. But anger had fled. He needed a haircut.

With the barest pressure on the remote, he closed the curtain, bringing the libidinous gymnasts back into view. He studied them without a trace of prurience. He and Lane had tried some of the positions themselves. That one, and that one, and a little of bit of that. It seemed like a lifetime ago.

The Pheasantry overlooked a golf course and the tame waters of a man-made lake. At the door was a college kid in a gravy-stained-blazer, greeting customers with rehearsed enthusiasm. Charlie and the two girls breezed by without a glance and took the last open table by the window.

The room was crowded with young, brightly dressed diners. There was a festivity about them that Slater thought must be temporary. It could not be maintained in the face of what life had to offer.

"Heaven on earth," Tracy said. It turned out she was reading from the drink list. The other woman, Shannon, was Rose's friend from the *Tecumseh*. The one who wouldn't put her hand in the drop box.

"What did you say your name was again?" Shannon asked him.

Charlie answered before Slater could speak. "This here is Slate the Great, my sister's old new meat. And my close personal friend."

Tracy kept her eyes on the menu. "You don't have close friends, Charlie. You have contacts."

"I have as many friends as the next guy."

The women looked at Slater.

"Listen," Slater said, "I appreciate you giving me a place to stay and all—"

"And loaning you my shirt," Charlie said. "Don't undersell the shirt."

Slater was wearing a white rayon shirt with large pink

birds. He opened his palms toward Charlie. "Whatever. The thing is—"

"Listen to this guy suck up," Charlie said. "Maestro, a little suck-up music, please."

Before Slater could continue, Shannon stood up and made her way toward the restrooms. She was taller than anyone in the room; several heads turned as she went.

"Seven o'clock and all's well," Tracy said. "She has to wash her fucking hands every hour on the hour. You can set your watch by it."

"We're not here to judge," Charlie said. "Remember, we like addictive behavior."

Tracy told Charlie to get screwed.

"Now there's an idea. I used to do that on a regular basis. I'm quite familiar with the entire procedure."

When the waiter appeared, Charlie ordered an expensive pinot gris. After it came, he turned to Slater. "You were in the middle of some kind of opening statement, I believe? A declaration of some sort?"

Slater shook his head, giving up. Nothing could get through Charlie's cloud of bullshit.

Shannon, returning from the restroom, created another trail of turned heads. "Want to stay healthy and have a good life?" She held up her wineglass so Charlie could pour. "Just wash your hands once an hour. It works."

"With all due respect," Charlie said, "if it's the good life you seek, I offer a far better alternative."

"What's that?" Shannon asked. "The life of a dealer? Pimping? Selling drugs?"

Charlie shushed her, then turned to Slater. "Think of it this way, pal. When it's snowy and you've been out on the slopes all day, and you stayed up all night the night before hitting on some chick, and you want to stay up all night again hitting on some other chick, because when it comes right down to it the first one wasn't all that charming and it's cold as a motherfuck out, what do you need? You need a pick-me-up. More precisely, you need someone to stop by with a pick-me-up." He poked a fork in the air. "And that person is you, Slate. Twenty-four-hour delivery. Ten percent off the top. You already have the perfect car for it."

Slater looked out the window, trying to ignore him. Outside, two golfers were chumming it up on the fairway.

"Mike Slater, See You Later. Johnny-on-the-spot with the pills and the whatnot. Think about it." He winked. "Plenty of free you-know-what."

Shannon poured him some wine, and he took a sip. It didn't seem to matter whether he answered or not. Charlie was all send and no receive.

Jesus, Slater thought. He completes me.

"I have two penises," Charlie said, midway through dinner. He pointed his fork at Shannon. "One's just for special occasions."

"Really?" Shannon didn't look up. "Like Christmas and stuff? New Year's Eve?"

"Uh-huh." He chewed a piece of veal. "I have a higher co-pay, of course, but otherwise, it's great. Women love it."

"You sure it's not just extra work for them?" Shannon asked.

"Or something else that gathers dust," Tracy added.

"Funny," Charlie said. "You ladies are a riot."

Slater glanced at his watch. It was five minutes to eight.

"And what about you?" Charlie said to Shannon. "What's your story?"

She took the napkin from her lap and dabbed her mouth. She sat with her spine perfectly straight. "I don't have any," she said. "Penises, that is."

Charlie and Tracy exchanged a glance.

"That's great," Charlie said. "Terrific. The world could use more people like you. More dickless girls. Don't you think, Trace?"

"If it's true," Tracy said. "We have to take her word for it."

Charlie cut a bit of veal but didn't eat it. "Well, there's a point. We've never really seen, have we? I mean, you seem to be having a good time lately. Soaking up the sun, and all. But I've noticed you like to stay more or less covered up. Fully dressed, so to speak."

"So that makes me a freak? Because I don't like to get high and prance around nude like everyone else?" She looked nervously toward the restrooms.

"Hey, you can dress like a nun and read the Bible all day. To each his own. We're an accepting lot at Hidden Mist. I was just wondering if there's something we could do to make you feel more. . ." He picked up his fork and swirled his bite of veal in the air. "I don't know. More comfortable."

"Less uptight," Tracy said. "Not so frigid."

"Maybe she's the only one around here with any morals left," Slater said.

Charlie put the fork on his plate. "You cut me to the quick, my friend." He clapped his hand over his heart. "Seriously. I'm wounded."

Shannon stood up. "Or maybe I just prefer to keep my clothes on."

She went off to wash her hands. For a tall woman, she had a way of walking that was almost like floating across the room.

"She's a slave to it," Tracy said. "Her hands aren't even dirty."

Charlie pushed his plate away. "There are worse things."

"Really," Tracy said. "Name five."

"Withdrawal. Being broke. Insulting a man after he befriends you and loans you his shirt. Sleeping in a cardboard box behind the Dairy Queen. Clowns. How many is that?"

Tracy took out a cigarette. "You're a sick man, Charles."

"I keep hearing that from people who depend on me for sustenance." He turned to Slater. "Stinkin' drunk clowns who put their hands everywhere. *That's* immoral. I'm providing a service, for crying out loud. What exactly are you providing?"

Slater looked from Charlie to Tracy and back. "Okay. You got me."

"We knew that," Tracy said. "The question is, for how long?"

The runner-up for the Miss Auto World Expo was coming in as they were going out. She wore five-inch heels and a silver, shimmery dress, and she nodded at Charlie as they passed—a customer, Slater guessed. In the front seat of the BMW, Charlie and Tracy debated whether she had achieved a state of Perpetual Fuckability.

"She's not fake enough," Charlie said. "She comes across as too real. For PF, you need a Barbie Gone Bad kind of look."

"Not true," Tracy said. "That's not where fuckability is. It's all in the eyes."

"Only if you're an eye man," Charlie said. "Some say it's the voice. Anyway, men don't really want PF. In fact,

PF kind of turns us off." Charlie glanced over his shoulder, including Slater in his theory. "Always fuckable is never fuckable, right, champ? I mean, where's the arc? We want to see the kitten become the tiger. It's a Zen thing."

"How would you know?" Tracy said. "Maybe we should ask someone who's still in the game." She hooked a thumb at Slater.

"He doesn't count," Charlie said. "He's been with my sister."

"So?"

"All roads lead to Rome with Lane. Love is a many-phallused splendor for that girl."

Tracy snorted. "News flash, Charles. They don't call it 'Rome' anymore. They never did." She pointed a thumb at Slater. "Anyway, he doesn't seem to have an opinion."

"I've noticed that," Charlie said. "You have to poke him with a stick to get him to speak." Charlie met Slater's eyes in the rearview. "That's what I like about you, Slate. You're so mellow. I envy that."

"I sincerely doubt that," Slater said.

"Sure I do. I envy everything. That's what gets me out of bed in the morning. I'm envious of rich and poor alike. I envy the wino his buzz."

Slater looked at the back of Tracy's head. The dark roots. Even from behind, her head looked like a wicked place. Made of polyester, tinsel, and wax.

"I envy your reticence," Charlie said. "I wouldn't want it personally. But I enjoy envying it."

The car turned down the dirt track through the woods.

"Perhaps you've heard my story," Charlie said. "Once I felt bad because I had no shoes. Then I met a man who had no feet."

"Did you envy his stumps?" Slater asked.

"I sold him some drugs. The next day he wanted more, and I envied his need." The extravagant outdoor lights of Hidden Mist shifted spookily as the two-track curved through the trees. "Anybody else try that new speed?" Charlie asked. "My snot's been orange all day."

When they got back, Slater went straight to his room. He lay on the bed fully dressed and reviewed the destruction, the screwups he had caused since coming back. It was intolerable, unfaceable.

He should leave, of course. Nothing was stopping him except the conviction that Harp would come back. And the idea that he might somehow see Lane.

He had almost dozed off when the rap came on his door, swift and explosive. He jumped, expecting the police. Surely he was about to be arrested. Instead the door opened slightly and Shannon poked her head inside.

"You mind?" She entered and closed the door behind her. "They're shooting up down there." She jerked her head in the direction of Charlie's room. "I hate that."

"Really? I thought—" He stopped himself before he could do more damage.

"Because I'm living here for a while, you thought I was a junkie?"

"No." Slater got the remote and brightened the overhead lights. "I mean, I don't know what I thought."

Shannon walked over to the full-length window. The darkness beyond it sent her reflection back toward Slater. The slider was still off its track and let the night breeze in.

"Charlie's Snatchatorium. That's what Rose calls it. The House on Snatchview Lane. I'm not a permanent resident. I'm just hanging out for a while." She found Slater's eyes. "Like you. You're not a junkie, are you?"

"Not to my knowledge, no. Not the last time I checked."

She sat in the room's only chair, a thin-limbed piece of art that looked like half a teacup. It made her look even taller than she was. "Do you think he really has two penises?"

Slater didn't smile. It would be easy to hurt her. "I took it as a joke. Don't you think?"

She pulled the curtain out a little, unfurling two lovers. "I don't know. Some people have extra body parts."

When she let go, the lovers went back into the fold. Slater pictured her with her foot behind her ear and was immediately ashamed. Maybe it's the shirt, he thought. He still had Charlie's shirt on.

Shannon tapped a little heels-together, toes-together rhythm with her feet.

"Could I ask you a favor? You want to drive me somewhere? For drinks."

"We've just had drinks."

"I know. But I need to see Jimmy."

"Where's the Karmann Ghia?"

"Jimmy has it. It's his, actually."

Slater didn't need much convincing. It was something to do. Anything was better than being alone with his regrets. "Sure. Let's go see Jimmy. I'm all about that."

Partway down the stairs, Charlie intercepted them. He was wearing red, white, and blue boxer shorts and a T-shirt that said *Shake Well*. "You two through with Ding Dong School already?" he asked.

"Leave us alone, Charles," Shannon said. "We'll be back later."

Charlie snapped the band of his boxers. "Take care of that shirt, champ."

They got all the way to the driveway before Shannon turned around, going back inside to wash her hands.

Slater eased the Ford out of the shed while Shannon waited outside on the gravel. When he opened the door for her, she bent and picked up something off the ground.

"Gross." She threw a hundred-dollar bill at him. "I can't believe I touched it." She sat stiffly in the Ford, waving her hands in the air as if to dry them.

Slater put the bill in his shirt pocket. "Must be Charlie's. I guess drinks are on him tonight."

Shannon took several deep breaths. When she calmed down, she said. "Jimmy will mix doubles at the price of singles. He's my ex."

"I guessed that."

He kept his eyes on the winding track though the woods. When they reached Highway 22, Shannon gave him directions to the Windship.

"We used to work there together," she said. "After we separated, I mean. Jimmy hired me."

"As a waitress?"

"Dessert chef. Chocolate tortes. Key lime pie, some nights."

"Don't your hands get dirty making tortes?"

She ignored the joke. "It was a bad situation. I couldn't be around him with all that food. All those ingredients."

She pointed left down a dark road. In the distance was the floodlit outline of a roof.

"Ingredients?"

"Food was a big part of our sex life. The main part,

really. It's so tactile. Have you ever really *felt* food?"

"I don't know. I guess not."

"That's the way we used to do it. Jimmy and me." She looked out at the dark. The empty road was a place for confidences. "He rubbed spaghetti on me and I disappeared."

The Windship had imitation gaslights out front. Slater parked in the lot and looked at her.

"I'm not a freak," she said. "Don't think anything like that."

"I was thinking you have a nice smile." It was only partly true. In fact, he was thinking about kissing her.

"I don't have the right kind of lips for smiling."

The exterior lights of the Windship flickered and caught the dings in the windshield. Slater held on to the wheel, though the Ford was stopped.

"People do terrible stuff," she said. "Including me. I've done terrible stuff to people. I just want to do something good."

"I'm sure you have," Slater said. "We all have."

"You helped us on the ferry. You didn't have to."

"I was just being friendly."

"Rose said you'd do it. She said she had your number."

He realized she was waiting for him to open the door. She didn't want to touch the handle. He got out, walked around, and opened it.

"I was wondering how close you are with Rose," he said. "She has something of mine that I'd like to get back."

"The knife. Charlie told me."

"Why does Charlie care about my knife?"

Shannon hunched her skinny shoulders. "He cares because he knows you care. If he has something you want, he can control you. That's how he is."

"The knife's not worth anything," Slater said. "But if you could get it for me, it would mean a lot."

"Rose is pissed at me. She thinks I'm ruining my life by staying at Hidden Mist. I don't know when I'll see her again."

She turned and did her float-walk to the door. When Slater opened it, a group of six or eight people streamed out, all laughing and tanned.

Shannon straightened her shoulders and made herself even taller. "Spaghetti and Mountain Dew," she said. "God, it was like nothing on earth."

You Can Lead a Horse to Water, the scrawl above the urinal read, *I'll Wait Here with Your Wife.*

There was a small window in the men's room and Slater opened it, breathing the night air. The Windship was awash with privilege and alcohol. After Shannon introduced him around, he fled. He couldn't stand the blood-filled faces of her friends, and they would no doubt find him depressing. He found himself depressing. Seeing it reflected in the faces of strangers would only make it worse.

By the towel dispenser was a corkboard protected by a sheet of Plexiglas. Behind it were Polaroids and snapshots of topless women, customers apparently. A card at the bottom offered a free pitcher in return for racy snapshots. An amazing number of women were willing to strip for the camera. Many of them held pennants with team names. A woman with centerfold measurements wore only a necktie. Her photo did nothing for Slater. The ones he liked best were simple shots—women who seemed to admit their nudity without comment, without making it into a costume.

Near one corner was a woman who looked quite a bit like Lane, but shorter and flat-chested. Someone had added a mustache. The photo weakened him, as if someone had opened a plug and drained his spirit.

A wave of laughter rose from the Windship. Outside the window, he could hear the hissing, buzzing night. In another moment, he gathered his senses and left the bar. Shannon would find a friend to drive her home, surely. She was that kind of girl. He got in the Ford; without making any real decision, he found himself headed to Wolverine.

The road was nearly empty. Every so often, a pair of headlights appeared around a curve and Slater would hit the dimmer. When the opposing car passed, he moved his foot again and flicked on the brights. Dimmer, brights. Dimmer, brights. There was something simple and satisfying to it, a night code shared with other solitary souls.

On River Road he stopped outside the house. Upstairs, a light shone in Lane's room.

The front door wouldn't be locked. Rose might or might not be inside. She had forbid him to enter the house. "You've been defanged," she told him. "How does it feel?"

The answer was, it felt bad. He should have fought Rose tooth and nail, but he didn't. He was never that fanged to begin with.

After a while, the light in Lane's room went out.

Slater waited a little longer. Then he drove back to Hidden Mist listening to nothing but his breath, dimming the lights and flicking them up.

He could drive that way forever, he thought. Just steering the car, just moving his foot, just watching the road—that would be enough, he thought, that would be okay, that would be alright.

—31—

IN THE UPPER Peninsula, Harp walked through Rapid River. Dirt road, abandoned houses, derelict Esso. A single track, well-worn, led to a one-room trainman's shack. Harp tramped up to the open door, scaring up grasshoppers as he walked.

Inside, a red-faced man with a crew cut sat reading a paperback titled *Heroes of Iwo Jima*. Crumpled carbon forms littered the control board. The man saw Harp but didn't speak.

"Any trains coming through?" Harp asked. "Maybe something going north?"

The operator didn't turned his head or look up from his book. Harp stood in the doorway of the airless room and waited. "Be a while," the trainman finally said.

The Buddha of Rapid River, Harp thought. He left the shack and found an empty boxcar on a siding.

The rest of the morning simply evaporated. Harp did nothing. He didn't eat; he didn't sleep. Everything stopped;

the afternoon and evening disappeared. He had been moving; now he was still. There was no correlation to the clock. He was on the underside of the interval, so there was no way to measure it.

Eventually dark fell and the Buddha drove off in a bone-white Chevrolet. When an evening breeze swept up, Harp noticed that the shadowed troughs of farmland were moving and that he was somewhere other than Burnt River.

Railroad time. Different from ordinary time.

From the balcony, Charlie had a satisfying view of the Spreadables on the sundeck. Tracy, topless. A new girl, name forgotten, but naked. Always a good sign. And Shannon, in absurdly modest beachwear.

Sweet, obsessive Shannon. She had finally come through for him.

Charlie scooped a handful of macadamia nuts from a dish and contemplated his options.

He didn't really care about seeing Shannon's body anymore. He'd seen bodies before. He picked up another macadamia nut and wondered about the odds of landing it directly in the new girl's navel. It could be an interesting party game. Get some girls, load 'em with 'ludes, lay 'em out, and sell the nuts. A dollar a toss. Get the Nut in the Navel.

What the heck. It sounded fun, even to him.

He tossed and hit Tracy in the forehead. She charged into the house. A minute later she was on the balcony and in his face.

"What the hell are you doing? You could have put my eye out!"

"I didn't mean to throw it," Charlie said. "It slipped."

"Are you a child? What kind of fool do you think I am?"

Charlie ignored the question. "In case you're wondering, Trace, I'm through throwing pine nuts at pussy. It was fun, but I have to give it up. I've found a new passion in life."

"What are you on, Charlie? You're high on something."

"Power." He picked up a large manila envelope. "Shannon brought us a little present."

He reached inside and pulled out the Blue Dart. "Welcome to Charlie's Bullshit Emporium," he said. "Open for business."

Rose left the sheriff's office in the late afternoon, shutting the door behind her after six hours of bored vigilance at the dispatch desk. The Town That Crime Forgot. There was a 10-91—Stray Horse—out past Slouka Road, and Lazenbeck called in a half dozen 11-95s—Temporarily out of Vehicle. Which meant he was either collecting envelopes or making booty calls. Other than that, the only excitement was an Unable to Locate involving a half-empty jar of Coffeemate in the break room.

As she stepped outside, Rose felt the cool air from the Lake on her face. She paused for a moment, looking at the wavy reflection in the window of Jerry's Donuts across the street. When she was done, she found her car and headed to Lane's house.

It had been a Stray Horse kind of week—everything a little bit out of place. On Tuesday, Shannon had shown up unexpectedly, past arguments forgotten. She washed her hands twice as much as usual and spent a long time in the kitchen complaining about Charlie. Rose could tell she was scared about something. They went upstairs, but Shannon was edgy. Rose went downstairs for a bottle of wine and before she could uncork it, Shannon was out the door.

The whole week had gone that way. Sometimes you could just smell it.

At Lane's house, she could tell there was trouble before she even got up the steps. The screen door was ripped, as if someone had fallen against it from the inside. The TV, which usually ran without sound, was off. The stereo buzzed loudly.

She found Lane at the kitchen table, head down, barely conscious. By her feet was a bag of glue.

"Oh, babe," Rose said. "Fuck."

Her lungs would be full of fumes, starving her brain of oxygen. Rose moved behind her and dragged her toward the door, expecting Lane to die in her arms.

"It's all black," Lane said. "I can't see anything." She threw up halfway across the living room, leaving a trail of vomit on the floor.

"You goddamn fool," Rose said. "You stupid, goddamn fool." She dragged her slack body to the Jeep, stuffing her limb by limb into the passenger seat as Lane pissed herself.

The emergency room was a twenty-minute drive. Too long. Rose drove to the marina instead, running every stoplight. She parked with one wheel on the curb and burst into the rinky-dink dive shop. The stoner clerk sat on a stool behind the counter. He looked at Rose, the town lesbian, like she was stump rot. "Come for a dive?" he said, mocking her.

She pointed at the Jeep. "Oxygen. Now."

Rose cleared Lane's mouth of vomit while the clerk

got a rebreather tank. He pushed the mouthpiece in while Rose held Lane's nose. It wasn't hospital oxygen but it was all they had. Rose knew the trick from working dispatch.

After seven or eight breaths, Lane blinked. She looked around, surprised by the world. Her dress, covered with puke, was up around her thighs. Rose pulled it down to keep the stoner's eyes off Lane's piss-soaked panties.

They gave her another ten minutes on the tank. Rose opened her purse and gave the clerk a twenty, following him into the shop for her change. When she came back, Lane was wiping her face.

"I'm sorry," she said. Her voice was barely audible.

"No you aren't. Not yet."

She slapped Lane once, twice, ten times, swearing with such ferocity that the stoner came back out to watch. "You will, never, ever do another tube of glue!" Each word had its own slap until they both were sobbing.

At the house, Rose opened every drawer and dumped them out. She went through cupboards and ransacked Lane's room, checking pockets, shelves, the jewelry box, while Lane shivered on the bed. Five tubes of glue went into a plastic garbage bag. She found the collection of un-built freight cars and smashed them into the living room vomit for Lane to clean up later, a lesson.

When she was done, she went back upstairs and made Lane get out of bed. "I am going to save your sorry, messed-up, shitty life," she said. "Whether you want me to or not."

The cover band at the Hiawatha Club finished "TV Eye" and began "Lucifer," channeling the ragged energy of Detroit. The music inspired Harp to call for another tequila, but when it arrived he realized he was too drunk to drink it.

The woman at the next table kept barking his name. Her rap hit all the high spots: her boyfriend just trashed his Camaro, the band sucked, the waitress was a cunt. She danced with a girlfriend, then went shoulder to shoulder with a wedgehead. The woman wasn't square. She was the kind who might end up in the men's room and not find it especially degrading if the guy was halfway nice. But not with me, Harp thought. Not tonight.

When the music stopped, he carried his gear to the sidewalk, strapped on his pack, and steered himself to the freight yard.

A string of empty auto carriers lined the edge of the yard. The sides were perforated steel—only the ends were open. From inside, he could see down the entire string, like looking through a tunnel. He unrolled his bag and passed out instantly, visited by dreams from an interior drunk tank.

Deep in the night, an air horn blasted him awake. The death star of an engine was bearing down on him, coming through the tunnel. Thinking he had fallen asleep across the tracks, he scrambled down the car, leaving his boots behind. As he jumped wildly to the gravel, the illusion burst. The oncoming train was just a truck on a nearby road, its headlights sweeping through the sides of the auto carriers.

After picking himself up, Harp couldn't stop shaking; his chest was full of pounding mallets. On a moving train, a screwup like that might have killed him.

To punish himself, he left the yard, right arm swinging wide, and trudged off to sleep in the park.

Against the emptiness of Hidden Mist, Slater developed a routine. Every afternoon, he downed a shot of Jim Beam, got stoned, and took Charlie's Nikon into the Lake, to the shallow water.

In the viewfinder, the waves were little miracles. Focus, click. The grass and whiskey curled up and crashed gently in the same rhythm as the waves. He never looked at the pictures. It was just something to do.

At night, he went to the nearby bars. The local women were interesting to watch, though none of them seemed to come from the same world as Lane. One night, a woman in a sequined dress did a sexy dance by the jukebox with two oversized yachtsmen. Outside, a hard rain bounced off the road. When the song ended, the woman picked up her purse and left, walking through the rain in no particular hurry. Halfway across the street, she knelt and kissed the pavement. No one except Slater seemed to see.

The nights ended in the hideous bedroom, next to the curtain with the gymnastic lovers. A tag at the bottom of the curtain read *Drill Me Faster, by Here, Doggy of Hollywood*, followed by a toll-free number.

What a poisonous, enchanted place the world had turned out to be, Slater thought. A commerce of money and bullets, with "Drill Me Faster" as the mantra. They ought to put it on every dollar in place of "In God We Trust."

One night Slater saw Dickinson in the darkness, nearly naked and frozen with the cherries. Dickinson in a Stetson, Dickinson on top of Cassie. All those pounds, all those poundings, and for what? A sore pelvis where love was supposed to be. Her baby-making equipment exposed and making loneliness instead.

In the next moment he found himself down the hall in the empty bathtub, fully dressed and crying, and trying not to make any noise.

— 32 —

MATTHEWS HAD AN empty Rolling Rock and he flipped it like a baton, catching the neck. One rotation, a blur of green, the smack of the bottle on his meaty hand. Slater was working on the surveillance tape from Erickson's office, trying to find a signal.

"Jefferson plagiarized from the Iroquois right and left," Slater said. "The Founding Fathers were trying to piece together a government, and the savages already had one."

Matthews grunted. "The history of white men. Steal some land, buy some niggers, powder your wig. Is this all news to you?"

Flip. Smack.

Slater had finally managed to finish *The Price of Beaver*. The hero, Etienne Brulé, was not the saint he pretended to be. Some said he was working for Champlain against the Hurons, or for the Hurons against the Iroquois. No one knew for sure. All agreed he was addicted to Huron women; eventually the Hurons murdered him for it. He put his spear where it didn't belong; they put a hatchet in his head.

Then Brulé was boiled and eaten. Digested, later to become fertilizer, as all men do. He made love to the women and he was shat upon the land. An old story, but a good one.

Slater hit EJECT and took Matthew's spy tape from the deck. There was no control track, no time code. "It's blank," he said. "I'm sorry."

Matthews looked at the cassette, front and back. He rattled it, held it up to his ear, and put it on one of Slater's shelves. "So what are we left with?"

"Good question."

From some other office, a phone rang faintly and then stopped. Matthews sat for several more minutes. Not speaking, not flipping the bottle. Just breathing. It was a trick he had, Slater thought. His doing-nothing trick. When it was over, Matthews stood up and laid a hand on Slater's shoulder. "I'll see you around, Mike. Don't stay in the dark too long."

Slater heard the bottle smack all the way to the elevator. An electronic ping sounded and the doors slid open. He waited until the floor was completely silent, then opened his drawer.

A knife. A book. A container of speed. A postcard from Harp. That's what we're left with.

Harp woke on a picnic table in the mangy park, wet with dew. Black-winged birds swarmed on willow trees all around him, more birds than he had ever seen. There were hundreds of them, and not enough trees. For a moment, he had no idea where he was.

The tequila hangover hit as soon as he stood—the Mescal Train, still roaring, a pulsing headache behind his eyes. He remembered the drunken screwup on the auto racks, the woman from the Hiawatha Club who kept calling him to dance. Red lips and donkey voice.

Clearly, demons were loose in the world. He needed coffee bad.

Under the weight of his pack, he retraced his steps, but downtown St. Ignace was still asleep. Only the Pancake Shanty was open.

Maybe just this once, he thought. Just a short stop in hell.

Inside, it was as bad as he feared. Three steps in, he was assaulted with pleasantries. A pigtailed waitress greeted him, seeming not to see his freight clothes or his agony. She led him to a booth and recited the dinner specials, "should you be in our vicinity this evening."

A different girl sloshed coffee on his table, filling his cup. He sipped it twice with eyes closed; when he opened them he was still at the Pancake Shanty. An unfinished short stack sat on the table next to his. Still Life with Flies.

He stood up and watched his hand bring the sticky cakes to his mouth. The pigtailed waitress and a boy in a paper hat stared. He finished the stack in three bites and rinsed his fingers in a glass of water.

He'd been riding dead-enders and one-a-days too long. It was time to get over that.

A rack of postcards sat by the cash register; each showed the plastic Shanty Boy with bib and spatula. Harp took one and wrote Slater's name on it along with a message. When he turned to leave, a worker in a paper hat asked him where he thought was going.

"Hudson Bay," Harp said. "Want to come?"

Charlie found Tracy lounging in the Jacuzzi. "Lazenbeck's here," he said. "Things are escalating."

"Here?" She sank deeper in the tub. "Is he out of his mind?"

"Upstairs, in fact. We have a problem, Trace. We're gonna have to get a little finesse-y, I'm afraid."

From the dock came the sound of an outboard motor starting up.

"I thought you had everything wired."

"I did," Charlie said. "But Rose is out of control. She's got the goods on Lazenbeck. All his so-called *royalties*. Apparently she's got proof and she's threatening to take him down."

Tracy looked over her shoulder, then spoke quietly. "Remind me why we care about that?"

"We care because you and I will go down even harder. She'll finger him and he'll finger us. We'll go to jail for the rest of our lives."

"That doesn't sound right," Tracy said. "How is that fair?"

"Basically, we're criminals," Charlie said. "So certain people want to lock us up. It's crazy, I know. But there it is."

"Spare me the bullshit, Charlie."

"We don't have a choice," Charlie said. "We have to shut Rose up."

"We?"

"Actually, me. This one's better if I do it alone."

Tracy turned off the jets and reached for a towel. "What do you have in mind?"

They were silent for a moment. Charlie was a statue looking out at the Lake, his nervous energy gone. When the engine at the dock revved, he turned back to the house.

"You're sure about all this?" Tracy asked.

"She brought it on herself. It's not our doing."

"She's gay," Tracy said. "Couldn't you just blackmail her?"

"People aren't ashamed of that anymore. It's practically a badge of honor."

"You could scare her."

"She doesn't scare. She got shot in the head and lived." Charlie let his shoulders slump for an instant, then recovered. "Leave it to me. Just go upstairs and take care of Lazenbeck for me. Calm him down."

She got out of the tub, toweled off, and stood naked in the sun. "Nuh-uh. I'm not bobbing for apples with the undersheriff."

"He thinks he has to arrest us. Do what you can to scrape him off the ceiling. We don't need him going apeshit."

"What's he thinking, coming out here? Does he have an ounce of sense?"

"I got Shannon and Mike out of the house. I'm having Leonard take them out."

Tracy turned, startled. "Out? As in *out*?"

"Christ, no," Charlie said. "This isn't the Mafia. Yet. He's taking them out in the boat. A little pleasure cruise."

"Pleasure." She let out a scornful little puff and looked at Charlie until Charlie looked away. "When's the last time we had some of that?"

Shannon sat in the rear of the Apache, hands in her lap. When Slater boarded, she gave him a look that he couldn't decode. They hadn't spoken since the Windship.

Leonard gunned the boat aggressively, slamming into waves with maximum violence. He chugged beers and tossed the empties overboard. Occasionally, he looked back to check out Shannon. Never once did he glance at Slater.

After a half hour of reckless boating, he abruptly cut the engine.

"Piss break," he said.

He walked past Shannon, unzipped, and pissed over the side. When he was done, he turned to her. "Your turn."

"I don't have to go," Shannon said.

"Whatever," Leonard said. "But if you expect to get back to land today, I'm gonna need to see some skin. You've been holding out long enough."

A set of oars was secured at the bow. Slater got up and moved toward them.

"No need to be shy," Leonard told her. "You got it. Why don't you flaunt it?"

"Why don't you fuck off and leave me alone?"

"I'm down with that," Leonard said. "When I'm done with your sweet ass, I'll leave you alone like you never existed."

He turned to share this bravado with Slater. The oar was already on its way. The flat part caught him across the face and knocked him backwards into the lake. While he was flailing in the water, bleeding, Slater got the Apache going. They tossed him a life ring as they left.

Slater found Hidden Mist on the shore and managed to tie up with only minimal damage to the boat. As he was helping Shannon out, he slipped and dunked himself in the Lake. She hurried inside, went immediately to the bathroom, and turned on the taps.

Slater went upstairs. "I Wanna Be Your Dog" came from his room, though the door was closed. Opening it, he found Tracy, pants-less and wearing a red push-up bra, on an older man's lap. The man was naked, with gray hair and a Roman nose. He turned toward Slater, a glint of panic in his eyes.

"Don't worry about that loser," Tracy told the man. "He's nobody."

— 33 —

LANE SAT ON the back porch on a metal folding chair, looking peacefully over unmowed grass. A paper bag was at her feet. It had started to rain, and the wet light changed everything—the axe and the firewood and the galvanized pipes of the outdoor shower. Dull, dark shine everywhere. She thought about taking off her clothes and standing in the rain. But it was already four o'clock, and Rose was due any minute.

There was a squirrel's nest in a spruce tree behind the house, and for some reason the rain made her think of it. Sometimes when she went walking, she found coyote scat full of fur.

The paper bag held two cans of Schlitz. She took one out and pulled the tab. Now that she had given up glue it seemed like she was always buying beer.

The red squirrels were bullies, anyway. She wasn't on their side.

The ax, out in the rain, was no longer usable. Harp had left it wedged into a piece of hard maple and she couldn't get it out. She pictured him with the blade overhead, driving it down, burying the head in the grain. She missed him sometimes, but not as much as she thought she would.

The bag was the perfect size for glue. Before Rose, she would have covered the bottom with epoxy and huffed until her whole body radiated. Then she'd take off her clothes and stand in the outdoor shower. You couldn't really be naked indoors, she thought. Stoned and in the rain—that was having a body and knowing it.

But Rose had stopped all that. She'd taken Lane to every hobby shop and hardware store within twenty miles. At each one, Rose marched her up to the counter so Lane could leave a photocopied picture of herself. *Tell all your clerks that I'm an addict*, she recited as Rose stood by her side. *If I try to buy glue here, call the police.*

It was touching, when she thought about it right. Rose was not to be messed with. She was on the undersheriff's case as well. Today was Stick It to the Man Day. She was blowing the whistle on the payoffs and other dirty stuff. After that, they would move to Boston. That was the plan.

Her last tube of glue—the one Rose hadn't found— was on top of the workbench. If it had been hidden, she would have felt guilty keeping it. But who could blame her for some glue that was sitting in plain sight?

She waited another half hour for Rose and then filled the bag. The first breath she took seemed to last forever. I'm sick, she thought. Sick is my name, and it's your name too.

When she was a baby, she used to lick sugar off her brother's finger. Her mother used to say.

She opened her eyes and the backyard came back. Beech trees and pine. The soggy cord of wood. Did it really matter if the firewood went to waste? Only Harp would care, and Harp was gone.

It was very possible, she thought, to meet yourself somewhere in the world. Your exact self in another body. What happened was that you died, and your soul went up to heaven. Time was different up there—there was no yesterday, no next week in heaven. Just eternity spreading out. So when your soul came back, it could come back anywhere in the past, present, or future. It might even come back on the very same day you were born, but in another body. Then the same soul would be in two bodies and the two of you might meet.

That was how she'd felt about Harp, once. Or maybe she was fooling herself. It was hard to remember anymore.

Rose was late. Lane took another hit from the bag. She felt an ant crawl across her foot.

That was what people meant when they said soulmates. When you met someone and felt like you'd known them all your life. One soul, two bodies. Very possible.

She went to the bag a third time and afterward she felt something on her chin. Too cold to be blood. She rubbed her face and looked at her fingers. She was drooling. Not a positive sign. Her spit tasted sharp and she washed it with beer.

You could share a soul for sure, and who knows who you might share it with.

But not me, she thought. No one wants my soul but me.

Charlie waited down the street from the sheriff's office until Rose stepped onto the sidewalk. When she got in her car, he followed, hanging far enough back to stay out of her rearview. They ended up at her house. He circled around, letting her get inside before he parked.

He was not very experienced at this sort of thing, he realized. But it wasn't hard. Anyone could do it.

On the steps of her long wooden porch, he checked out the sight lines. It was screened on three sides by a trellis, shrubs, and a lilac tree. Perfect. Custom-made for a crime.

Instead of knocking, he sat on the porch swing and waited. No need to hurry. He'd catch her by surprise when she came out.

The shade of the porch felt a little damp, he thought. The swing wouldn't be much good in the afternoon. It was more of a sunrise swing. He thought about putting it up at Hidden Mist—it would be a nice addition to the balcony. If he'd had a swing like that a few months ago, the Sara Lee girl might still be alive.

The front door opened after about twenty minutes. Rose came out carrying a day pack. She couldn't have expected to see him there, but neither did she seem surprised.

"Charlie," she said. She had her keys out, but she didn't lock the door behind her. "Get away from me. You'll only make things worse for yourself."

Charlie stayed in the swing. She'd have to walk past him to escape. "I'm not here to make things difficult," he said. "I'm here to make them easier."

"Then leave."

"I was just thinking about Pinocchio." He kept one hand hidden from Rose. "Have you heard the one about Pinocchio and the dumb blonde?"

Rose looked past him. "Did you hear the one about private property?"

Charlie pushed with his feet, swinging a little higher. It was a pleasant feeling. Like Sunday after church, 1950. If such a time had ever existed.

"Pinocchio is going south on this blonde, okay? A little mouth-to-muff resuscitation." He found her eyes. "You know all about that number, am I right?"

"Get off my porch, Charlie."

"Now, Pinocchio doesn't even know this little missy's name, but he's got his nose right up there in Grand Central where she can feel it nice and tight. He munches a while, then he stops and says, 'I love you.' His nose grows and he gets back to work. Then he stops and says, 'I'll always love you.' His nose grows some more. The blonde is diggin' it. She goes, 'More, more.'"

Rose coughed. Charlie dragged a foot and stopped the swing. "So Pinocchio looks up and says, 'More licking?' And the blonde says, 'No, you freakin' toothpick. More lying!'"

Rose stepped forward and Charlie stood up.

"I'll bear that in mind," Rose said. "Next time I fuck a puppet."

"Do," Charlie said. His right hand was still behind his back. "You see, everyone likes the lie. We all get off on it. It's how we get our jollies. Then someone like you comes along and tries to tell the truth. It's a major bummer."

She was cradling her lame hand, but there was no trace of fear in her voice. "You're blocking my way, Charlie."

He brought his hand out and showed her the blade. "Yes," he said. "That's the idea." He was surprised to find he had a hard-on for the first time in years.

Outside the boxcar, Harp pissed on the wheels and felt the sun on his back. He'd been riding quarter-mile all morning—rolled rail, each section a quarter-mile long, laid over concrete ties. Smooth as shit, and very fast.

At the siding stop and afterward, he found himself thinking of Lane. It went along with feeling strong again, maybe. He sat on a piece of cardboard as they picked up speed and remembered making love to her, the big rail map on the wall behind his head, the cherry cannons booming in the hills. He rubbed tequila on her lips; her eyes were lit like a hundred megawatts. She looked at the ceiling, not at him. Toward the end, something slipped from her face as chaos crept in. Lane in bed was like a person letting go of a rope. The change was wonderful to watch: it was half of what he fucked her for.

When he used to. In the old days.

At Sudbury he changed cars and rode through the afternoon. The new boxcar had only one door open; the other was rusted shut. Riding blind in one eye, he called it.

The train was headed to Oba. A wind whipped in the car, alarmingly fresh. It was a good wind. It was the kind of wind that said *Now*.

Charlie lined the long cedar chest with two layers of plastic, taping the corners to make sure it was watertight. He left it next to the freezer and went to the garage, where he humped eight bags of party ice onto a dolly, which he rolled to the basement, locking the door behind him.

The rest was sweat work. He restacked the ice and worked the cedar chest onto the dolly. Half the ice went inside. It made a nice, neat bed. Cold, but cozy. Then it was Sara Lee time.

To protect himself, he took a rain slicker from a hook, then thought better and traded it for one of the thick yellow squall jackets, zipped to his chin. He found some neoprene gloves that turned his hands into big orange cartoons. Holding his breath, he unlocked the freezer.

She wasn't any worse than before. The right side of her body, crushed by the fall, was ruined. But the brown glaze was covered in most places with a festive and sanitary frost. And she didn't stink. That was a plus. To his surprise, she wasn't that hard to move. He lost his footing once and banged her head on the edge of the freezer, but he managed to get her into the cedar chest in one piece. He had imagined much worse. Eruptions. Legs and limbs dropping off. He put the remaining ice bags in and held them in place with another layer of Visqueen. At the very top, he arranged three kilos of sugar and a baggie with eight grams of cocaine. Enough for possession with intent to distribute. He closed the lid and tied it shut with twine. Don't melt too soon, he told Sara Lee. You've got one more walk-on, darling.

Leonard and one of the other screwups were in the bongo room watching porno. Leonard was still pissed that he hadn't been allowed to kill Slater. It had taken hours to convince him that a more painful and useful fate was in store.

Charlie stepped in front of the screen to get their attention. "You fine fellows ever score with three chicks in one day?" he asked.

"Three in twenty-four hours?" Leonard asked. "No."

The other freak didn't even look up. "Nah."

"And you never will," Charlie said. He sent them out grumbling to load the chest onto the Ford Ranchero.

In a few hours, it would be Triple Play day for La-zenbeck. The undersheriff had arranged for a multicounty sting. He'd arrest the smooth and silky Chance Ballinger downstate receiving eight grams of coke, courtesy of Slater. Lazenbeck would get some airtime on the evening news; Chance would get ten years. The sad and slender body of Sara Lee would also be discovered. Another victory for the undersheriff. Depending on the breaks, Lazenbeck would also arrest Slater as an accessory. Or, if the timing worked out, retrieve his corpse from the driveway. Chance was expecting three kilos of coke and would not be amused to discover that most of the bags contained sugar. For all his charm, Chance had no sense of humor. And he always shot the messenger.

So it was a triple play for Charlie, too. Rose, Chance, Slater. Nicely fucked in one day.

Upstairs, he knocked on Slater's door and went in without waiting for an answer. Empty. The dumbass was usually sitting there staring into space. When a quick room-to-room turned up nothing, Charlie started to swear. Slater had a leading role in the docudrama he had so carefully planned. Without him, they were screwed. Finally, Charlie spotted him out by the Lake. The dipshit was up to his knees in the water, pointed toward Wisconsin. Charlie grabbed a black plastic bag and went out to round him up.

The Lake was flat and Slater was standing there like a big upright turd. He held a Nikon away from his body. For a full minute, he didn't move. Charlie crinkled the bag. Nothing.

"Full of zing today, aren't we, champ? You stoned?"

Slater did a slow pivot. "I'm looking at the water."

"Ask a silly question." Charlie waded partway out to him, stopping before the water reached his shorts. "This is embarrassing, but I have to ask you a favor. I need you to make a delivery."

"Not interested," Slater said.

"Really? I talked to your friend Rose today. What a good old gal she is."

Two dead alewives floated behind Slater, tangled in a patch of stargrass. "Rose is not a friend of mine."

"Then you won't miss her. She's on her way to Boston."

Charlie brought the knife out of the black bag. "Funny how everyone wants this. Rose wants it, you want it, Lazenbeck wants it." He looked at both sides of the blade, as if eyeing a suspicious piece of fruit. "It doesn't look that special to me."

"That's mine," Slater said. "Give it."

"I've got a beautiful cedar chest that needs to be stripped and refinished. These guys down by Alma do a bang-up job. Real craftsmen. Thing is, I'm short a driver." He put the knife back in the bag. "Once you deliver that chest, you come and get what's yours. Fair?"

Slater stood there looking at him. They all did that. Calculating the odds before they stepped off the cliff. Slater did it longer than most.

Charlie shooed a beach fly away, waiting.

"How could you do it?" Slater asked. "Fuck your mother."

"You're a guest here," Charlie said. "We don't talk about that."

"Topic's taboo, is it?"

"Yes, it is."

Slater advanced the film and fiddled with the lens of the Nikon. "I would have thought screwing your mom was the taboo thing. Maybe I've got that wrong."

Charlie took a breath, holding his anger in. "You've got a lot of things wrong. I'd explain them to you, but I'm a little pressed for time."

"I have all the time in the world."

"Actually you don't, champ. None of us do. So let's put this behind us."

"Let me take your picture, Charlie. The Boy Who Loved His Mother."

As Slater raised the camera, Charlie looked down at his feet. The Lake and the sunlight made them shimmer. "If I weren't in such a good mood, I might take offense at that."

The shutter clicked. "Loved his mom and made his sister clean up the mess."

I decide when we fight and when we don't, Charlie told himself. Regardless, he took a step toward Slater. "You're concerned about sis," he said. "I can dig that. Tell you what. Do this little errand for me. When you come back, we'll sit down and talk it all out."

Slater took another picture. "Tell me about it now, Charlie. What did it feel like when you slipped it in her? The ultimate power trip?"

"You're a moron," Charlie said.

"Did you make her come? Did she call you Jesus? Or was she just another one of your Spreadables?"

Slater was adjusting the lens when Charlie's right hook caught him. The Nikon flew into the water. Everything Charlie had been holding back, the punch unleashed. It was followed by a second and a third until Slater staggered back and went down. When he raised his head from the water, he was bleeding at the mouth.

"You think I was some ignorant douchebag who didn't know right from wrong?" Charlie yelled. "Some dumbfuck with two teeth who barely knew what his cock was for? Well, I was! Of course I was! I was as dumb as a fucking stone. A flat-out loser. And she was lonely. You want to judge me for that? Judge the whole goddamn world."

Charlie kicked up a spray of water. The two dead alewives bobbed by Slater's head. One of his flip-flops was floating out to the Lake.

"Nobody ever gave me a fucking hand! Nobody ever said, 'Here Charlie, let me help you. Let me show you how things are done.' Bullshit. I made my own way and I left a trail of crap behind me. You think I don't know that? You think I'm not aware? And what about you? What mark have you made on the world? None. Now get up."

Charlie stood over him and put out a hand. Slater got up without taking it.

"You're a fucking moron." Charlie walked into deeper water and fished out the camera. Water drained from it as he held it up. "You're afraid of your freakin' shadow and you cry about it with every breath you take. You let some self-righteous lesbian kick you out of your bed without a peep. At least I know what I did. I got in bed with a woman who wanted to get in bed with me, and since then everyone's tried to tell me I'm a monster. Like the whole world shits vanilla ice cream except for me."

"I didn't say that," Slater said.

"What a fucking hypocrite," Charlie said. "You would have wanted it just as much as I did. But you would have been too afraid to do anything about it."

Charlie shoved the Nikon at his belly. Slater flinched, taking the camera with both hands to protect himself.

"You want this knife?" Charlie asked. "Do what I say. Otherwise, rot in jail." He pulled an amber bottle from his shorts, tapped four pills into his hand, and swallowed them. He stuck the bottle in Slater's shirt pocket. "It's a long drive," he said. "You're gonna need some of these."

The drive was south. Slater kept his foot on the gas as the Ranchero shimmied. The Smiling Os that Charlie had given him and the sharp afternoon light made right angles out of everything.

His mouth was crusted where the camera had cut him. But the speed made the pain feel different—muted and solid, like something he could touch with his tongue.

Past Mesick, the road cut around a dozen small lakes, each with a skirt of cottages. Dirt drives led to back doors, rusted boats bobbed in high grass. Every cottage he passed had a crazy name. Thistle Dew, Sunsets and Schulers, Shure Nuff. The signs enraged him with their ignorance, their insistence on a dull comfort in such a barbed and vicious world.

What Charlie had said about him seemed like the truest thing he'd ever heard. He'd made a mess of his life. Hurt others with his pointless fear. Turned away from love. Fought for nothing.

Angry at himself, he stepped on the gas, pushing the needle higher. The cedar chest slid in the bed of the Ranchero, hitting the side panels when he cornered. He passed very few cars.

The farther south he drove, the more gravity tried to pull at him. The roads got bigger and the trees smelled like newsprint. When he stopped at a Dairy Queen in Mt. Pleasant, he recognized the drill. Reality. Cast of thousands.

In the parking lot, he resisted the temptation to open the chest. It would be filled with drugs, of course. But if he didn't open it, he could legitimately say he didn't know. Not that any cop in the world would believe him. Particularly with Charlie's pills in his pocket. He took another one, went inside for a cone, and watched two kids in colorful hats making sundaes. They were idiots and they had better lives than he did.

Time to run, he thought. Stick out his thumb and head for the hills. Instead, he got back in the Ranchero. As he drove, the radio played Seger, the early antiwar song. Five-note intro and then the voice.

Yes it's true I am a young man, but I'm old enough to kill . . .

Listening, a determination came over him. He'd do this for Charlie, then he'd get the goddamn knife and go back to Lane. Rose could do whatever she wanted, but she wasn't going to stop him.

Outside Alma, a fount of flame burned atop a pencil-thin smokestack. The smokestack marked the invisible boundary between northern and southern Michigan. South of Alma, the days were counted in an order that never varied. But not for me, Slater told himself. I'm not going that far.

Charlie's directions, scribbled on a pharmacy pad, said to take Meary Road past Drake's Restaurant for three miles, and then left past the bridge. Slater tried it three times but never came to a bridge. Finally, he went back to Drake's and pulled in. The restaurant had plywood over the windows and a phone booth that smelled like sewage. Charlie had told him not to call him under any circumstance. After nine rings, Shannon answered in a panic. Her voice was shrill, lurching from word to word. The crappy receiver made her sound like she was on the moon.

"Rose is dead," she said. "He killed her."

"What? Who killed her?"

"Charlie's gone crazy. He went to see Lane. I have to get out of here before he gets back."

The black mouthpiece brushed Slater's lips. "Don't hang up," he said. "What's going on with Lane?"

"She called. She knows about Rose. He said he'd kill her too if she didn't shut up."

"Shit."

"Don't come back here."

The line did the awful, empty hum of phones when no one talks.

"He made me steal your knife," Shannon said.

Slater got in the car and spun the Ford around, sending a cloud of dust over Drake's. On the highway he swallowed another of Charlie's pills and bent into the wheel. The afternoon light was cracked and yellow. He pushed the Ford to seventy-five.

Near Mesick two deer stood in the road. They jumped away as he slammed past. The cottages and their stupid signs sped by. The Jacob Vanderhands, the Preston Faylords. His fingers tapped five-stroke drum rolls on the wheel, one after another. The cadence drove him insane, but he couldn't make himself stop.

The Ford topped out at eighty-five. One cop car and he would be done for. They'd pull him over and open the chest. But he didn't slow down.

At the county line, maples crowded the shoulder. Their thick canopy turned the road into a tunnel. He felt light-headed, like he might pass out. The low afternoon light strobed on and off as the road snapped from shadow to sun.

As he rounded a curve, the maples parted and came to life, taking the form of a deer, a real one. For one frozen second, he could see its fur, a white crest over its ribs, dead center in the road.

The deer leapt for its life, but not in time.

In slow motion, Slater could see the damage, what broke, what burst, what shattered. The Ford whirled, a spinner flicked in a childhood game. The radiator exploded. Slater's head cracked against the windshield. Flying through the warp was a spray of blood and money and a dark-haired girl he thought must be Lane—airborne, like she'd been smacked out of his head and into the swirl. The next thing he knew, his eyes were filled with blood and all he could hear was the horn.

He wondered, then, why he wasn't dead.

When he managed to get out, he fell to his knees. The pavement under his hands was strangely still. Charlie's drugs were all over the road and all over his hands. He licked a fingertip. It tasted like sugar.

The woman who had been launched in the whirlwind wasn't Lane. She was younger and shorter, and she was lying in the road in a mess of bloody hundred-dollar bills. Plastic around her feet was stapled to broken pieces of Charlie's chest; her head was half gone. Someone had left a message on her belly. *There are no problems, only solutions.*

She had been a pretty girl once. He touched her skin and it was cold. She terrified Slater, but what scared him most was the money. It covered the road, as if the collision itself had produced it. It had to be Dickinson's. He didn't know how he knew, but he knew.

Shaking, he began scooping up bills. He got handfuls of them and filled his pockets. As he stuffed them into his pants he realized how bad his leg hurt, even through the speed.

The deer that brought it all forth—the magic white-crested deer—was no longer there, but a splatter of blood led off the side of the road. It was in the brush somewhere, dying.

Slater bent to the road again, favoring his left leg. Most of the bills were soaked in blood. Even as he reached for them, he knew he should run, and before he could gather many more, the sound of a motor rose behind him. In the distance, a pair of headlights appeared. They'd be cottage people, the Preston Faylords or the Thistle Dew folks. They'd call the police.

Slater took a last glance at the Ford and hobbled stiff-legged into the woods. If the Preston Faylords caught him now, it would be the end of everything.

Going north to Oba, Harp grabbed a woodchip car. It was an easy hop; the train never knew she'd been boarded. He climbed to the top, carved a hollow in the mound of wood-chips, and lay back. The night was warm, stars everywhere. Nothing better, he thought.

But by the first siding stop he was bored. He climbed down and walked along the train until he found an open boxcar. Clean, with a metal floor. He swung in easily and took out his map, looking again at the crosshatched line of the Northern Arrow. The final names along the route were printed in the smallest possible type. In the circle of his flashlight, they gave the impression of icy loneliness: Weir River, Bylot, Digges, Tidal. Past them, past everything, was Hudson Bay. As far as you could go by rail.

A minute later, the train was barreling at top speed. Harp folded the map and stood by the door. He still thought of Lane once in a while. And part of him always missed Slater. But the wind would take care of that, at least for now.

A deer path through maple and birch brought Slater to Dupertail Road. He limped along the pavement for twenty minutes, and no cars passed. When his head began to pound, he took another of Charlie's pills.

Finally, an unmuffled engine sounded in the distance. He turned and put out his thumb as a blue Torino sped past. It shimmied to a stop, then backed up at high speed, scattering gravel. The passenger door came open.

In the front were two men in their forties. The driver wore a torn white T-shirt, sweat-stained. The other man was in tie-dye. He leaned forward so Slater could slide in back. The car stank of booze and Aqua Velva. The instant he was inside, the Torino took off, fishtailing.

The driver eyed Slater suspiciously in the rearview. "You look like shit," he said. "What type of pussy are you?"

The passenger passed a can of Old Milwaukee over the seat to Slater. "Don't mind him," he said. "I'm Vic. Where you headed?"

"Wolverine," Slater said.

The driver shook his head, deepening a crease in the back of his neck. "We can't take this rig into Wolverine," he said. "Mister Nasty might find us."

"How close can you get me?" Slater asked.

"Not very."

A bowling bag sat on the floor of the backseat next to a dozen empties. Slater was certain the car and the ball did not belong to the men.

The driver jerked a thumb at Vic. "Barf-breath here wants to go to Traverse City and get another tattoo. The police love that, don't they? Identifying marks. Makes their job easier."

"I guess." Slater's leg cramped painfully. He considered offering the men money to take him to Wolverine—one hundred, two. But if he started pulling out bills, they'd beat him and take it all.

"You a cop?" the driver asked.

"Not me."

"Then how would you know?"

A butterfly hit the windshield and made a jellylike smudge.

"He ain't a cop, asshole," Vic said. "He's a speed freak. Look at him blink."

The driver checked him out in the rearview. Slater tried not to blink.

"Looks like Mr. Nasty already found him. You got any speed on you?"

"No," Slater said. He had a handful of Smiling Os in his shirt pocket.

"You lying sack of shit," the driver said. "Don't lie to people who are helping you."

"Maybe he's not a speed freak. Maybe he's a pussy, just like you said."

The men talked back and forth about a cabin in the Upper Peninsula. A woman they called Candy. The passenger got angry about something and started throwing empties out the window. Slater convinced them to drop him by the two-track that led to Hidden Mist.

"Goodbye, fuckface," Vic yelled before he was out of the car.

Hell must be a big place, Slater thought, to have room for such mountains of shit and still smell like cheap aftershave. He waited until the Torino was out of sight before walking into the woods.

The flies found him immediately. He chewed more of Charlie's speed and limped along the two-track. As he walked, he kept seeing the girl on the pavement, her head a half-eaten melon. He was ready to drop when headlights came around a curve and stopped. The Karmann Ghia. Shannon ran the passenger window down and leaned over to stare at him.

"Oh my God," she said. "Did Charlie do that?"

Slater touched his forehead. The cut from the windshield was bleeding.

"I'm okay. Take me to Wolverine." He opened the passenger door.

"No," she said. "Stay out."

Slater slid in anyway, fouling the white leather seat. He pulled some bills from his pockets and tried to give them to her. "I have to see Lane."

Shannon cringed against the door. "Get those away from me!"

Her face, lit by the dash lights, looked pale and scared; her eyes puffy. She wore a dark blazer over a white blouse.

"I'm sorry," he said. "I promise I won't touch you. But I need to see Lane."

She looked at him and he saw how filthy he was in her eyes. She drove slowly along the two-track. At the main road, she put the Karmann Ghia in park and lowered her head until it rested on the wheel. "I stole your knife," she said. "I took it from Rose and gave it to Charlie."

"It doesn't matter."

"He killed her with it."

Reflexively, he reached out to touch her shoulder but pulled his hand back. "It wasn't your fault."

She started to sob. "I'm a terrible person."

"That's not true," Slater said. "Just take me to see Lane."

"I can't." She pulled the blazer tight around her.

"Just do this one thing."

Her shoulders jerked, but the rest of her sobs were silent. He was about to take the wheel from her when she stopped crying and sat up. She put the car in gear and turned toward Wolverine.

"I'll take you there," she said. "But I'm not getting out of the car. I don't want to see Charlie."

Slater nodded. If he said anything, he thought, even a word, she would change her mind. He tried to close his eyes, but he couldn't keep them shut. The night smelled like skunk—it mixed with the speed and made his mouth taste bitter. The drive took forever.

Not far from the house, her composure broke, bursting like a dam. She jerked both knees toward her chest and let go of the wheel. "I'm so dirty," she cried. "I'm such a dirty person."

Slater grabbed for the steering wheel. She shrieked as he pushed his leg over hers, trying to get at the brake. His foot found the gas instead and they sped down River Road. Shannon screamed. Slater, fiercely fucked-up, pulled at the wheel, making zigzags and barely staying on the road.

"Stop touching me!" Shannon cried.

He found the brake for an instant before losing it. As the house shot up, the Karmann Ghia left the road. They clipped the mailbox and came to rest in a stand of saplings, barely missing the large maple. The passenger door was boxed in and Slater had to climb over Shannon to get out.

"I'm sorry, I'm so sorry," he told her, but Shannon didn't react; she'd gone into some other part of herself.

The sky was black; tiny stars made nervous streaks over the house. The downstairs was dark but spilling over with guitar. Hendrix at high volume. Slater scanned the living room in jerky, disconnected glances, searching for something he could use as a weapon. There was a fork on the floor. He picked it up and climbed the stairs.

The door to Lane's room was open. Charlie was leaning against the wall by the bed. He'd been drinking or crying—his face was red. Tracy was rummaging through the closet. From below, "All Along the Watchtower" was ending.

Slater took a step inside the room and stopped. There was a body on the bed, covered by a sheet. A bare foot was sticking out.

Tracy saw him first.

"Oh, this is cute." Her words were slurred. She pointed at Slater. "What gives, Charlie-boy? I thought he was supposed to be incarcerated. Or dead. He doesn't look dead to me."

Charlie was holding a gun. "What's the fork for?" he said. "You here to do her one last time? While she's still warm?" He pointed the gun at Slater.

"That I'd like to see." Tracy was holding a pair of Lane's shoes; she had skirts draped over her arm.

"You killed her," Slater said.

"No." Charlie said. "You killed her. You're the one who let her fill her brain with fumes. With poison. You could have stopped her, but you didn't. She was gone when we got here." He raised the gun. "Where's that cedar chest I entrusted you with?"

"In the middle of the road." He could feel the drug coiling up inside him. Gun or no gun, in a moment he was going for Charlie.

"So you met my friend Sara Lee."

Slater took a step toward the bed—toward Lane—and felt a hand on his shoulder. Shannon had followed him up the stairs.

"Fuck a duck," Tracy said. "It's the Bobbsey Twins. Maybe we'll finally get to see her tits." She pointed the shoes at Shannon. "Make her take off her shirt before you shoot them."

Slater took a step toward Charlie. He couldn't make himself stop. "Are you going to kill us like you killed Rose?"

"Rose had a boating accident." Charlie took a bottle of whiskey from the nightstand and drank.

"Here's the story," Tracy said. She pointed at the sheeted figure. "Lane comes home, finds Mikey and Miss Shannon going at it like hump-rats. She shoots them both. Then ODs. Double murder with suicide."

"Lazenbeck would love that," Charlie said. "You'd need a good strong sheriff to clean up a mess like that." He waved the gun in a jaunty little spiral, a flourish to show he was a real sport. "But I'm not worried about Shannon. She can walk. She's not the type to tell secrets."

Tracy smacked the shoes together, making everyone jump. "Don't be stupid."

Charlie took another slug of whiskey. "I would like to see her undress, though. Just once for Uncle Charlie." He aimed the gun at Shannon. "Then I'll let you go."

"He's lying," Slater said. "Don't do it."

Shannon hunched her shoulders and let them drop. "I don't mind," she said. "I'm not shy."

Everyone watched as Shannon took off her jacket and handed it to Slater. She stepped to the foot of the bed and unbuttoned her shirt.

"You're a pervert," Slater said to Charlie. "A freak."

Charlie told him to shut up.

Shannon folded her blouse carefully and placed it neatly on the bed near Lane's feet.

"This ain't a fashion show," Tracy said. "Hurry it up."

Slater drew his breath in, still holding Shannon's jacket. It was heavy and weighted on one side. The handle of the Blue Dart was sticking out of one of the pockets.

"Please don't laugh at me," Shannon said. She bent her arms around her back, unhooking her bra. Slater tested the weight of the knife secretly and adjusted his feet.

"We'll laugh all we want," Tracy said. "Take it off."

They all kept their eyes on Shannon, but in the corner of his vision, Slater watched Charlie. A tremendous smirk lit his face as Shannon took off her bra. She had an extra nipple on her right breast, near her armpit.

"Whoa, Nelly," Tracy said.

For a moment, everyone stared at Shannon's tits.

In one motion, Slater threw. Before Tracy could speak again, the Blue Dart was in Charlie's chest. His head hit the wall with a thump. Tracy turned to see what had made the noise, and Shannon covered herself.

"Shoot him," Tracy said. "Kill him now."

Instead, Charlie dropped the gun and fell to the floor, the handle of the Blue Dart twitching in his chest.

"Fuh," he said.

One last fricative. Then he quieted.

Hendrix did the solo to "Voodoo Child" as Charlie bled himself to death. Slater retrieved his knife. At the bed, he pulled the sheet back and took Lane's hand. Her face was slack, her fingers cool. No more in this world.

Tracy backed up toward the closet, her face white. "You're a freak," she said to Shannon. "A lot of guys would go for that."

When he finished saying goodbye to Lane, Slater picked up Charlie's gun and backed Tracy against the wall with it, watching the fear in her eyes.

"Say your name," he said.

"Tracy Shepherd."

"Your other name."

Her voice was childish, a mouse squeak. "Vulva Voom."

He held the barrel of the gun against her forehead until she peed. Then he walked away.

—34—

IN HIS DREAM, a carnival man with a cigar and a holstered gun stirred a tub of ducks. Fairgoers paid a quarter per duck to pick them from the tub. But the game was rigged—all the ducks had the same number. The man's daughter had shown him. She pulled Slater behind the rides for a kiss. Now the man wanted to shoot him. The midway was narrow with an irrigation ditch on one side. Slater plunged into the ditch with the man in pursuit. Lawn chairs floated by.

The sound of an incoming train tore a flare of alertness through his dream. Slater got out of his sleeping bag and went to the door of the boxcar. A northbound had pulled into the small, wet yard and was sitting on the high track. It cast slanted shadows from the arc lights behind it.

It was the train Slater had been waiting for. There were three open boxcars. He was headed to Oba, and the northbound would take him there.

He had discovered the Shanty Boy postcard in Wolverine, after Tracy fled. The card was on the kitchen table by a plate of cold macaroni and cheese. *The Northern Arrow*, it said. *Don't be late.*

From Traverse, he had picked his way through Grayling and Mackinac, hitching rides until he could grab a freight to Sault Ste. Marie, and then to the Sudbury yard. Charlie's pills kept him going. He never slept; when he closed his eyes he went somewhere else. He saw people who weren't there. He kept expecting to see Harp.

The Shanty Boy card said Oba on the eighth. Looking at the northbound, Slater added up the days. The eighth was tomorrow.

If Harp was on the northbound, he'd be in the boxcar toward the back of the train. That was the rule. Stay close to the caboose. The cars near the engine were the first to get set out.

Crossing the wet gravel, rain hit his face. He'd lost his gloves somewhere; the back of his hands were cold and cracked. A little colder and the rain would be snow.

He checked the two forward cars and was not surprised to find them empty. Air hissed in the hoses as he walked along the train to the third boxcar, a Southern Pacific. Slater got his flashlight and swept both ends of the car with its beam.

Nothing. The empty was empty. A boxcar of emptiness shipping north. He climbed in and switched off the light. An hour later he was rolling.

The main obstacle to riding was fear. It made you miss the ladder, made you twist your ankle on the jump. Fear sent you to the wheels. One instant, you're a living, breathing sack of flesh. Then, for a few minutes while you're under the train, you're a rhythm—a cadence the cars make while they slice you in halves, fourths, eighths, sixteenths. Finally, you're nothing. Maybe down the road, a worker notices a little bit of you on the wheels, a little brown and red left behind. He aims a hose at you and washes you off.

On speed, Slater never felt the fear. It was a strange feeling to ride without it.

He crawled into his bag and went to the place where sleep used to be. Because of the cold, he kept his head inside the sleeping bag. He felt heaviness of loin and limb.

In the morning, a ridge of snow had formed inside the rolling boxcar. More snow was falling outside.

Fine, then. Through snow, through fire. That would be the way Harp would like it. Into the teeth of it. Make you feel alive. He slipped out of his bag and stood as close to the door as he could.

At first, he worried that he had already passed Oba. When he saw a milepost, he discovered he was still fifty miles away.

It took the train two hours to cover the distance, and by then the snow was deep. The yard at Oba consisted of a half dozen tracks, a scattering of freight and the mainline. Wet snow covered everything except the rails and a small path around the crew house. From his box, Slater could see the entire yard.

Through the early afternoon, he kept a lookout. When the cold became too much, he put on his pack and hiked to the town's only café, next to the crew house. A girl of eight or nine poured him a cup of coffee and asked him questions in a language he didn't understand. Eventually, a woman who seemed to be her mother came out of the back and took his order. Her tag said Donna FiveMoons. She had a birthmark on her arm that looked like a goose.

No other trains arrived on the eighth. Slater slept in an empty toolshed at the edge of the yard. During the night, he had more bad dreams. A scream of wind melted his skin and blew through his mouth and eyeholes. The sky rained metal and broken glass. Even with his eyes gone, the air had its own brightness.

When he went to the coffee shop in the morning, Donna FiveMoons told him the news. Slater caught a ride in the back of a crew truck to White River, twenty miles south.

The derailment was straight from his dream. Fire had burnt a huge ring of mud in the snow. A dozen freight cars were strewn across it. Smoke rose from the center of the pile. Workers and firemen coiled hoses; some wore masks over their faces. The broken cars were tankers, gons, and boxcars. A pile of twisted junk ringed a broken silver tank car.

There were no clues about Harp. The derailment had happened on the ninth. His card said Oba on the eighth. If that didn't mean Oba on the eighth, it meant nothing at all.

Workers raised a tent with a generator and folding chairs and long tables where equipment and boxes were stacked. A coffee urn was set up. Slater wandered in and out, lost in the confusion.

Dark poured out of the torn cars and all around was snow and sun. The contrast made everything glow. What a strange light for the end of the world, Slater thought. He wished there was a tomorrow where he could tell Lane about the light. But he was all out of tomorrows like that.

None of the workers knew anything about transients on the train. But cars were still piled up, and the snow kept falling, burying the uncleared areas. Slater pitched

in, spreading tarps and carrying electrical cables as three
men tried to stabilize a generator. He moved plywood and
helped erect a smaller tent where workers could get warm.
Many of them were zombies, stoned on disaster. He helped
serve spaghetti at lunch. No one asked his name; he was
anonymous even to himself.

That evening, a meal was served in the high school
gym. A dozen or so cots lined the walls and Slater slept
a while. When he woke, the waxy air was filled with man
talk and good-natured complaining. A card game had developed nearby.

"Some blast," said one voice.

"Biggest I seen."

Slater kept his eyes closed. In the last hours of the day,
he fell into a hard, narrow wedge of sleep. In the morning,
a well-intentioned lady told him that the pancakes were
nearly gone.

"He's not one of the workers," another woman said.

Slater sat up and snorted viciously. Without speaking
to anyone, he walked to the White River bus station. One
bus a day went south.

Waiting, he discovered he had Harp's eyes. He could
see through lies.

He walked through town, using them. At the town ball
field, he sat on a bench and contemplated the untrampled
snow of center field.

Black Fly Park, the scoreboard read. Home 0, Visitors 0.

Good thing it's not summer, he thought. We'd all be
eaten alive.

The ride south was dismal. A constant rain streaked
the windows and the coach smelled like exhaust. His fellow

passengers were sleepers, snorers, and ghosts. People with parts of their lives missing.

On the floor, next to a crust of bread, was a copy of *The Watchtower* with various, overlapping boot prints. A fire raged on the cover. The headline asked "Is Hell Hot?"

Last time I checked, Slater said.

The man across the aisle turned to see who had spoken.

Outside the town of Kapuskasing was a blank billboard, paper peeling from the corners, the sales message faded to white. *Jana D. Fucks All* was spray-painted across the board.

Slater rode blank-eyed the rest of the way, the whir of the highway conducting his stupor. *Jana D. Fucks All* was a mantra in his head: a four-car train on a circular track—engine, coal car, boxcar, caboose. Made of white wood and no sharp corners and the last car was the best. Not some, not many, but *all*. He saw it as a revelation, a headline in the morning paper, something blurted over dinner. *Jana D. Fucks All*. It held the bitterness of men in bus stations everywhere. Including me, he thought.

The next morning, at Sudbury, the driver woke him and walked him by his arm to the door. "There you go, commander," he said, putting him off.

He was left to walk through drizzle. In town, he passed a row of storefronts. A tiny man with a broom whistled at him.

At an all-night diner near the border, a trucker offered Slater the tomatoes from his salad. "I'm not a tomato man," the stranger said.

Slater speared the red wedges, then hitched a ride to Wolverine.

River Road had a new yellow line down the middle. The war paint of developers. Money came, and men put stripes on blacktop, dividing things. Slater tried not to see it, but he had Harp's eyes.

When he saw the *For Sale* sign, he knew the house would be empty.

The front door was locked, so Slater let himself in through an upstairs window. In the bathroom, Lane's cup was still by the sink. He held it up. Fearless now, he let himself picture Lane taking a sip before bed.

Downstairs, the living room was empty. When he stood in the middle of the room and spoke her name, his voice bounced on hard walls. It was the kind of echo that could fuck you up forever.

Unless Lane was in the kitchen, he was the only one. He told himself there might be a note on the refrigerator, a single word in the hand he had known, but there was no note. There was no nothing. The refrigerator was gone.

Chicago was a maze of on-ramps. Slater stood by one with his thumb out and watched a dented van come to a stop.

The driver was a black man with large shoulders and eyes that seemed to miss nothing. The van was piled with electronics, computer monitors, and cables. John Coltrane played as Slater climbed inside.

"Join the passing parade," the man said, putting out a hand. "Name's Matthews."

When they were a mile down the interstate, the man asked him where he was headed.

"Tucson," Slater said. "Or vicinity."

Matthews swiveled his head, taking a look at the messed-up soul who had joined him.

"I'll take you as far as New York City," he said, "if you can drive a stick. You're on the wrong road for Tucson."

Slater listened to Coltrane's *A Love Supreme*. "You sure?"

"There's a map in the glove box," Matthews said. "Check if you want. But ain't nothing ever sure."

— 35 —

THE DAY AFTER Matthews was fired, Slater left his edit suite in the middle of the day. The sidewalk buzzed with distraction. A gun shop invited Luger Lovers to come in and ogle the collection. Sport shirts in gaudy colors were fanned in the window of the Shirt Xplosion. The street musician stood at his usual spot on the corner; the cord from his Gibson fell to the sidewalk and lay there, connected to nothing. As Slater passed, the player swung his guitar behind his head and shredded a classic, silent solo, eyes wild.

The man was a genius, Slater thought. A master of the form.

In Wolverine, the trees would be changing. Ten shades of orange, the color of creation. But Slater didn't want colors anymore. He wanted to suck the color out of everything. He wanted to go blank.

When he stepped into Paradise Squared, the warm concoction of shame and talcum washed over him. The bar was a place where losers could lose themselves.

The first body to float up, the bouncer, was scrawny and skeletal. Another speed freak. Are you me? Slater thought. Am I you?

"Eight-buck cover," the bouncer said. "Dig deep."

Slater pulled out a twenty and handed it over. "Are the girls nude and naked?" he asked. In his experience, many bouncers could not talk and make change at the same time. Sometimes, their errors worked in his favor. On those occasions, he was actually paid by the club to watch women undress.

"As nude and naked as women get," the bouncer said.

Moving farther into the fragrant gloom, he saw the loitering dancers. He had known all along that they would not be naked. They wore bracelets and lingerie. One wore a Yankees cap. You had to pay another twenty dollars to get them to take their underwear off. Then they put it back on and you had to pay again. A man's work was never done. Everyone seemed to be okay with the system.

Slater sat down and closed his eyes as the Yankees girl climbed onstage. Another good thing about Paradise Squared was that the girls never pretended to like you. You stayed in your hell and they stayed in theirs.

When he opened his eyes after a couple of songs, he saw a young executive at the next table. The man wore a suit with a white shirt that appeared Day-Glo under the lights. He twisted his head like an owl to watch whichever woman was slouching by. Slater felt a deep dislike for the businessman. The guy wasn't there to lose himself. He was there to see some titties. The idea repulsed Slater.

Hey you, Slater told him. I don't like your face. He got no response, and it seemed possible that his voice had sounded only inside his head. His mouth wasn't moving, so that was a clue. I hate your car, he told the man. I hate your wife's bored suburban daydream. He picked up his beer and moved to a darker table. I hate the tassels on your shoes.

Translucent, jittery gangsters drew their guns on screen three, oblivious to the talking head that was superimposed over their scene. The head was a flack for International Can. While the gangsters broke down a door, the talking head yammered on about the world aluminum market and the high cost of labor.

"Double exposure," Slater said. "Ghosts. And this is the master. It's ruined."

Dimi looked over at the screen. "You can't get them off?"

Slater shook his head. "Matthews did this. He was wiring a new box when he got the news. Now look."

The ghost gunmen mowed down a stoolie, while the flack blamed cutbacks on a bar chart.

"The only hope would be to sell the client on it. Tell them it celebrates Hollywood. You'd have to change the music, though. I don't think they would buy it."

He tapped some keys, but the gunmen were there to stay.

Dimi had brought Slater a small pumpkin, not much bigger than a softball. It sat provocatively on his console, its blatant vegetable nature naked against the technology.

"There must be a way to undo it," she said.

Slater swiveled his chair to look at her. There was an efficient, mechanical whir as he erased the tape.

We're all double exposures, he tried to say. Two, three, four stories going all at once. Stuff on top of stuff. "We shouldn't be surprised when it turns out weird."

She stood beside him, her hand on his shoulder. "Weird could be good," she said. "Weird might be fun."

When he stood up, he saw in her eyes the current he had followed before. It led to a house of horrors. A kiss and a scream behind every door. The small diamond that she wore in her nose was an interesting touch, though. Different.

He glanced briefly at the console. The screens looked empty, but you never knew. Crossing bells were sounding in the distance.

"Then there's always the present," Dimi said. "You remember the present, don't you? Where you and I are standing right now?"

Slater put a hand on the pumpkin. It was smooth and cool, with secret folds. There was a walk for starting over. It was a hard walk, but you pretty much had no choice. When you got down to it, there was no other transport.

Cautiously, he touched her and felt the present. Its circuitry buzzed under his fingertips, firing electrons trapped in his skull since Detroit. They would always be trapped there, he thought. Their burred edges would cut him again and again. He didn't care.

"Sure," he said, "I remember."

From somewhere, the crossing signals rang their odd, uncertain rhythm—two bells, a fraction out of sync. The sounds started separate and grew closer; they came together and rang as one and separated again. And came together, And separated.

When he kissed her, the diamond in her nose caught the light. He was falling, but that was okay. He was halfway down and he still had a long way to go.

I AM GRATEFUL to many for their assistance and support, especially: Stevan Allred and Joanna Rose; and Sheila Hamilton, Bruce Barrow, Randy Cepuch, Jessica Poundstone, Julie Mancini, Carolyn Sparling, and Chris Shelton. I am also grateful to Jesse Burkhardt and Tom Lacinski for freights and Northern Michigan; Jack Cady; and Lee Montgomery, Tony Perez, and everyone at Tin House.